To all the seekers
who strive to understand the past,
to help them make sense of the present,
and allow them to shape the future.

This is book is brought to you by Bear & King Publishing.

Second edition 2016
© Gabriel Farago

The right of Gabriel Farago to be identified as the author of this work has been asserted by him in accordance with the Copyright Amendment (Moral Rights) Act 2000.

Cataloguing-in-Publication entry is available from the National Library of Australia: http://catalogue.nla.gov.au

Author:	Farago, Gabriel Geza
Title:	The Empress Holds the Key
ISBN:	978-0-9945763-2-3 (paperback)
Subjects:	Fiction; Adventure stories

Cover design and layout by Vivien Valk.
Images from iStockphoto.com

THE EMPRESS HOLDS THE KEY

Gabriel Farago

To Dori and Tibor for instilling in me a great love of reading
and a sense of curiosity and adventure,
and for having taught me to always keep an open mind,
and strive for excellence.

A writer's journey ...

Becoming a writer is a long, and often tortuous journey, especially for a non-native speaker like myself; English is my third language. A special thank you must go to my wife Joan who, sitting next to me at university many years ago, taught me the many intricacies and often baffling nuances of this wonderful language. Without her encouragement, unwavering support, perseverance and guiding hand, *The Empress Holds the Key* would not have seen the light of day. It is therefore as much her book as it is mine.

Gabriel Farago

Author's note

We carefully removed the last stone blocking the entry to the burial chamber, and held our breath. Peering inside, we saw a large sarcophagus partially covered with sand. No other treasures – tomb robbers had probably seen to that centuries ago. Silent, we entered and approached the stone chest, its exquisite hieroglyphs whispering to us from the distant past.

Our professor pointed to the inscriptions on top of the broken lid, his hand shaking with excitement. Barely able to speak, he said they told stories of great battles, conquered lands and glory. It appeared the tomb belonged to a general close to the pharaoh. Our spirits soared; a discovery like this only comes along once.

After the excitement had died down, the Professor cleared his throat, a smile on his face. 'This isn't bad, guys, but don't get too carried away,' he said, pulling us back down to earth. 'What do you think would be the ultimate find?' he asked, throwing us a challenge.

I'm sure he was only teasing, but a heated debate erupted at once, the ensuing discussion continuing well into the evening as we waited for the boat to take us back across the Nile to Cairo.

At first there were many suggestions, but then, quite unexpectedly, we all agreed that one particular artefact, which had mysteriously disappeared from the pages of history a long time ago, would qualify for that distinction.

This was remarkable, because scholars from different parts

of the world rarely agree on matters like this. However, on this occasion, all of us – Christians, Muslims, and Jews – had somehow come to share the same view.

It was an unforgettable moment; it turned into a moment of destiny and became the inspiration for this book.

Gabriel Farago
Leura, Blue Mountains, Australia

If we don't believe in something greater than ourselves,
we are destined to remain forever small.

Benjamin Krakowski

Contents

Part I

WAR CRIMES

Swiss-German border; November 1944

The major looked affectionately at the sleeping Doberman curled up on the seat beside him. Slowly, he took off his gloves, stroked the dog's shiny coat and then ran his fingers playfully along the open violin case resting on his knees.

After a while, he looked out the window and, recognising where they were, tapped his driver on the back. 'Stop the car and wait for the others. We're almost there.'

The driver slowed and pulled the powerful Mercedes to the side of the road. After switching off the engine, he unfolded a large map and began to look for the inconspicuous track he remembered leading down to the lake.

Meanwhile, the major turned and watched the armoured personnel carrier slowly crawling up the pass behind them. He pulled out his silver cigarette case engraved with a small swastika that Himmler had given him. *If Heinrich only knew what we'd just done!* he thought, *all hell would break loose.* By driving through the night and using only back roads, they'd managed to avoid patrols and roadblocks. Himmler, of all people, would know that leaving Auschwitz with two prisoners without the necessary permits wasn't easy, even for a member of the SS. And then there was the precious cargo ...

Benjamin Krakowski tried to shield his brother from the icy wind rocking the open truck. He put his arm around his brother's bony shoulders and pulled him towards his chest.

'Where do you think they're taking us?' asked his brother,

3

staring up at the snow-covered peaks ahead of them.

'Shut up, David! Do you want them to beat us again – or worse?' whispered Benjamin. He glanced anxiously at the guards sitting on wooden crates in the back and squeezed his brother's arm.

'No,' replied David, huddling closer.

Fear could no longer keep Benjamin awake. Almost delirious from hunger and the numbing cold, he closed his eyes and drifted into a restless sleep his exhausted body craved so much. Unable to relax, he again heard his father beseeching him: 'Benjamin, listen carefully ... There isn't much time! Promise me you'll do exactly as I tell you ... You must finish what I've begun ... *You are the one* ... Do you understand? And remember, *the Empress holds the key* ...'

'I promise, father,' murmured Benjamin. 'Yes; the *Empress* holds the key ... '

The personnel carrier followed the black Mercedes down to the lake and stopped in front of a jetty.

'Wake up, you lazy scum!' shouted one of the guards, kicking Benjamin in the back. 'Unload the crates. Move!'

One by one, the two young prisoners lifted the heavy wooden boxes off the truck and carried them across to the jetty.

'And when you're finished, start digging a trench over here,' the guard yelled.

'We're digging our own graves,' hissed David, driving his pick into the hard clay. 'We've seen it all before. We *have* to make a run for it – now! Into that forest before it's too late!' he continued, pointing towards the pines with his chin. 'Come!'

'Are you *mad?*' said Benjamin. 'They'll shoot us before we make it to the first tree.'

David ignored his brother's warning and slowly worked his way towards the guard standing closest to the trench. Then, lifting his pick, he slammed the pointed end into the back of the guard's knee. Taken by surprise, the screaming soldier lost his balance, dropped his gun, and fell against the crates, splitting one open. Three shiny gold bars tumbled unnoticed into the mud.

Benjamin froze. Instead of running after his brother, he stared at the soldier thrashing in agony on the ground in front of him.

Startled by the scream, the major looked across to the jetty. He unleashed his dog, raised his arm, and pointed to the prisoner running towards the forest. '*Arco* – there. Catch!' he shouted.

Before the other guards had realised what had happened, David was lying face down in the mud. Pinned to the ground by the major's Doberman on his back – fangs bared and snarling – he was certain he was about to be torn apart.

The major pointed to a dead tree. 'Take him over there,' he ordered. 'Strip him!'

The angry guards ripped the threadbare prison rags from the boy's thin frame. Terrified and shaking, David looked like a cornered animal as he tried in vain to cover his genitals with bleeding hands.

'Now, string him up from the tree over there,' shouted the major. 'The way we saw the Ukrainians reward deserters – remember? That'll teach him a lesson.'

'Why don't we use this instead?' suggested one of the guards, pointing to an iron cross wedged into the rock behind the tree.

'A crucifixion?' said the major, laughing. 'That *would* be most appropriate; he's a Jew after all. Look, it's too small, even for a miserable wretch like this – see? Pity.'

Suddenly, a motor boat materialised out of the mist and approached the jetty. A tall young man in a fur coat waved his slouch hat, jumped ashore, and hurried towards the major.

'Is it all here?' he asked.

'See for yourself, Anton,' replied the major. He pointed to the crates and embraced his friend.

Anton began to examine the markings on the lids by tracing the familiar German eagle with the tip of his finger. Satisfied, he turned towards the major. 'Congratulations!' he said. 'I don't know how you did it. Let's get them on board. Quickly!'

The major opened the door of the Mercedes and lifted the violin case off the back seat.

'Taking music lessons?' teased Anton, smiling.

'No. This has nothing to do with music. This is an instrument of history,' the major replied gravely, patting the case. 'Come, let's go; they've almost finished loading the crates.'

The two friends hurried down the embankment and stopped in front of the dead tree. Despite the horrific beating, David was still alive. The major reached for his holster.

'Hold it right there,' said Anton. He pulled a camera out of his pocket and took a photo. 'One for the family album?' he added sarcastically.

The major pointed his Luger at David's head. 'Can you hear me?' he demanded.

David nodded without opening his eyes.

'You cannot run away from destiny,' the major whispered calmly, and shot David in the temple. The virgin snow, turned crimson by the hot droplets of David's splattered blood, began to weep.

When he turned around, the major saw Benjamin staring at him from across the trench. Their eyes locked and contempt met fear. Then, slowly, the major lifted his gun, took aim, and pulled the trigger. 'Neither can you, Jew boy,' he snarled, calmly slipping the Luger back into its holster.

'Bury them,' barked the major. 'Heil Hitler!' He hurried across the gangplank and saluted his men standing to attention by the jetty.

As soon as the powerful diesel engines had roared to life, Anton gave an order. Two sailors armed with machine guns stepped out of the wheelhouse and opened fire on the major's men. Torn apart by the unexpected hail of bullets, the hapless men collapsed, their arms still raised in silent salute.

Anton looked at the major. 'No witnesses – remember?' he said with a shrug and climbed below deck.

Benjamin opened his eyes. Darkness. He quickly closed them again. Silence. Licking his lips, he tasted blood. Barely able to breathe in the confined space, he tried to move his aching limbs but couldn't; something heavy was pressing on his back and shoulders. It was the arm of a dead soldier lying on top of him. Slowly, the numbness drained away and his whole body began to throb with pain. Flashes of memory returned: *Benjamin realised he wasn't dead!*

Fear gave him strength. Slowly, he began to claw through the loose clay towards the top. Breathless and retching, he pushed his head out into the open and gasped for air.

The sleet hitting his face like icy needles revived him. He opened his mouth, a silent scream on his parched lips, then searched all around him, squinting through half-closed eyes into the blinding daylight, scanning the empty clearing. The soldiers were all gone, the crates had disappeared and there was no boat at the jetty. The burnt-out shells of the armoured truck and the Mercedes smouldered in the mist, filling the bracing cold air with an acrid stench of burnt rubber. Over the brooding lake the mountain fog hovered like a shroud. Benjamin cautiously turned his aching head, and began to look for his brother's tree. It was just behind him, with part of a severed rope still tied to one of the branches.

'David!' Benjamin cried out. 'Noooo.' He covered his face with blood-stained hands, fell to his knees, and began to pray.

1

The thunderstorm blew in from the south, sending dark clouds racing across the night sky like a celestial pirate fleet raiding the stars. Suddenly, a bolt of lightning struck an old eucalypt; it split its trunk in half and set it on fire. The rugged sandstone cliffs trembled as the thunder roared across the dry valley. At first, the flames struggled to ignite the tough bark of the doomed tree. Soon however, nourished by a gust of wind, they formed a blazing ring around the base of the giant and began their deadly ascent towards its parched crown. Defeated, the burning trunk crashed to the forest floor, sending a cloud of lethal sparks dancing towards their next victim. The bushfire had begun.

Two Rural Fire Service volunteers, their eyes firmly fixed on the fire spreading through the gullies below, stood on an exposed escarpment high above the burning forest. They knew the real danger was always the wind, and the wind was picking up. The old timber cottage behind them stood directly in the path of the advancing blaze. Unless the wind changed direction, the fire would soon reach the cottage. A third volunteer – a young woman in sweaty yellow overalls – was kneeling on top of the roof. Frantically cleaning out the blocked gutters with her bare hands, she too was anxiously watching the fire.

The wind didn't change direction. The fire jumped across a

waterfall and burst into a densely wooded gorge just below the cottage. Trapped in the narrow gorge, the wind intensified, funnelling the blaze upwards. As it reached the top of the escarpment, the firestorm roared out into the open and raced towards the cottage. Moments later, the cottage drowned in a sea of flames.

Jack Rogan raced along the motorway in his MG and was fast approaching the foothills of the Blue Mountains, a popular holiday retreat, 100 kilometres west of Sydney. He enjoyed driving fast, but not that morning. A familiar feeling began to claw at his empty stomach – danger. Chewing his bottom lip, Jack smiled; danger had a twin – excitement. Jack loved excitement. The bright morning in Sydney suddenly gave way to a gloomy twilight – yellow-red and foreboding of the bushfires that lay ahead. The sun had disappeared behind a giant mushroom-shaped cloud of smoke, and visibility was poor. Large flakes of ash rained down from above, smudging the windscreen. Singed gum leaves carried along by the hot wind surged towards him like swarms of hungry locusts ready to attack. Jack switched on his headlights.

As he neared his destination, Jack carefully threaded his way through a convoy of fire engines and water tankers heading up the mountains and then suddenly stopped in front of a row of police cars blocking the road. Jack got out of the car, the smoke and intense heat making it difficult to breathe. The destruction ahead reminded him of a car bomb site he'd photographed in Kabul the year before. The smouldering tree trunks looked like the chimneys of a destroyed village buried under a carpet of powdery ash. *Accusing fingers pointing to angry gods who had forsaken the faithful*, thought Jack.

Jack walked up to a policeman and asked for the fire chief. The agitated policeman ordered him to get back into his car and leave the area. Jack's press ID didn't help. Neither did the baggy green shorts, crumpled t-shirt and thongs.

'It's all right, Officer, there's a way around the fire,' came a familiar voice from behind him. 'He can come with me.'

The policeman shrugged and turned away.

'Will!' Jack exclaimed, barely able to recognise his friend in his sooty yellow overalls and battered fire helmet. 'Sorry it took so long; I know you said it was urgent but the traffic was diabolical.'

'No worries. If we hurry, we might just get through,' said Will. He handed Jack a helmet and jacket, and pointed to a four-wheel drive with its engine running. 'Hop in. It'll get a little rough, I'm afraid. Shoes would have helped, mate,' he added, shaking his head. 'You'll never change.'

Will turned the car into a narrow fire trail leading into the bush. 'As long as the wind stays like this, we should make it,' he said, wiping his brow with a wet towel. 'One of our girls died in the firestorm this morning, just up the hill from here. Horrible; burnt beyond recognition. She was trying to save an old cottage. I've known her since she was a little nipper in kindergarten,' he added. 'Her father doesn't know yet. He's fighting the fire on the other side of the mountains and can't be reached. Poor bastard.'

'I'm sorry.'

'But that's not why I called you. It's what we found *under* her body you'll find interesting,' said Will, barely missing a smouldering tree trunk.

'What is it?' asked Jack, frowning.

'Wait and see. We're almost there.'

A shiver raced down Jack's spine. Often the best stories found *him* in the most unlikely places. He was wondering if he was heading for just such a place.

What was left of the body of the young woman was covered with a wet tarpaulin. A group of dejected looking fire fighters stood next to it, staring into space – waiting.

'The police chopper's on its way,' said Will. He guided Jack through the smoking ruins of the cottage towards a brick chimney leaning precariously to one side – the only structure still standing. The corrugated iron roof had collapsed and all the walls had burnt to the ground.

'That's what we found when we moved the body,' said Will, pointing to a small green tin lying in the rubble next to the fireplace. 'I think it was hidden somewhere inside the chimney – that's why it hasn't buckled.' Will cleared away the ash next to the tin with the tip of his boot. 'We're supposed to leave everything just as we find it,' he continued, lowering his voice, 'but, well, you know how it is ... curiosity ...' he said, picking up the box and opening it. 'Here, have a look at this.'

Jack stared at a sepia photograph, slightly singed around the edges but otherwise undamaged.

'A bit brutal, wouldn't you say?' said Jack, holding up the picture. 'He's only a kid, for Christ's sake.'

Will pointed to the back of the photo. 'Look, there's a date here – November 1944.'

'Anything else in the box?' asked Jack.

'Yep. All this weird stuff here, look.'

'Interesting ...'

2

Jana Gonski peeled back the ivy, opened the iron gate, and walked up the moss-covered stone steps. Then she pressed the doorbell, and waited. She wasn't surprised when no-one answered. In one way, she was quite relieved. She hadn't seen the guy in years, and their parting had occurred under circumstances – she was sure – he'd prefer to forget. Taking a deep breath, Jana looked around: the terrace house appeared deserted. Crumpled envelopes – chewed around the edges by snails – bulged out of the letterbox. Several mouldy, rolled-up newspapers were rotting on the landing.

'I don't have to remind you how important this is,' she recalled her boss saying. 'The press is having a ball, the minister is screaming for answers and the Director of Public Prosecutions is breathing down my neck. Need I go on? As usual, the journalists seem to know a lot more than we do. We must get to the bottom of this – now. Do what you have to do, but do it fast – I need results!'

As the agent in charge of Special Projects Jana was used to pressure. She dealt almost exclusively with the sensitive and the unusual.

Jana was just about to leave when the door opened and a man in faded jeans, torn at the knees, and a striped pyjama top unbuttoned to the waist, squinted out at her.

'I can't stand getting up this early in the morning. What do you want?' he demanded, running his fingers through his unkempt hair.

'Still chasing that big story, Jack?'

'Jana?' asked Jack, shielding his eyes from the sun. 'Well, what a surprise! What have I done wrong this time?'

Jana laughed. 'You've done nothing wrong except not returning my calls,' she said. 'I've left several messages on your answering machine.'

'Is that a federal offence now?' he asked.

'Seriously, Jack, I want to talk to you about a dead fire fighter, a newspaper article, and a photograph.'

'You'd better come in,' he said. 'But I have to warn you, my cleaning lady took the week off ... '

'I can see ...' said Jana, smiling.

The tiny lounge room on the ground floor looked like it hadn't seen a cleaner for at least a year. A scratched coffee table was covered in empty beer cans, bottles and crushed milk cartons, and the sofa in front of the fireplace was barely visible under layers of old newspapers, magazines and various items of crumpled clothing. A lonely ironing board stood in the middle of the room with a basket full of limp washing nearby. Newspaper cuttings littered the floor.

'It's been, what, five years?' asked Jack, clearing a space on the sofa for Jana to sit down. 'I was just making coffee – would you like some?'

'Let me help you. Is this the way to the kitchen?' asked Jana, pointing to the back of the house.

'It is, but even I'm a little afraid to go in there just at the moment,' said Jack. 'You stay right here. And besides, I make excellent coffee ... remember?'

'Sure,' said Jana, crossing her legs and smiling at him.

'Poison,' said Jack, touching his nose with his finger.

'Beg your pardon?'

'Dior, you're wearing Dior's Poison. I hope it's not an omen.'

He's good, thought Jana, sitting down on the sofa.

She's obviously working out. She looks great for the wrong side of forty, thought Jack. Her simple black dress accentuated her trim, athletic body, and her short honey-blonde hair showed off her dark tan.

After a lot of clattering around and cursing, followed by a long silence, Jack swept into the room balancing a steaming coffee plunger and two mugs on a tray. He'd put on a fresh shirt and combed his hair, Jana noticed.

'When I take on an assignment, I often work through the night nowadays,' he said, pouring the coffee and searching the room in vain for a cigarette. 'I hate distractions. I haven't listened to my answering machine since my divorce last year. My ex and her lawyers used to call all the time and leave messages. Every time I called back, it cost me money. Then I just stopped listening,' he rambled on. 'It worked, you see. They don't bother me anymore.' Jack drained his mug of black coffee and sat down next to Jana.

'Single again?'

'Sure am. So, what would you like to know?' asked Jack.

'Your article in last Sunday's *Herald* ruffled a few feathers in Parliament ...'

'That's gratifying; I like my readers to show interest.'

'Your pictures were rather provocative.'

'Quite deliberately so; it was a shocking death.'

'Surely your point wasn't the death of the unfortunate woman, but where and how she died. "Whose property was this brave young volunteer trying to save? What is the meaning of the Nazi memorabilia found in the ruins of the house? Who is the SS officer in the photograph?"' said Jana, quoting from the article.

'Not bad. A little selective and out of context perhaps, but still impressive,' Jack replied. 'It's just an interesting story to be read on a Sunday morning on the terrace with your latté and croissants, that's all. In a week or so it'll be forgotten. It's always the way.'

'Really? Then why are you working on a follow-up article?'

'We are well informed.'

'Your editor talked ...'

'I should have known. The old fart could never resist a pretty face and a short skirt.'

'Spoken like the true blue chauvinist you are. Honestly, you haven't changed at all, Jack. In actual fact, my tools of trade are a little more sophisticated than that.'

'You're the one leaning on me,' Jack replied, pointing to the door.

'All right, all right. Truce please?' said Jana, holding up her hands.

'It's your call.'

'You seem convinced that there's a connection between the officer in the photo and the owner of the cottage,' said Jana, coming straight to the point. 'What makes you so sure?'

'Instinct.'

'Instinct alone isn't enough, you need proof.'

'I'm aware of that, but in my line of work instinct is important.'

'Let me think ... what was it last time? Accusing the Archbishop of paedophilia without sufficient evidence? I stopped you just in time, remember?'

Jack frowned, annoyed. 'Thanks for reminding me; I was just wondering when you'd get around to that.'

Taking chances – often big ones – was part of Jack's makeup. If it wasn't risky, it wasn't fun. If it wasn't fun, he lost interest. Jack was used to being in trouble.

Jana put her hand on his arm and smiled at him. 'It's okay. I think your instincts are right, by the way, this time.'

'And what makes you so sure?' Jack asked.

'Instinct,' she replied, and they both burst out laughing.

'Okay, we both agree instinct is important,' Jana continued, 'but we do need more. So what have you found out so far?'

'Why should I tell you?' asked Jack. 'If I remember correctly, last time I took you into my confidence, I almost got my balls cut off.'

'Oh yeah? I'd have thought a few little bruises to that tiny little ego of yours was preferable to a couple of years in the clink. Get over it, Jack!'

'Shit, here we go again ...' said Jack, shaking his head.

'You don't have to, but I think you will,' said Jana, changing tack.

'Am I that predictable?'

Jana shrugged. 'No. I think you will because of what I'm about to propose.'

'You certainly don't waste time do you?' countered Jack.

'I suggest we share information,' said Jana. 'If I come up with something worthwhile, you get more material for your article.'

'And you, what's in it for you?' asked Jack.

'I move a little closer to ... let's call it, my subject, so we both get what we want,' said Jana.

'What exactly are you investigating? The fiery death of a young volunteer? Come on ...' said Jack.

'That's a matter for the coroner.'

'My point exactly. What then?' asked Jack.

'My brief is wider than that,' said Jana.

'What are these Special Projects you're in charge of anyway?'

'I investigate ... sensitive matters ... usually involving politicians, judges, high-profile individuals, even police officers ...'

'Or possible war criminals?'

'Yes,' Jana conceded.

'What, like Special Branch or Internal Affairs ...?'

'Something like that.'

'Sounds a bit cloak and dagger to me,' said Jack, raising an eyebrow.

'Of course there would have to be certain conditions about how you use the information I give you – understand?'

'Bossy as usual,' mumbled Jack.

'What did you say?'

'Nothing. I think you forgot something rather important.'

'What's that?'

'Trust. It won't work without trust ...'

'You're right,' she agreed. 'And trust has to be earned.'

'Quite.'

'About earning trust ...' said Jana, reaching for her briefcase and taking out a silver ring, which she passed to Jack. 'We found this near the fireplace in the cottage. I'm surprised you missed it. You'd been through everything else before the police arrived, right? What do you make of it?'

Jack took the ring and walked towards the window. Just as he reached it, the window exploded, splinters of glass whistling through the air like jagged missiles, one of them imbedding itself in Jack's cheek, barely missing his eye. A house brick landed on the floor in front of him.

'What on earth was that?' cried Jana, jumping up and running towards Jack. Glancing out of the broken window she caught a glimpse of a boy pedalling away on a pushbike.

'Are you all right?' she asked.

'Yeah, I'm okay,' said Jack, pulling the splinter out of his cheek and trying to stem the flow of blood with a handkerchief.

'Let me have a look.'

'It's nothing, just a scratch.'

'Jesus, Jack. You could have lost an eye. Still treading on the wrong toes?'

He shook his head. 'Just street kids, leave it alone. I had a problem here the other night ...'

'What do you mean?'

'Someone vandalised my car. You know, scratches, smashed brake lights, slashed tyres, stuff like that. I asked around ...'

'And?'

'Nothing; forget it.'

'Let me get this straight: someone throws a brick through

your window in the middle of the day, barely missing your head, and you just want to forget it?'

'Exactly.'

'As you wish,' said Jana, shaking her head.

Jack bent down, picked up the ring, and held it up to the light as if nothing had happened. 'Well, well,' he said after studying it for a while, 'how extraordinary. This is a *Totenkopf* ring, the honour ring of the SS. Usually awarded personally by Himmler for special services for Reich and Fuehrer. It was extremely rare and highly prized.'

Jack proffered the ring to Jana. 'It's made of silver. Look, you can see the skull and crossbones and there are some runic symbols engraved on the band. It was manufactured by a firm in Munich – Otto Gars.'

'I'm impressed,' said Jana. 'You've certainly done your homework on the SS.'

'Sure have. My first assignment as a rookie journalist was tracking down an SS thug living in Queensland. You never forget your first assignment, especially one that went spectacularly wrong,' replied Jack, laughing. 'Have you checked the inside of the band? The inscriptions?'

'Of course.'

'The band should be engraved with the letters "S.lb", which stands for *Seinen Lieben*, the date of presentation, a facsimile of Himmler's signature, and most importantly ...'

'The recipient's name,' interrupted Jana.

'Well?'

'See for yourself.'

'Bummer! The name's been chiselled out.'

'I'm afraid so.'

'That would have been too easy, I suppose. In any case, this ring shouldn't be here.'

'What do you mean?'

'Well, it should either be on the left ring finger of the recipient, if he's still alive that is, or ...'

'Or what?'

'In the event of death, the ring should have been removed for preservation at Himmler's castle at Wewelsburg in memory of the ring holder.'

'Fascinating.'

'You know, the rings of SS officers fallen in battle were kept at a special shrine at the castle. In 1944, Himmler ordered the rings to be sealed inside a mountain near Wewelsburg to prevent their capture by the advancing Allies. The rings have never been found.'

'What a story.'

'I think it's my turn now,' said Jack, handing back the ring. 'Let's go upstairs to my study. I want to show you something.'

'How exciting, not etchings I hope,' Jana joked, following Jack up the narrow stairs leading to the attic.

'No. I only show my etchings to young chicks.'

'Thanks, Jack.'

3

The study was tidy and well designed, with lots of light flooding in through a large dormer window facing the courtyard. 'Welcome to the engine room,' said Jack, pointing to a long work-bench crammed with computer screens, laser printers, a fax machine and an array of photographic equipment. Several large photographs were pinned to a whiteboard next to the window.

'How come your study's so tidy and the rest of the place is such a mess?' said Jana, looking around.

'Priorities. It still amazes me what you can do with computers these days,' said Jack, ignoring her. 'Let me show you what I've found out so far,' he added, reaching for a laser torch and pointing it at one of the photographs on the whiteboard.

'As you can see, this is an enlargement of the photo from the cottage. I took a close-up of it with my digital camera and enhanced it. This is it here. Let's begin with the man in the uniform. Tell me what you see,' Jack suggested.

'I see a German officer wearing the uniform of the SS. Highly decorated, with a *Ritterkreuz* – a Knight's Cross – right here.' Jana pointed to the throat of the officer in the picture.

'Rank?'

'*Sturmbannfuehrer* – Major.'

'Age?'

'Young. Early thirties I'd say.'

'Go on, how tall?'

21

'Quite tall, but I'd have to guess of course ...'

'I can tell you he's at least five foot eleven inches,' Jack explained.

'How can you be so precise?'

'Do you see this arm band?' he asked, holding up another enlargement showing only the upper body of the officer. 'This is the Adolf Hitler arm band on his cuff. It was worn only by members of the Leibstandarte SS Adolf Hitler – Hitler's bodyguard, the pride of the Waffen SS, the cream of the Aryan super race. They had to be at least five foot eleven to be eligible to join. Tall lads, as you would expect. Goose-stepping shorties just wouldn't have been quite the same – right?'

'Certainly not.'

'This is interesting. Come, look at the hand holding the gun.'

'He's wearing a ring. This one you think?' Jana asked, holding up the Totenkopf ring.

'Looks like it. I didn't notice it before. This ties in with the other contents of the box. I took photos of everything.' Jack pointed to a group of smaller pictures on the board in front of them. 'The most impressive item is the medal – the Ritterkreuz. See, the officer in the photo is wearing one just like it – here.'

Jana nodded.

'It was awarded for acts of great courage,' said Jack. 'Now, what about the unfortunate boy. What do you see?'

'I see a naked youth – about fifteen I'd say – hanging upside down from a tree branch with the rope or wire wound around his testicles. It's the only thing holding him up. It's horrific. Also, his hands are tied behind his back and his head is shaved. He's frightfully thin. Look at his ribs,' she said, and shuddered. 'You can count them!'

'What else?'

'Well, there's a gun pointed at his head, and a nasty Doberman,' said Jana, tracing the outline of the large dog crouching on the ground next to the boy.

'What about the geography?'

'Alpine, I'd say. Stunning. Those mountains are massive and that's heavy snow cover on top and pine forests down to the edge of a lake ... Austrian or Swiss perhaps? Rather large, judging by the size of the boat over here.'

'Not bad,' said Jack, clapping his hands in mock applause. 'It's a Swiss lake actually.'

'Oh? How do you know that?'

'The boat. Here, look. I've prepared several enlargements. Unfortunately I couldn't disperse the fog to get a better image. Computers are good, but not that good – yet. That's a powerful motor cruiser tied up at the jetty; fast, sleek, expensive. The sort of thing you'd expect to find moored in front of one of those exclusive hotels on a Swiss lake. And here's the proof,' he said, pointing to the stern of the boat.

'A flag. But I can't make out any pattern or design, it's too blurred.'

'Try this.' Jack handed her another enlargement.

'It's a cross; the Swiss flag!' Jana exclaimed, getting excited. 'This is really quite something. I've told you before, you're in the wrong business. You should be a sleuth.'

'There's more,' said Jack. 'The officer has something tucked under his arm. See?' he said, pointing. 'It's an unusual shape. That's what intrigued me.'

'It's too small and most of it is hidden. I can't see what it is.'

'Then try this, Inspector, it's one of my more sophisticated tools of trade,' said Jack, handing her a magnifying glass.

'Amazing. It looks like a violin case.'

'Precisely. Not exactly what you'd expect to find, is it? A gun in one hand and a violin case in the other. Quite a guy.'

'You said it. Surely, there can't be any more, I'm exhausted.'

'Just one more item, and a fascinating one at that,' Jack promised. 'Here, look at the dog. Look at his collar. It's wide and shiny, possibly made of some metal, and there are pointed studs and a leather band underneath.'

'You're right, it must be metal,' Jana agreed, looking through the magnifying glass.

Jack was tempted to stroke her hair, but pulled back his hand. Standing so close to Jana, seeing the gentle curve of her neck, the tiny shell of her ear, smelling her familiar scent – musky and exciting – brought back memories of lazy Sunday mornings wickedly spent in bed a long time ago. But that was in another life, he reminded himself.

'How unusual,' said Jana. It's engraved on the top here. You can just see the letters R–E–I. I wonder what it means.'

'It could be initials, or the end of an inscription. A name perhaps, with the rest of the writing continuing on the other side of the dog's neck,' Jack suggested.

Jana walked to the window and looked down into the overgrown courtyard below. 'Jack, have you been able to find out who owns the cottage, or rather what's left of it?' she asked.

'That wasn't hard; my title search is right here. The property is registered in the name of Wotan Holdings Pty Limited. The shareholders and directors are Eric and Heinrich Newman.'

'Apparently, father and son. Sir Eric has agreed to see me; I have an appointment with him tomorrow at his home.'

'It's *Sir* Eric, is it?' It was Jack's turn to look impressed. 'I don't suppose I could come along?' he asked hopefully.

'That wouldn't be such a good idea. It'll be a formal police visit.'

Jack's face sank.

'Come on, Jack, don't look so disappointed.'

'Easy for you. Just flash a badge and walk straight in.'

'I'll tell you all about it after. We have a deal, remember?'

'We do?' Jack asked. 'I didn't know we'd agreed.'

'Let me put it this way, if we have, you can come with me to visit Miss Abramowitz if you like. I'm going to see her now.'

'And who might that be?'

'She's the lady who wrote to your editor claiming to have recognised the officer in the photograph,' Jana replied casually. 'The paper notified the police straight away. That's really why

I came to see you,' she explained.

Jack looked thunderstruck. 'The bastard didn't tell me. You're joking, surely?'

Jana opened her handbag and gave Jack a copy of the Abramowitz letter. He read it and hurried to the door.

'Bloody hell, what are you waiting for?' he reprimanded her, looking for his car keys.

'What about the window?'

'I'll fix it later, let's go!'

4

Jana enjoyed sitting next to Jack in his MG with the top down. It reminded her of carefree student days at the Police Academy. Looking relaxed, she let the wind play with her hair. Not even the heavy morning traffic crossing the Harbour Bridge seemed to bother her.

'Great car, don't you think?' asked Jack, lovingly patting the dashboard like a proud first-wheels-teenager. 'I guess I was lucky.'

'How come?'

'Dreadful marriage, great divorce. I ended up with this old thing and the boat, and my dear wife got the town house and the mortgage. She's a stockbroker, you see, obsessed with real estate. Negative gearing, capital gain, all that stuff. That's just not me, I'm afraid,' he explained, enjoying the sun on his face and the closeness of the exciting woman sitting next to him.

'Any children?' Jana asked casually, looking down at the Opera House.

'No, only careers. Oh yeah, and a cat. She took the cat, thank God! Travelling journalists and cats don't mix. Nine lives just wouldn't be enough.' Jana began to laugh. 'What about you?' he asked.

'I seem to have been spared domestic bliss. The Police Force isn't exactly a good place for such things ...'

'Single?' Jana nodded. 'Career girl, eh?' said Jack, looking sideways at her.

'Did you say girl?'

'Beg your pardon, Ma'am. I bet you're a good shot as well.'

'The best. Now try to keep your eyes on the road.'

'What's that bastard doing?' asked Jack, looking in the rear view mirror.

'What do you mean?'

'The car behind us ...' Suddenly, a black four-wheel drive with tinted windows veered to the right and began to overtake. 'Here he comes.'

'Look out!' shouted Jana. Jack could feel the heavy car on his right bump against the driver's door and begin to push him off the road. 'Jesus!' Jack cried out and hit the brakes, almost smashing into the guardrail to his left. The black car, its number plate covered in mud, accelerated, changed lanes and disappeared into the traffic.

'That was close,' said Jack, turning to Jana. 'Are you okay?'

'This was no accident, Jack! Are you going to tell me what's going on here?' asked Jana, taking a deep breath.

'I really don't know.'

'Sure. You must have pissed someone off big time, that's all I can say. The vandalised car, the brick and now this? Come on, Jack, we both know this fits a pattern.'

'I think it's some kind of a warning ...'

'Warning about what?'

Frowning, Jack bit his lip. 'I'm not sure – honest.'

Jana didn't believe him. 'You keep ignoring this, you could end up in deep trouble and you know it.'

'Yes, Ma'am.'

'You haven't learnt a thing, have you, Jack?

'The car has to go to the panel beater anyway, for the scratches – right? They can fix the door at the same time,' Jack replied, grinning. Somehow, danger always seemed to follow Jack, Jana remembered. Yet somehow, he always got out of it – just. Lucky guy.

Bloody larrikin, thought Jana. 'Have it your way. But

remember, I did warn you,' she said gravely.

'Yes, Ma'am.'

'And you can cut out the "Yes, Ma'am" crap.'

'Yes ...'

Lena Abramowitz lived in a tiny flat in a neglected block of units in Rose Bay, a Sydney suburb popular with European immigrants of her background and generation. She spoke broken English with the heavy guttural accent of the Eastern European, and was difficult to understand.

'Sit here, I bring cake,' she said gruffly, after Jana had explained the purpose of their visit. The musty room was cluttered with all kinds of furniture that once must have graced a much larger home.

Display cabinets filled with heavy Bohemian crystal and porcelain figurines lined the walls. Dashing hussars on horseback and girls in rococo dresses smiled through the smudged glass. An assortment of threadbare Persian rugs piled on top of each other covered the floor. A large old radio stood prominently in the middle of a badly scratched dining table covered in dust.

'You say in your letter, Miss Abramowitz, that you recognised the man in the uniform,' began Jana, handing the old lady a copy of the photograph. 'What can you tell us about him?'

'He came to *lager*, how you say? – camp, often, with his *hund*, dog – a big dog. He always came with *Kommandant*; he was important man, you know.' Her face lit up. 'I see him now. He like music. We had orchestra in *lager*, you know. They played when the trains arrived. So many people, so many *zuege* – trains – so many dead. *Schrecklich!*' She paused and stared at the photograph in her lap. '*Wiener musik*, you know,' she continued softly, her voice barely audible. '*Waltzer, polkas, Strauss*. He always spoke to musicians and asked for special *musik*.' She paused again. 'I work in *Canada* section sorting clothing of people from trains. Mountains of shoes, mountains of scarfs, gloves, *brillen,* ah, spectacles, you know.' Her voice trailed off and the photograph fell to the floor.

'He just stand there with his *hund* as the trains came into *lager* and listened to music; always *Wiener musik.* "Juden raus, schnell, schnell! Links, rechts!" I can hear it now; Jews get out! Women and children, right; men, left.' She waved her thin bony arm about. When she let her arm fall back into her lap, Jana noticed a set of small, faded numbers tattooed into her forearm. For a while, the old lady just sat there with her eyes closed.

'Where was this, Miss Abramowitz?' Jack asked.

'Auschwitz.'

'Can you remember his name?' asked Jack, holding his breath.

'The *Kommandant* called him, Herr *Sturmbannfuehrer,* you know. I had a *zwilling,* a twin sister, Miriam, but she was not any longer with me then,' continued the old lady, drifting away from the question. 'She died after medical experiment. *Doktor* Mengele, *der teufel,* monster! She was only fifteen. We have many twins in Auschwitz, the doctors very interested in twins, you know. All that pain, all that pain.' She paused again and her head sank slowly against the back of the chair.

'Is there anything else about Herr Sturmbannfuehrer you can remember?' Jana asked, bending over the old woman in the chair. There was no reply.

'I think she's fallen asleep, we better go,' Jack suggested, standing up to leave.

'The *hund,*' replied the old woman softly, barely moving her lips. 'He has shiny silver collar with writing on it. I can see it now.' Jana looked at Jack staring at the woman in the chair.

'Can you see the writing?' Jana asked quietly. The old lady had slipped into a trance-like state, suspended, not quite awake, yet not quite asleep.

'*Ja,* Miriam. Remember, we often joked about it, *Arbeit macht frei.*'

'What did she say?' Jack asked impatiently. 'I couldn't hear.'

'She's talking to her dead sister. *Arbeit macht frei,*' Jana answered, her voice sounding hoarse. 'The motto of Auschwitz – *work sets you free*, written on a dog's collar, would you believe.'

'Now, that's what I call cynical.'

They left the flat without disturbing the sleeping old lady. Folding his lanky frame into the driver's seat, Jack reached across to the glove box and took out a small notebook. 'Old habit,' he explained, jotting down a summary of their conversation with Miss Abramowitz. 'Write it down straight away before your memory plays tricks on you, as my first editor used to say.'

Jack suggested lunch at a small seafood restaurant. 'Everything she told us about Auschwitz was accurate, you know,' he observed. 'She may not have given us a name,' continued Jack, 'but she did provide a credible link between the man in the photo and Auschwitz. Assuming she didn't really recognise the officer, she certainly recognised his dog, or rather that collar. She couldn't possibly have noticed the engraving; we could barely see it with our magnifying glass in the enlargement.' He took another sip of wine and reached for his notebook.

Jana looked dreamily across the sparkling harbour, enjoying the warm sunshine caressing her face. 'Something puzzles me, Jack.'

'Oh?'

'Why are you so interested in all this ...? Aren't wartime stories rather passé? This isn't really your kind of stuff, is it?'

'What makes you say that?' Jack was watching her carefully from behind his dark sunglasses.

'Well, you have quite a reputation for investigative journalism of a rather different kind.'

'And what kind might that be?'

'You know exactly what I mean. Religion, the Church, faith, history, and always with your particular twist. You like to provoke, isn't that so? You're the challenger, right?' Jack did not reply. Instead, he topped up their glasses.

'*A Day In The Life Of The Pope – The Da Vinci Code Phenomenon – The Mary Magdalene Conspiracy*,' Jana rattled off the titles of some of his recent articles.

'Not bad. More inside information from the short-skirt-loving editor of mine trying to keep you by his side a little bit longer, I bet,' quipped Jack.

'No, just a little research on an old rascal I used to know. Seriously, Jack, why this story – to be read on a Sunday morning with a latte and croissants, and then to be forgotten? You aren't usually that flippant with your work, are you?'

'Even journalists have to eat. Most purists are starving.'

'Is it really that simple? Something tells me there has to be more ...'

Jack looked at her. He'd only told Jana enough about his own investigation to keep her involved. He hadn't told her about one of life's unexpected little coincidences. He hadn't told her about what else he had found in the ashes of the cottage ...

'It's a good story, that's all,' Jack repeated casually, reaching for the bottle.

Jana wasn't convinced. 'Really? I wonder ...' she mused, shaking her head. Despite the warmth of the sun, she suddenly felt quite cold.

Back in his attic study, Jack called one of his mates at the BBC in London. His friend had contacts in the Vatican Radio and had helped before. As he waited for his mate to come to the phone, Jack wrote three names on his notepad – Berenger Diderot, Marie Colbert and Francine Bijoux.

31

5

The Newman family residence stood concealed from the road by a green umbrella of tall Moreton Bay figs. The familiar summer-hum of cicadas near the fountain appeared particularly shrill and hypnotic in the stillness of the hot afternoon. Apart from a young man polishing a vintage Bentley parked under the trees, the expansive grounds were deserted. Aware of the searching eye of the CCTV camera trained on her from above, Jana took a deep breath before pressing the doorbell.

Inside the house it was pleasantly cool. As she followed the quietly spoken housekeeper down a long corridor, Jana recognised several of the paintings hanging on the walls. *Brett Whiteley, Norman Lindsay, Sidney Nolan*, she thought. *Not bad.*

The housekeeper stopped in front of a wood-panelled door and opened it. 'Inspector Gonski, Sir Eric,' she announced and stood aside. When Jana entered the room, three men seated on leather chesterfields by the fireplace stood up.

'I'm Henry Voss, the family solicitor,' said one of the men, politely extending his hand. 'We spoke earlier. Let me introduce you, Inspector. Horst and Heinrich Newman,' he continued, pointing to the two younger men standing next to him. An awkward silence followed.

'And I am Eric Newman,' Jana heard someone call out from behind. A tall, lean man with a striking head of white hair – neatly parted in the middle – walked slowly towards her. 'You are obviously interested in art, Inspector. I noticed your eyes went straight to my friend over here. Right?' he asked, running his hand playfully over the top of a large stone bust on a pedestal. 'A little frightening, isn't he?' he continued without waiting for an answer. 'And so he should be. He is a demon after all; the Hebrew demon, *Asmodeus*.'

'How fascinating.'

'Do you know who he is?'

'No,' replied Jana, shaking her head.

'Protector of secrets and minder of hidden treasure.' Newman motioned casually towards a mahogany sideboard. 'Please, do sit down. A cool drink perhaps?'

How extraordinary, thought Jana. *He's totally at ease and in complete control. And he's trying to put me off balance.* Within moments, Newman had taken over. As he came closer, Jana noticed that his eyes, behind a pair of small, gold-rimmed glasses, were still clear and ice blue. *Quite remarkable for a man of eighty-seven*, she thought. He shook her hand with a grip that was both firm and gentle. His hand was cold and dry and she found his touch unnerving. He spoke perfect English, with only the slightest hint of an accent occasionally betraying his foreign origin. Jana tried to resist his obvious charm. She did not want to be distracted by the easy, polished manner of this urbane man, or to be side-tracked by pleasantries or trivia.

'You are mistaken, Sir Eric. I was actually looking at the photographs over here,' Jana said, pointing to a group of photographs on top of the mantelpiece. 'Photos can tell so much, don't you think?' She gave him her best smile. *So much for charm*, she thought. Jana opened her briefcase, took out an enhanced copy of the photograph showing the naked boy and the SS officer, and pushed it across the coffee table towards Newman. *And so much for pleasantries*, she thought, carefully observing the expression on his face.

'You know of course why I'm here, Sir Eric,' Jana said casually, coming straight to the point. 'Have you seen this photo before?'

33

'Only in last Sunday's newspaper,' Newman replied, without actually looking at the photograph. The expression on his face had changed; he appeared suddenly tense. The affable, debonair manner had vanished.

'But it was found in your house. How do you suggest it got there?'

'As I have just told you, Inspector, I saw it for the first time in the paper.'

'I understand that you built the house back in the sixties as a holiday home for the family,' Jana pressed on.

'Yes, it was mainly for the children. You are obviously well informed. You will therefore be aware that it was rented out for many years after my children grew up. We had numerous tenants. You can check with my agent if you like.'

'I see.' Jana continued undeterred, reaching for her briefcase. 'What about this, Sir Eric, do you recognise any of these items? This box was found under the body of the young woman who lost her life fighting the fire.' Jana was tempted to say, *protecting your property*, but checked herself. She opened the box and emptied the contents onto the wooden tabletop in front of her. 'A Ritterkreuz, a Totenkopf ring, insignia and buttons belonging to the uniform of a Sturmbannfuehrer – just like the one in the photo here – and a cigarette case with an engraved swastika.'

'Fascinating. And you say all of this was found in our cottage? How odd.' Sir Eric picked up the silver cigarette case and turned to his sons. 'Have you seen this before?' he asked, tracing the small swastika with the tip of his finger. They glanced at it briefly and shook their heads. 'There, you have your answer, Inspector. As you can see, we cannot help you.' Newman put the cigarette case back on the coffee table and looked calmly at Jana. 'Is there anything else?'

'You have a beautiful home, Sir Eric,' Jana replied, changing the subject. She realised that somehow she had to get under the old man's guard. As time was running out, she decided to gamble. She was going to bait him. 'And such a lovely family,' she continued, pointing to the photographs on the mantelpiece. 'You said earlier that you built the cottage for your children. I presume that includes your daughter?' Jana asked, watching Newman carefully. The rift between Sir Eric and his high profile daughter was public knowledge; it had been dragged through the social gossip magazines only the year before. Newman sat up abruptly, as if prodded from behind, and turned towards Jana. A shadow of anger flashed across his face. It only lasted an instant, but Jana noticed and decided to press on.

'She doesn't appear to feature in any of the family snapshots over here, yet you have every reason to be proud of her. Wasn't it only last year that she received the Order of Australia for her work?'

'You appear to know a lot about my family as well, Inspector Gonski, I am flattered. But please tell me, what has all this to do with your inquiry?' Newman asked.

'Perhaps nothing at all,' Jana replied. *Two can play this game*, she thought. It was obvious that the interview could not progress much further. She put one of her business cards on the table next to the photograph and stood up. 'In case you do remember something, Sir Eric, please give me a call,' said Jana, with more than a hint of sarcasm in her voice.

Newman frowned. 'Please do sit down, Inspector; I think it is time we stopped beating around the bush and put the *real* cards on the table,' he said frostily. It sounded more like a command than a request. His solicitor began to squirm uncomfortably in his seat and was about to say something, but Newman held up his hand. It was obvious who was in control. His solicitor sat back and said nothing.

'As you wish,' Jana replied and sat down.

'What you are really here to find out, Inspector, is whether the man in the photo next to the Jewish boy is me. Right?' Jana did not reply. 'You are really asking whether this Nazi honour ring – as you call it – and all these other curios allegedly found in our cottage, belong to me.' Newman took off his glasses and began to polish the lenses with a white handkerchief. Jana was fascinated by the old man's calculated performance. Newman put his glasses back on, leant slightly forward and looked directly at Jana.

'The answer to both of your questions, Inspector Gonski, is no. No, I am not the man in the photo, and no, these things are not mine,' he said in a quiet, yet almost threatening tone of voice. The air in the room felt suddenly hot and oppressive. Jana's hands and neck began to perspire. She realised that this impeccably dressed old man sitting opposite her was both unpredictable and dangerous; a man who, if challenged or threatened, would instantly turn into a resourceful and vicious adversary. She also sensed she had been told a lie. Despite her discomfort, Jana held his gaze.

'How do you know the boy in the photograph was Jewish? There was nothing in the article to suggest that,' Jana said, looking directly into the old man's ice-blue eyes. For a while Newman did not respond.

'If you look carefully, Inspector, you will see that the boy has been circumcised. In Germany at the time, only Jews were circumcised.'

'I must congratulate you, Sir Eric. You have remarkable powers of observation. You barely looked at the photograph here and the unfortunate boy's private parts were masked in the paper.' Newman just looked at her without saying another word. The meeting had obviously come to an end.

Jana walked towards the door and stopped in front of the bust of the demon Asmodeus. 'One can only hope, Sir Eric, that the demon hasn't lost his powers,' Jana said, without turning around. 'To guard secrets and protect hidden treasure, that is,' she added quietly and left the room.

Arrogant bitch, thought Newman, a flash of anger clouding his eyes.

6

Jana reached for her mobile and dialled Jack's number. 'Where are you?' she asked. 'I can hear water.'

'Sailing. Hold on, I have to tack.' Jana could hear the tinkling of the sheet running through the steel block as the boat came about. 'That's better. The ferry came a little too close. How did it go?'

'Buy me a drink and I'll tell you.'

'That bad, eh? You're on. Hop in a cab and come to Watsons Bay. I'll pick you up at the wharf in half an hour. Have to go.' Jack's words almost drowned in a clatter of flapping sails and gurgling water.

Watsons Bay, a popular suburb located at the entry to Sydney Harbour, was teeming with tourists. Jana got out of the taxi and looked around: seeing Jack's familiar boat tied up at the end of the wharf conjured up memories of long balmy nights spent on the harbour.

'Permission to come on board,' she shouted, waving. Jana kicked off her shoes and jumped on board. Jack pointed to the tiller. 'Hold this,' he said, lowering the jib. 'Let's head back. There, thunder; could be a storm.' Jack looked up at the dark clouds rolling in from the south. The wind freshened and the temperature dropped rapidly. Draping his favourite old sailing jumper over Jana's shoulders, Jack took back the tiller and looked at her.

'Well, Sir Eric is an impressive man. It's hard to believe he's almost eighty-seven. Sharp, quick-witted, no Alzheimer's there, I can tell you! He was courteous, yet his politeness didn't feel genuine – quite the opposite, if you know what I mean.'

Jack nodded. 'What about his appearance? Any resemblance to the man in the photo?' he asked.

'He's certainly the right height and the correct age, but that's about all. The picture *is* more than fifty years old; appearances change. But there was something about his eyes ...' Jana stopped mid-sentence. 'It's difficult to articulate – something mocking, something cruel,' she explained. 'I can't be more specific I'm afraid; it's only a feeling. Yet, when I look at the man in the photo, I have the same feeling. Not very helpful, is it?'

'On the contrary, first impressions are most valuable and often surprisingly accurate. Go on.'

'Of course he denied all knowledge of the photo and the Nazi stuff, just as we expected. But the way he did it was quite extraordinary.'

'What do you mean?'

'I think he was really telling me that of course he was the man in the picture, but that I would never know for sure and would never be able to prove it. It appeared quite deliberate, like a game. No, not a game; more like a challenge.'

When they tied the boat to the mooring, the first heavy raindrops began drumming against the deck. Soon, the raindrops turned to hail, making it difficult to row ashore in the small dinghy. By the time they reached the jetty, they were covered in ice-balls the size of marbles, and shivering.

'Not a bad kitchen for a bachelor. How's your cooking, nowadays?' asked Jana, looking for a place to put down the wet paper bags filled with groceries.

'Patience, and you'll find out. How about something quick,

spicy and Asian. A stir fry perhaps?' Jack opened a bottle of wine and handed her a glass.

'Promises, promises,' Jana joked.

'If you're prepared to help, we could be eating in half an hour.' Jack placed the wok on the gas stove and began to arrange his ingredients next to the chopping board. 'I forgot, career women don't cook, do they?'

'Just give me a moment and I'll surprise you. But I have to get out of these wet things first. May I borrow something of yours? And a quick shower perhaps?'

'Be my guest. My entire wardrobe is at your disposal,' Jack replied, pointing to the stairs with his glass.

'Did you say wardrobe? Come on, Jack, you never had a wardrobe. Checked shirts and jeans and a couple of old jumpers – threadbare at the elbows – if I remember correctly, that's about it. And of course, I almost forgot, that leather bomber jacket – right? You've still got it, I bet.'

'You know me too well; piss off.' Jack took another sip of wine and began to chop the chillies.

When Jana returned wearing one of Jack's checked flannel shirts, thin strips of chicken were sizzling furiously in the wok, and the kitchen was filling with the aroma of frying onions and ginger. Jana noticed that Jack had almost finished the bottle. 'I was right,' she said. 'Your stuff belongs in a charity bin.'

'Stop whingeing. You obviously don't mind wearing it – see? First my favourite sailing jumper and now my shirt. What's next?' Jack asked, grinning.

'Do you mind?'

'Of course not. Wearing anything underneath?'

'I won't tell you.'

'Teaser!'

'Look who's talking.'

'Enough! Make yourself useful and chop something. There's lemongrass, then you can get to the coriander and a little more chilli.' Jack opened another bottle and watched Jana fumble with the chillies. He noticed that his shirt was a little too short to be entirely decent, yet long enough to tease his imagination. Her wet hair, combed straight back, accentuated her prominent cheekbones and the graceful arch of her neck. Her long legs, still flushed from the hot shower, had a soft, pinkish glow.

'Not like that! I thought I told you to chop the chillies, not destroy them,' Jack complained, shaking his head. 'What am I going to do with you?' Jana looked up, raised an eyebrow, but said nothing. Jack walked over to her, took the knife out of her hand and kissed her on the back of the neck. Jana did not pull away; instead, she turned slowly around, opened her mouth just a little and began to lick her lips with the tip of her tongue. Putting her arms around his neck she lifted herself onto the kitchen table directly behind her.

'Any ideas?' she purred, her voice sounding seductively husky.

7

Jana switched on the bedside lamp and answered the phone. She recognised the tone of voice instantly; desk sergeants on night duty sound the same anywhere, especially at four o'clock in the morning.

'Inspector Gonski?'

'Yes.'

'You know Jack Rogan, the journalist – right?'

'Yes.' An eternity seemed to pass before the voice continued. 'There's been a burglary ...'

'Jack?' was all she could say. Her mouth went dry.

'He's been injured.'

'How bad ...?'

'He's on his way to hospital.'

'But I only left him a few hours ago.' Jana's voice sounded shrill.

'I'm sorry.'

Jack was in the operating theatre. The night nurse was tight-lipped and uncooperative. Even Jana's police ID was no help. She found waiting difficult at the best of times, but sitting in casualty early in the morning, next to bleeding drunks and incoherent druggies was almost unbearable. But worst of all was the uncertainty.

To calm herself, Jana began to read the fax she'd received from her research assistant the night before. It contained background information on Newman and his family.

Dr Erich Neumueller, (he changed his name by deed poll to Eric Newman in 1947), arrived in South Australia in December 1946 by boat from Genoa. There is a letter of introduction from a certain Monsignor Brandauer addressed to Bishop Honegger in Adelaide. His immigration to Australia was apparently arranged and sponsored by the Vatican. However, when I requisitioned his immigration papers to find out more about this, I came across something odd – classified information. I was denied access. I will try the Freedom of Information Act to get around this, but as you know, this will take some time. In the interim, I have asked for his divorce file, which should tell us a little more. Until I receive that, I'm afraid this is all I have been able to come up with. Strange, isn't it ...?

'Inspector Gonski?' Jana looked up. 'The doctor will see you now,' the nurse said. A very tired looking young intern in a dark green operating gown was examining X-rays in the far corner of the brightly lit room.

'You're the investigating officer, I take it? I think we've saved his eye,' the doctor said casually before Jana could contradict him. 'He has some rather nasty injuries though,' he continued, 'there will be permanent scarring, here and here.' He pointed to the X-rays in front of him. 'He received a terrible beating; it's one of the worst I've seen for a long time. He had a bad fall as well and lost a lot of blood. There was considerable internal bleeding, several broken ribs, extensive bruising, abrasions; his face is a mess.' The doctor looked at his notes and rattled off the injuries like items on a shopping list. 'He's lucky to be alive. He could easily have broken his neck or his back during the fall. The alcohol didn't help either. You'll have my full report in the morning.'

'When can I see him?'

'Not for quite a while, I'm afraid, perhaps in a few hours when he comes out of the anaesthetic. Now, if you'll excuse me ...' The doctor reached for the pager in the top pocket of his gown and hurried out of the room.

Jana returned to the hospital just before noon and was shown to Jack's room. She had made many a hospital bedside visit during her career and thought she'd be well prepared for what was to come. She wasn't.

At first, she couldn't recognise him at all. The top of his head, the left eye and part of his face were completely covered in bandages. A ring of dark bruises circled his other eye, which was bloodshot and almost closed. Through a small gap between the bandages, Jana could see that his head had been shaved. Several plastic tubes protruded from his nose and various monitoring devices were connected to his right arm. A fine line of small, neat, zipper-like stitches ran from the corner of his mouth along the jaw to his ear.

When Jana walked towards the bed, Jack winked at her with his good eye, a hint of a smile creasing his mouth.

'Can he talk?' Jana asked the nurse.

'Yes, he's actually quite alert; aren't you, handsome?' the nurse said, giving Jack's good hand a gentle squeeze before leaving the room.

'That was some dessert last night,' Jack whispered, moving his lips slowly and carefully. 'Look at me.' He managed to raise his hands a little. 'Next time, I want a smaller helping.' Jana laughed and wiped a few tears from her cheeks. Jack's unexpected humour had broken the dark spell of the awkward moment.

'What on earth happened?' Jana asked, regaining her composure.

'I really don't remember too much, I'm afraid. I fell asleep in the chair. Something woke me. I think it was a noise coming from upstairs. At first I thought it was you, but you'd already gone. Apart from the light in the kitchen, the house was in total darkness. That should have alerted me, I guess, but then I was still half asleep and not thinking straight. I wasn't entirely sober either ...'

'Five more minutes,' said the nurse on her way past. 'I have to change the dressing.'

'The rest happened very fast,' Jack continued. 'He was waiting for me at the top of the stairs.'

'Who?'

'My mystery sparring partner.' Jack closed his eye. 'He came at me fast, like a cat, and hit me several times in the stomach. I think I fell against the handrail. Then he hit me again, hard. My knees gave way and I went down. I remember this tremendous blow to the side of my face here.' Jack pointed to his jaw and traced the stiches. 'The last thing I remember is falling backwards down the stairs. He must have kicked me in the head, I suppose.'

'Is that all?' As soon as she said it, Jana realised just how foolish this sounded.

'I'll try to do better next time, promise.'

'Sorry. But why? Did he say anything?'

For a while, Jack did not respond. 'Yeah, I think he did say something ...'

'Can you remember what? Come on Jack, this is important.'

'Something to do with the past. Digging up the past, or something. Digging up the past can ...' As the medication wore off, the pain returned and Jack's whole body began to throb. Exhausted, he closed his eye. Ignoring the pain, he tried to recall the man at the top of the stairs. '... *can make the present* ... *very* ... *dangerous*. Yeah, that's it.' The nurse returned with fresh bandages and began to adjust Jack's drip.

'What would he have meant by that?' Jana asked.

'I think he was warning me.'

'Warning you? About what?'

'I'm not sure.'

'Newman? The article perhaps?'

'Possibly.'

'It's all related, isn't it? The car, the brick, now this.'

'Yep ...'

'What was he doing upstairs?'

'Looking for something. He came out of my study. This was no ordinary burglar, that's for sure. This guy was a pro. He knew exactly what he was doing.'

'What do you think he was looking for?'

'Something to do with my work, I'd say. But the strange thing is ...'

'What?'

'I didn't call the ambulance. I was unconscious.'

'You think he did?'

'Who else?' Gasping for air, Jack fell back against the pillow.

'You never learn, do you?' Jana said, clenching her fist in frustration. 'You ignored the signs, now look at yourself!'

'That's enough!' the nurse said curtly. 'I think it's best if you go.' She pushed Jana aside, pulled the curtain around Jack's bed and began to change his dressing.

8

'Mr Farim is in reception, shall I show him in?' asked Horst's secretary.

'Has my father arrived?'

'Yes, he's waiting in the boardroom with your brother.'

Newman only came into the office on special occasions and left the day-to-day running of the family business to his sons. However, he still insisted on being consulted regarding all major decisions affecting Newmans Colonial Bank. After all, he was the founder. On matters of real importance, he had the final say.

For the past two weeks, Horst had been working on a business venture with great potential. The unique proposal had been put to him recently in London by one of his father's art dealers.

'Thank you for coming all this way just to see me, Mr Farim,' Newman said affably, extending his hand. 'My son would have told you, I rarely travel these days.' Abdullah Farim bowed politely and shook hands. He was a stocky, broad-shouldered man of middle years with thick, oily, blue-black hair combed straight back.

'It's been a pleasure to come to your beautiful city. I can see why you are reluctant to leave it,' Farim replied in perfect English. He spoke softly, with the melodious accent of the well-educated Arab.

'I have heard a great deal about you, Mr Farim,' continued Newman, well aware of the polite, circuitous exchanges that were expected before it was considered proper to turn to the subject of real interest. Newman had dealt with Arabs before and was familiar with their customs. Farim recognised this immediately and relaxed a bit. However, his dark eyes, always restless and alert, never smiled.

'I understand that you wish to put a business proposal to us, Mr Farim,' began Newman after his guest had finished his second tiny cup of strong, Turkish coffee.

'Quite so. May I speak frankly?' asked Farim, slowly stroking the pointed beard framing his narrow face.

'Please do,' replied Newman, 'it is the best way.' He watched Farim carefully.

'I represent a small group of Egyptian patriots who believe that their country is heading in the wrong direction and wish to rectify this lamentable situation.' Smiling, Farim paused. He wanted to give his words time to have the desired effect. 'In order to achieve this,' he continued, 'my principals wish to purchase certain merchandise ...'

Newman understood exactly what Farim was telling him. Farim was really saying that he was the agent for a group of Islamic fanatics who were about to embark on a campaign of terror to force the government of their country to alter its politics.

'We are financiers, not merchants, Mr Farim,' Newman pointed out quietly. 'I cannot see how we can possibly be of assistance to you.'

'Quite so, but it is a financier we seek. A financier with certain – shall I say – inclinations and connections. In short, a financier just like you.' The calm, almost infuriating smile did not leave Farim's face. However, the tiny beads of perspiration on his brow and the eyes darting nervously around the room divulged his anxiety.

'You speak in riddles, Mr Farim. What is it you want from

us?'

'We have heard that you have participated in similar transactions before, Sir Eric.' Farim paused and reached for a glass of water on the table in front of him. 'In Kampuchea and Sri Lanka, for instance, and more recently in Ethiopia ... financing the purchase of certain sensitive goods in ... rather creative ways,' he continued, haltingly feeling his way. 'And that you are well connected with the Russians,' he added, lowering his voice.

'I think what Mr Farim is trying to say,' Horst cut in, coming to Farim's assistance, 'is that we may be able to arrange the purchase of certain merchandise of a military nature.'

'Precisely,' Farim agreed, nodding gratefully.

'I am intrigued, Mr Farim. There are many financiers much closer to home and much more experienced in matters of this kind than our small bank, yet you have travelled halfway around the world to talk to us. Why?'

'The answer, Sir Eric, lies in the unique nature of the proposal I have been instructed to put to you,' Farim replied, gaining confidence. 'Let me come straight to the point: My principals are simple people of the desert with no access to the amount of Western currency that would normally be required to finance a purchase like this. However, they have the means to pay *in kind* – and rather handsomely too, I might add – just like the Khmer Rouge.' Farim was, Sir Eric thought, clearly well informed about the family's past dealings and it appeared the latest proposal was similar.

'How?'

Farim sensed Newman's interest and took his time. 'With antiquities,' he said at last. The expression on Newman's face told him he had chosen the correct approach. Encouraged, he pressed on. 'As you know, the ancient sands of Egypt still hold many treasures and my principals have – shall we say – ready access to their heritage.'

'Are you suggesting that we provide you with arms in return

for antiquities?'

'Precisely.'

'Where's the profit?'

'I admire your candour, Sir Eric,' Farim said, stroking his beard. 'We propose to sell the antiquities to you for a quarter of their market value. My agents tell me you are very well connected in the art world and would have little difficulty finding willing buyers. Needless to say, how, and for how much you sell the items, is of course entirely a matter for you.' Farim made an expansive gesture with his right hand. 'And besides, I understand you are quite a connoisseur yourself,' he added cunningly, 'who likes to keep some of the best pieces for his own collection.'

'What about the arms? How do you suggest we agree on price there?'

'We will pay market price. That shouldn't be too difficult to establish,' Farim replied without hesitation. 'I understand there is some sort of black market price list for such things.' Farim had done his homework.

The proposal was both ingenious and simple. It had its risks, but that was to be expected. No risk, no profit; Newman understood that. A few years earlier he would have embraced the deal without hesitation, but times had changed.

'I have to disappoint you, Mr Farim, you have knocked on the wrong door I am afraid. Our bank is not in a position to assist you,' Newman said sternly.

Horst began to fidget in his chair. 'But shouldn't we at least ...' he interjected. Newman silenced his son by raising his hand without looking at him and stood up. The meeting was over.

'As you wish,' Farim said, bowing politely towards his host. It was the reply he had expected. It was time to bait the hook. 'But before I leave, there is one more matter ... I almost forgot, how foolish of me,' Farim added smoothly. 'Something I'm sure you will find most interesting ...'

'And what might that be?' Newman asked.

'I don't quite know how to put this. I hope you will not misunderstand ... I have strict instructions from my principals ...'

'Please, Mr Farim, try to get to the point,' Newman interrupted impatiently.

'To tell you ... but only you ... privately that is ...' Farim continued haltingly.

'Really! Come now, let us not play games. Whatever it is you want to tell me you can tell me in front of my sons. We don't have any secrets here.'

'I do apologise. I didn't mean to offend you, but as I said before, my instructions ... I cannot ... Please understand this is not my decision.' Farim stroked his beard one more time and a troubled look clouded his face.

'In that case, Mr Farim, I would rather not know. Horst, would you please show Mr Farim out,' Newman said curtly, annoyed by Farim's persistence.

'This is most regrettable,' Farim said casually, following Horst to the door. 'I believe you have been looking for information about *Armand de Blanquefort* for a long time.'

Newman tried to get up and almost knocked over the glass of water in front of him. 'What did you say?' he demanded. Farim stopped at the door and slowly turned around. He was smiling again.

'Armand de Blanquefort – the Templar – in Egypt,' Farim answered calmly.

'Sit down, Mr Farim. Horst, Heinrich, please leave us.'

9

'Good evening, Horst,' said the housekeeper, 'your father's waiting in the study.'

'I am curious,' Newman said, adjusting his dressing gown. 'You told me it was urgent.'

'It is ...'

'Well?'

'I don't quite know how to tell you this ...' Horst began. 'I did something foolish the other day, something I know you won't approve of.' Newman walked to the sideboard and poured two whiskies. 'I arranged a ... um, well ... a search, yes a search of ...'

'You sound just like our Mr Farim this morning. Do try to get to the point. Here, have this, it might help.' Newman handed Horst a scotch.

'That journalist's house – you know that chap Rogan ...' Horst gulped down his drink. Newman looked at him without touching his glass. 'There's more, I'm afraid. Can I have another one?'

'Help yourself.'

'I just wanted to find out what he knew ... with the float coming up, you see, and teach him a lesson.'

'What kind of lesson?'

'You know, persuade him to drop the story, make him see sense ...'

'Sense? Let me get this straight. Are you telling me that you hired someone to break into the journalist's home, search the house, and rough him up a little to make him see sense?' Horst nodded sheepishly, and gulped down his second scotch.

'I know it sounds bad.'

'You cannot be serious. Who did you use?'

'Cramer.' *At least that was good news*, thought Newman. Cramer was a Vietnam veteran turned private investigator who could be trusted.

'You must have been out of your mind. Do you realise what this could mean? Do you? If this is in some way linked to us, and that inspector, that crazy policewoman, gets wind of it ...' hissed Newman.

'Not a chance!' protested Horst. 'You know Cramer, we can rely on him.' Horst did not mention Rogan's injuries and hospitalisation.

'Up to a point. You know what really puzzles me?'

'What?'

'Why you're telling me all this now? I know you Horst, this is not like you. Why tell me at all?'

'Why? Because of this,' Horst replied, reaching into his pocket. He pulled out an envelope. 'Cramer found this in the journalist's study next to the photo the policewoman showed us here yesterday.' Horst opened the envelope and handed a badly damaged black and white photograph to his father.

Newman put down his glass and held the photo under the light of the desk lamp. He examined it for a long time without saying anything, turned it over and read what was left of the singed inscription on the back, 'Montse ...'

'And this was apparently pinned to the photo,' Horst explained, handing his father a piece of paper. Three names were written on it – Berenger Diderot, Marie Colbert and Francine Bijoux – and a notation underlined in red: Newman in Montsegur?

Newman paled.

'Obviously the journalist thinks this is you,' said Horst, pointing to the officer in the photograph. 'I thought you should know ...'

'Can I keep this?'

'Certainly.'

Looking at the photo on his desk with his back to his son, Newman said, 'Now, listen carefully. This whole woeful episode must go no further, is that clear? You will not discuss this with anyone, and you will promise me not to do anything without consulting me first, understood?'

'Absolutely. Whatever you say. I was only trying to help,' Horst said lamely, relieved to be getting off so lightly. 'There's something else you should know.'

'You have more?'

'Cramer saw that policewoman and the journalist – together – at his home last night. Apparently they were rather intimate ... you know ... on the kitchen table ... Cramer took some photos. I haven't seen them yet, but ...'

'For heaven's sake Horst, this is not a divorce case,' Newman interrupted impatiently.

'I suppose Cramer just couldn't help himself. He's used to investigating infidelities. You never know, the pictures could come in useful one day ...'

'Perhaps. But not now. Have you spoken to Farim?' Newman asked, changing the subject.

'Yes, he was obviously pleased with your decision. He's making arrangements for the first delivery straight away. It should only be a matter of a week or so.'

'Good. The sooner we know where we stand, the better. Now, let's get some sleep, shall we? It has been a long day.' Newman walked to the front door with Horst.

'Why did you change your mind?' Horst asked, stepping outside into the cool night. 'What did Farim tell you? If I'm going to be dealing with him, I think I should know.' Newman looked at his son. Horst was right; sooner or later he had to know. This was as good a time as any.

'What I am about to tell you will remain strictly between us, is that clear? That means not even telling your brother.'

'Absolutely, you can rely on me.' Horst would have gladly crawled over broken glass for an opportunity to be taken into his father's confidence.

'Farim offered me something I've been searching for ... for a long time.'

'What?'

'Information about a warrior-monk, one of the Knights Templar,' Newman explained.

'What information?'

'Proof that the Templars travelled through Egypt in the fourteenth century.'

'Are you serious? What kind of proof?'

'A dagger found in Egypt, which once belonged to the knight ... and something else ...'

'You changed your mind because of an old dagger?' interrupted Horst, shaking his head. 'Why?'

'Because ... of a quest begun a long time ago ... and a pact made between friends. There is more, a lot more ...' Newman started to explain but quickly checked himself. 'I'll tell you about it another time. Good night, Horst,' Newman replied curtly and closed the door.

Newman returned to his study and looked at the photograph of the young officer standing in front of the castle tower. Why had Horst arranged that clumsy burglary and turned up this old snapshot in the process? Newman began to smile. Another sign? A pointer perhaps, or something more?

He opened the top drawer of his desk, took out a magnifying glass and the small sheet of paper Farim had given him that afternoon. It was a photocopy of a single page written in French. The writing had faded but was still legible.

'*These are, I believe, the last words I will be able to record before our enemies overwhelm us. We are surrounded, escape is impossible,*' he began to read, running his finger slowly along the two lines.

The rest of the text, except for the signature, had been masked.

But the name and date at the bottom of the page – Armand de Blanquefort – was the item of real interest. Newman examined the signature through the magnifying glass and carefully traced each letter. Forgery seemed unlikely.

How extraordinary, he thought, that after almost half a century of futile, painstaking search, Blanquefort should find him, virtually on the same day the Abbé Diderot had reappeared out of the past. Newman did not believe in coincidences, only destiny.

10

Cardinal Brandauer reached for his cane and walked slowly across to the large window overlooking the dome of St Peter's Basilica. It was four o'clock in the morning and most of the Vatican was still sleeping. As head of the Vatican Congregation of the Doctrine of the Faith and Dean of the College of Cardinals he only allowed himself four hours sleep a night. He had just knelt on his pew and folded his hands to pray when the phone rang. Annoyed, the Cardinal stood up. Reaching for the black Bakelite receiver, he noticed that the private line indicator was blinking on the panel; only a privileged few knew the number.

'Pronto.'

'Good morning, Sebastian. I am sorry to disturb you this early, but something important has just come up,' Newman said, coming straight to the point. He knew the Cardinal would like it that way.

'Eric. What is it?'

'Armand de Blanquefort.'

'What? Did you find something?'

'Yes. A dagger with his family crest engraved on the blade.'

'Are you sure?'

'I have seen it. There is more,' added Newman excitedly.

'What?'

'A letter written by Blanquefort was found with the dagger ...'

'Where?'

'Egypt. There is a signature and a date! October 1305.'

'Where in Egypt?'

'I don't know yet ...'

'How extraordinary! After all these years, who would have believed it?'

'There are some complications ... I will need assistance.'

'In what way?'

'I only have a few lines of the manuscript at this stage – that was free – no doubt to whet my appetite and loosen the purse strings. The rest I have to buy. You know how these things work.'

'You need assistance, you said.'

'Yes, with authentication, translation and so on. I do not want to involve outsiders.'

'Understood.'

'Something else has come up unexpectedly, something out of the past I have to deal with as well – urgently and discreetly.'

'Can you be more specific?'

'Diderot ...'

'Are you serious?

'Absolutely.'

'That is strange. Only yesterday the BBC contacted the Vatican with a request for certain information ...'

'Information about what?'

'The German excavations in Montsegur during the war, and ... Diderot and the Templars ...'

'Surely not another documentary?'

'We weren't told.'

'Coincidence?'

'Hardly. Destiny, I would say. Wouldn't you?'

'What are you going to do about it?' asked Newman.

'I put a lid on it of course. No information will be released.'

'Good.'

'I will send Father Habakkuk,' the Cardinal said. 'He's an expert on the subject; resourceful and totally reliable.'

'Excellent.'

'Please keep me informed and be careful. We cannot afford to ...'

'I know. Thank you Sebastian.'

The Cardinal returned to his pew – a present from his mountain village in Bavaria – and ran the tips of his fingers over the smooth, three-hundred-year-old wood. Looking out the window, he digested the astonishing news. Should he tell the Pontiff about the unexpected discovery or should he wait? What if Eric was mistaken? *Better to wait until Habakkuk evaluates the situation*, the cautious diplomat in him counselled.

The Cardinal unlocked the bottom drawer of his desk, took out a bundle of old manuscripts and began to arrange them carefully on the tooled leather top. Some of the documents reached back several centuries to the bloody days of the Inquisition. The old threat had surfaced again.

Blanquefort in Egypt, he thought, *could it really be? After all this time — a step closer perhaps?* As he leafed through one of the manuscripts, the Cardinal found some of his old notes written many years ago. He held up the crumpled pages and began to read aloud:

'In 1119, nine French knights, the founding fathers of the Poor Knights of Christ and the Temple of Solomon — the Templars — travelled to Jerusalem. They were welcomed by King Baldwin who used the Al-Aqsa Mosque as his own palace, and invited them to establish their headquarters on the Temple Mount. The knights asked the king for permission to occupy part of the mosque for their own use. Curiously, this extraordinary request was granted. For the next seven years, the knights remained in Jerusalem and rarely left the mosque.'

The Cardinal put down the page, looked out the window and watched a flock of birds circle the dome of St Peters. *What were the Templars doing there during all this time?* he asked himself, playing with his pencil. *There's a clue*, he thought. *The recent archaeological excavations! A tunnel found under the mosque. The*

Templars were digging! They were looking for something! But what? And did they find what they were looking for?

The Cardinal began to search through the pile of manuscripts on his desk. He was looking for one of the first documents the Vatican had obtained from Diderot; he'd not looked at it for several years, but his hands began to shake just thinking about it. He found it pinned to one of the manuscripts at the bottom of the pile. '*There is only one ...*' he read.

Crushing the piece of paper into a tight ball, the Cardinal threw it on his desk without reading the rest. There was only one plausible explanation for the Templars' baffling activities on the Temple Mount, he thought: a search. A search that lasted seven long years and failed. Why? Because the monks were looking for something that was no longer there, something that had disappeared long before their arrival in Jerusalem.

The Cardinal took a sip of water to calm himself. But they did find it later on, he reminded himself, in Africa ... or did they? Shaking his head, he pressed the bell knob on the side of his desk. His secretary appeared almost instantly. 'Please get Father Habakkuk,' said the Cardinal, 'now.'

'You wanted to see me, Eminence,' said the black priest, standing in the doorway of the Cardinal's study. The Cardinal pointed to the leather chair facing his desk.

'I have some news you'll find interesting ...' The Cardinal paused and reached for the document he had earlier crushed into a ball. 'A letter written by Armand de Blanquefort has been found,' he added, watching the black priest carefully. Habakkuk sat up, his eyes fixed on the Cardinal like a snake about to strike, but said nothing. Slowly, the Cardinal smoothed out the creases of the crumpled page. 'You have to go to Sydney immediately to talk to Sir Eric.'

'Did he ...?'

The Cardinal held up his hand. 'Later,' he said. 'Brother Frumentius arrived from Addis Ababa yesterday.'

Habakkuk looked shocked. 'Frumentius ... is ... here?'

'Yes. He had a message for me ... from ...' The Cardinal stopped in mid-sentence.

'Another petition? He doesn't give up, does he?'

'Frumentius wants to see you,' said the Cardinal, ignoring the question. 'He will be waiting in the gardens at sunrise. Apparently you will know exactly where. It's almost light; better hurry.'

The Cardinal put his hand on the familiar pew and knelt. By the time the first rays of the morning sun illuminated the top of Michelangelo's architectural masterpiece, he knew exactly what he had to do.

11

'Is that all you've been able to come up with?' George Cunningham, the Director of Public Prosecutions, leafed through Jana's report, obviously unimpressed. 'I'm sorry, but it's not much, is it? You say you're convinced Newman was lying about the photograph, yet you offer no proof, no evidence. Then there's Mrs Abramowitz? Her story is certainly intriguing but, again, nothing tangible; it doesn't link the man in the photo to Newman. The attack on the journalist is of course regrettable, but most likely has nothing whatsoever to do with this matter. Burglaries happen all the time. In short, your conclusions are not convincing. I'm sorry ... I just can't let you continue an investigation based on gut feeling and speculation.'

Jana knew Cunningham was right. She also knew what her instincts told her. She sensed that all she needed was a little more time and an opportunity to speak to Newman's daughter.

'You're asking me to back a hunch,' continued Cunningham. 'Why? Convince me.'

'Surely we can't solve everything through reason alone,' Jana argued. 'Not everything in life is logical or rational. I mean ... sometimes, Sir, a feeling, or a hunch, can provide that missing link that reason alone ... Occasionally, we must trust our instincts if we want to reach that little bit further ...'

Cunningham put down the report and took off his glasses. 'You've said you want to speak to Newman's daughter,' he said and peered at Jana. 'Tell me about her.'

'She's a famous ophthalmic surgeon. Her late husband, Professor David Rosen, established the Rosen Foundation – surely you've heard of it, Sir? They used to work together, treating eye disease in Third World countries. Two years ago she was named Australian of The Year and last year she received an Order of Australia for her work.'

'So ... I'll be ... that's Newman's daughter. How extraordinary,' said Cunningham.

'She's the daughter of his first marriage; it's all in the report,' Jana pointed out. 'She doesn't fit into the Newman family picture at all. Apparently, she married a Jewish doctor – one of her university lecturers – against her father's wishes. Her parents divorced when she was still a teenager; I had a look at the court file. Newman has cut her off completely. He behaves as if she doesn't exist.'

'What's she doing now?'

'Her husband died in a plane crash in Ethiopia a few years ago. Since then, she's carried on his work on her own,' Jana said. 'The Foundation relies entirely on donations and bequests. She's either operating in poor countries or campaigning for the Foundation. I understand she's in great demand as a guest speaker.'

Cunningham was slowly turning the pages of the report. Jana was, he thought, one of his best agents; she had had spectacular results in the past.

'How much time do you think you need?'

'A few more days should do it,' Jana replied casually, hoping not to be questioned about the length of time.

'Why a few days? Can't you contact her straight away?'

'Well, she's a little difficult to reach right now.'

'Why?' Cunningham asked apprehensively.

'She's somewhere in the jungle.'

'Jungle? Where?'

'New Guinea.'

Settling into the flight to Port Moresby, Jana unbuckled her seatbelt, turned on the reading light and opened her backpack. She was itching to find out what her research assistant, Melanie, had come up with. Jana pulled out the sheaf of papers Melanie had hurriedly thrust into her hand in the taxi and settled back in her seat. She was intrigued to learn how an apparently impecunious refugee from war-torn Europe had managed to establish a successful merchant bank with assets worth many millions scattered across three continents.

Newman met his first wife, Ingrid, reported Melanie, *the daughter of a Lutheran pastor, during his stay in Hahndorf soon after his arrival in South Australia. They married in December 1947 and moved to Adelaide. Newman went to work for a stockbroker.* Melanie had obtained most of this information from Newman's divorce file.

A daughter, Bettany, was born in 1949. There were no other children. In 1962, the family moved to Sydney and a year later Ingrid Newman sued for divorce. So far, so good. However, the period between his arrival in December 1946 and his marriage the following year is still a blank. Until we get our hands on his immigration file – the classified section – we'll just have to be patient. I've made the Freedom of Information application and told them it was urgent.

Breathing heavily, the quiet young man with the striking halo of fuzzy hair had his eyes closed. There were beads of perspiration glistening like tears on his cheeks. He hadn't touched his food.

'You should really try the dinner,' said Jana, turning to her dark-skinned neighbour, 'it's quite good.'

'I'm not hungry, thank you,' replied the young man politely, keeping his eyes closed and increasing his grip on the armrests.

'Are you returning home?' asked Jana, trying to keep the conversation going.

'Yes.'

'This is my first trip to New Guinea.' There was no reply. 'I'm going to Bundi; it's somewhere in the Highlands I believe, do you know it?'

'To Bundi?' repeated the young man. He opened his eyes and looked at Jana for the first time. 'So am I.' He introduced himself as Daniel Kunduna, a medical student returning to New Guinea for the holidays. His parents still lived in a small village near Bundi, he explained. When Jana mentioned Dr Rosen's name, Daniel became quite excited. Dr Rosen was revered in the Highlands as a great healer, he told her. She had encouraged him to study medicine and had helped him win a scholarship.

The remaining hours of the long flight passed quickly. Daniel entertained her with fascinating stories of *wana perena porois* – ancestral spirits – and sorcerers called *wei kumos*. He spoke of ancient rituals and traditional *sing sings*. Her suddenly chatty neighbour appeared to have lost his fear of flying altogether. Not only did he devour his next meal, but was happy to accept part of hers as well.

Jana spent the night at the Australian embassy in Port Moresby. There were only two flights a week to Bundi. Weather permitting, the next one was due to leave in the morning.

The small plane was filled to capacity. Jana's seat was at the back. How everyone – including Daniel – had managed to board before her was a mystery. To get to her seat, she had to push past noisy natives prattling excitedly in Pidgin English and step over children playing on the floor. Nonplussed, Jana stared at her seat. It was already occupied – by a small pig in a crate.

'Don't worry about it,' said Daniel, waving from the back. 'Just push it into the aisle and sit down; this is New Guinea.'

Father Schaffer, the missionary in charge of the Bundi outpost, met every flight. He was waiting at the end of the runway, holding a big umbrella. He had bad news for Jana. Dr Rosen had gone to a remote mountain village, he explained, and wasn't due to return for several days. Jana's spirits sank.

'Dr Rosen is still up in the mountains?' asked Daniel, butting in. 'I can take you to her if you like. My village is on the way. I'm leaving in the morning.'

'I must warn you, Ms Gonski, the terrain here is very rough and almost completely isolated. Everything will have to be carried, you understand,' explained Father Schaffer. 'Uphill, for most of the way.' He pointed to the mountains covered in seemingly impenetrable rainforest behind the mission. 'A journey like this is not without danger. There are no paths; you will have to climb into deep gorges and cross many streams. I'm told some of the old suspension bridges have been washed away by the heavy rains we've had recently. It happens every year.'

'I can see you're trying to frighten me, Father,' Jana said. 'You're forgetting I'm a police officer. You should see some of the training we have to do. For once, it may actually come in useful.'

Father Schaffer had not exaggerated. It had rained heavily for weeks, making the ground muddy and treacherous. Slippery tree roots hidden under a thick carpet of rotting leaves criss-crossed the forest floor like giant spider webs waiting to ensnare the unwary. Within minutes of leaving the mission, Jana was soaked to the skin. The humidity was intense. Without the porters and Daniel's resourcefulness, the journey would have been impossible.

Jana lost count of the frightening bridges and icy streams they had to cross because the bridges were no more. Daniel set a gruelling pace, anxious to reach the village before nightfall.

'Can you smell it?' he asked, grinning at Jana.

'What?' Jana was near breaking point and could hardly speak.

'Smoke, and as they say, where there's smoke, there's fire. Cooking fire,' he said, smacking his lips. When they entered the silent village it was almost dark. 'Up there.' Daniel pointed to a small clearing above the village. 'That's Dr Rosen's tent.'

Clambering up to the tent, Jana thought she could hear music. At first, she didn't trust her ears. However, as she came closer, the music became louder and clearer; unmistakably Mozart. Ignoring her aching back and burning feet, she stood in front of the tent and listened. When she tried to lift her stiff arms to take off her backpack, she heard footsteps approaching from behind.

'Let me help you with that,' someone said. Jana turned around. A tall, middle-aged woman holding a lantern came walking towards her out of the shadows. 'Tea?' she asked.

'Oh yes, please,' Jana replied gratefully.

12

Habakkuk knew exactly where to find Brother Frumentius. They had met in the Vatican gardens many times as young men, always at the Fontana Della Galera, the Galleon Fountain. Frumentius sat on a stone bench facing the fountain and watched the water cascade out of the gun ports of the ornate galleon in the centre. The galleon, covered with wet moss, reminded him of a ghost ship rising out of the deep.

'I was trying to remember. I think it's been fifteen years,' Habakkuk said, walking up to Frumentius from behind. The grey-haired man stood up, turned around and embraced Habakkuk.

'They called us the black twins, remember?'

'Always together, always laughing, impossible to tell apart.'

'Look at you, you haven't changed at all,' said Frumentius, shaking his head.

'Neither have you.' They both knew it wasn't so. They linked arms and began to stroll through the gardens. 'What brings you here?' Habakkuk asked. 'After all these years?'

'I came to deliver a message to the Cardinal – from the Guardian.'

'In person? It must be important.'

'It is.'

'Another petition?' asked Habakkuk, raising an eyebrow.

'Yes, and a message. I have a message for you as well ...'

'Oh?'

'I suppose it's more of a reminder than a message,' Frumentius continued quietly.

'A reminder, how curious. You are to remind me – of what?' bristled Habakkuk.

'Of who you are, where you belong.'

'Isn't that a little presumptuous? I know who I am.'

'I'm only the messenger ...'

'If I remember correctly, we had a similar discussion about this very topic, in this very garden, many years ago. Just before you went back,' said Habakkuk.

'Quite.'

'And the petition?'

'Access to the archives.'

'Again?'

'Yes. You know we should be given permission ...'

'I disagree,' Habakkuk interrupted. 'The interests of Mother Church are paramount; *you know that.*'

'Here we go again! Suppressing the truth is not the way!'

'Preventing the faithful from falling into error is our duty! The Church has done so, many times – I can point to countless examples, and so can you.'

'Yes, of bloodshed and torture, bigotry and ruthless persecution – all tried and tested tools of the Inquisition – the end justifies the means,' snapped Frumentius. 'Eradicate heresy at all cost – the Albigensian Crusade, the burning of the Cathars at Montsegur – do you still believe that? We are no longer in the Dark Ages, you know.' Habakkuk didn't reply. 'I see. We agree to disagree, nothing has changed.'

'He's turned you down, again?' asked Habakkuk.

'I'm not at liberty to say.'

'You don't have to; I can work it out for myself ...'

Frumentius looked sadly at Habakkuk. 'You have a lot of influence, I hear; especially with the Cardinal. Could you ... perhaps ...?'

'I'll see what I can do. Are you staying in Rome for a while?'

asked Habakkuk, watching his friend carefully. He was well aware that Frumentius had a great deal of influence himself, in very powerful circles. Habakkuk knew he had to be careful.

'I will stay here until you come back from Sydney,' replied Frumentius calmly. 'Armand de Blanquefort could be telling us something new,' he whispered.

Habakkuk shook his head, laughing. 'I shouldn't be surprised, but I am. My conversation with the Cardinal was less than half an hour ago. I don't know how you do it.'

'You once told me, the Vatican has the highest concentration of keen ears in the world,' replied Frumentius, pointing a finger at Habakkuk. 'No whisper is too soft, no gesture too subtle, no language too exotic to be safe. Your words. We used to joke about it, but it's true.'

'Well, it doesn't really matter, I suppose.' Alarmed by the detail and accuracy of Frumentius' intelligence, Habakkuk sensed danger. Obviously, Frumentius had sources close to the Cardinal. Very close ...

'Remember when we used to run barefoot through the mountains back home in Axum; remember we pretended to be marathon runners?' asked Frumentius, changing topics.

'Dreaming of the Olympic Games ... look at us, great runners we turned out to be – eh? Black cassocks and sandals and no running shoes or shorts.'

'We are still running, my friend, believe me. Only the race has changed and the stakes are higher,' observed Frumentius quietly.

'All right. How about this: Wait here until I get back from Australia. If I find anything worthwhile, I'll tell you. I will also speak to the Cardinal about the archives ...'

Frumentius looked up, surprised. This wasn't what he had expected. 'The Diderot papers ... I must ...'

'I know.'

'Why are you doing this?'

'Why? Because I believe I can persuade you ...'

'Persuade me?'

'To follow the right path,' Habakkuk reminded his friend.

'Isn't that a little presumptuous?'

'Touché. Perhaps it is.' They both burst out laughing.

13

'You've surprised me. I didn't expect you to come all the way up here to find me,' said Dr Rosen, pouring boiling tea into a mug. 'I received a cryptic note from Father Schaffer about you the other day.' She smiled encouragingly at Jana. 'What would bring an Australian Federal Police officer to this remote part of the world, I have to ask myself. Another nomination perhaps? I've already been Australian of the Year once,' she joked, sipping her tea.

'It's nothing like that, I'm afraid,' Jana replied, searching for the best way to broach the sensitive subject. The hot rim of the mug scalded her lips but she didn't flinch. As she looked at the confident, composed woman sitting in the canvas chair opposite, Jana sensed that candour would be best. 'I'm here about your father ...'

Dr Rosen paled. 'My father? In what way?'

Jana pulled a manilla folder wrapped in plastic out of her dripping backpack and opened it. 'It got a little wet,' she said, holding up a large photograph. She dried it with her sleeve and handed it to Dr Rosen. The mood in the small tent changed abruptly. The music stopped and the blunt gramophone needle scratched across the record. Coming to rest in a cracked groove, it continued to go 'round and 'round with annoying monotony.

'Where did you get this?' whispered Dr Rosen, her voice sounding hoarse.

'I don't think I have to ask if you've seen this photograph before,' Jana said quietly, 'do I?' Dr Rosen didn't reply.

'May I come in?' Daniel asked, opening the flap of the tent. 'Can't you hear the drums? The dancing is about to start. Come, quickly.'

The two women followed Daniel down the hill. Fires had been lit in front of the ceremonial men's hut in the middle of the village. Walking into the circle of light, Jana noticed they were surrounded by excited villagers watching them from all sides. Pushing through the crowd, Daniel walked towards a group of elders squatting next to the fires.

'If you sit here you will see everything,' he said, pointing to a grass mat. Dr Rosen bowed and said something to one of the elders. They sat down next to a toothless old man with a large pig's tusk through his nose.

'This is the chief of the village,' Dr Rosen whispered, turning to Jana. 'Sitting here is quite an honour, especially for a woman. We are very privileged to witness this, you know. There aren't many places left where they perform the *kiama* the traditional way.' Daniel sat next to Jana. Chanting, what Jana later learned were magic spells, a group of drummers came towards them, their naked, muscular bodies glistening with sweat.

'How my husband would have loved this,' said Dr Rosen. 'He was fascinated by these ceremonies. He thought of them as little windows, a brief glimpse into the true soul of the people.' The drummers formed a semicircle in front of the chief.

'Here they come,' shouted Daniel. A ripple of excitement washed over the villagers. Three young men wearing costumes of tapa cloth, colourful feathers and tiny shells stepped into the light. Slowly, they began to dance.

'My husband was Jewish, as you no doubt know, and almost twenty years older,' began Dr Rosen, turning the conversation back to the photograph. 'He was a Holocaust survivor, one of the few who emerged out of the horror with his humanity, his compassion and his ability to love intact. Not only was he a gifted healer and a wonderful teacher, he genuinely loved people. You were, of course, quite right; I've seen the photo before – a long, long time ago,' admitted Dr Rosen. 'As you can see, you caught me by surprise. I didn't expect to see it again – ever.'

I knew it, thought Jana, finding it difficult to control her excitement, *Newman lied!* The first crack in his smug, arrogant denial had appeared.

Balancing a pole decorated at the top with long feathers, a dancer called the *kovoi* joined the drummers. 'The pole represents the kovoi tree, the home of the bird-of-paradise,' explained Daniel. A young woman holding a thick rope attached to the top of the pole began to dance around the make-believe kovoi tree.

'Where did you see it?' Jana pressed on.

'I don't know where this is leading,' replied Dr Rosen, sidestepping the question. One of the drummers jumped over the fire, furiously beating his *kundu* drum.

'To the truth, if we have the courage,' said Jana quietly.

'The truth, my dear, is not always easy to find and often when we do – sometimes quite accidentally – we don't like what we see. But there's no turning back. The truth can be dangerous and destructive. It has the power to change us, and our lives, forever.'

'Is that what happened?' Jana asked.

'I must have been about twelve or thirteen at the time,' began Dr Rosen. 'A visitor from South America – one of my father's closest friends – was staying with us. I remember; he came almost every year. How I dreaded those visits. My father used to turn into a different man when he was with his friend. He became loud and rude and aggressive, especially towards my mother. He and his friend drank a lot and talked about the War and their *Kameraden*, their mates. When they got drunk, which was often, they used to sing German songs; always the same songs. I can still remember one of them – the Horst Wessel song. For some reason my mother hated it with a passion. Why am I telling you all this?' asked Dr Rosen, turning towards Jana. 'I haven't spoken about this in years.'

'My mother believed that all of us experience moments of destiny, when we say or do things not because we want to, but because we must. Perhaps this is such a moment,' ventured Jana.

'A moment of destiny?' repeated Dr Rosen pensively. 'Perhaps. I can still remember this clearly: It was a rainy evening in summer, oppressively hot and humid. My father and his friend sat on the veranda of our holiday cottage in the Blue Mountains. They were drinking beer as usual. I went into my father's study – I can't recall why – and there on his desk was this horrible photograph. His friend must have given it to him. I showed it to my mother and she confronted my father with it. That was certainly a moment of destiny; he hit her so hard she fell to the ground, bleeding. I will never forget it. After that, our life changed. The terrible fights began; the shouting, the long silences, the violence. My mother had discovered something she wasn't supposed to know.' Dr Rosen paused. 'Whatever it was, it ultimately destroyed her,' she added quietly.

Finding it hard to keep awake, Jana watched the sweating bodies of the dancers merge into a wild spectacle of colour and motion. Overcome by exhaustion, she closed her eyes, resting her head against Dr Rosen's shoulder.

Jana was woken by the hum of strange voices. Bright sunshine flooded into the tent, almost blinding her. She sat up in the hard camp bed and looked through the open flap. Dr Rosen stood outside, examining an old woman.

'Welcome to my surgery,' said Dr Rosen, without turning around. 'I left you some breakfast, help yourself. I'm almost finished.' Supported by two boys, the last patient hobbled away. 'Congratulations, you slept through the entire morning consultation. My patients were most intrigued,' Dr Rosen said, taking off her white gown. Jana felt a little drowsy and disorientated. Everything looked different in daylight.

'Unlike you, I couldn't sleep at all,' said Dr Rosen. She walked to the small camp table in the middle of the tent and began to rummage through her papers. 'I thought about those moments of destiny you mentioned last night.' She found the photograph and held it up. 'Ultimately, we cannot hide from ourselves, nor can we deny the truth.' Jana sensed that the right moment had arrived to pose the big question.

'In that case, let me ask you this: Is that your father?' Jana pointed to the photo in Dr Rosen's hand.

'You have no idea how often I have asked myself that. You see, my mother thought so. No, I should really say she sensed it, I suppose,' she corrected herself. 'But I? I honestly don't know.'

'Would you like to know?' asked Jana.

'That's a very dangerous question. Some things in life are best left alone, especially after such a long time. My mother's dead, but old wounds can still bleed.'

'Is that what you really think?'

'No, that's what I would like to think.'

Dr Rosen looked suddenly very tired. The sleepless night, the painful memories, the soul-searching, the agonising doubts and recriminations were finally catching up with her. During the long, lonely hours of the early morning she had reached into every corner of her heart. Conjured up from the distant past by the extraordinary photograph, feelings and memories she had suppressed for years had reappeared as powerful and real as ever. 'What happens now?' she asked.

'I prepare a report,' replied Jana, smiling reassuringly at Dr Rosen.

'And then?'

Jana shrugged and reached for the manilla folder on top of her backpack.

'That's for others to decide.' When she opened the folder,

several photographs fell out. 'What are these?' asked Dr Rosen, pointing to the floor.

'Enlargements of certain sections of the photo. Here, for instance, is one of the boat in the background,' explained Jana. 'And here, a detail of some of the crates with markings of the *Reichsbank*, and over here a violin case, of all things, under the officer's arm. Isn't it curious? Somehow it just doesn't seem to fit.'

'A violin case?' Dr Rosen looked stunned. 'Show me!' Jana handed her the photograph.

'You can't really notice it in the original; it's too small and almost hidden under his coat. But here in the enlargement it's quite obvious,' explained Jana, pointing to the violin case.

Dr Rosen's face had turned ashen. 'Please forgive me,' she said, wiping away a few tears, and hurried out of the tent.

Jana followed Dr Rosen down to the village and found her kneeling on the ground by a stream. She was washing her face in the clear, cool water.

'Before you go, I'd like to show you something,' said Dr Rosen, drying her face with a handkerchief. 'Come.' She stood up, and took Jana by the hand.

Jana followed her into the forest. After a short climb they came to a small clearing and looked up. A waterfall roared out of a moss-covered cave in the side of the mountain high above them and cascaded down into a deep, almost circular rock pool. Fingers of bright sunlight reached hesitantly through the gloom and came to rest on the smooth surface of the wet rock below. A spray of tiny droplets rose high into the clear, morning air and formed a rainbow. Overcome by the breathtaking beauty of nature's timeless perfection, the two women stood in awe, watching.

'I come here often,' said Dr Rosen, 'somehow, it's never the same.' She had to shout to make herself heard. 'The morning is my favourite. There's something divine, something cleansing about the first light of a new day. It's like a rebirth, a new beginning. I came here at dawn to think about my father. After a while, everything became clear. I realised that I do want to know; must know,' she added calmly, reaching for Jana's hand. 'Come, there's something I have to tell you about that violin case.'

14

Horst walked over to Farim waiting in the hotel lobby. 'Welcome to Istanbul,' Farim said, extending his hand. The Egyptian's appearance surprised him: a crumpled sports jacket and baggy trousers had replaced the slick business suit he had worn in Sydney. The top two buttons of his shirt were missing, showing a hairy chest and a gold chain around his thick neck. Badly in need of a shave, and with dark shadows under his eyes, Farim looked like a man who hadn't slept in a week.

Horst motioned towards the bar and ordered coffee. 'I can only stay for two days,' he explained. 'My art expert is arriving from Amsterdam this afternoon to value the – samples. Will you be ready?'

'Excellent! The artefacts will arrive by boat from Alexandria tonight. I just spoke to the captain. What about the Russian?'

'You will meet him tomorrow,' snapped Horst, 'provided everything is in order.'

Newman had insisted on a sample before going ahead with the deal. The antiquities had to be authenticated and valued by an expert of his choice – Jan VonderHaar, an old business contact. Not only was VonderHaar a leading Egyptologist working as a restorer in the National Museum of Antiquities at Leyden, but, more importantly, he was prepared to provide his services – for a generous fee, of course – without asking too many questions. He understood the intricacies of the fickle antiquities market, was well connected and knew how to keep his mouth shut.

It was almost midnight by the time the *Sobek*, a small wooden fishing vessel named after the ancient Egyptian crocodile god, steamed up the Golden Horn, and berthed near the Galata Bridge. Farim went aboard first and embraced the bearded captain waiting for him on deck. The two men spoke excitedly in Arabic and went below, leaving Horst and VonderHaar standing on the wharf. Farim reappeared moments later carrying a small wooden crate under his arm and waved them on board.

Horst followed Farim into the tiny wheelhouse. He found the nauseating smell of unwashed bodies, rotting fish and diesel fuel almost unbearable. Farim placed the crate on the chart table and began to attack the lid with a crowbar. The crate was filled with pieces of sackcloth, crumpled newspaper and strips of old rags. Slowly, he lifted a vase-like object the size of a small doll wrapped tightly in sheets of bubbled plastic out of the crate, and placed it carefully on the table.

'Please, open it,' Farim said, turning towards VonderHaar.

'This is superb,' VonderHaar exclaimed, unable to control his excitement. Peeling away the plastic, he exposed a pair of pointed ears belonging to *Duamutef*, the jackal-headed deity. When he held it up against the lantern, the alabaster vessel appeared almost translucent.

'Definitely New Kingdom, approximately 1500 BC. Splendid workmanship,' announced VonderHaar, caressing the smooth surface of the jar with his fingertips. 'If the set is complete, it would rival some of the best I've seen.' He put the lid back and began to unpack the next parcel.

'Please explain, what is it?' asked Horst.

'You don't know?' asked VonderHaar, surprised by Horst's ignorance. 'These are Canopic jars. There should be four of them. They were used by the ancient Egyptians to preserve the internal organs of the deceased, which were ritually removed from the body during mummification,' lectured VonderHaar.

'Well, what do you think, Professor?' Farim asked impatiently.

'Museum quality; the best I've come across for a long time.' VonderHaar was itching to ask where Farim had got them from, but knew better.

'Is there a market for these?' enquired Horst eagerly. VonderHaar's enthusiasm was infectious.

'Certainly,' VonderHaar replied without hesitation.

'How would you sell them?'

'That depends. If you wanted to sell quickly – no questions asked – you could approach one of the dealers I can introduce you to. They could easily place a set like this with a private collector. To get the best price, however, you would have to go to auction. Either in London or New York. To go to auction you have to be able to substantiate title.' VonderHaar raised an eyebrow and looked at Farim. 'In other words, provide provenance,' he added emphatically.

'Well, can you?' asked Horst. Farim raised both hands in a gesture of surrender, and smiled.

'No provenance then, I suppose,' said VonderHaar. 'This will significantly influence the price, you understand.' Farim nodded, but didn't reply.

'I know a dealer in Switzerland who could provide a credible provenance for the jars,' suggested VonderHaar on their way back to the hotel. They were alone in the taxi; Farim had remained on the boat with the captain.

'How would it work?' Horst asked.

'A bit like a forged passport, I suppose.'

'Would that make a difference?'

'It could more than double the price.'

'Any risk?'

'There's always risk, but if you deal with the right people and offer the right amount of money, the risk should be minimal. Interested?'

'Certainly!'

The waiter at the door eyed Farim suspiciously: the odour of sweat and diesel fuel didn't quite fit into the refined atmosphere of the Pera Palace Hotel dining room. Farim pointed to Horst sitting at a table near the window and explained that he was expected for breakfast. Reluctantly, the waiter ushered Farim across to the table. He pulled up another chair, turned up his nose and left.

'Let me introduce you,' said Horst, 'this is Colonel Sorokin.'

The well dressed, elderly man sitting next to Horst put down his serviette and stood up. 'Please call me Gregori,' said the Colonel, in a strong Slavic accent. Broad-shouldered and stocky, with a pockmarked, yet strangely handsome face, the Colonel radiated the confidence and authority of a man used to being obeyed. But his prospects had changed; the collapse of the Soviet Union a few years earlier had destroyed his career and left him destitute. Unemployed, and without much hope, Sorokin had drifted towards the rapidly growing black market controlled by a thriving underworld – the new Russian *Mafiya*. His contacts and intimate knowledge of the armed forces ensured a meteoric rise within the organisation.

'Gregori can provide everything from a Kalashnikov to a submarine,' said Horst, laughing, 'as long as you pay him in US dollars. Please tell him what you need.'

15

Sheikh Omar stepped out of his grandfather's tomb, unrolled his prayer rug and knelt down. Facing east towards Mecca, he began to pray. His family's modest mausoleum stood just behind the tombs of the Mamaluk Amirs and their princesses. Sheikh Omar was proud of his ancestors. They had fought alongside Saladin in 1187 and captured Jerusalem. They had defeated the Crusaders. Sheikh Omar yearned to do so again.

Far removed from the noise and traffic of modern Cairo, Sheikh Omar and half a million fellow necropolis-dwellers lived in one of the huge cemeteries at the edge of the desert. The tombs were the only shelter the poorest of the poor could find; the dead cannot evict the living. The twisted alleys and countless courtyards of the labyrinthine city of the dead provided both anonymity and safety. As the founder and spiritual leader of the *Islamic Brotherhood for the Liberation of Holy Places* – a new radical Islamic movement – Sheikh Omar needed both.

Accompanied by his two young bodyguards, Sheikh Omar walked to the bazaar. He turned into the familiar lane leading to the spice-seller's store used by the Brotherhood as a safe-house and stopped in front of the baker. This was part of his morning routine. The baker waved from inside, put some flat bread into a paper bag and handed it to him through a hole in the wall. Sheikh Omar enjoyed simple things: the heat from the open fire in the bread oven, the mouth-watering aroma of freshly brewed coffee and the hum of the bazaar in the morning.

The storekeeper had already opened the wooden shutters and began to arrange his wicker baskets and sacks filled with fragrant spices, nuts and coffee beans along the narrow footpath. The familiar smell of the spices reminded Sheikh Omar of his grandmother's kitchen in Alexandria. Walking to the back of the store past sacks filled with cardamom, nutmeg and turmeric, he picked up a cinnamon stick and crushed it between the palms of his hands.

Sheikh Omar sat down behind a row of jars brimming with olive oil and poured himself some coffee. When he turned his head, he saw Farim walk into the store. Farim, dressed in a turban and a long *jalabiya,* looked just like one of the many morning shoppers flooding into the bazaar.

Farim took off his dark glasses and allowed his eyes to adjust from glare to gloom. Like every trader sniffing a new deal, he felt elated, the expectation of easy profit making his cheeks glow with excitement. The meeting with Horst and his art expert in Istanbul had gone better than he could have wished for.

'I bring good tidings,' began Farim, after he had finished his second tiny cup of strong coffee. 'The dollars and the guns have agreed to do business.'

'Allah be praised.' Sheikh Omar raised his hands. 'Was it difficult to arrange?'

'Not really. The greed of the infidel is both transparent and predictable and thus easy to manipulate,' Farim explained with a sly smile. Sheikh Omar nodded. He was well aware that Farim's own avarice not only matched that of his Western business associates, but was in a category quite of its own.

'And the dagger?' Sheik Omar asked, frowning. 'Is it safe?'

'Here.' Farim pulled the Blanquefort dagger out of his sleeve and handed it to Sheikh Omar. 'It had its desired effect, just as you predicted. All I had to do was show it to him. The bait was taken, the hook swallowed. Sir Eric is prepared to do business and wants to buy the manuscript.'

'What about the son and our samples?'

'All went as planned. The son wants to prove himself in his father's eyes and is eager to proceed.'

'Excellent! When can we begin?'

'As soon as you wish; everything is ready.'

'How quickly can you deliver the weapons and explosives we need?' asked Sheikh Omar, watching Farim carefully. He didn't trust Farim, he only trusted the man's greed. It was greed that made slaves out of men, and slaves could be owned and disposed of at will.

'You've already obtained the merchandise then,' Farim replied eagerly. 'Can I see it?'

'That's my concern. Keep your voice down! You will have everything you need,' snapped Sheikh Omar, 'when I decide ...' Farim realised he had almost gone too far.

'I can deliver in a week,' he said.

'Good. Just in time ...'

'In time for what?'

'*Aida*,' Sheikh Omar replied thoughtfully, stroking his beard. Farim didn't understand the meaning of the cryptic answer, but wisely decided against asking for an explanation.

16

'Great eye patch. Suits you,' Jana joked, walking up to Jack's wheelchair. She put down her duffel bag and kissed him on the cheek. 'And so does the scar. The thing missing is the earring. You should audition for the Pirates of Penzance.' Jack waved at her clumsily with his bandaged hand, but looked otherwise comfortable and relaxed. The week in the private rehabilitation clinic had done wonders for his recovery.

'You've obviously never heard me sing, or you wouldn't make such a reckless suggestion,' Jack replied, laughing. 'Now, tell me about Dr Rosen.' By leaning forward a bit, Jack released the pressure on his painful back and made sitting still a little easier. 'And thanks for putting this pathetic invalid out of his misery by coming straight here from the airport. I couldn't have waited much longer, I tell you. The suspense is killing me.'

'And then, the next morning,' Jana explained, 'just as I was leaving, she took me to this beautiful waterfall deep in the forest. I think it was her own private – no, more than that, her spiritual place. It was there she told me about the violin.'

'You showed her the close up?'

'Yes. Apparently her father had this violin – some family heirloom he had brought with him from Europe after the War – which he kept locked away in his study.'

'This is supposed to help us?' interrupted Jack.

'Patience please. Don't you want to know what happened to

it?'

'Sure.'

'Just before her parents separated and she was sent to boarding school, the violin was sold for a lot of money – something to do with charity. They were still living in Adelaide at the time and, listen to this, she believes there was actually an article about it in the paper.'

Frustrated by his lack of mobility, Jack tried to sit up in his wheelchair. 'Now we've got something,' he said excitedly. 'Did she recall the year?'

'Around 1961. The violin wasn't sold in Australia, but sent to England to be auctioned,' Jana added. 'That's what the article was about.'

'If she's right, we should be able to find the article without too much trouble,' Jack said, squirming in the wheelchair. 'Perhaps even trace the sale and its new owner. A valuable instrument like this doesn't just disappear.'

'Exactly.' Jana peeled one of the oranges she had brought for Jack and held a piece up to his mouth. 'There was another curious thing about all this,' she said. 'As soon as Dr Rosen saw the violin in the photograph, she became quite emotional. It appeared to me that to her it represented some kind of proof ...'

'Go on.'

'That the man in the photo was really her father. I think she was actually relieved when she saw it. Even after such a long time, after so much ...' Jana paused, searching for the right words, 'sadness, I suppose, it provided that important link. I know, it sounds vague, yet – there was something there, something real.'

'Good work,' Jack complimented her, 'but is it enough?'

'No, but we have a hell of a lot more than before. It's still rather patchy and circumstantial. Too many snakes, not enough ladders, as my boss would say.' Jana looked deflated and ran her fingers nervously through her hair. 'I really don't know Jack, are we doing the right thing here? I mean, after all these years. Look at Dr Rosen with all her soul-searching; look at Miss Abramowitz – old wounds can still bleed, remember? They both want closure. Are we achieving anything by digging up the past like this – by opening up the wounds? Perhaps we should just stop right here and walk away.' Jana sighed. 'Perhaps I'm just tired.'

Jack put his bandaged hand gently on hers. 'If you wheel me back to the terrace we can have lunch,' he suggested, changing the topic. 'Don't think for a moment while you were playing detective in exotic places that I've been the idle patient. We have a deal, remember?'

'What do you mean?'

'Lunch first, I'm feeling weak.'

'You're an impossible tease, Jack.'

'Having to stay in bed – alone that is – can have its advantages,' said Jack, winking at Jana. 'It certainly gives you time to think. God, I could kill for a fag.' Jana reached for her bag.

'Are you out of your mind? Not here, not even outside. Do you see that nurse over there, the big, tough-looking one? She's Irish. I think she'd break my arm if she caught me smoking,' he joked.

'Jack Rogan, actually afraid of a woman? Well, who would have thought that?' Jana began to laugh.

'You've seen the second article, I take it – with the picture of the Totenkopf ring and the Ritterkreuz?' Jack asked, ignoring the remark.

'I have. I read it in Port Moresby on my way back. It was rather provocative. Mentioning Newman's family company as the owner of that – what did you call it? – that tragic house of hidden secrets, must have caused quite a stir.'

'It did, just as we predicted. My editor's phone hasn't stopped ringing. Newman's lawyer is threatening all sorts of things. I guess I did put a little spin on the story,' Jack added mischievously.

'The bit about Newman's German background with the obvious Nazi innuendo, next to the picture of the SS honour ring and other Nazi memorabilia found in his house was quite naughty. I loved it,' said Jana, leaning back in her wicker chair. 'And then, the Knight's Cross on top of that charred roof beam – carefully arranged for effect, no doubt – looked like a Nazi propaganda shot. "Valour conquers all" it seemed to say. You could just see the body of the dead woman being lifted into the helicopter in the background. Very clever.'

'Thanks, now listen to this,' continued Jack, turning serious. 'An American attorney from New York called me yesterday – Sam Greenberg.'

'A Pulitzer Prize nomination already, how exciting!' Jana joked.

'Not quite, something a little more sobering I'm afraid. He's representing a group of Jewish Holocaust survivors in a class action against a number of Swiss banks. He found the article on the internet and contacted the paper with certain information.'

'Oh? What information?'

'Let me tell you a little story: It's June 1944; and the war is almost over. A Jewish family – a doctor, his wife and young daughter – are rounded up in Budapest in the middle of the night, herded to the railway station, packed into a goods train with hundreds of others and taken to Auschwitz. The parents are gassed, the girl survives; four hundred thousand others who were deported in the summer of 1944 from Hungary do not.' Jack paused and took a sip of water. 'Before the war, the doctor – a cautious and quite rich man – had deposited a substantial amount of gold bullion into a Swiss bank. Foolishly, as it turned out, he was relying on the integrity and reputation of the Swiss to safeguard his assets.' Jack began to drum his fingers nervously against the frame of the wheelchair. 'Instead of honouring the bargain, the bank assumed the doctor and his family had perished in the Holocaust and simply appropriated his assets. However, to the bank's considerable embarrassment, the daughter survived and appears to have all the necessary documentation to back up her claim. She's the principal plaintiff in the American class action.'

'I don't understand; what has this got to do with us?' interrupted Jana.

'Just listen. It all started with the fiftieth anniversary of the death camp liberations by the Allies. Researchers working for the World Jewish Congress began to sift through mountains of records in the US National Archives. They concentrated on material dealing with "Operation Safehaven", a secret American wartime spy operation monitoring the staggering flow of Nazi loot into Switzerland. What they found was extraordinary and will certainly change the way the world looks at Switzerland and the Swiss from now on.' Jack pushed his wheelchair forward a little, to get out of the hot sun.

'A wealth of information about dormant bank accounts belonging to thousands of Holocaust victims has come to light. According to the US attorney, the records seem to suggest that the doctor's gold deposit – together with those of many others like him – was conveniently labelled, "abandoned", by the Swiss bankers. Do you know what they did with the assets?'

'Tell me.'

'Apparently, they added half to their own coffers, and credited the other half to certain bank accounts set up by the Nazis.'

'What, they divided the loot?'

'Meticulously.'

'You can't be serious!'

'There are documents ...'

'I'm sorry, but I still don't see the relevance,' Jana interrupted again, shaking her head.

'Your turn to be patient; here comes the best. As you can imagine, most of the Nazi money left Switzerland a long time ago and is now impossible to trace. However, a substantial chunk of it has been identified. It's still in a Swiss bank account set up by the Nazis and is accessed regularly.'

'So?'

'The American investigators claim that the money trail is leading from Switzerland via Spain to certain German corporate interests in South America and from there, to a bank – wait for it – right here in Australia,' Jack added quietly. 'All part of a sophisticated, highly organised international money-laundering operation.' Jana looked stunned. 'A kind of sophisticated superannuation fund for ageing Nazis.'

'Surely you're not suggesting Newman's bank is somehow involved?' she asked quietly.

'It could be, but now comes the bad news. The transactions involved are deliberately complex and murky and at this stage unfortunately inconclusive. Not surprisingly, Spanish and Swiss cooperation has been less than enthusiastic. The Argentineans are outright hostile and don't want to know about the matter at all. They've buried everything in red tape. You can imagine this is a sensitive and potentially extremely embarrassing matter with major international political ramifications. The Americans have suspected for some time that there was an Australian connection, but had virtually no clues, no leads at all; until they found my articles about Newman, a banker, with a possible Nazi past, that is. They're taking the matter quite seriously and are looking into it.'

'I need a drink,' Jana said.

'This is a hospital not the Ritz, remember? But if you're really nice to me and wheel me inside, I'll tell you more ...'

17

'Mr Blackburn will see you now,' said the Attorney-General's PA, putting down her phone. Jana straightened her skirt, took a deep breath, and knocked on the door.

Meeting Robert Blackburn, the Attorney-General, in the flesh was always a surprise. Slim and tanned with short blonde hair, he looked more like a tennis pro than a senior public servant. George Cunningham, Director of Public Prosecutions, sat in front of the Attorney-General's desk with a copy of Jana's report on his lap. He took off his glasses and smiled encouragingly at her.

'Good work,' Blackburn began, complimenting Jana, with his clever opening remark. Commending Jana in front of her superior, he was actually praising them both. He knew how to get cooperation without wasting time.

'Thank you, Sir.'

'Let's get straight to the point: I don't know where you find your sources, but only this morning – and this is strictly confidential, you understand – the American Ambassador has requested our assistance. The Americans want to investigate certain financial dealings involving Newmans Colonial Bank. Apparently, it has to do with court proceedings instigated by Holocaust survivors against a Swiss bank in the US. Yet, here you are, raising the very same issues in your report. Impressive.' The Attorney-General paused and pointed to Jana's report on the desk in front of him.

I owe you one, Jack, thought Jana, suppressing a smile.

'You should know that this latest development throws quite a different light on the Newman investigation. Even if we wanted to close the matter now, we cannot do so. I've already spoken to the Prime Minister about this and he agrees that the American request makes it imperative that we continue to investigate Newman fully and urgently. This has now become a political question, and a rather sensitive one at that, which will no doubt receive a great deal of publicity in due course.'

Blackburn put his hands in his pockets and began to pace up and down behind his desk. 'Consequently, not only do we have to actively pursue every reasonable avenue of inquiry, it must also be apparent that we do so. Do I make myself clear?'

'Absolutely, Sir.'

'Excellent.' Blackburn stopped and reached for Jana's report. 'I have a few questions regarding the Swiss wartime banking connections with Nazi Germany you mention here,' he said politely, changing direction. Jana had been warned about this. Apparently Blackburn had a phenomenal memory and carefully read every relevant document before a meeting. He expected his staff to be fully briefed on all issues and frequently tested their knowledge and level of preparation with probing questions. Jana sensed that this was such an occasion.

'You state here,' he said, 'that: *According to recent research carried out by the World Jewish Congress, the Nazi war machine could not have rolled across Europe without access to an international banking system. It could not have purchased the raw materials needed to keep its foundries, its shipyards and munitions factories operational, without a regular supply of hard currency acceptable to its trading partners. Throughout the war the Swiss supplied both, the Swiss franc as the much coveted and internationally acceptable currency, and their banks to facilitate payment. Huge amounts of gold were transferred by the Nazis to Switzerland, mainly through the Reichsbank, or smuggled into the country by various clandestine means.*

'*Most of the gold was looted from the conquered treasuries of occupied countries, or stolen from murdered Jews. The gold was purchased by the Swiss with Swiss francs, thus providing Berlin with the currency it needed to keep its industry functioning.* Have the banks involved been identified?' asked Blackburn, watching Jana carefully.

'Yes.'

'Unbelievable!' said Blackburn, dropping Jana's report on his desk.

'The documents speak for themselves, Sir,' Jana pointed out, reaching for her own copy of the report. '*During his trial in May 1946*,' Jana read from the research material she had obtained from the World Jewish Congress, '*a very contrite and well informed Emil Puhl, the vice president of the Reichsbank, testified that his superior, Walther Funk, the president of the Reichsbank, was in charge of the grizzly SS gold deliveries from the concentration camps. Apparently, the gold looted from the victims' possessions on their way to the gas chambers, and after their murder from their bodies, was melted down, often mixed with gold from other sources to disguise its true origin and given a new, "respectable" identity acceptable to the Swiss bankers, before being transferred to "neutral" Switzerland.*' Jana closed the report and looked calmly at Blackburn. 'These controversial gold deposits and the fortunes paid by trusting Jews into Swiss banks prior to the war are the subject of the current investigation by a New York Senator. They form the basis of the American class action against the Swiss.'

'I wish to make one thing very clear,' announced Blackburn. 'If a war criminal is in fact hiding in our country, this government is totally committed to bringing him to justice. We have the legislation, the power and the will. Is that understood?'

'Perfectly, Sir.'

Spoken like a true politician; he can't help himself, thought Cunningham. 'How do you wish us to proceed?' he asked, well aware that he would now be personally responsible for the future conduct of the investigation. He was determined to obtain clear instructions in such a delicate matter before the meeting was over and Blackburn was otherwise occupied.

'I think we need a senior prosecutor, immediately. He should consider all the available evidence so you'll involve him in the investigation from the very beginning. This way, he can get an intimate knowledge of all the facts. Ultimately, he'll be in an excellent position to determine whether or not an indictment is warranted. We cannot afford half measures here.'

'I entirely agree,' Cunningham concurred, obviously relieved by Blackburn's suggestion. This meant that the responsibility would now be shared from the outset. 'Do you have anyone in particular in mind?'

'In my view, this case calls for an outside appointment. What I mean is, we should turn to the private bar and brief a senior criminal specialist rather than hand the matter to a public prosecutor employed by the State. That way we can't be accused of bias. We must appear totally fair at all times. Transparency, we must have transparency! We need someone really special; tact and experience is what I'm looking for. Can you recommend someone?'

'It's an excellent idea, Sir,' Cunningham replied, playing for time. 'Let me see ...' He sensed danger. In asking for his recommendation, Blackburn was placing the responsibility for the selection of the prosecutor back on his shoulders. This was a serious matter. A successful public servant had to make sure he was always covered.

'Marcus Carrington would be a good choice, Sir. He acts mainly as a defender as you know, but as you will recall, he has successfully prosecuted a number of high profile cases for the Crown – complicated ones. He has also served as an acting judge.' This was a shrewd suggestion. As Cunningham well knew, Marcus Aurelius Carrington QC was one of Blackburn's closest friends. They had gone to law school together and shared the university medal in their final year. If Blackburn approved the appointment, he was unlikely to criticise the recommendation later on. And besides, Carrington was one of the best criminal barristers in the country.

'You're right; Marcus would be an excellent choice for a number of reasons ...' Blackburn agreed. 'He's a terrier with brains – a rare combination, especially in the law. And we can trust his judgement. That's precisely what this case needs. He's our man.' As a close friend, Blackburn could hardly have put Carrington's name forward himself. Yet, Cunningham suspected it was Carrington that Blackburn really had in mind. As an experienced tactician, Blackburn knew exactly how to get what he wanted.

'It's settled then, but come to think of it, there's one little problem,' said Blackburn, turning towards Jana.

'A problem?' she asked.

'You'll have to deliver the brief personally and persuade Mr Carrington to accept the appointment.'

'Certainly, sir. I will try to see him tomorrow and do my best.'

'I'm sure you will *try*, but it will not be quite as simple as you think.'

'Oh?'

'I'm afraid you'll have to travel again. Marcus Carrington is presently overseas on sabbatical. He's taken some time off to pursue his great passion.'

Jana frowned. 'What is this great passion, Sir?'

'Archaeology.'

'May I ask where?'

'Egypt.'

18

The burial complex was deep below ground. A simple, hand-operated winch straddled the mouth of a narrow, vertical shaft connecting the tomb to the world of the living. Stepping into the canvas sling, Marcus Carrington signalled to the workmen to begin the descent. At the bottom, he adjusted his torch, collected his tools and turned towards the burial chamber. Except for a large sarcophagus with its lid broken, the tomb was empty. *Tomb robbers*, thought Carrington, pointing the beam of light towards the limestone chest.

The first thing he noticed was the unusual position of the sarcophagus. It should have been placed under the ledge cut into the back wall, not along the side of the chamber. *Perhaps it's been moved*, he thought, *or it was just left like that during a hasty burial?*

Carrington began to examine the hieroglyphs carved into the side of the lid. When he reached for the tracing paper, his pencil fell behind the limestone chest. Running his hand along the side of the sarcophagus, Carrington discovered a small gap between the chamber wall and the lid. He went down on his hands and knees and reached behind the chest. Searching for the pencil, he touched something hard and smooth sticking out of the rubble, like an accusing finger pointing out of the netherworld. *This is strange*, he thought, brushing the sand away with the palm of his hand.

Lifting the torch above the rim of the limestone chest, he

pressed his cheek against the chamber wall for a closer look. The weak cone of light crept along the floor and stopped in front of a piece of black polished stone protruding out of the rubble. Carrington's mouth went dry. There was a hole under the sarcophagus and something was buried in it.

Carrington returned with four Egyptian labourers armed with shovels, crowbars and pieces of timber. Easing the heavy limestone chest away from the wall, they exposed a small shaft filled with sand. Instead of using a shovel, Carrington continued to dig with his bare hands. Slowly, the stone began to take shape. *It looks like ... a crown*, he thought, *polished diorite. And a crown is never alone – it's worn on the head!*

The workmen stopped their chatter and watched in awe as the serene face of a young man began to rise out of the sand. 'This is not a man, this is a king!' shouted Carrington, uncovering the intricately carved false beard – one of the insignia of ancient Egyptian royal power. Leaning forward, Carrington's forehead almost touched the cool stone and he found himself face to face with a god-king staring calmly into eternity.

'Only the pharaoh wore the false beard and the crown. Come, Mustafa, help me.' Carrington stepped back from the haunting image, aimed the torch at the statue and smiled. The strange shape of the pharaoh's head and the peculiar features of his long face were unmistakable.

'Do you know who that is?' he asked Mustafa, standing next to the statue. 'Look at him carefully.' Mustafa shook his head. 'You don't?' Carrington traced the *uraeus*, the exquisite little cobra on the pharaoh's forehead, with the tips of his fingers. 'But I do!' he said, laughing.

19

'The Australians are over there, next to the English,' said the guard, pointing with his machine gun to a mound of rubble. Jana shielded her eyes from the glare and looked around. The whole of Saqqara – ancient Memphis just outside Cairo – was a hive of chaotic activity with teams of archaeologists from around the world excavating in their designated areas.

Forming long, human chains, Egyptian labourers were handing baskets filled with sand and rubble to each other. From above, they looked like giant caterpillars gorging on the detritus of ancient Egypt. The baskets were emptied into wooden carts waiting at the end of the line. There was no machinery of any kind; everything was done manually.

I should have worn my joggers, thought Jana, almost falling into a ditch. *Damn!* The labourers stopped and began to laugh. 'Who's in charge here?' she asked, rubbing her ankle.

'I am,' said a tall, middle-aged man, stepping forward. He took off his broad-brimmed hat and began to wipe his sunburnt neck with a small towel. In his faded khaki shorts, a chequered shirt with dark sweat stains under the arms and cuffed boots, he looked more like a shearer from outback Queensland than a QC on sabbatical.

'Marcus Carrington?' asked Jana.

'Someone from the Museum already; that was quick,' answered Carrington. He looked at the breathless woman standing in front of him and smiled. 'I suppose news like this does travel fast, even here. Well, do you want to have a look straight away?' he asked, before Jana could correct him. 'It's a bit rough going down, but I assure you it's worth it.' He began to adjust the ropes.

At first, Jana was a little taken aback by Carrington's appearance; he was completely different from what she had expected. His exuberance, however, was infectious.

'If you say so, but before I agree to descend into this dark hole with you, I think you should at least tell me what I can expect to find. One of King Tut's mummified relatives perhaps, with a golden mask?' Jana joked.

'Wrong time, wrong place, yet a lucky guess nevertheless. His father, actually. You're not from the Museum, are you? Forgive me, I should have noticed earlier,' apologised Carrington. 'This is a very special moment for us here as you can see. Discoveries like this only come along once in a lifetime. If you're lucky,' he added. 'What can I do for you?'

'Jana Gonski, Australian Federal Police.' Jana held out her hand. 'The Attorney-General has sent me to deliver a brief to you,' she continued. 'I have a letter that will explain everything.' Jana reached for her shoulder bag.

'The day is full of surprises! For Rob Blackburn to send you all this way on the public purse it must be important.' Carrington put his hat back on.

'It is.'

'Or he's in trouble again,' speculated Carrington. 'Another political fiasco no doubt; a major tax evasion case, I bet, involving an MP or a judge. That's my guess.'

'No. It's a little more interesting than that, I'd say.'

'Oh, what then?'

'War crimes,' said Jana quietly.

'War crimes? In Australia? You can't be serious!' Carrington frowned, shaking his head.

'I am. You need to read this, Sir,' Jana said, pulling the Attorney-General's letter out of her bag.

'Please, not now, if you don't mind. They sure know where to find you when they want to.' Sensing his irritation, Jana slipped the letter back into her bag.

'Well, are you going to show me this great discovery of yours or not?' she asked breezily, changing the subject.

Smart lady, Carrington thought, *she knows when to back off.*

'Come on then, step in here and hold on tight,' he said, spreading the canvas sling for her. 'Mustafa, where are you?' he shouted, calling the foreman. 'Somehow, they're never around when you need them,' Carrington complained. Shrugging his shoulders, he signalled to the men operating the winch to lower them into the shaft. 'Good help is hard to find in the desert. Put your arms around me.'

'What do you think?' Carrington asked, holding the torch high above his head. The workmen had dug the statue out of the pit and had lifted it onto a plank. Feeling a little dizzy, Jana placed her hand on the rim of the sarcophagus to steady herself.

'The mummy's still in there; the tomb robbers weren't interested in the remains of the poor departed, only his possessions,' Carrington explained. Jana quickly pulled her hand away without looking inside. 'And fortunately for us, they didn't find this.' Carrington pointed to the statue. 'He was buried under the sarcophagus.'

'Is this the owner of the tomb?' Jana asked, pulling herself together.

'Certainly not! This is a pharaoh,' Carrington announced proudly. 'A very special one. The owner of the tomb was a court official, not a king. Extraordinary ...' continued Carrington, tracing the elongated head of the statue with the tips of his fingers. 'This is Amenhotep IV, the Heretic King. He changed his name to Akhenaten. He certainly shouldn't be in here. I wonder ...'

'Why not?'

'Wrong place, wrong time. This is an Old Kingdom cemetery

dating from the third millennium BC. Akhenaten lived in the fourteenth century BC, fifteen hundred years later.'

'What's he doing here then?'

'Good question. He must have been hidden in here later to preserve his image from being erased forever. After all, the fate of heretics is persecution and oblivion.'

'A hidden heretic then,' observed Jana. 'How intriguing. What was the heresy?'

'Religious reform. In Egypt, that's about as serious as it gets. He became an outcast. Not only did he look different, he dared to be different and went against two thousand years of tradition.'

'How?'

'By abolishing the gods.'

'What do you mean?'

'Well, the centre of royal and religious power at the time was Thebes, the home of the god Amun,' Carrington explained. 'Thousands of priests served the gods there and wielded a lot of power and influence. They depended on the gods for a living. He changed all that.'

'In what way?'

'Legend has it that it all began with a vision. Apparently, the god Aten revealed himself to the pharaoh as light; the sun disk between two mountains. Akhenaten interpreted this as a sign from the god, Aten, to bring about change – change of a most fundamental kind. For the first time in recorded history, Akhenaten declared that there was only one God – Aten. In doing that, my dear, he did something ... something quite radical, alien, frightening even.'

'What?'

'Monotheism: the concept of a single, all-powerful god. Imagine, monotheism in Egypt? Only one god in a world ruled by so many? He abolished all the other gods, erased their images and destroyed their temples. This is about as radical as it gets.'

'Fascinating, I had no idea ...' Jana said, looking at the statue. 'You're right though, he does look quite different. Artistic style, I suppose.'

'Not quite. There's more to it than that. Experts have carefully studied the surviving images of Akhenaten and his family and have come up with a scientific explanation for his strange appearance.'

'What, medically?'

'Yes. Apparently, Akhenaten displays the classic symptoms of Marfan syndrome, a genetic defect. This here is a perfect example. Look. Long head, neck, hands and feet,' explained Carrington, pointing to the statue in front of them. 'Short torso, pot belly over here, heavy thighs. He has all the features. And thanks to the new art form he favoured, he was portrayed exactly as he looked; warts and all, as they say.'

'They tell me you're a barrister as well,' joked Jana, interrupting the lecture.

'Vicious rumour, ignore it. But the most fascinating thing about this statue is this here,' continued Carrington, pointing to the pharaoh's hands. 'Am I boring you?'

'Certainly not, Professor.'

'Look, he's holding a disk. This is a complete break with tradition. Normally, the pharaoh's arms would be crossed in front of the chest. He should be holding the flail in his left hand and the *heka* sceptre in his right. Those were the classic symbols of royal power; but not here. Akhenaten's source of power is the sun disk – Aten. Amazing, and perfectly preserved,' said Carrington. 'Well, almost perfect – a small piece of the beard has broken off right here at the tip as you can see. Pity.'

'The mystery still remains – what's he doing here?'

'Obviously he was hidden here much later, perhaps by secret Aten followers trying to protect the image of their god-king from tomb robbers, or more likely, the priests. This was not uncommon. Tomb robbers were a great menace in ancient Egypt right from the beginning. Superstition and fear of detection were no match for greed, even then. Mummies and statues of kings and royal family members were often hidden in other, less prominent tombs to preserve them. Speaking of tomb robbers, that reminds me. I've arranged for guards to patrol the site during the night. I just hope they arrive in time. We're moving the statue to the Museum tomorrow.'

'Guards? Is that really necessary? It's not as if you could just pick him up and carry him away from here, is it?' Jana joked.

'The world is awash with money. You'd be surprised what wealthy collectors would be prepared to do to acquire something as unique as this,' explained Carrington. 'I can tell you there are people who wouldn't hesitate to pay several million dollars – no questions asked, mind you – to own this treasure. Certain things haven't changed at all through the ages.'

'I had no idea it was so valuable.'

'Something like this is really beyond price. It cannot belong, or rather it shouldn't belong, to just one person. It belongs to humanity. It's irreplaceable. We can't just travel back a few thousand years and order another one, can we?' Carrington argued passionately. Jana enjoyed listening to him.

All of a sudden, Carrington's mood appeared to change. He was staring intently at the statue in front of him. For a moment he looked like someone who had glimpsed something frightening, something profoundly disturbing reflected in the serene features of the Heretic King.

Jana noticed the worried expression on Carrington's face and moved closer for a better look. The stone floor in front of the statue was uneven and covered with rubble. Stepping forward, Jana stubbed her toe against something hard and almost lost her balance. Carrington reached for her arm to steady her and looked down.

'I don't believe it! No, it couldn't be,' he called out and bent down to pick up a small piece of stone. Black in colour like the statue, it was smooth and polished on one side, jagged like a broken tooth on the other.

'What is it?'

'Have a look. Better still, here, hold it. After all, you found it. What do you think it is?' Carrington brought the torch closer. Turning it from side to side, Jana began to examine the piece of stone in her hand. Suddenly, her face lit up and she held the fragment carefully up against the broken tip of the pharaoh's beard. It fitted perfectly.

20

Mustafa nodded to the beggar guarding the entrance to the spice-seller's shop in the bazaar and hurried inside.

'What brings you here at this late hour, my son?' asked Sheikh Omar. He pointed to a stool and handed Mustafa a plate of dates. Running his fingers playfully through the cinnamon sticks in one of the spice sacks, Sheikh Omar sat down next to him.

'Good news. A find at Saqqara, a big one this time. I came as soon as I could,' Mustafa replied excitedly, stuffing handfuls of dates into his mouth. 'It's worth a fortune, I overheard them talking about it.' Sheikh Omar put more dates on Mustafa's plate without interrupting him. 'It's still in the tomb. They'll move it tomorrow, we have to be quick.

'What is it, my son?'

'A large statue.'

'Of a god?'

'No, a pharaoh.' Mustafa looked up and grinned, exposing a row of yellow, broken teeth.

'Allah be praised! It's a sign. He's showing us the way, my son. If we hurry, we can still make the boat.'

The *Sobek* was due to leave Alexandria the next day. It would sail to the Greek Isles to exchange its cargo of stolen antiquities for instruments of Holy War. If Mustafa was right, thought Sheikh Omar, the statue could be worth more than the entire hoard of antiquities the Brotherhood had painstakingly accumulated over the past two years.

Sheikh Omar decided to lead the raid himself. That way, he thought, nothing would go wrong. Two of his best young fighters had just returned from a training camp in the Sudan. They were hiding in the flat above the shop and were eager to prove themselves.

Heavily guarded by soldiers during the day to protect the foreigners, Saqqara was deserted by night. Shielding their faces from the sandstorm with their scarfs, the raiding party moved past the four-stepped pyramid of King Zozer and turned into the notorious *rue de tombeaux*. Sheikh Omar knew every stone in Saqqara and guided them through the maze of ancient Memphis. There was no sign of any guards. Usually, the dead did not require protection. When they reached the tomb, Mustafa moved forward alone.

'There are two soldiers behind those stone pillars over there, near the shaft,' whispered Mustafa, wiping sand out of his watery eyes. He pointed towards a narrow path leading to the tomb. 'I don't think there are any others.'

'My sons, this is *Jihad*. You are warriors now. You know what to do,' said Sheikh Omar gravely. He placed his hands on the shoulders of the two excited youths crouching next to him in the sand. 'Allah will guide you and give you courage. Go!'

Carrington was clutching the sweat-soaked blanket to his chest and kept turning restlessly on his narrow camp bed. The nightmare haunting his mind did not allow his exhausted body to relax. Instead, he found himself back in the tomb, alone with the statue of the Heretic King.

In the dream, the pharaoh spoke to him. Carrington could not understand the words, but the troubled expression on the king's face suggested a warning. Suddenly, the walls of the burial chamber began to bleed. Blood oozed out of gaps in the rock and dripped from cracks in the ceiling. The king raised his long right arm and pointed to the sarcophagus. Slowly, the heavy lid began to rise up all by itself until – suspended in mid-air – it was hovering weightlessly above the limestone chest. Drawn irresistibly towards the open sarcophagus, Carrington walked over to it and looked inside. At that moment, he was woken by his own scream and sat up. He could remember every detail of the dream, except for what he had discovered inside the sarcophagus.

Carrington turned on the light and looked at his watch. It was too early to return to the cemetery; he would have to wait until dawn. To calm himself, he reached for the manilla folder Jana had left with him the day before. He put on his glasses and, moving closer to the naked light globe dangling from the ceiling, settled back into his pillow and began to read about Sir Eric Newman.

21

He should have been here an hour ago, thought Jana, looking impatiently at her watch. She was about to leave when she noticed a man jump out of a taxi and come running up the museum stairs towards her.

'I can see you're mad – sorry,' Carrington said breathlessly. 'Something terrible has happened. Come, let's go inside.'

Carrington looked exhausted. He wore the same dusty clothes from the day before and had obviously not shaved. They entered a long hall crammed with statues of hawk-headed gods and feline goddesses. Carrington took a deep breath and sat down on a bench facing a gigantic granite effigy of the god Amun.

'He's disappeared; it's quite unbelievable,' Carrington explained, rubbing his bloodshot eyes.

'Who's disappeared?'

'The Heretic King is gone. Someone broke into the tomb during the night and stole the statue.'

'No! What about the guards?'

At first Carrington didn't answer. 'I asked for armed men, they sent two boys with guns. They're both dead, I'm afraid. I found them this morning with their throats cut,' he said quietly.

'How awful.'

'The site's been closed. The whole of *Saqqara* was swarming with soldiers this morning. All our workmen have been detained.'

'Why?'

'Not surprisingly, the police think it was an inside job. Apparently Mustafa, our foreman, didn't turn up this morning. They're looking for him. Everybody is to be interrogated. It was chaos and confusion as usual. Too little, too late; that's Egypt I'm afraid.' Carrington shrugged. 'I suppose that's it for the season,' he added sadly.

'I'm sorry, I really am, but with all those tourists in the country for that big musical extravaganza, you can't really blame them for being a little nervous, can you?'

Carrington shook his head. Jana sensed his dejection and felt a strange need to put her arm around his shoulders to comfort him. It seemed the most natural thing to do. She was about to raise her arm, but checked herself.

'You're right of course. I'm just disappointed, I guess,' Carrington replied. 'That's nothing really, when you think of the two lads who were murdered this morning. And all because of a chunk of carved stone – just like this one, only a little bigger.' Carrington pulled the small piece of Akhenaten's beard Jana had found out of his pocket and held it up towards the light. 'That's all we have left for now. Perhaps one day we can put it back where it belongs.'

'What will you do now?'

'My wife and daughter are on their way to Luxor by boat,' Carrington explained. 'A long overdue Nile cruise I promised them years ago. They'll arrive there tomorrow. I was going to join them in Luxor for the opera.'

'So, this thing is an opera – in Egypt? How exotic.'

'Yes. Verdi's *Aida*; it's quite an event. They're performing it in front of the Luxor temple with a cast of thousands, I'm told. Nubian slaves, elephants, lions, the lot.'

'How romantic,' Jana said with a mischievous sparkle in her eye and a hint of regret in her voice she couldn't quite conceal.

'Or reckless,' Carrington said quietly.

'What do you mean?'

'Nothing. Forget it, I'm just tired.' Carrington stood up and began to walk away from the approaching tourists. 'Let's have a look at Akhenaten while we're here, I think you'll find it interesting.' Jana had to smile; she had guessed the real purpose of their meeting all along. Carrington wanted to look at statues of Akhenaten in the museum and compare them with the one he had found in the tomb.

'If I remember correctly, you asked me yesterday to meet you here to discuss the brief,' Jana reminded Carrington jokingly, 'not to examine the strange features of pharaohs with ... what syndrome?'

'Marfan. We can do both, come.'

Jana followed Carrington through a maze of corridors and rooms filled with exotic treasures. She was sensing his change of mood and it made her sad. *What if he's already decided to decline? What if he just wants to let me down gently?*

'Here he is. What do you think?'

The similarities were striking: the same elongated face, the pot belly, the wide hips, the long arms. Carrington took Jana by the hand and guided her around the statue like an excited schoolboy showing something to his teacher. 'Apart from the workmen, you and I are the only two people who've seen him, you know,' he said. 'Imagine, a life-sized statue of the Heretic King, holding a sun disk in his hands. What a discovery!'

'Will they believe you?' Jana asked. As soon as she said it, she realised it was a rather tactless question and bit her lip. Carrington let go of her arm; reality had intruded into the fairy-tale.

'Without the statue, I doubt it. And besides, the authorities will do their best to cover up the whole incident. It's the last thing they need at this crucial time.'

'In that case, we'll just have to wait until he turns up again, won't we?' said Jana, trying to undo the damage.

Carrington began to laugh. 'Stranger things have happened in this country, you know. Come on then, let me show you some of my other favourites,' Carrington said, changing the subject. 'We shall continue this conversation as soon as our friend decides to show himself again, okay?' Jana nodded. 'You do know, of course, who his wife was?'

'Sorry Professor,' Jana replied, 'they taught us all about gunshot wounds and powder burns in the academy, not Egyptian dynasties.'

'Nefertiti, the most beautiful woman in ancient Egypt. Her famous bust is unfortunately in Berlin. It should be right here, next to him. The plunder of Egypt's heritage knew no bounds, just like the Nazi rape of occupied Europe.' Carrington pointed to a stone relief depicting the defeated Hittite army on the battlefield of Qadesh. 'Somehow, the strong always subjugate the weak; it's a timeless cycle of greed and lust for power. I can show you several examples right here in this room alone.'

'That's a little too fatalistic for me,' Jana said.

'Perhaps. But tell me about Sir Eric. Give me your impressions.'

Jana described the strange meeting in Newman's house on that hot, humid Sydney afternoon. She spoke of his ice-blue eyes and the strange hold he appeared to have over his two sons. Carrington was a good listener.

'How lucid was Lena Abramowitz?' he wanted to know. 'I've seen old people who couldn't tell you where they lived, or what day of the week it was, yet give accurate and reliable evidence about events half a century ago. Miss Abramowitz strikes me as one of those. It would be a mistake to disregard her story,' Carrington observed. 'The suffering of the Jews, now there's another timeless topic for you. This is the great Ramses himself, over here,' Carrington said, pointing to another life-sized statue of a seated pharaoh at the end of the corridor. 'Look at his face: the prominent cheek bones, the hooked nose, those piercing eyes, the intelligence radiating from his features. It's possible, you know, that this is the face of the man who spoke to Moses; the face of the pharaoh who allowed the Jews to leave Egypt – after a little divine persuasion, that is. Quite extraordinary, don't you think? It puts the true antiquity of these pieces into a rather different perspective. History carved into stone by the hand of man,' Carrington said quietly, 'right here for us to touch.'

'Did you sleep at all last night?' Jana asked. 'I know you promised to read the brief, but you didn't have to learn it by heart.'

'Years of cramming information into your head, somehow always at the last minute just before going into court, does wonders for your memory, I can assure you. The ever-present fear of embarrassment makes you remember everything you read,' Carrington explained, shrugging off the compliment. 'Don't look so glum. I can clearly see the question written across your face,' he continued, laughing. 'Let me answer it for you and put you out of your misery.'

'Is it that obvious?'

'It is, but you don't have to blush.'

Jana shrugged and managed a crooked smile. 'What's the verdict?'

'As any first year law student will tell you, to consider prosecuting a man after more than fifty years for a serious war crime, without a body, without a single reliable witness, without any credible identification, based on intuition, an old photograph and a little, I stress little, circumstantial evidence is nonsense.'

Jana's mouth went dry. As quickly as it had appeared, the colour began to drain from her face. 'The answer then is *no*, I take it?' she said quietly, unable to hide her disappointment. It was more of a statement than a question.

'No, it's not!' Carrington replied emphatically. 'Like you, I also happen to believe Dr Rosen is right. We just have to find a way to prove it.'

Jana reached for his arm and squeezed it hard.

'Ouch! Don't get too carried away. I still have to discuss it with my wife before I can give you a final answer. After all, it would mean the end of my sabbatical and the family holiday.'

'I understand.'

'Well then, why don't you come to Luxor with me and we can both talk to her. And you can work on Isabella,' he added. 'Now, there's a challenge for you.'

Jana's face lit up. 'Isabella?'

'My daughter – sixteen going on thirty-six. And besides, a few people around here owe me a favour or two. I'm sure I can wangle another opera ticket for a famous Aussie detective,' Carrington said, winking encouragingly at Jana. 'How about some lunch? I'm starving.' Taking Jana by the arm, Carrington steered her towards the crowded exit without waiting for an answer.

22

'Is this your first visit to Australia, Father?' Newman asked, sizing up the tall, black priest. It was impossible to guess his age, but the short wiry hair greying at the temples suggested a man in his fifties. Newman watched the priest's eyes – penetrating and cruel – and instantly recognised the look. He had seen it many times before; the look of a zealot. Newman waited for his housekeeper to leave the room before asking the next question. 'How is the Cardinal?'

'His Eminence sends his regards, Sir Eric,' answered Father Habakkuk politely, 'and his congratulations on your extraordinary find ... I believe you now have a copy of the complete text?'

'My son faxed it to me yesterday from Italy.'

'May I see it?'

'I understand you are Ethiopian, Father, and an expert on the subject,' Newman said, ignoring the question.

'Quite so. Ethiopian history is my specialty.'

'I have read your book on King Lalibela. The Cardinal sent it to me – fascinating. It would appear Lalibela was destined for great things from the very beginning. And his name means something like *the bees recognise his sovereignty?*' said Newman, deliberately showing off. If the black priest was in any way surprised by this demonstration, he certainly didn't show it.

'According to legend, a swarm of bees hovered over the infant just after his birth. This was seen as an omen,' Habakkuk explained calmly. 'Lalibela was the younger half-brother of King Harbay who was very superstitious and considered this prophecy a direct threat to his throne.'

'So much so,' interjected Newman, 'that he wanted Lalibela killed in infancy. Several attempts failed over the years, but ultimately Lalibela was poisoned, I think, and fell into a coma that lasted for three days.'

The priest nodded. 'During those three days, Lalibela was lifted to heaven by angels and taken into the very presence of God who assured him of a safe and glorious future.'

'As soon as he awoke, Lalibela fled Ethiopia and sought refuge in Jerusalem,' Newman interrupted again. 'He remained there for twenty-five years as a guest of the king – until 1185 to be precise – secure in the knowledge that as soon as the time was right, he was destined to return to his homeland and claim the throne. Not only that, he would build several extraordinary churches ...'

'Following precise instructions given to him by the Almighty ... I can see you are very well informed, Sir Eric. The Cardinal did warn me about this. It's always a pleasure to meet a fellow scholar interested in one's subject.'

Newman smiled; he believed in establishing ground rules from the very beginning. 'Well, here it is,' said Newman, changing direction. He handed the fax to his guest.

'*These are, I believe, the last words I will be able to record before our enemies overwhelm us. We are surrounded, escape is impossible ...*' the black priest began to read, casting his eyes eagerly over the lines. Newman noticed that Habakkuk's hands were shaking. '*If we have offended Thee, O Lord, forgive us; if we have failed Thee, O Lord, forgive us* ... But, this is a prayer,' said the priest, disappointment clouding his face.

'It would appear so, but please read on.'

'*Our mission to bring the Holy Relic back to France has failed – but not completely, thanks to Thee. The Holy Relic we leave behind is but a shell – empty, its very essence gone,*' Habakkuk translated. '*The _____* *of the Prophet are out of our enemies' reach; one is on its way to France with a dispatch recording the hiding place of the other, as commanded by Thee.* This is incredible,' whispered Habakkuk. 'Pity about the missing part here. Accidental damage or deliberate? We'll never know.'

Newman nodded, but said nothing.

'Protect our brother Bernard on his journey, guide him safely back to France, and give us strength to die with honour, serving Thee. This is it?' asked Habakkuk.

'Yes, that's the complete text. It does read like a prayer, as you say,' Newman replied. 'The testament of a man about to die. It must have been written in a great hurry. What does all this tell the expert historian?' he asked, throwing a challenge at his inscrutable visitor.

'The missing parts of the text refer to two specific items ... that fits. *One has been sent back to France with a dispatch recording the hiding place of the other.* However, the text doesn't tell us where it was written, and without knowing that, it's practically worthless. We must ascertain where it was found.' The black priest wiped his hot face with a white handkerchief and poured himself a glass of water.

'Are you suggesting that once we know where it was found we will also know where it was written because ...'

'We are surrounded, escape is impossible,' interjected the priest, quoting from the text. 'I think Blanquefort was making peace with God and hid the prayer and his dagger from his enemies just before he was killed. It has all the hallmarks of urgency and desperation you would expect in a situation like that.'

'A prayer and a dagger. Quite appropriate for a warrior-monk, wouldn't you say?'

'Yes. Above all else, they were Templars ...'

'And are you also suggesting that Blanquefort buried these things near the hiding place?' asked Newman.

'I do believe that is the correct interpretation. The knights died where they fell, virtually on top of, or right next to, the hiding place. The circumstances appear to suggest that,' explained Habakkuk, holding up the page. 'Ironic, don't you think?'

Newman looked at his visitor with new respect. 'But even if we are right about all that, we would still need the dispatch recording the actual hiding place, to find it.'

'Yes,' conceded Habakkuk, 'it would appear so. But we would have narrowed down the possibilities considerably, and who knows, perhaps all the clues put together are enough ...' Newman nodded, the point was compelling. 'Do you think there's a way we could ascertain, Sir Eric ...' Habakkuk asked hopefully, 'where this Blanquefort prayer was found?'

Newman walked across to the bust of *Asmodeus* and put his hand on the demon's head. He stood there for quite a while, as if waiting for inspiration. '*Blanquefort Prayer* – that is a good name for it,' he said. 'Perhaps there is a way ... As for the Holy Relic Blanquefort left behind, what do you think that might have been?' asked Sir Eric, carefully watching his visitor.

So far, neither of them had touched on that topic. In fact, they had deliberately avoided it. The black priest put the glass of water on the table in front of him and looked calmly at Newman. 'I'm sure you know, Sir Eric.'

23

Carrington hurried across the crowded deck of the *Nefertiti*, the largest of the cruise ships berthed at Luxor. Surrounded by a small flotilla of feluccas crowded with eager vendors offering gaudy souvenirs to the passengers promenading on the decks above, the *Nefertiti* reminded Carrington of a Mississippi paddle steamer – Mark Twain meets Agatha Christie.

'There she is, over there,' Carrington said to Jana, who was trying to keep up with him. He pointed to a tall woman waving a straw hat.

'Inspector Gonski?' asked Elizabeth Carrington, extending her hand before Carrington could introduce Jana. 'Now I can understand your enthusiasm for these arduous field trips, Marcus. Charming ladies as travel companions and exciting new discoveries – as long as they don't go missing, I suppose. Poor darling,' she teased, winking at Jana. There was no malice in her voice, only good-natured humour.

'It's tough being an archaeologist,' complained Carrington with a shrug, kissing his wife on the cheek.

Elizabeth Carrington was one of those fortunate women who in their fifties look forty and don't understand all the fuss about advancing age. Jana was fascinated by her natural grace and easy manner.

'Where's Isabella?' asked Carrington, looking around the deck.

'Down there by the pool with her admirers,' explained his wife, pointing towards the back of the boat. 'Now that you're here, you can help me fend them off. Good luck!' Carrington leant over the handrail and began to wave. A tall girl with long blonde hair jumped out of the pool and came running up the stairs, pursued by several tanned young men.

'Papa, you're here already,' she shouted, throwing herself into his outstretched arms. Laughing, she covered his face with kisses.

'I should go away more often,' observed Carrington, trying to disengage from his daughter's wet embrace. 'I'm not always this popular.'

Isabella, at sixteen, was her mother's clone. Mother and daughter could easily have passed for sisters. 'Cool. You're staying in my cabin, come,' said Isabella, taking Jana by the hand. Jana looked at Carrington.

'You'd better go, she won't take no for an answer,' he said. 'And besides, there isn't another bed in Luxor. We're all staying on the boat.'

Jana was too tired to fall asleep and stared at the low wooden ceiling of the tiny cabin. She kept turning restlessly in her narrow bunk, careful not to wake Isabella. After a while she got up and stepped outside, letting the cool breeze caress her damp face. The dark temple ruins behind the cruise ship loomed large and ominous in the ghostly light of the full moon.

When Jana looked across the moonlit Nile, she thought she could hear the chanting of priests drift across the still waters; echoes of a distant age of river gods, temple festivals and solemn funeral processions.

'I couldn't sleep either,' Jana heard a soft voice whisper from behind. 'Isn't it beautiful?' Elizabeth Carrington placed her hand on the rail next to Jana's. 'Marcus and I have discussed this fascinating case of yours. As you know, he's rather passionate about justice, about what's right and what is not.

He's quite naive about it at times, you know,' she explained, 'all black and white and full of zeal. Just like his daughter. But I guess that's what drives him. It's the fire within.' Elizabeth Carrington paused and placed her hand on Jana's arm. 'And besides, Marcus thrives on a challenge.'

'Does this mean you approve?' Jana asked hoarsely.

'I'll return to Australia with Isabella after the performance.'

'But do you approve?'

'I want what Marcus wants ...'

Jana perceived a hint of sadness in Elizabeth Carrington's evasive reply. 'You are very generous, thank you,' she said, kissing the older woman spontaneously on the cheek.

24

The interrogation cells in the basement of Chief Inspector Haddad's police headquarters in Cairo were reserved for prisoners requiring special attention.

'Stop! Can't you see he's unconscious, you fool,' shouted Haddad, stepping into the tiny cell. The surprised guard turned around, wiped the blood from his knuckles and adjusted the sweat-stained braces cutting into the muscles of his hairy chest.

Mustafa sat on a wooden stool in the middle of the whitewashed cell. His hands were tied behind his back and blood oozed out of the corner of his open mouth, showing a row of broken teeth. With his nose crushed and one of his ears almost severed, he looked like a sitting corpse. Haddad was afraid he was already dead.

'Water!' ordered Haddad. The guard hurried out of the cell. As the senior police officer entrusted with the impossible task of protecting the visiting dignitaries, Haddad had urged his superiors without success to cancel the Luxor performance. His reports had fallen on deaf ears and were considered a nuisance.

The bazaars and coffee houses were abuzz with rumours of conspiracies, new secret Islamic societies, and *Jihad* – Holy War. What Haddad needed was proof, not rumours. He was convinced that some kind of terrorist attack was imminent and suspected that the recent theft of the statue was somehow connected with it.

The guard returned with a bucket. Haddad poured a little water into Mustafa's open mouth and the rest over his lacerated head. The cool water appeared to revive the prisoner. Greedily, he began to lick his swollen lips. Haddad clenched his fists; time was running out. He should be in Luxor by now, not interrogating this pathetic prisoner. The performance was due to begin in less than twenty-four hours and the prisoner was dying. It was going to be a long night.

'You want the pain to stop, don't you?' began Haddad, whispering seductively into Mustafa's bleeding ear. The prisoner nodded. 'Then tell me, who stole the statue?'

Haddad looked anxiously at the departure board. He noticed that the early morning plane to Luxor was late as usual. Taking a deep breath to calm himself, he flicked impatiently through the pages of his notebook. He was trying to make sense of the incoherent snippets of information he had managed to extract from Mustafa during the night. Just before sunrise the prisoner had finally lapsed into a coma; further interrogation was futile. Haddad loosened his tie and ordered another coffee.

The statue had been smuggled out of Egypt and had already been sold on the black market; so much was clear. The word *Jihad* – Holy War – was mentioned several times, together with the mantra 'Death to the Great Satan'. Haddad tried hard to concentrate and stared bleary-eyed at his notes.

'The world will hear the music and see the blood of the Great Satan flow into the sand. Many will die,' he read aloud. *'The evil stain of blasphemy will be erased from the holy shrines and the true word of the Prophet will be victorious.'*

'What does it all mean?' he asked himself. This sounded more like a prophecy than a confession. Was this a clever riddle based on some disguised truth, or merely the ravings of a hallucinating wretch close to death? Had the prisoner been toying with him? Haddad cursed the careless guard for his ignorant brutality, closed his notebook and boarded the plane.

For several years the Egyptian government had tried in vain to persuade the world that it was safe again to travel through the land of the pharaohs. Despite all the assurances, the tourists stayed away. Obviously something more was needed.

An entrepreneur from California recognised an opportunity and came up with a unique idea: an opera performance on a grand scale to showcase the monuments of Ancient Egypt. The obvious choice was Verdi's *Aida*; the venue, the Luxor temple. By engaging the best singers, a famous conductor and a cast of hundreds of locals to provide colour and authenticity, *Aida by the Nile* would become the social event of the year. The man was prepared to spend millions in return for the television rights.

The proposal was enthusiastically embraced by the Egyptian authorities and the few sober voices counselling caution and restraint were swept away by the overwhelming support for the imaginative plan. Generous payments into the right pockets, the promise of lucrative local employment and future flow of tourist dollars, sealed the deal. Suddenly everyone had short memories. Forgotten were the atrocities of the past, the bombings, the shootings, the burning tourist buses, the gutted hotel foyers and maimed bodies. The obvious risks and dangers were simply ignored. The only thing that really mattered was to have an invitation.

When Haddad arrived at the Luxor temple, the final preparations for the evening's gala performance were nearing completion. He was stunned by the size of the production. TV crews from all the major networks – especially Europe and the US – were setting up their equipment. Local porters were hauling gear up steel ladders leading to the top of purpose built towers. Strategically positioned around the temple forecourt, the towers were there to provide the best possible vantage points for the cameras. Surrounded by a maze of cables criss-crossing the forecourt, technicians were adjusting mobile satellite dishes for test transmissions; massive generators were humming in the background.

Seated inside a pit in front of the stage, a symphony orchestra from the UK was rehearsing in the glare of the noonday sun. *Only mad dogs and Englishmen*, thought Haddad, shaking his head. Suddenly, an army dressed in exotic costumes came marching through the portals, the cheering soldiers waving at rows of empty seats. An excited little man holding a sun umbrella was shouting directions through a megaphone.

'This is madness,' mumbled Haddad. He had done his best to warn his superiors. However, he had to admit that the little information he had finally been able to piece together after Mustafa's disappointing interrogation, sounded rather vague and speculative. Not surprisingly, his report had been ignored. Fanning his flushed face with his hat, he stared at the countless rows of seats crammed into the temple forecourt. Once seated, the spectators would be vulnerable and trapped, Haddad noted unhappily. He rubbed his aching neck; if he wanted to stay alert, he had to get some sleep. When he looked up at the colossal statue of Ramses towering above him, he could still hear Mustafa's slurred words: *The world will hear the music and see the blood of the Great Satan flow into the sand; many will die, but not I. I will go to paradise.* Haddad clenched his fists in frustration, turned around and hurried back to his waiting car.

Sheikh Omar wiped the sweat from his brow with the end of his turban and walked across the empty stage. As one of the few English-speaking volunteers helping the organisers communicate with the locals, he had free access to all the facilities. A group of bored soldiers stood aimlessly around the temple forecourt. They paid no attention to the workmen preparing to go home. As far as the soldiers were concerned, the rehearsal was over.

'The victory procession will enter over there,' explained Sheikh Omar, pointing to a gap in the temple wall. 'The elephants and the drummers will come through here,' he said and walked towards another opening in the wall behind the orchestra. 'And the torch bearers through that arch over there. It will be chaos, I promise you.' He smiled at the young martyrs hanging on his every word. 'Now, let's go over it once more,' he said, 'and remember, timing is everything.'

During the past few weeks, the Brotherhood had successfully infiltrated the entire opera cast. Members of the Brotherhood would be marching in the victory procession, handling elephants and showing the guests to their seats. Two suicide bombers were even playing in the orchestra. The elaborate rehearsals had provided an excellent preview of the carefully choreographed performance to come.

While Radames and Aida were planning their stage death in the crypt below the temple of Vulcan, Sheikh Omar was plotting real death and mayhem on a scale that would have challenged the imagination of even the most ambitious librettist.

25

'*A caleche!* How did you manage this?' asked Elizabeth Carrington, letting go of her husband's arm. She pointed to the horse-drawn open carriage pulling up in front of the jetty. The other passengers leaving the cruise ship were eyeing them enviously; they were piling into old buses without seats.

'If I'm fortunate enough to go to the opera with three charming ladies, the least I can do is provide proper transportation, don't you think?' replied Carrington, laughing. He walked across to the carriage, took a bow and opened the door for his wife.

'How romantic. Another one of your local contacts, no doubt,' observed Jana, squeezing into the narrow seat next to Isabella. 'I don't know how you do it.'

'It's quite simple, really. What you see at work here, my dear, is the power of *baksheesh*,' Carrington joked. 'Isn't that right, Abdul?' he added, leaning conspiratorially towards the driver. The grinning coachman turned around and winked at him. Carrington said something in Arabic and Abdul lashed out with a long whip. To everyone's amazement, the scrawny horse was able to pull the carriage with relative ease and even managed a reasonable trot. 'The power of fear, no doubt,' said Carrington, leaning back in his seat.

The short trip from the wharf to the temple took over an hour. Threading its way through the raucous crowd choking the road, the carriage was mobbed by curious locals eager to get a glimpse of the foreigners flocking to the temple. Adding to the chaos, army trucks crammed with soldiers tried to push past frightened donkeys and temperamental camels returning from the fields.

'This is better than any opera,' shouted Carrington, turning around. 'There, look.' He pointed to a street urchin hitching a ride on the back of the carriage. Grinning mischievously, the boy was playing with Isabella's long blonde hair. Elizabeth Carrington placed the palm of her hand affectionately against her husband's cheek. Jana noticed that the shadow of sadness she had observed the night before had not left Elizabeth Carrington's face.

'Contrary to popular belief, *Aida* was commissioned by the Khedive of Egypt for the opening of the Italian Theatre and *not* for the opening of the Suez Canal,' explained Carrington, joining the long queue in front of the temple. Sudanese boys dressed in billowing pantaloons, embroidered vests and bejewelled silk turbans were showing the guests to their seats. Jana recognised several famous faces in the crowd. Somewhere in the background, an orchestra was playing a medley of Verdi melodies.

'We're a little early, come, let's go through there. I want to show you something,' said Carrington, pointing to a narrow opening in the temple wall.

'Someone's coming,' hissed Sheikh Omar, adjusting the suicide vest of the young man standing next to him. 'Hold still!'

'I seem to remember you can get to the court of Ramses and the Great Colonnade of Amenhotep through here,' explained Carrington. 'And, would you believe, there's a mosque in there as well – Abu el Hagag.'

'Good evening, Sir,' said Sheikh Omar, stepping out of the shadows, 'I think you're going the wrong way.' He bowed politely. 'All the seats are over there ...'

'I know; I just wanted to show my wife the Hypostyle Hall before the performance. I seem to remember it's just in there ...'

Jana looked at the man in the striking blue robe and exotic turban. *He must be part of the cast*, she thought.

'You cannot go through here,' explained Sheikh Omar, blocking the way, 'not tonight, I'm afraid – preparations. I'm sure you understand.' He smiled at Jana. 'You should try that way.' He pointed to the other end of the forecourt. *He has beautiful hands*, Jana thought, *and what a voice!*

'Thank you, perhaps later then,' replied Carrington, turning around.

'Enjoy the performance,' said Sheikh Omar, touching his forehead.

'What a fascinating man,' Jana observed, walking back into the crowded forecourt. 'He could have stepped straight out of a nativity scene ...'

'You mean, as one of the Three Wise Men bearing gifts? Which one would you suggest – Caspar, Melchior or perhaps Balthazar?' Carrington joked.

'Exactly. He does have an almost biblical face, don't you think?' Jana asked. 'White beard and all; I'd go for Balthazar.'

'And those eyes ...' Isabella interjected, 'like burning coals ...'

'Carefully chosen for the performance, no doubt,' ventured Elizabeth Carrington, 'and already dressed for the occasion.'

'All right, guys, enough. I get the picture. He's probably a tour guide in real life,' Carrington said, showing their tickets to one of the cute black boys.

'Are you enjoying yourself?' asked Carrington, turning towards Jana.

'The best seat in the house and an opportunity to rub shoulders with the rich and famous. What more could a woman want? Thanks Marcus.'

'Don't thank me, this is the man who arranged it all,' replied Carrington, pointing to a short, barrel-chested man in a white linen suit and Panama hat. 'You're sitting next to him.'

'Good evening, Naguib,' said Carrington, embracing the little man. 'This is Chief Inspector Haddad, our host,' he explained, introducing his friend. 'You two have a lot in common, professionally speaking, that is,' Carrington said to Jana, lowering his voice. 'Both of you chase bad guys for a living. He's the one who organised your ticket. Be nice to him.'

'How come you know him so well?'

'We've been friends for a long time. We met at a legal conference in London a few years ago. My passion for Egypt was irresistible ...' joked Carrington.

Jana towered over Haddad. She looked at him and smiled. He looked at her long legs and thought, *How wonderful*, and smiled back.

26

Sheikh Omar covered his face with his scarf and looked through the gap in the temple wall. *Excellent,* he thought. The late arrivals were being seated. *Let the show begin!*

A hush fell over the excited spectators, anticipation growing with every heartbeat. Then, softly at first, Verdi's stirring music began to rise up. Instead of a parting curtain, beams of coloured light washed over the stage. Slowly, the performers materialised out of the gloom and the spellbound audience began to clap and cheer.

The high priest, Ramfis, an Italian bass, was telling the Captain of the Guard, Radames, a famous American tenor, that the gods had already made their choice. *Celeste Aida,* the sublime aria, brought the house down.

'I don't like it,' muttered Haddad, scanning the empty space under the TV transmission towers with his opera glasses. He was searching in vain for the security guards supposed to patrol that area.

'But he was magnificent,' protested Jana, applauding enthusiastically.

'I'm not talking about the singing.'

'What do you mean?'

'Gut feeling; you know how it is. After a while you see trouble brewing everywhere,' replied Haddad quietly, without removing his glasses. 'This place is one big trap and we are sitting right in the middle of it.'

Something cold tingled down Jana's spine. There was an odd familiarity about the feeling and she reached instinctively for the scar on her left shoulder. The old bullet wound was a permanent reminder of a stake-out gone terribly wrong. This only heightened her apprehension and tiny beads of perspiration began to appear on her upper lip.

Danger, she thought. *There's real danger here. That's what he means.* Jana turned towards Carrington, sitting to her right. She wanted to warn him about something, but didn't know how. Her throat went dry and she began to cough. Carrington looked at her and smiled without noticing her distress. Gradually, the applause ebbed away, the lights went out again and the wonderful music continued.

Then suddenly the darkness parted and a procession of torchbearers marched through a narrow gap in the temple wall. They were followed by Sudanese drummers wearing only leopard skin loin cloths, their black bodies casting flickering shadows across the spectators sitting in the front. The highlight of the opera, the famous Victory March, had begun.

By the time the decorated war elephants made their entry, the cheering crowd was on its feet. The producers had achieved their objective: the spectators had spontaneously turned into participants. Jana, too, was swept up by the excitement of the moment, temporarily forgetting the disturbing premonition.

The first explosion almost went unnoticed. A grenade dropped from the top of the TV transmission tower at the back of the audience ripped into the unsuspecting spectators applauding below. Sheikh Omar looked at his watch and nodded. 'Allah, be praised, it has begun,' he whispered excitedly and reached for the scimitar hidden between the copious folds of his robe. The touch of the razor-sharp blade appeared to calm him. It was a promise of things to come.

Haddad's trained ear had picked up the vibrations of the unusual thud. Turning his head, he saw a flash of yellow light out of the corner of his eye. He realised instantly what it was. Then a second grenade exploded, spraying the spectators with a deadly shower of hot shrapnel and body parts.

The orchestra is next, thought Sheikh Omar, listening to the screams of the maimed and dying. The young suicide bomber playing in the orchestra turned towards Mecca, prepared himself for paradise and detonated the explosives strapped to his chest. The force of the blast turned musical instruments into whistling messengers of death and sent twisted kettle drums and trombones flying – some with hands still attached and dripping with blood. A piece of the harp severed the power cables under the stage. Spewing sparks and hissing madly, the cables twisted and turned like a headless hydra fighting a phantom.

A young man marching behind the elephants whispered '*Allah akbar*' and pulled a grenade out of his robes.

'Get down!' shouted Haddad. He reached for his gun and began to fire. As the gun went off, Jana tripped, hit her head on the metal seat next to her and fell face down to the ground.

Haddad shot the man holding the grenade in the head, but was a fraction of a second too late. Just before he died, the young martyr pulled the detonation cord attached to his suicide vest and turned himself into a human bomb. A particularly nasty bomb, designed to cause maximum damage at close range.

A long, bent nail grazed Carrington's forehead, glanced off his temple and entered Isabella's eye. Instinctively, Elizabeth Carrington threw herself forward, trying to shield her injured daughter. Moments later, a handful of ball bearings slammed into her back, killing her instantly. Bleeding profusely, Isabella collapsed on top of her unconscious father, her body ripped apart by a second blast of deadly shrapnel just before she died.

The trained elephants turned into frightened beasts and began to stampede, carving a trail of destruction through the rows of screaming spectators. Instead of protecting the guests, the bewildered soldiers were adding to the confusion by firing their weapons aimlessly into the air, unable to identify their foe.

The stallions pulling the chariot bolted. Radames lost his grip on the reins and was thrown sideways onto the burning stage. Momentarily trapped by the chariot, the terrified elephants smashed the wooden cart with the lions' cage to pieces. The cage tipped over, pinning Radames to the ground under its heavy frame.

One more, thought Sheikh Omar, just as the last suicide bomber blew himself up at the exit, *and then it's time!* Satisfied, he looked around: the carnage was complete. The right moment had arrived.

Sheikh Omar took a deep breath and reached for his sword, his hand trembling with excitement. To show his followers that he was truly the *Chosen One*, he needed an act of symbolic significance. He was determined not disappoint them. What he was about to do, in plain view of the world watching his every move, would be etched into the memory of millions for decades to come.

Before stepping out of the shadows, he adjusted his turban and scarf to hide his face and then walked slowly across to Radames.

The Captain of the Guard was still alive. Standing over him like an avenging angel, Sheikh Omar raised his gleaming scimitar up high. For what seemed an eternity, the razor-sharp blade stood still, reflecting the flames devouring the stage behind him. Then, shouting, '*Allah akbar*,' he brought the heavy blade swiftly down, cutting off Radames' head with one clean stroke.

The triumphant executioner turned towards the TV cameras – face concealed, but eyes burning with zeal – and pointed the tip of his sword to the bloody head lying at his feet. It was an unmistakable message sent to the living rooms of a gasping world. For an instant he stood quite still, like a statue, and then vanished into the darkness, like a ghost.

Part II

SECRETS

Carcassonne; February 1944

The black convertible Mercedes pulled up in front of Villa Bethania. Brushing a speck of dust off his tunic, the major adjusted his cap and got out of the car. 'Announce me,' he said.

The driver walked across to the villa and rang the bell. A small, elderly woman opened the door and squinted at him through her lorgnette. She looked like a surprised owl scrutinising its prey, unsure whether to pounce on it or let it go.

'Madame Colbert?' asked the major, stepping forward. The woman nodded. 'Sturmbannfuehrer Wolfgang Steinberger,' he said, clicking his heels together. 'May I come in?' He followed the woman into the drawing room on the ground floor.

'You have heard of our little excavations?' The woman nodded again. 'Good. I am sure you know what we are looking for.' The woman shook her head.

'Very well then.' Annoyed, the major scrutinised the little woman in front of him. 'You were Abbé Diderot's housekeeper for many years. No, that's not quite right, is it?' the major corrected himself. 'You were much more than that. Companion and confidante would be far more accurate, don't you agree? In fact, you were at his side when he died. Now, as his sole beneficiary you were privy to all his secrets – correct? And he was certainly a man of secrets and intrigue ...'

'You are obviously well informed, Monsieur.'

The major smiled; Madame Colbert was about to find out just how well informed he really was. 'The abbé refused to explain

137

the source of his sudden – dare I say staggering – wealth and this caused a lot of controversy at the time. Not only in the parish, but with his superiors in the Church as well, I believe. So much so,' the major continued, 'that for a while he was suspended by his bishop for alleged simony, but later reinstated by the Vatican on appeal.' The major paused and lit a cigarette. 'What a silly accusation; selling masses to his parishioners. He was selling something quite different, was he not, Madame?'

Madame Colbert paled, visibly shaken, but once again did not reply.

'To remain silent is not helpful, Madame. Allow me to assist. The Vatican was involved in all this – correct?' The major was beginning to enjoy himself. He was well versed in the subtle art of interrogation and knew exactly how to create the impression that he knew a lot more than he did. Fear would usually do the rest and loosen the tongue.

'You must understand all this was a long time ago. I'm just an old woman living here alone. Why ...?'

'And quite comfortably I can see,' interrupted the major. 'The abbé left you a beautiful house, Madame. A house full of memories *and secrets*. I am sure you wouldn't wish to leave it,' he said quietly, introducing the threat.

'No, I would not,' whispered Madame Colbert, playing nervously with her lorgnette.

'And there is no reason why you should have to,' the major reassured her, 'if you help me, that is.'

'What do you want from me, Monsieur?'

'We are beginning to understand each other – good. The Fuehrer has taken a personal interest in this matter, the importance of that speaks for itself. So let me be frank.' The major ground the stub of his cigarette into the ashtray on the table. 'The abbé discovered a cache of old manuscripts during the restoration of his village church in the 1890s.' Madame Colbert sat up as if pricked by a hot needle from behind. 'The Church authorities became very interested in this discovery, right? However,' continued the major, leaning across to Madame Colbert sitting opposite, 'there was more, much, much more ...' he whispered.

The major thought he detected a flicker of fear in the eyes of the otherwise calm woman. 'The documents the abbé found in the hollow altar pillar were only the beginning, is that not so? The first few pages pointing the way, so to speak, to a treasure trove – the legendary archives of the Knights Templar.' The major paused, to allow the words to find their mark.

'In fact,' the major paused again, enjoying the suspense, 'the abbé was selling the Templar archives to the Vatican. That was the true source of his wealth, am I right?'

For a while, Madame Colbert sat quite still, without looking at the major. Then slowly, she nodded her head. The major began to smile; the door had been opened.

'The abbé was – shall we say – a cautious man. He sold the documents in instalments, one bundle at a time, keeping back some of the more important ones for later. No amount of inducement or threat could persuade him to do otherwise. Rather ingenious. However, his sudden death in 1917 brought all this to an abrupt end, did it not?' Madame Colbert nodded again. 'The obvious question remains: Where are the documents he did not sell to the Vatican? Can you help me with that?'

'No! I don't know where they are. He died suddenly. He had his secrets. I ... I ... don't ...'

'But not from you, Madame,' interrupted the major, raising his voice. Madame Colbert began to search for her handkerchief.

'Please calm yourself. It is quite simple really. If you cannot help me find the remaining archives you will force me to look for them myself – right here.'

'What do you mean?'

'This villa will be taken apart, brick by brick, until I find what I'm looking for. The Templar archives are somewhere right here – here with you!'

'You are mistaken, Monsieur!' shrieked the old woman.

'You have until tomorrow to give me your final answer. I will return in the morning. Please think it over – carefully.' The major stood up. 'One of my officers will stay with you – just as a precaution – I am sure you understand.' The major turned on his heels and walked towards the door.

'Not even Asmodeus here will be able to protect the secrets of this house,' said the major, pointing to the bust of a hideous-looking demon on a pedestal, 'should we have to pull this place apart. Good day Madame.'

The major returned the next morning and found a composed Madame Colbert waiting for him in the drawing room.

'The documents you seek – what's left of them that is – are hidden in Montsegur,' she said calmly. 'There is a cave under the ruins of the castle ... I can show you where.'

'A most prudent decision, Madame,' replied the major, obviously pleased with himself. This had turned out to be a lot easier than he had expected. 'In return, I will personally guarantee your safety and undisturbed stay here in the villa,' he announced.

'There's one complication,' said Madame Colbert quietly.

'Oh?' The major was about to light up, but changed his mind and put the cigarette back into its silver case. 'What complication?' he demanded.

'As you obviously know, the documents the Vatican was so interested in related to one matter in particular ...'

'Quite so. Something very old, something mentioned in the Old Testament. It is something, we hear, that could rock the Church to its very foundations ... if the manuscripts tell the truth, that is,' interrupted the major. He could never resist an opportunity to show his knowledge.

'Monsieur, I'm afraid the documents you really want have gone,' explained Madame Colbert.

'What do you mean?' The major sensed danger.

'I was not the only beneficiary ... the abbé has a son ...'

'*What? A son?* Are you serious?'

'Absolutely. I can see you don't believe me, but it is so.' The old woman stood up and hobbled across the room to a small desk by the window. 'Just before he died, the abbé gave me this.' She opened one of the drawers, took out a neatly folded sheet of paper and handed it to the major.

'*By the time you read this, my dearest, I will be in the Lord's hands,*' the major began to read aloud. He spoke slowly, because Diderot's tiny handwriting was difficult to decipher. '*There is one last act of kindness I ask of you, one that is more important than all the others you have shown me over the years. You know of my son; you know where to find him. Go and visit him and give him my letter and these parchments. Please, I implore you, you must hand them to him personally. My letter will explain everything. One day he will understand what they mean. They have the power to change the world. With love, here and in eternity, Berenger Diderot.*'

The major folded the sheet of paper carefully along its creases and looked at Madame Colbert; he noticed she was crying. 'Please,' he said, quietly, 'tell me about the son.'

Madame Colbert shook her head.

'The son!' bellowed the major.

Madame Colbert looked up, frightened. 'Soon after the abbé discovered the manuscripts hidden in the church, he took them to Paris.'

'Why?'

'To show them to ... some learned people with rather exotic interests,' explained Madame Colbert. 'One of them was Francine Bijoux. Do you know who Francine Bijoux was, Monsieur?'

'A famous singer, I believe.'

'Yes; she was a celebrated diva ... probably the most well known at the time. She was also an occultist, you know. They became infatuated with each other ...' Madame Colbert pulled a handkerchief out of the sleeve of her dress and began to wipe away the tears. 'Please forgive me. She visited here often, and then ... she ... had a son.'

'When was that?'

'1892. It was all hushed up of course. Having an illegitimate child didn't quite go with her glamorous career. The abbé's involvement was covered up as well.'

'What happened to the child?'

'She didn't keep the boy; he was put up for adoption virtually straight away. Close friends of hers – a childless couple, musicians I believe – took him in and raised him.'

The major stood up and began to pace up and down in front of the window. 'When the abbé died, the boy would have been – twenty-five, am I right? Did you go and see him?'

'Yes, I visited him in Paris and gave him the parchments and the letter, just as the abbé had wished.'

The major stopped in front of the window and looked out into the garden. He began to squeeze his hands behind his back until the knuckles turned white. 'Have you kept in contact with him?' he asked, without turning around.

'Only for a few years. When I met him in Paris he was already an accomplished musician. After that, we lost touch. He got married and moved to Warsaw, I believe.'

'What's his name?'

Madame Colbert did not reply.

'His name, Madame,' the major asked again, raising his voice. 'I want his name.'

'Krakowski, the name of his adoptive parents. Russian émigrés – a Jewish couple.'

The major continued to look out the window. 'And his first name?'

'Berenger; after his father.' Madame Colbert kept pressing the handkerchief to her trembling mouth.

She had told the major enough to convince him she was telling the truth – but inside she was smiling. She had not told him everything. She had not betrayed the abbé's trust. She had not told the major what else she had given Berenger in Paris after his father's death. Just thinking about it after all these years made her tremble. There was nothing about it in the letter she'd shown the major; the subject was far too dangerous.

'I will now take you to Montsegur, Madame, and you will show me where the Templar archives are hidden,' said the major, turning around. 'As for Berenger Krakowski ... if he's still alive and somewhere in the Reich, I will find him.'

27

Carrington stood in front of the cathedral with the other pallbearers, waiting. A single bell tolled in the steeple above – the solemn reminder of mortality announcing the arrival of the hearses.

Jana was shocked by Carrington's appearance. Straining under the weight of his daughter's coffin, he looked vulnerable and frail. *Even the coffin is weeping*, she thought, looking at the raindrops glistening like tears on the polished wood. Jana hadn't seen Carrington since the Luxor massacre. *Could grief age a man so much, so quickly?*

Jana only remembered fragments of what had happened at the temple that night. Most of her recollections were a blur of panic and confusion. The funeral service brought the painful memories flooding back all at once: the screams, the fear, the maimed bodies, the smell of death, the blood.

The pallbearers placed the two identical coffins on top of the biers waiting in front of the altar and stepped back. Without the pallbearers, the coffins looked like two lonely islands floating in a sea of flowers.

Jana tried in vain to block the haunting image of Isabella's mutilated face, and the terror in Elizabeth Carrington's open eyes, frozen in death. Jana covered her face with both hands and tried to pray. She hadn't prayed in years and the only words that came to her were those of a simple childhood prayer. The long-forgotten, yet still familiar words began to calm her.

During the chaos after the carnage, Jana had assumed that Carrington had been killed as well. When Haddad found her at the airport and told her that Carrington was in fact alive and recovering in a military hospital in Alexandria, she cried with joy. But to visit him there was out of the question, Haddad had explained.

After the burial, Carrington thanked each of the mourners personally. Jana was one of the last to file past the two mounds of wet clay grieving in the rain. The wilting flowers and muddy wreaths reminded Jana of mortality, decay and the relentless passage of time. Momentarily overcome by the sadness of the moment, she couldn't speak.

'Thank you, Jana,' she heard him say, his voice sounding distant. He brushed his cold lips fleetingly against her cheek and, putting his arm around her, slipped something into her hand.

'Please keep this for me,' he whispered, and let her go.

Jana looked briefly at the object in her hand, then asked Carrington quietly, 'Remember the man with the biblical face we met at the temple before the performance?'

'The one we called Balthazar?'

'Yes. Haddad showed me some film footage ... The man was a terrorist – most probably the leader.' Carrington didn't reply and Jana couldn't be sure he had heard her.

Jana threaded her way through neat rows of muddy graves and hurried back to the car park. She took cover under the lichgate and wiped away the tears. When she opened her hand, she recognised the small tip of Akhenaten's beard.

'Come,' said the priest, putting his hand on Carrington's shoulder, 'it's time to go.' Carrington didn't hear him and kept staring at the graves. After a while, he turned around and followed the priest out of the deserted cemetery.

Carrington hadn't slept in days and was feeling quite ill. Sitting alone in his empty study, the crushing realisation of what had occurred that morning began to overwhelm him. He had just buried his family; his wife and daughter were gone forever. He would never see them again or be able to touch their faces; their laughter was but a memory. Carrington began to shake. For the first time since the massacre he was able to let go. Tears streamed down his wan face. He felt dizzy and had to hold the desk to steady himself. He closed his eyes and drifted into a restless slumber.

Suddenly, the serene face of Akhenaten floated out of the shadows. The pharaoh raised his long right arm and pointed to the sarcophagus, just as he had done in the dream back in the boarding house in Saqqara. The heavy lid began to lift slowly all by itself until it was suspended in mid air, hovering weightlessly above the limestone chest. Once again, Carrington found himself irresistibly drawn towards the open sarcophagus. He walked over to it through pools of blood and looked inside. This time, however, he was not woken by his own screams. Instead, he was staring at his dead wife and daughter lying side by side on a bed of flowers.

The fax machine on the desk clicked into action. A single page fell into the tray with a beep, signalling the end of the transmission. Carrington woke with a start, switched on the light and wiped his burning face with his handkerchief. Reaching for his glasses and the page simultaneously, he began to read:

My dearest friend,

As you will have realised by now, I have unfortunately been unable to make it to the funeral after all. Please forgive me. That you have lost your family in such barbaric circumstances in my country fills me with deep shame and regret. You have my solemn promise that I will not rest until the perpetrators are brought to justice. I know this is cold comfort just now, but you should know that we have made some progress. I think we may have found the stolen statue.

Carrington's vision blurred and the hand holding the fax began to shake.

I am presently waiting for confirmation and will call you later tonight, your time. I may need your help with identification. My thoughts are with you, and remember, even in the middle of the darkest night, the bright light of the morning is never too far away.

Your grieving friend,
Naguib.

Carrington crushed the fax into a tiny ball with his right hand until the knuckles turned white and his fingernails dug deep into his palm. 'Thank you, Naguib,' he whispered. 'I owe you.'

28

The remote beach house, built of corrugated iron, scavenged driftwood and glass, had an uninterrupted view of the sea. Jack limped out onto the terrace, picked up his binoculars and began to watch a pod of dolphins glide through the surf close to shore.

Jana checked the address again and then tried the door. It was unlocked. She opened it and walked inside.

'There are obviously no active burglars in *this* neighbourhood,' Jana called out, kicking off her shoes. She could see Jack standing on the terrace.

'Only seagulls and dolphins,' replied Jack, turning around. 'Come, say hello to my friends.' He pointed to the dolphins. Jana dropped her overnight bag and flew into his outstretched arms. 'Careful now, I'm an invalid, remember?' Jack warned, hugging her tightly.

They made love that whole afternoon with a passion that was both furious and tender. Jana desperately needed to feel alive after Luxor and the funeral. Jack sensed this and responded to her need, despite the pain in his chest and the cramps in his leg.

The bandages had been removed from his head and his hair was slowly growing back. Jana told him he looked like an American naval recruit with an ambitious crew cut, one who'd recently been in a fight with his cutlery – and lost. The scars were healing well. Jack didn't tell her that his internal injuries were still painful and occasionally bleeding and that the limp could be permanent; she might have regretted their lovemaking. The doctors recommended rest and exercise. An architect friend had given Jack the keys to his hideaway on the far North Coast and told him to stay as long as he liked.

Strolling along the deserted beach with Jack, Jana relaxed. Slowly, she began to tell him about Egypt.

'What happens now? Will Carrington continue?' Jack asked.

'I really don't know. He just buried his family; I guess no one had the courage to ask him. I told his clerk where I was going and left my phone number. Just in case.'

'Have you spoken to your boss?'

'Sure. He was of course shocked by it all, but noncommittal. He suggested I take a few days off to let things settle down.'

'Excellent advice. Thank you boss,' Jack said, kissing Jana on the neck.

'What about you? Have you found out anything else?'

'For the first few days up here, the only surfing I was able to do was on the internet,' Jack explained, laughing. 'It paid off. I have something to show you, come.'

'Can't it wait until tomorrow?' Jana purred softly, walking the tips of her fingers slowly down Jack's back.

'Don't look at me like that, you hear. Can't you see I'm an invalid? Have you no pity at all?'

'No! Just leave it all to me. You won't have to do a thing. Well, perhaps just a little ...'

'Oh yeah? Promises, promises. Last time ...'

'Is this a complaint?'

'Not really.'

'In that case, follow me.'

Jana woke with a fright and propped herself up on her elbows. A phone was ringing somewhere in the dark. Jack was asleep next to her, breathing calmly. She remembered the last time she was woken by a phone call in the middle of the night and began to shiver. She put her hand on Jack's shoulder to reassure herself that he was really there. Jana recognised the ring tone of her mobile. She got out of bed, walked into the hallway and answered the phone.

'Hello?' Jana said hoarsely, trying to calm herself.

'Jana, is that you?'

'Yes, who's this?'

'Marcus Carrington. I'm sorry to wake you at this hour, but it's quite urgent I'm afraid.'

'What's happened?' Jana sat down on the floor.

'Haddad just called with some extraordinary news.'

'What about?' Jana asked, suddenly wide awake.

'Apparently, they've found the statue.' A light came on in the bedroom and Jack appeared in the doorway.

'Where?'

'In London.'

'In London?' Jana repeated, unable to hide her surprise. Jack knelt down behind her and began to massage her neck. 'It's Carrington,' she explained.

'You have company, I'm sorry,' Carrington apologised. Jana noticed a subtle change in the tone of his voice. It had lost some of its intimacy and had become a little frosty and formal.

'It's all right, really, please go on,' Jana said, trying to put him at ease.

'Shall I call back later?'

'No. Please, it's fine,' she assured him.

'Our pharaoh is about to be auctioned.'

'What? Auctioned? When?'

'Day after tomorrow.'

'So soon! How do we know it's him?'

'Well, we cannot be absolutely sure, but wait till you see this. Do you have your laptop with you?'

'Yes, I'll turn it on.'

'This is what alerted Haddad,' Carrington explained. 'I'll email it to you now and you can tell me what you think.'

'What is it?' Jana asked, waiting for the email to come through.

'An addendum to an auction catalogue with a picture of the statue on the back.'

'It's here,' Jana said. The image was quite blurred, but the outline of Akhenaten was clearly visible. The photo was taken at an angle, showing the unusual face almost in profile. Jana noticed that the bottom part of the king's beard was missing.

'What do you think?' Carrington demanded impatiently.

'The beard – I think it's him!' Jana almost shouted.

'So do I.'

'What happens now?'

'We go to London and stop the auction.'

'Who's we?' Jana asked. As soon as she said it she realised just how foolish it sounded.

'You and I, of course. We're the only ones who can identify him, remember? Haddad is convinced the theft of the statue is somehow connected with the terrorists,' Carrington pointed out. 'I've already spoken to the Attorney-General,' he continued, anticipating her next question.

'And?'

'He wants you to come with me. The Government has received an official request for assistance from Egypt and the CIA,' Carrington explained. 'The Americans are about to bomb a terrorist training camp somewhere in the Sudan in retaliation for Luxor. Believe me, they need every lead they can get, but please, keep this to yourself,' he added, lowering his voice. 'We're booked on a Qantas flight to London leaving at 8 pm tonight. Haddad will meet us in London. It's cutting it fine, but we should just make it. Can you get back to Sydney in time?' Carrington asked anxiously.

'Yes, I think so.'

'Excellent, and don't forget to bring the missing piece of the beard,' he reminded her and hung up.

Jack was cooking breakfast while Jana packed her bag. 'I can see clearly now how our arrangement is going to work,' observed Jack, stirring the omelette.

'What do you mean?'

'Well, you get all the glamorous assignments – Cairo one day, London the next – and I get the drudgery. Wading through endless newspaper articles, doing the research, staring at computer screens all day long, exciting stuff like that – with the occasional bit of encouragement thrown in to keep me motivated, I suppose,' he added mischievously. Jana threw a pillow at him through the doorway, narrowly missing the frying pan.

'You want your omelette fluffy then, I take it,' Jack chuckled. Jana tiptoed quietly up to him from behind and put her arms around his waist.

'Careful now. Remember what happened the last time you interfered with my cooking?' Jack warned, waving his spoon at her. 'My kitchen table will never be the same again,' he complained with a sigh and continued to stir the omelette.

'Jack.'

'What?'

'I feel so happy here,' Jana said quietly. 'I really don't want to go.'

'Do you have to?' Jack asked hopefully.

'You know the answer as well as I do.'

'I guess so, but I don't have to like it.' Jana began to nibble his ear. 'Enough of that now. No more smooching or you'll really miss your plane. Go and do something useful. Squeeze something, preferably an orange, or set the table.'

'Remember how Dr Rosen thought there was an article in an Adelaide paper about the violin at the time her parents got divorced?' Jack reminded her.

'What of it?'

'Look under your serviette.' Jana lifted her serviette and found a neatly folded piece of paper under it. It was a photocopy of a newspaper page dated October 12, 1962. In the bottom left corner was a small article with the heading:

Charity violin to be auctioned in London.

'Where on earth did you find this?' Jana asked, holding up the page.

'The fruits of drudgery are occasionally quite sweet,' Jack replied with a grin.

'*Prominent Adelaide stock broker, Eric Newman, has donated a precious violin to bushfire victims in the Adelaide Hills. The violin, a treasured heirloom, has been in his family for generations, he said,*' Jana began to read out loud. '*The magnificent instrument – thought to be a genuine Stradivarius – is to be sent to England for auction. A representative of the auctioneers – McCormack & Sons of London – has indicated that there was already considerable interest in the unique instrument, which is expected to fetch several thousand pounds.*'

'I thought, while you're in London, you could look up the auctioneers and ask them to search their records,' Jack suggested. 'It could be useful to find out what's happened to the violin. A Stradivarius doesn't just vanish without a trace.'

Jana nodded and read the article again. 'This is very exciting, Jack. Dr Rosen certainly told us the truth.'

'And there's more,' Jack said, reaching for another slice of toast.

'What do you mean?'

'That American attorney called again. You know, the class action in the US?'

'Green ... something ...'

'Yeah, Sam Greenberg from New York. Apparently the investigators had a breakthrough with the Swiss authorities. The international pressure had its desired effect. The banks concerned have agreed to cooperate and open their ledgers and, hopefully, their vaults. Well, at least the ledgers; the vaults will take a little more persuasion, I believe.'

'Does this help us?'

'It could. Remember I told you about a particular bank account set up by the Nazis that is still being accessed regularly from Argentina?'

'Yes.'

'The Americans are now almost certain that an Australian bank is involved. They're talking to a potential witness in Buenos Aires right now – a former Nazi. It's all very hush-hush, but who knows?'

'How extraordinary.'

'It gets better.'

'It does?'

'Greenberg and I have made a deal, as the Americans would say.'

'What kind of deal?' Jana looked puzzled.

'We exchange information. Sound familiar? I keep him up to date about our Newman investigation over here, and he keeps me informed about the Swiss bank proceedings and the new witness.'

'You learn quickly.'

'I have a good teacher.' Jana began to laugh. 'And the best bit,' Jack continued, leaning forward, 'my paper has commissioned a series of articles about the US class action and the Holocaust victims with their *abandoned* Swiss bank accounts. You never know, if it turns out that an Aussie bank *is* involved, well ... In any event, it's a good story and we stay ahead of the game, don't you think?'

'Congratulations!'

'And,' Jack paused, rubbing his hands together, 'I negotiated a fat advance. I don't make this kind of money often. After falling down those stairs, my bank balance appears to have fallen with me – quite alarmingly so in fact. My kind of journalism is a fickle business, you know. You certainly wouldn't do it for the money.'

'That's my Jack: always charming, always broke, but ready for anything.'

Jana looked out the window of the small plane and saw Jack standing at the end of the runway. He was waving at the plane with both hands. Jana waved back, well aware he couldn't possibly see her.

29

'Ladies and gentlemen, we now come to the item many of you have been waiting for,' the auctioneer announced with a flourish. He paused, giving his audience time to settle down. He adjusted his yellow polka-dot bow tie with carefully manicured fingers and scrutinised the potential bidders. 'A magnificent life-sized statue of a famous – dare I say notorious – pharaoh, exquisitely crafted from black granite by royal Egyptian sculptors 3200 years ago.' The auctioneer turned around and signalled to his assistant. The blue silk sheet covering the statue was lifted off and a ripple of excitement washed across the room.

'Ladies and gentlemen, I'm sure you will agree that many a museum would be proud to display such a splendid piece in its collection. Yet, here you are with a unique opportunity to own it yourself,' continued the auctioneer. 'No doubt you have all read the fascinating history of the statue in your catalogues and would have noticed that it forms part of the deceased estate of a Swiss collector. It's offered for sale here today by his executors. Ladies and gentlemen, the beneficiaries want their money; the statue must be sold,' joked the auctioneer, shrewdly weaving a reference to the provenance of the item into his opening remarks. The auctioneer paused again and reached for his gavel. Somehow, this gesture appeared to silence the excited crowd.

'I'm in your hands, ladies and gentlemen. Do I have a million pounds to start? A million pounds for a piece of eternity? A million pounds I have, thank you, sir,' said the auctioneer, pointing to a well-dressed, elderly gentleman standing at the back of the room. Curious heads turned in his direction.

'Any advance on a million pounds? A million I have, a million pounds. A million and two hundred thousand; thank you, madam,' said the auctioneer, bowing politely towards a young lady sitting in the front row. 'It's against you now, sir. One million five hundred thousand; thank you, sir. That's the spirit. One million and a half I have, a million and a half for a real pharaoh. It's a bargain at this price. Any advance on a million and a half?'

The taxi crawled through the heavy London traffic. Carrington looked at Jana sitting next to him and pointed to his watch.

'How much further?' Jana asked the cabbie.

'We're almost there, Miss. I'm going as fast as I can,' the driver assured her.

At the next intersection the traffic came to a virtual standstill in the pouring rain. Their flight had been delayed in Singapore. Carrington had phoned Haddad from the airport and was told to go straight to the auction; there were complications with the injunction ...

The taxi inched a few feet forward and then stopped completely. Carrington looked again at his watch, reached for his mobile and dialled Haddad's number.

'Where are you?' asked Haddad.

'Still in the taxi, where are you?'

'Still at court with the ambassador and the lawyers. How close are you?'

'How much further, driver?' Carrington asked.

'Just there, guv,' replied the cabbie, pointing to the other side of the intersection.

'Very close.'

'Run for it!'

'And what do you suggest I do when I get there?'

'You're the barrister, you'll think of something. Buy us time. Anything, just hold up the sale. I'll come with the ambassador as soon as I can,' Haddad said, and hung up.

'Great! Come on, Jana, let's go,' Carrington shouted and opened the door. They ran across the intersection and almost bumped into the liveried doorman standing in front of the auction house. 'Where's the auction?' Carrington demanded breathlessly. The doorman pointed towards a pair of open doors at the end of a long corridor.

'Four million pounds I have, four million, four million pounds,' the auctioneer droned on, trying to keep the bidding momentum going forward. He knew that any interruption to the flow could be fatal. 'It's against you now, madam. This is the opportunity of a lifetime, ladies and gentlemen. Four million pounds for a unique piece of history.' The auctioneer paused, dabbing his brow with a red handkerchief. 'I will take advances of one hundred thousand. Four million one hundred thousand I have; thank you, Sir Edmond,' said the auctioneer, acknowledging one of the regulars. 'I'm sure your tenacity will be well rewarded.'

Eager to see what was happening, curious spectators had gathered in the corridor outside the auction room. Carrington ignored their protests and began to push past them.

'Four million six hundred thousand once,' said the auctioneer, holding up his gavel. 'Four million six hundred thousand twice. This is your last opportunity, ladies and gentlemen; the Heretic King of Egypt will be sold. Four million six hundred thousand pounds, are you all done?' asked the auctioneer for the last time. All eyes were on the raised gavel.

As soon as he saw the black granite statue on the podium, all of Carrington's niggling doubts evaporated. 'Stop!' he shouted from the back of the room and held up his hand.

'Are you bidding, sir?' asked the surprised auctioneer, lowering his gavel.

'Please, let me through,' Carrington said. The auctioneer put the gavel back on the lectern.

'Please, sir, answer me. Are you bidding?' demanded the auctioneer again.

'Mr Auctioneer, the lot you are about to knock down is stolen property and rightfully belongs to another sovereign country. It cannot be sold!' Carrington said, climbing onto the podium. With his wet hair plastered across his forehead and rainwater dripping from his trench coat, he looked like the Pink Panther under secondment to MI5.

'This is a trick. Throw him out! This is intolerable. Do your duty, auctioneer,' shouted angry bidders from the floor below. The crowd was turning hostile. The auctioneer motioned to the security guards at the back of the room.

'Don't make a big mistake, I have proof,' Carrington warned, looking the auctioneer straight in the eye.

'He has proof,' shouted someone in the front row.

'He has proof,' repeated others further back. The auctioneer hesitated, uncertainty clouding his face. Carrington took a deep breath. *We may have just bought a little time*, he thought.

'What proof?' asked the auctioneer. 'Who are you?'

This is just like a court performance, thought Carrington, turning confidently towards the agitated crowd. He held up his hands and tried to calm the ruffled patrons. 'My name is Marcus Carrington. I found this statue three weeks ago, buried in an ancient tomb at Saqqara, in Egypt,' he explained calmly, addressing the crowd like a jury. He paused, and pointed to the smiling pharaoh. 'It was stolen from the tomb the night after I discovered it. The statue was under guard. Two young soldiers were murdered trying to protect it.'

The crowd fell silent. The security guards approached the podium and looked at the auctioneer. He waved them away; throwing the man out now would solve nothing.

'Anyone can say that,' shouted a man at the back. 'Mr Auctioneer, I demand you continue with the sale immediately.' Jana looked at the man and instantly recognised Horst Newman. She wanted to tell Carrington but he was on the podium arguing with the auctioneer. Jana kept looking at Horst to make sure she wasn't mistaken.

'The Egyptian ambassador will be here any moment with an injunction,' Carrington said.

'You have proof?' asked the auctioneer, now also trying to buy time.

I believe I have an ally here, thought Carrington. *How quickly things can change.*

'Yes, what proof?' repeated someone in the front.

'Put up, or shut up,' shouted someone else.

'I do have proof. Please listen to me.'

'Order!' shouted the auctioneer, hammering the lectern with his gavel. 'Ladies and gentlemen, please. I'm sure we can resolve this quickly. Let us hear what Mr Carrington has to say.'

'Let the man speak,' yelled someone in the back.

'Yes, let him speak,' chorused the crowd and calmed down.

'This is a farce,' shouted Horst, 'get on with the auction.' The auctioneer ignored the remark.

'Keep quiet!' barked a man standing in front of Horst. Colonel Sorokin put his hand on Horst's arm. 'The auctioneer won't proceed with the sale, let it be,' he said quietly. Sorokin was anxious not to attract any more attention. Horst paled and turned to Farim standing next to him.

'Well, what do we do now?' he demanded angrily.

'We keep calm and see what happens,' replied Farim, looking for the nearest exit.

'When I discovered the statue three weeks ago buried in a tomb, it was exactly as you see it here before you now – with the tip of the beard broken off,' explained Carrington, pointing to Akhenaten. All heads turned towards the statue and looked at the beard. 'When we tried to move it, we found the missing piece ...' The podium had become a stage and the bidders had turned into a spellbound audience. *I feel like a circus magician,* thought Carrington. He already knew the verdict of this jury; all he had to do was present the evidence. By deliberately taking his time, Carrington let the tension mount.

'I have the missing piece right here,' he announced, holding out his hand. Jana reached into her bag and handed the piece of black granite to him. When she turned around, Horst recognised her. They stared at each other until Horst lowered his eyes. Jana continued to look in his direction.

'I don't believe it,' mumbled Horst, 'what on earth is she doing here?' He looked suddenly alarmed. 'Do you see that woman over there, in the front?' Horst asked Sorokin. The Colonel nodded. 'Do you have someone here who could follow her?'

'Sure, but why?'

'I'll tell you later. Please, just do it,' pleaded Horst, looking nervously around the room.

'Okay.'

'Please take it,' urged Carrington, handing the small piece of stone to the perplexed auctioneer. 'After all, it's part of what you're trying to sell. If it fits, I think you have your proof, don't you agree?'

The crowded auction room turned deathly quiet. All eyes followed the small, shiny stone fragment in the auctioneer's hand. The tension grew. For an instant, the auctioneer hesitated, as the magnitude of his predicament began to dawn on him. *What if it fits?* he asked himself. *There'll be one hell of a scandal and I'm right in the middle of it.*

'Go on, see if it fits,' urged one of the bidders impatiently. The auctioneer realised he was no longer in control and began to fumble with his bow tie. He walked across to the statue and carefully placed the piece of polished stone against the broken end of the pharaoh's beard. It was a perfect fit. At first there was complete silence, then the room erupted.

'That was quite a performance; you should try Shakespeare next,' Haddad said, putting his arm around Carrington's shoulder. 'I really enjoyed the show.'

'How long have you been here?' asked Carrington, surprised to see his friend. He had to shout to make himself heard.

'You were doing so well, I didn't want to interrupt,' Haddad replied, sidestepping the question. 'The ambassador is serving the injunction right now, the auction is over, come.'

Jana pushed through the excited crowd towards Horst. He saw her coming and hurried towards the exit. When she finally made it to the door, Horst had disappeared.

30

'Congratulations,' Jack said on the other end of the line. 'I'd like to have seen the auctioneer's face when you two burst into the room crying foul. Here they come again.'

'Who? What are you talking about?' Jana asked. 'Have you been drinking?'

'The inquisitive dolphins, silly. They've turned up every day since you left – what a sight! I think they're looking for you. That's what happens when you walk around starkers on the terrace. You see, they remember those firm, well-rounded ...'

'One more word and I hang up,' interrupted Jana, choking with laughter, 'and you won't find out who bought Newman's violin.'

'What? You know? Tell me. Dolphins go away!'

'There were no records. They don't keep them that long. But a nice lady in the auctioneer's office gave me the address of an old fellow who valued musical instruments for McCormack & Sons for decades. I went to see him. He remembered the violin well. As you can imagine, a Stradivarius coming from Australia was quite a novelty at the time. The violin was apparently bought by a Lady Ashburton for her young son.'

'Is she still around, you think?'

'She's not, but her son is. I'm meeting Lord Ashburton later this morning at his country estate near Bath. He's even sending his driver to meet me at the station.'

'Jolly nice of the chap. Good luck! Are you ready for the

plodder report now? You're not the only one making progress, you know.'

'I miss you – plodder,' Jana interrupted.

'What did you say? I couldn't quite catch that,' Jack pretended, 'we must have a bad line.'

'I miss you,' Jana repeated, louder this time.

'This must be my bit of long-distance encouragement,' Jack speculated. 'It's not quite the same, but I guess it's better than nothing. For now, that is.'

'Seriously, Jack, how do we explain Horst turning up at the auction – eh?'

'I'm just as puzzled as you are. There has to be a connection, we just can't see it, that's all. What does Marcus think about all this?'

'He's making inquiries. Apparently, the Egyptian secret service had the auction under surveillance.'

'How exciting; turbans and dark glasses? Were they bidding?'

'You're an incorrigible larrikin,' Jana said, laughing.

'And you're a relentless teaser. Now, listen carefully. Do you have pen and paper?'

'Sure, why?'

'Write this down. J–a–k–o–b F–i–n–k–e–l–s–t–e–i–n.' Jack spelled the name and gave her an address in Warsaw.

'Who's Jakob Finkelstein?' Jana asked.

'A Holocaust survivor, and ... a former member of the Auschwitz welcoming orchestra. He was in the camp until the end and was liberated by the Allies. A young GI befriended him and later wrote a book about the musicians of Auschwitz based on Finkelstein's memoirs.'

'You truly amaze me,' interrupted Jana. 'How on earth did you find him?'

'On the internet. I found the book first, then I tracked down its author – a retired journalist living in Colorado. He was most helpful and gave me his friend's address. They still correspond regularly.'

'If Miss Abramowitz's recollections are accurate, this could be quite a lead,' Jana said. 'I suppose you want me to look him up, is that it?'

'If you have time.'

'I should ... Marcus is tied up with the lawyers and the injunction. Apparently he'll have to give evidence. It'll take a couple of days.'

'I'm going crazy here, all on my own,' said Jack, changing direction.

'You've got your dolphins.'

'Not quite the same.'

'You need to rest.'

'Bullshit! I need to be with you.'

'I wish you were here ...'

'You mean it?'

'You know I do.'

'Be careful.'

'Why's that?'

'Because wishes can come true.'

'But you're an invalid, remember? You told me so yourself,' Jana reminded Jack, laughing.

'Enough! Incidentally, Finkelstein seems to be quite a character,' Jack warned. 'In the book he's referred to as the Watchman of Warsaw.'

'How strange. Why?'

'Patience. You'll find out when you get there.'

31

Lord Ashburton cantered across the frozen meadow, followed by a brace of large Irish wolfhounds. He jumped off his steaming horse and threw the reins to the waiting groom.

'I'm so sorry to have kept you waiting,' he apologised, holding out his hand. 'You should have gone inside, it's freezing.'

'I've enjoyed walking through the gardens. They're magnificent, even in winter,' Jana said, introducing herself.

Lord Ashburton waved his hand dismissively at the manicured grounds. 'Let's have some tea to warm us up, shall we?' he suggested, leading the way to the entrance of the imposing residence. Hamilton Park had been in his family for over three hundred years.

Everything about Lord Ashburton was a little odd. His arms were a little too long, his head and ears a little too large and his mouth too wide. Yet, at fifty, he still had a youthful, rather school-boyish look about him. He gave the impression that he consisted of several ill-fitting parts belonging to different people.

'Splendid. James has lit the fire for us, good man,' said Lord Ashburton, pulling a large leather chair closer to the fireplace for Jana. The wolfhounds settled down in front of the chair and refused to move. 'Now, some tea.' On cue, the old butler appeared, dressed in a morning coat. It was the same man who had earlier collected Jana from the station in a vintage Rolls Royce.

'You said on the phone that you wanted to talk about the Stradivarius my mother bought. I must say, you made me curious. How can I help you?'

'It's a bit of a long story, I'm afraid,' Jana said, reaching into her handbag. She handed the photograph of the German officer and the naked boy to Lord Ashburton and began to explain how and where it was found.

Lord Ashburton was an attentive listener and didn't interrupt. Jana told him about Dr Rosen and gave him the Adelaide newspaper article to read.

'How extraordinary,' said Lord Ashburton. 'But there's no doubt we're talking about the same instrument here. We always knew it came from Australia. I suppose the real question for you is, of course,' he speculated, 'whether the violin case in this photograph contained the same instrument.'

'Correct. If the man in the photo is Sir Eric, well ... it's a long shot, I know.'

'Amazing.'

'Do you still have the violin?'

'In a way – yes. My mother gave it to me when I was still a boy being groomed for the concert hall. Regrettably I wasn't the virtuoso type ... All my tutors finally gave up in despair because I was more interested in horses and hunting than violin practice. I was a great disappointment to her I'm afraid,' he said, staring into the fire. 'I was sent to Eton and hardly ever saw her after that. She lived in Italy for many years. All her lovers were musicians. My father was much older; they lived separate lives. You know how it is ...' he added quietly.

'Where's the violin now? May I see it?'

'For years it was kept over there,' he replied, pointing to a glass display cabinet in the far corner. 'Mother left it to the conservatorium in Florence as part of a trust arrangement. There's an annual competition and a prize that bears her name. The winner gets a scholarship and is allowed to keep the instrument for a year. It travels all over the world, you see.

Maximum exposure, I suppose, and all that.'

'What a wonderful idea,' Jana said, 'but it's gone then. It's no longer yours – right?'

'Not exactly ...'

'What do you mean?'

'I'm the sole trustee.'

32

Jana knew she was lost. Warsaw in winter was grey, damp and freezing and the empty, cobblestoned backstreets all looked the same. She walked up to an old woman at a bus stop and asked for directions. Jana's childhood Polish was a little rusty, but adequate. When she finally found the tiny shop it was almost dark.

'Jakob Finkelstein – Watchmaker,' said the faded sign above the door. A torn blind covered the narrow shop window; there was no light inside. A nauseating smell of boiled cabbage and sewage filled the air. Jana pulled the brass bell knob next to the door. She could hear a bell ringing in the back of the shop, but nothing happened. After a few minutes, with no one coming to answer, she tried the bell again.

'Yes, yes I'm coming,' a voice called out from inside. Someone fumbled with a key in the lock. Finally, the door opened with a creak and a small, wizened old man squinted at Jana through thick glasses. 'I'm closed, can't you see? I'm eating dinner. What do you want?' said Finkelstein gruffly. Jana smiled at him and mentioned the name of the American GI who wrote the book. The old man's demeanour changed abruptly. 'Don't just stand there; come in,' he said, pointing down a dark corridor leading to the back of the shop.

The walls of the room in the back – Finkelstein's world – were covered with all kinds of clocks. Old Viennas were busily ticking next to elaborately carved cuckoo clocks from the Black Forest. Marble mantle clocks and bracket clocks of all shapes and sizes lined the shelves. In the far corner of the room an elegant English mahogany grandfather clock was rubbing shoulders with an old Dutch lantern clock that had once been to sea. The dimly lit room was full of movement and sound. Fascinating shadows crept along the walls following polished brass pendulums in mesmerising unison. The regular tick-tock of a hundred intricate mechanisms was near deafening.

Finkelstein lived surrounded by his treasures – each reminding him of former customers. He could still remember all their names, yet he could barely recall the name of someone he met only the day before. Most of the clocks had been brought to Finkelstein for safekeeping during the war. Unlike their unfortunate – predominantly Jewish – owners, the clocks survived the Holocaust, securely hidden in the spacious cellar under his shop.

'My faithful friends,' said Finkelstein. 'They are all special, but I do have my favourites of course. Take this one for instance,' he continued, running his hands affectionately along the gleaming mahogany case of a tall grandfather clock. 'Made in Glasgow in 1820; magnificent workmanship. It took me three weeks to repair it. It was very difficult. It needed new parts. I make all the parts myself, you know,' he explained. Jana smiled at him. 'It belonged to Professor Horowitz, a great man. Ah, and over here I have something really special. Come, look.' Jana followed the little man to his workbench. He pointed to an exquisite porcelain table clock on the shelf above. 'Meissen china, the best. It once stood in King Ludwig's dining room in Neuschwanstein castle. Wait until it chimes – superb.' Finkelstein became quite animated and began to stroke the tip of his white goatee. 'Forgive me, but I can see you didn't come here to talk about my clocks.' He motioned towards a threadbare sofa next to the workbench. 'Please, take a seat.'

Jana glanced at the steaming bowl of evil-smelling broth on

the bench and sat down. 'Would you like some? It's borscht, I made it myself.' Jana declined politely. Finkelstein climbed onto his stool in front of the bench and continued to eat his dinner. 'If it's not clocks, then what brings you here?'

'Auschwitz.'

Finkelstein put down his spoon and looked wistfully at Jana through his thick glasses. 'It never really goes away, does it?' he said at last, wiping his mouth with the back of his shaking hand. 'It just goes on; the ghosts are still with us.'

'You were playing in the camp orchestra until the end, I'm told.' Finkelstein nodded, a haunted look clouding his wrinkled face. 'Can you ...?' Silence. 'Can you tell me about it?' prompted Jana quietly.

Finkelstein nodded again. 'They made us play at the camp entrance when the trains arrived,' he said. 'Mainly cheerful Viennese music, would you believe. A polka to sweeten the march to the gas chamber; terrible. The things one did to stay alive ...' Finkelstein shook his head. 'But I was still a young man then, full of hope. One of the lucky ones, I thought at the time. I was sent to Auschwitz with my wife and two small daughters soon after the ghetto revolt in forty-three. The orchestra needed another musician; my clarinet saved my life. I thought it would save theirs as well,' he added sadly. 'It didn't.'

Suddenly, a cacophony filled the room. The clocks announced the hour with an exotic melange of whistles and bells, hooting owls and chipper cuckoos, sonorous gongs, lullabies and folk tunes. It was seven o'clock.

'No matter how hard I try, I can never quite get them to do it all on time,' shouted Finkelstein, 'there are always a few slow ones.' The chiming went on for several minutes until the last of the stragglers finally caught up.

Jana opened her handbag and pulled out the photograph. 'Do you recognise this man?' she asked, pointing to the German officer in the photo. Finkelstein took off his glasses, adjusted the lamp on the bench and pressed his round watchmaker's magnifying glass to his right eye. He examined the photograph for a long time and Jana noticed that he kept coming back to the dog in the picture.

'Do I recognise this man?' repeated Finkelstein, putting down his magnifying glass. 'Strictly speaking, no. As you can see, his face is barely visible under the visor of his cap.' He pointed to the officer's head. 'Yet, there's something familiar about him. His stance, his arrogance, I can't really explain it. And then of course, there's the dog ...'

'What do you mean?'

'Well, there was a German officer who visited the camp regularly. He used to come to the train station with his dog, and often spoke to us about music before the trains arrived and the selections were made. He was always looking for new arrivals with certain special skills. They were taken to another camp close by. He had a dog just like this one.' Finkelstein pointed to the snarling beast in the photo. Jana recognised echoes of Miss Abramowitz's recollections. Holding her breath, she leant forward. 'The dog had an unusual metal collar with an inscription on it,' he explained.

'What inscription?' Jana asked hoarsely.

'Ah, yes, I do remember now: *Arbeit macht frei*. Crazy. We didn't know what to make of it. Typical SS, they were all mad.'

Jana could barely contain her excitement. 'Is there anything else you can remember about him?' she asked hopefully.

'Not really. It was a long time ago and my memory isn't what it used to be, I'm afraid.' Finkelstein shrugged, and handed the photograph back to Jana.

'Do you know of anyone else who might?' she asked casually, almost as an afterthought.

'Strange you should ask; I was just thinking the same thing. There was this musician at the Auschwitz remembrance service – you know, the fiftieth anniversary of the camp's liberation. I was there.'

'What about him?'

'Well, he used to play in the camp orchestra as a young boy with his father. Perhaps he can remember something. You see, he survived – his father didn't. I spoke to him afterwards. It was all very moving.'

'Did you recognise him?'

'No, but I did remember his father. He was a well-known music teacher right here in Warsaw before the war.'

'What was his name?'

'I knew you would ask that. I'm sorry, but I just can't remember right now,' said Finkelstein apologetically. 'I'm rather bad with names ...'

'Please ... you must!' Jana almost shouted, unable to control her frustration. She put her hand on the old man's shoulder. He shook his head sadly. Embarrassed, Jana withdrew her hand.

'Wait, there is someone who might know,' said Finkelstein, waving his finger at Jana. 'My friend Moritz was with me at the liberation ceremony. We spoke a lot about it at the time; he might remember the name.'

'Where's your friend?'

'He lives close by; we play chess almost every day. I will ask him in the morning. Why don't you come back tomorrow and we'll see ...'

When Finkelstein showed Jana to the door the clocks chimed again –eight o'clock. Jana turned up the collar of her coat and looked around. The narrow alley was dark and deserted. There was only one street light. Preparing herself for the long walk back to her hotel, she hurried towards the light.

Jana thought she could hear footsteps behind her. The footsteps stopped when she stopped, and started again when she walked on. She looked quickly over her shoulder and caught a glimpse of a figure darting into a doorway. Certain she was being followed, she began to run towards the intersection at the end of the alley. Looking ahead, Jana saw another shadowy figure coming towards her from the intersection. *A trap*, she thought, her heart racing. She knew she had to get past the man in front. If he didn't have a gun, she had a chance; her hand-to-hand combat skills were excellent. Jana slowed to a walk and clenched her fists, ready to attack. As the man came closer, a flash of recognition raced across her mind. *No way!* she thought. She couldn't see the face, yet there was something familiar about the shape of the body and the outline of the head lit up from behind. The man stopped, so did Jana, bracing herself for an assault. 'I did warn you,' said the man, 'wishes can come true.' The man limped into the pale cone of streetlight and held up his hands. 'I surrender, Inspector.'

'Jack?' asked Jana, refusing to trust her eyes.

'And for a moment I thought you were running into my arms,' said Jack, laughing.

Staring incredulously at Jack, Jana tried to catch her breath. 'I'm being followed,' she croaked.

'Yeah, by those two guys over there.'

'We've got to get out of here; quickly!'

'Sure. My cab's waiting 'round the corner, come.'

As she sat next to Jack in the taxi, Jana began to relax. 'What on earth are you doing here?' she asked, running her fingers through Jack's short hair struggling to grow back. 'Just look at yourself, Scarface.'

'Someone had to scare the villains away. And besides, I got sick of sitting on the beach. Dolphins aren't much company, believe me. To tell you the truth, I was bored shitless.'

'How on earth did you find me?'

'I spoke to Carrington. He told me you had gone to Warsaw, you weren't at your hotel, I had Finkelstein's address ... here I am.'

'But your injuries ...'

'A few stitches and a limp; big deal.'

'And the rest.' Jana traced the red scar running across Jack's cheek with the tip of her finger. 'You can't afford any more knocks, mate. Trust me.'

'I'm fine, really.'

'Aren't you freezing?'

'What do you mean?'

'Favourite bomber jacket and t-shirt in winter? This is Poland, not the Sunshine Coast!'

'It was summer when I left home and I was in a hurry – so? And I did bring a jumper ...'

'Really? Where is it?'

Jack looked sheepish. 'Well ... I didn't have a chance to unpack yet,' he said.

'You're incorrigible, Jack Rogan. You know that, don't you?'

Jack realised he was losing and looked out the car window. 'What about Finkelstein? What did he tell you?' he asked, trying to change the subject.

'Later. Shut up and kiss me.'

33

After the auction debacle, Farim panicked and left London. Returning to Egypt, however, had quickly turned into a nightmare.

Haddad was getting worried; Farim hadn't provided him with a single piece of useful information since his arrest at Cairo airport the day before. The interrogation was going nowhere. It was time to turn up the heat.

'You haven't written a single word,' Haddad shouted, pointing angrily to the blank page on the table. Farim didn't reply.

'No names, then. I thought you were smarter than that.' Haddad turned around and called the guard.

'Wait, I want to make a deal,' Farim pleaded, barely able to see. The swelling around his broken nose and battered cheeks had almost closed his eyes.

'You are in no position to bargain with me, you miserable cur,' thundered Haddad.

'I've been given very little encouragement to help you,' Farim continued undeterred. 'If I tell you everything I know, I will rot here in jail – possibly for the rest of my short life – and if I don't, you put me back on the streets and circulate rumours that will almost certainly get me killed. Hardly an attractive choice, is it?' Haddad looked at Farim and frowned. He was convinced that Farim knew the mastermind behind the Luxor attack. To see him dead would achieve nothing. On the other hand ...

'What's on your mind?' Haddad asked, lighting a cigarette. Farim managed a smile. He could see that Haddad was interested.

'A little nicotine would certainly assist my memory,' suggested the irrepressible Farim. Haddad gave him the cigarette and lit another for himself. Farim inhaled greedily.

'Well?'

'I know the man you're after and I can take you to him.' He paused, allowing the words to find their mark. 'It will not be easy, but I think I can do it. In return, I want a new passport, a new identity and permission to leave Egypt – for good.'

'Is that all?' Haddad looked at Farim with grudging respect. He had to admit, the man had courage and knew how to bargain. If he could deliver what he claimed, the deal was worth considering.

'How long would it take you to find him?'

'I'm not sure. He's no longer in Egypt, you see ...'

'What do you mean?' Haddad asked, watching Farim carefully.

'The man you want is the founder of the Islamic Brotherhood for the Liberation of Holy Places. He's the one who decapitated the American singer at Luxor.'

'I know all that,' Haddad interrupted impatiently. Farim smiled at him and shrugged.

'Perhaps so. But you may not know that immediately after the Luxor incident he joined a caravan and went on a pilgrimage; a pious man, no doubt. No wonder his followers believe he is the "Chosen One". He's in Mecca right now, directing his mullahs from there.'

Haddad looked impressed. *This 'Chosen One' is obviously not only an utterly ruthless fanatic, but a clever, well-organised leader as well*, he thought. To hide in Mecca was quite ingenious. To reach him there – even with Farim's help – would be virtually impossible.

'What's his name?' demanded Haddad.

'Not so quickly,' Farim replied, enjoying himself for the first time since his arrest. He could sense he was slowly gaining the upper hand. 'Do we have a deal?'

'His name.'

'His followers call him the *Defender of the Faith*. That's all I know.'

'A *nome de guerre*, how original,' Haddad said sarcastically. 'What about his real name?' Farim shrugged again, implying he knew more. 'And this Australian banker, the one who was with you and the Russian at the auction? What's his part in all this?'

'Tell me we have a deal and I'll tell you all about him as well.'

Haddad began to pace up and down in the tiny cell like a caged animal. It was the same cell Mustafa had died in three weeks before. He didn't like having terms dictated to him, especially by someone as despicable as Farim. It was humiliating. He also realised he had little choice. Farim was by far his best lead, his only lead.

He remembered Elizabeth Carrington lying on top of her dead daughter with her eyes wide open, looking accusingly, he thought, at him. He remembered his friend Marcus farewelling the two lonely coffins at Cairo airport. He remembered the promise he had made; he could not afford to lose this opportunity.

'It's a deal,' Haddad said reluctantly. He stopped in front of Farim and grabbed him roughly by the hair. Farim winced. 'Listen carefully. You double-cross me once, only once ... and I will tear you apart with my own hands. Do we understand each other?'

'Perfectly,' Farim replied, grinning at Haddad. 'May I have another cigarette?'

34

The front door of the shop was open. Jana rang the bell and looked inside. 'It's so quiet,' she said to Jack standing next to her. 'Where are all the clocks?'

'Mr Finkelstein,' she called, walking towards the room in the back. There was no reply. The fine hairs on the back of her neck tingled. She reached the door at the end of the corridor and stopped to listen. Silence. 'I don't like this, Jack.' The door was ajar and she pushed it slowly.

Finkelstein was lying face down in a pool of blood with something grey and sticky-looking oozing out of his crushed scull. Next to his head on the floor was a piece of marble covered in blood. All the clocks in the ransacked room had been smashed to pieces. The floor was littered with broken glass, twisted pendulums, dented brass weights, steel springs and splinters of wood.

'Jesus, look at this!' Jack cried out. He knelt down and felt for the old man's pulse. There was none. He looked at Jana and shook his head.

'Don't touch anything. Let's get out of here,' said Jana. She was turning around to leave when the front door slammed shut. 'Did you hear that?' Standing perfectly still, she listened to the creaking floorboards – footsteps, coming closer. The footsteps stopped. Jana turned her head and saw a large figure standing in the doorway.

'Looking for something, Inspector Gonski?' asked a man in

a high-pitched, almost feminine voice. The man lit a cigarette. He was completely bald and grotesquely fat. Jana could hear him exhale and saw a puff of smoke drift slowly into the room. Instinctively, she reached for where her shoulder holster would normally be. Of course there was no gun. 'And who have we here?' continued the man, looking at Jack. 'The intrepid Mr Rogan. Out of hospital already? I'd be careful if I were you.' The man began to laugh. Jack's eyes darted around the room, searching for another way out. There was a back door. He grabbed Jana's arm and was about to make a run for it when the door opened and another man entered, blocking the way.

'Poor old Mr Finkelstein, what a sad way to go,' continued the falsetto voice. 'You shouldn't have killed him.'

'We didn't,' Jana contradicted the man, her voice sounding shrill.

'I know that, but others may not believe you.' The man began to chuckle.

'What do you want from us?'

'What a sensible question; I can see we'll get on famously.' The man sucked noisily on the cigarette. 'Here are the rules; quite simple really.' The man inhaled again, smacking his lips. 'The police will arrive in about twenty minutes. They will find you here alone with the body. Your fingerprints will be all over the murder weapon – that piece of bloody marble over there on the floor. Needless to say, you will be the prime suspects. Clear so far?'

'But we didn't do anything,' protested Jack.

'You will have to explain that to the police – try to explain, that is. This is Warsaw, Mr Rogan, not Sydney. If you're lucky, it will only take a few weeks to clear this up. If not, well ... our jails here are very – basic. I'm sure you know what I mean. And the wheels of justice turn slowly, very slowly,' chirped the man, 'and require a lot of oil ...' He paused and lit another cigarette.

'What do you want from us?' demanded Jana hoarsely.

'Such impatience. I see, of course, the time. Tick-tick-tick;

twenty minutes can be so short. Back to the rules then,' falsettoed the man, 'all you have to do is answer a few questions – truthfully of course; lies are very costly – and you will leave before the police get here. Simple, isn't it? What shall it be?'

'What do you want to know?'

'I like sensible women,' continued the man, blowing smoke in Jana's direction.

'Let's begin. What is your interest in Benjamin Krakowski?'

'Sorry, never heard of him.'

'Come now, this isn't helpful. Benjamin Krakowski, the famous Auschwitz composer you discussed with poor Mr Finkelstein here last night? Does this jog your memory?' the man asked sarcastically.

The Auschwitz musician – of course! *Thank you fat man*, thought Jana, smiling. Unwittingly, the man had given her the very name she had been looking for.

'You find this amusing?' snapped the man.

'No, only surprising.'

Jana and Jack answered the questions fired at them by their well-informed interrogator. All had one thing in common: the Newman investigation. Jana began to bite her lower lip as the minutes ticked by. It was the only visible sign of her growing anxiety. Suddenly, the questions stopped. The man lit another cigarette and kept staring at her.

'Well, are we finished? What about the police?' Jana asked. The man began to laugh.

'Police? We are the police, Inspector Gonski. A piece of friendly advice,' continued the fat man, lowering his voice, 'if I were you, I'd get on the first plane back to Australia and forget all about this. Next time you won't be this lucky; understood?' The man inhaled deeply and blew smoke into the room. 'You are both free to go,' he said after a while and left the room.

'You see, I told you Vassili would get all the answers,' Sorokin said, handing Horst another scotch. 'He didn't lay a hand on them – just as I promised. The man is a genius, you must admit,' he continued, raising his glass. 'One of my friends from the old days – KGB,' explained Sorokin, laughing. 'We don't call him *Little Beria* for nothing.'

Horst looked wistfully at Sorokin. He had witnessed the entire interrogation from his vantage point behind the fat man in the corridor. It had been far too contrived and theatrical for his liking. *Had the policewoman and the journalist been telling the truth?* How could he be sure? They appeared to be completely unaware of the Newman-Farim connection and the Egyptian arms deal. However, the policewoman's baffling presence at the auction still worried him. Her explanation that she was helping the Egyptians recover the stolen statue because it had been found by an Australian archaeologist seemed somehow fanciful and implausible.

'Do you think she told the truth?' he asked.

'That's a matter for you to decide,' Sorokin replied. 'But if you ask me, I think so. You saw the fear in her eyes. Fear never lies.'

Horst wasn't convinced.

35

Carrington was waiting for Jana at Heathrow airport.

'You look terrible,' he said, helping Jana with her luggage. 'Where's Jack?'

'He flew to Zurich to meet the American attorney. Apparently there's been some kind of breakthrough with the Swiss money trail. He'll be back tonight.'

'What happened in Warsaw?'

'Buy me a drink and I'll tell you – better have a stiff one too, you'll need it.'

'That bad, eh?'

'Warsaw was full of surprises.'

'This guy stood there and questioned me about a Benjamin Krakowski,' explained Jana, massaging her aching temples. 'At first the name didn't mean anything to me, but then it clicked. He wanted to know why I was interested in Krakowski – the Auschwitz musician Finkelstein was talking about the night before? I had no idea he was a famous composer.'

'Krakowski – the name he couldn't remember?' Carrington interjected.

'Quite.'

'You mean to say Finkelstein was killed because you asked him about Auschwitz?'

'No, it's more complicated than that,' Jana replied sadly. 'The questions changed.'

'What do you mean?'

'Suddenly it was all about you and me and the London auction. This guy wanted to know what we were doing there. He wanted to know about you. And then, listen to this ... he began to ask about the Newman investigation. He knew a hell of a lot about it. And he knew a great deal about Jack. The beating he received, his hospitalisation – it doesn't make sense! A total stranger tries to frame us for murder and interrogates us in Warsaw about Newman? I don't get it,' Jana said. 'Where's the connection?'

'That's interesting,' Carrington said, 'it actually fits better than you think.'

'It does?'

Carrington handed Jana a photograph. 'This was taken by one of Haddad's agents after the auction. Do you recognise anyone?' The photo was a close-up of three men leaving the auction house.

'Yes, this is Horst Newman,' said Jana, pointing to the man in the middle.

'And I can tell you who the other two are. The one on his right, the stocky one with the pockmarked face, is Colonel Sorokin, alias Gregori Molotov. He's a Russian Mafiya boss who apparently supplied the weapons and explosives used in the Luxor massacre. He's most probably also the one who arranged to have Finkelstein killed and had you interrogated. He operates mainly out of Warsaw and Odessa. Interpol has a dossier on him as thick as a telephone book: child pornography, arms, body parts, sex slaves; need I go on?'

'You're kidding!'

'Far from it. The other one, here, is Abdullah Farim,' continued Carrington, pointing to the photograph, 'another unsavoury character. He's an Egyptian wheeler-dealer who'll do anything for a buck. Allegedly, he purchased the arms for the terrorists who committed the atrocities.'

'How on earth do you know all this?'

'Haddad called. It looks like you weren't the only one being questioned last night.'

'What do you mean?'

'Farim made a big mistake. He returned to Cairo after the auction. He was arrested as soon as he set foot on Egyptian soil. Haddad interrogated him last night.'

'But where does Newman fit into all this?'

'It would appear he financed the arms deal, and the sale of the statue was somehow part of it. That's why all three showed up at the auction.'

'I don't believe it!' Jana almost shouted.

'That's what Haddad was told. Look, the three of them are getting into the car – together. The photo doesn't lie! Neither did Farim, I believe. Haddad's methods are very effective.'

'I need another drink,' said Jana, suddenly feeling very tired, 'and some sleep. This is all a little too much for me right now.'

'Newman's involvement is still rather baffling, I must admit. First the Newman investigation in Australia, then an arms deal financed by Newman involving Egyptian terrorists and the Russian Mafia, followed by a London auction of a stolen statue. Not any statue, but the same one we found three weeks ago at Saqqara.' Carrington shook his head. 'I don't believe in coincidences like that; there has to be a link, *a common thread*. We just can't see it.'

'And now this Warsaw mess. A murder, a crazy interrogation, and a warning. They obviously want us to back off. What does it all mean, Marcus? Where do *we* fit into all this?'

'We should know more soon. Haddad expects to question Farim further, later today – if he's well enough, that is,' Carrington added quietly.

'What do you mean?'

'The methods of the Egyptian police are effective, not gentle,' he explained, shrugging his shoulders. 'Apparently they worked him over quite a bit ...'

'How bad is he?'

'He's in the prison hospital.'

Jana leant back in her chair and closed her eyes again. 'All this violence,' she said, 'it goes on and on. It's like a quagmire. Once you step in, you can't get out. I'm caught, and sinking fast.'

'What about this Jewish composer – Krakowski? Are you quite sure he's Finkelstein's Auschwitz musician?'

'Why don't we ask him? I looked him up on the internet. Quite a famous man by the way, with an impressive website. Best of all, he lives right here in London.'

36

'I know that most of you have mastered the technical challenges of this extraordinary instrument,' Professor Krakowski told his master class. 'I've heard many of you play and have little to teach you when it comes to technique. What I will try to do, however, is to show you how to reach that little bit further, but in a different direction.' He held up his violin and walked to the front row. 'Who would believe that a small wooden box like this, with four simple strings,' he paused, pointing to the instrument with the bow in his right hand, 'is capable of producing such sublime sound? Sound, which can be deliriously joyful or profoundly sad; sound, which can reach into the very soul of man. You know why it can do all these marvellous things?' he asked. 'Because it has help. Help from you, the musicians who play it. It's quite simple really; it is you who give it life.' The professor began to pace up and down – violin under arm – followed by the adoring gaze of his mesmerised pupils.

'My father was a wonderful teacher. He believed that music could express things mere words could not. He believed that it allowed man to communicate on a different, intensely personal level. One of the last things he said to me more than fifty years ago in Auschwitz,' he added quietly, 'which I have never forgotten and would like to share with you here, if you will permit me, was this: When you play, reach deep within yourself, let the music flow from your heart into your fingers and from your fingertips into the strings. Make them sing.'

Jana turned towards Jack sitting next to her in the back row and whispered, 'It's him.'

'Like this.' Professor Krakowski lifted the violin to his chin, closed his eyes and played a short passage from Mozart's second violin concerto. He played with total concentration and technical brilliance yet made it appear easy and uncomplicated. He left the final note floating in mid air and placed the violin carefully on top of the lectern. 'There was one more thing my father said one had to do,' Krakowski explained. 'I'll tell you what it is: practise, practise, practise ...' He shrugged apologetically. The students began to cheer and clap, giving their beloved professor a standing ovation.

'Thank you for inviting us to your class. It was fascinating,' Jana said, holding out her hand. Carrington and Jack stayed deliberately in the background, watching.

'Ah, yes, Ms Gonski.' They shook hands. 'I must say, I was intrigued by your questions about the musicians of Auschwitz,' Krakowski said, closing his violin case.

'I understand you were once one of them ...'

'Are you a journalist?' Krakowski asked, looking a little apprehensive. Jana decided to come straight to the point.

'No. I'm a police officer from Australia investigating a possible war criminal.'

'A war criminal? Who?'

'This one,' Jana explained. She put an enhanced copy of the photograph showing the German officer and the naked boy on top of the lectern. Krakowski reached for his glasses and looked at the photo. Carrington leant forward, watching him carefully; Jack took a deep breath. Krakowski began to tremble and had to reach for the lectern to steady himself.

'David,' he muttered at last and kept staring at the photo. 'Where did you get this?'

'Could we go somewhere a little more private?' Jana

suggested. Krakowski nodded and shuffled slowly towards the exit. Suddenly, the vitality of the gifted teacher had evaporated; all that remained was an old man remembering a painful past.

37

Jana knew the future of the case hung in the balance. The Cattle Baron was Carrington's favourite London restaurant. With a view across to Tower Bridge it was a bit touristy, but the steaks came from Down Under. That was the attraction, even if the prices were eye-popping.

Jack had gone back to Zurich to meet Sam Greenberg, and Jana was anxiously awaiting Carrington's decision. She wasn't sure whether Carrington had chosen the venue to let her down gently, or to enjoy a meal he knew they would both like.

Carrington handed the wine list back to the waiter and ordered a bottle of Shiraz – all the way from South Australia. 'Funny how we gravitate towards the familiar,' he said.

'We all do,' replied Jana.

'I've decided to carry on with the investigation,' announced Carrington, coming straight to the point.

'Oh? Has Krakowski convinced you?'

'Convinced me? No. There are too many coincidences here for my liking. To me, the whole story has a sense of destiny, almost inevitability, about it. Not very scientific is it? I'm not explaining this very well, am I?'

'Not really,' Jana replied, obviously relieved, 'but I know exactly what you mean. I have the same feeling. It's almost as if someone is guiding us, leaving clues, showing us the way, urging us on.' Carrington nodded. 'What's our next step then?' Jana asked.

'We need a body.'

'What do you mean?'

'I phoned Krakowski this afternoon. He's prepared to take part in a search for his brother's grave.'

'That's great! But where do we start?'

Carrington pulled a crumpled map out of his pocket and placed it on the table in front of him. 'Right here,' he said, pointing to a lake on the border between Austria and Switzerland. 'In 1944 this was all part of Greater Germany, today it's Austria. And remember, the Swiss border hasn't changed,' he added.

'And Krakowski told us yesterday,' interrupted Jana, 'that he and his brother were taken out of Auschwitz – here.' Jana pointed to the map. 'In the evening, he said, after dark.'

'Correct. And they drove through the night and ended up at this lake here in the morning. Right on the Swiss border; that fits. Unfortunately, he's quite vague about what happened after that. Too traumatic, I suppose.'

'What's next?'

'I've already spoken to the Attorney-General. He will request the help of the Austrian ambassador later today. You know, cutting through the red tape and all that. The notorious Austrian bureaucracy,' explained Carrington, rolling his eyes. 'You have no idea – there's a department and a permit for everything and it all takes ages. And besides, the whole thing is rather delicate. Everyone is tired of digging up the past – in this case quite literally. Understandably, the Austrians are very sensitive about these things.' Carrington ordered another bottle of wine.

'If we do find the grave with his brother's remains in it, that would certainly substantiate Krakowski's story,' observed Jana. 'But it still doesn't link Newman to the officer in the photo – it doesn't link him to what happened at the lake, does it?'

'No, unless Krakowski can provide the missing link and identify him.'

'Do you think that's likely?'

'The simple answer is no. An experienced cross-examiner would eat him alive if he tried. Even if Krakowski could honestly identify Newman as the officer in the photo, even if he would be prepared to say on oath: "This is the man who shot my brother", there would have to be some convincing independent corroboration before a jury could accept his testimony.'

'You're right of course. But then again, look where we were a few days ago,' observed Jana. 'We didn't even know Krakowski existed. And a man had to die ...' she added.

'I know.'

Carrington signalled to the waiter and suggested coffee by the fire. 'With all we've been through in the short time we've known each other,' Carrington began, changing the subject, 'I feel that I know you, but I hardly know anything about you. Strange, isn't it?' He raised his glass and looked at Jana. 'I'd like to know more.'

'What would you like to know?' asked Jana, staring into the flames.

'The usual things, I suppose. Growing up, career, relationships, plans for the future ...' Most people are flattered when someone shows interest in them and need little encouragement to talk about themselves. Not Jana. On the contrary, delving into her past filled her with dread. Still, she wanted to open up and tell this fascinating, lonely man sitting next to her about her real self. She drained her glass and took a deep breath.

'This may surprise you, perhaps even shock you,' she began quietly and put down her glass. 'Mum was a single mother, an alcoholic. I was taken away from her when I was quite young and went to live with an aunt. That didn't work out either. I grew up on the streets after that. When other girls my age went to ballet classes and had piano lessons, I was doing drugs and

193

stealing food. I was a feral street kid; so much for family. Can I have some more?' asked Jana, pointing to her empty glass.

'I'm sorry, I didn't mean to pry,' Carrington said.

'Of course you didn't.' Jana managed a faint smile. She hadn't spoken about this part of her life to anyone in years. But now that the worst was out in the open, she felt better and wanted to continue. 'Then, one day, I broke into this small cottage ...'

'Stop! I should really warn you about self-incrimination now,' Carrington joked, raising his hand. 'Are you sure you want to continue?'

'Yes, Your Honour. I was looking for food. I was very weak by then and must have fallen asleep. The next thing I remember is waking up in a real bed with real pillows and sheets. I thought I was dead. That was the day I met Mrs Gonski.'

'This sounds a bit like a fairytale,' observed Carrington, smiling.

'Perhaps, but let me tell you about Olga Gonski. She was a tiny, middle-aged woman from Poland. She had migrated to Australia with her young husband shortly after the war. He was killed in a mining accident soon after. They had no children. She was a wonderful person, she ...' Jana paused and looked at Carrington, '... she radiated love, if you know what I mean.'

Jana felt suddenly at ease; the earlier tension disappeared. Remembering Olga's kindness had given her confidence. 'She hardly spoke English, so I learnt Polish; so much for my Polish background, hey?' Jana explained, laughing. 'She became mother, friend, teacher and confidante, all wrapped into one. She may not have given me life, but she certainly gave it back to me.' Jana paused and looked into the dying embers. 'I lived with her for ten years – until she died of leukaemia. I still have her cottage; it's in Sydney. I only live in Canberra for work. That cottage is my real home; I'll show it to you one day.'

'That's quite a story,' Carrington said, reaching for her hand. 'I must say, you've surprised me – again. I had no idea. And the name?'

'I changed mine to Gonski – in her memory. And you know what's really scary?'

'Tell me.'

'I'm now about the age she was when she took me in.'

Carrington squeezed her hand. 'You never married?' he asked.

'No. The white knight hasn't found me in time, I'm afraid,' Jana said, adding, 'This damsel has turned into a matron, see?'

'Nonsense!'

'Well, I think I've shown you enough skeletons in my dusty cupboard for one evening,' she joked, leaning back into the soft cushions. 'There must be at least a few bones rattling around in yours.'

Carrington began to laugh. He had not laughed since Luxor. Something about the vivacious woman with the surprising past and warm, engaging manner made him feel strangely alive.

'I can't compete with your adventures, I'm afraid. My father was a rather eccentric academic, a professor of ancient history with a consuming passion for Ancient Rome. I grew up in a large, totally bohemian household. Imagine six children, two spinster aunts, one imperious grandmother ruling us all like the proverbial matriarch, several exchange students of various nationalities and a whole menagerie of animals – all under one roof. We were all given Latin names. I ended up with Marcus Aurelius, one of my father's heroes. We even had to speak Latin at the dinner table.'

'How do you say, "May I have another glass of wine, please" in Latin?' interrupted Jana.

'That's obviously a hint,' replied Carrington, reaching for the bottle.

'Why criminal law?'

'Criminal law is about people, everything else in law is about money. I prefer people; simple as that. Incidentally, have you been to Austria?' asked Carrington, changing the subject.

'No, but I've always wanted to see Vienna.'

'You're about to. We're meeting the Australian ambassador in Vienna to discuss the arrangements for the search.'
'When?'
'Tomorrow.'

38

Dr Otto Gruber was waiting for them in the hotel foyer with the Australian ambassador. He was a senior public servant with the curious title, *Oberregierungsrat*. In Austria, the title was more important than the salary. Dr Gruber was in charge of some obscure department for the preservation of monuments and someone in the government had decided that the exhumation permit which, if the truth be known, was considered an irritating nuisance, came under his jurisdiction.

'Welcome to Vienna. Is this your first visit to Austria?' the ebullient Dr Gruber asked in perfect English.

'No, I've been here several times before, mainly on legal conferences and one ball – the *Opernball*,' explained Carrington. 'And Professor Krakowski here is certainly no stranger to your wonderful concert halls,' he continued, pointing to Krakowski standing next to him. 'He conducted the New Year's Concert only last year, I believe, as guest conductor right here in Vienna. You might remember?'

'Of course.' Dr Gruber smiled, nodding his head in pretend recognition. 'Where is Mr Rogan, the journalist?'

'He'll join us tomorrow,' replied Jana.

'And you, Inspector Gonski, are you also a Viennese veteran?'

'I'm afraid not. This is my first visit.'

'In that case, perhaps you will permit me to show you a little of our city before we leave tomorrow. But we can discuss all this later,' continued Dr Gruber, motioning towards the exit. 'In Vienna we eat first; sightseeing comes later. Parks and museums on an empty stomach – unthinkable,' he said. 'I've taken the liberty of reserving a table for lunch in a small restaurant close by. We can walk if you don't mind.'

Dr Gruber was not only an excellent host, but as it turned out, an extremely efficient organiser as well. All the necessary permits had been sealed and stamped, transportation arranged and the local officials notified of their arrival.

'A guide will meet us at the lake with a patrol boat. He's an experienced border guard. As you can imagine, our border guards know every corner of the terrain,' Dr Gruber explained. 'Incidentally, I agree with Professor Krakowski's suggestion entirely. We should start the search by boat. As you'll see, the snow cover is still very heavy and it would be extremely difficult to explore the shore on foot.' He paused and looked at the menu. 'For the all important dessert, may I suggest the *Gundl* pancakes; a specialty of the house.' Everybody ordered pancakes.

'What's an *Einspaenner*?' asked Jana, reading from the menu.

'A coffee – delicious. You should have one with your pancake,' suggested Dr Gruber, delighted to have been asked. 'The army has provided engineers to assist with the exhumation, should we locate the gravesite.' He continued, lowering his voice, 'They are standing by.'

'We are indebted to you, Dr Gruber,' said the ambassador, tucking into his second pancake filled with apricot jam and walnuts covered with generous lashings of whipped cream. 'No doubt the Attorney-General will thank you personally in due course.' Dr Gruber looked pleased; formalities were important. After all, this was Austria.

39

Jack opened his briefcase and put several enhanced copies of the photograph on the map table. The border guard began to pore over them immediately.

'This has obviously been taken from the Austrian side,' he explained, pointing to the mountains in the background. 'The peaks in the photo are clearly those over there, but viewed from a different angle. I think I know where we should begin.' He started the engine of the patrol boat.

Carrington put on his beloved hat and stepped outside. 'Do you always travel with this funny thing?' asked Jana, pointing to Carrington's battered Akubra. 'It looked okay in Egypt, but here ... really, Marcus, what will the Austrians think? It's full of holes ...' she pointed out, lowering her voice.

Carrington shrugged. 'Habit. Do you think it's, well, a little eccentric?' he asked, frowning.

'Marcus, look at yourself ...' Jana replied, laughing.

Krakowski was very quiet and looked pale. This was the first time he'd returned to the lake since the war. Back in London a few days before, it had somehow seemed the right thing to do, but now, here at this brooding lake, he was no longer so sure. He was suddenly afraid of what he might find; afraid of the past. Carrington sensed his disquiet and took him aside.

'This cannot be easy for you, Benjamin,' began Carrington, adjusting his hat, 'but if you turn back now you'll always wonder. You will ask yourself what if ...' Krakowski looked at Carrington.

'You must have been reading my thoughts,' he replied, no longer feeling quite so alone. 'I was thinking the same thing. You see, it's an eerie feeling being back here on this bright, clear, cold day ...' He left the sentence unfinished and began to scan the shore with his binoculars. 'I find it hard to believe that more than half a century has passed since that day. The world has changed, but the lake looks just the same.'

'How did you get away from here – all by yourself? Where did you go? You never told me,' Carrington asked. Krakowski put down the binoculars.

'I remember running into the forest. All I wanted to do was leave that horrible place and hide in case the Germans came back. It was raining heavily and I recall sinking deep into the mud. I must have walked for hours because it was beginning to get dark by the time I heard it.'

'Heard what?'

'Someone was chopping wood. I followed the sound and came to a clearing.'

'And?'

'An old man was splitting wood and loading it into a cart. When I walked towards him he raised his axe and swung it at me. I must have looked like a ghost, I guess, in those striped rags covered in blood and filth. He was obviously afraid of me at first, but then he must have realised I meant no harm, because the next thing I remember is lying in the cart on top of the wood with an old blanket wrapped around me. It was almost completely dark by then and the old man was leading the horse towards a small farmhouse. I can still see the lights of that house; they looked so beautiful and so safe.'

'That's quite a story,' Carrington said, surprised by the detail of Krakowski's recollection.

'I haven't thought about this in years, you know. It must be this place. It seems to bring it all back – quite strange really.'

They explored the shoreline throughout the morning. They pulled into every cove, investigated every pebbly beach, held up the photo every few minutes and looked at the mountains for clues and direction. The heavy snow cover made everything look the same. In the afternoon, the fog drifted in and the mountains disappeared in the mist.

'It's no use,' said Krakowski, his voice a mixture of disappointment and relief.

'Is there anything else you can remember that might help?' Jana asked. Krakowski shook his head.

'We should really turn around and head back,' said the guide, pulling into a narrow inlet. 'It's getting late.' Krakowski turned up the collar of his overcoat and stared at the rocky shore. Suddenly, he felt very cold and began to shiver. Dr Gruber reached for the thermos and poured some steaming coffee into a cup. 'Perhaps tomorrow,' he said, handing the cup to Krakowski.

'There!' shouted Krakowski, pointing to a rock. 'Stop!' Startled, Dr Gruber looked up and almost spilt the coffee. 'The cross – there, on top of that rock,' continued Krakowski.

'What about it?' asked Jack.

'I remember standing at the edge of the pit facing – that way,' Krakowski explained without taking his eyes off the cross. 'The officer was walking towards the boat moored at the jetty – somewhere over there.'

'And then?'

'He stopped in front of David and pointed his gun at ...' Krakowski began to choke, 'at his head. He held it there and ... fired.' Krakowski covered his face with his hands. 'Then he turned towards me ... The last thing I remember is ... looking at ...' Krakowski reached for the handrail to steady himself.

Jana walked over to him and put her arm around his shoulder. 'It's alright, Benjamin. What did you look at?' she asked quietly.

'That cross over there,' replied Krakowski hoarsely, pointing to the small, black, iron cross. 'After that, everything goes blank.' Without being aware of it, he began to rub the thin white scar where the bullet, having grazed his temple, had missed his forehead because he had looked up at the cross.

They returned to the inlet early the next morning. Having not slept at all, Krakowski looked tired and tense. The blanket of fog had lifted and it was clear and sunny. The army engineers had already arrived and were waiting for them at the lake. Drifting towards the shore, the police launch bumped against something in the shallow water. When they investigated they found several submerged posts – remnants of an old jetty.

The border guard explained that the cross marked the spot where a boat had capsized during a storm on Good Friday in the 1850s. There were no survivors. The bodies had not been found and the superstitious locals still believed the place was haunted. *A perfect location for a clandestine operation*, thought Carrington.

When he stepped ashore and looked back across the lake towards the snow-covered mountains, Krakowski knew he had found the right place. He held up the photograph and began to orientate himself.

'Come, have a look,' he said to Jack, 'you can see the cross in the photo. It's right here, behind the officer.' What had looked like an innocent tree branch on top of a rock, took on the shape of the iron cross, now that one knew what it really was. 'The tree was over here,' he continued, 'but it's gone of course.' Krakowski picked up a stick and broke it in half.

'We know the jetty was over there. We stacked the crates right in front of it, about here.' He pushed one of the sticks into the snow as a marker and began to walk towards the forest. He stopped and stared at something on the ground.

'Where was the pit?' Carrington asked. Krakowski turned slowly around and pushed the second stick into the snow.

'Right here.'

It was a shallow grave. The engineers only had to dig through two feet of frozen clay before they found the first bones. Krakowski watched until a human skull appeared.

'There, Marcus, the prosecution has a body,' said Krakowski, pointing to the skull. The skull was well preserved and intact. There was no sign of a bullet hole.

'It would appear so, Benjamin, but whose is it?'

'Let's wait and see ...' Krakowski shrugged, turned up the collar of his coat and walked back to the boat.

An hour later, Dr Gruber took Carrington aside. 'There are several bodies buried in there. Here, look at this.' He showed Carrington a piece of a grey cloth with metal insignia still attached to it. 'This is from an SS uniform ... There's more: buttons, belt buckles, even side arms ...'

'May I take these for a moment?'

'Sure.'

Carrington gathered up the muddy items. 'I'd like to show these to Mr Krakowski, if you don't mind.'

'I thought you might.'

40

The first pack of news-hungry journalists descended on the village by the afternoon. Word of a newly discovered Nazi mass grave travelled fast, especially in Austria.

'I've been asked by my superiors in Vienna to make a statement to the press tomorrow morning,' announced Dr Gruber back at the hotel. 'It would be best if you stayed in the village. Except for you, Inspector Gonski; I would be grateful if you could come with me. After all, we are here because your government requested it ...' Dr Gruber smiled at Jana standing next to him. 'It's up to the experts now,' he explained. 'I'm sure you understand. I have arranged for the police to seal off the area. The media attention will be considerable and I don't want this to turn into a circus.'

Dr Gruber gave Jack a stern look; it was obvious he didn't trust journalists. He wasn't quite sure why Jack had been included in the search party in the first place, but was too polite to ask. 'The pathologist is already at the site with the forensics team to investigate the find. We are treating it as a potential crime scene.' Dr Gruber turned towards Krakowski leaning against the bar. 'If your brother's body is among them, the pathologist will be able to confirm that rather quickly I imagine – you know, the DNA test we spoke of before ... It shouldn't take long.'

Krakowski put his hand on Carrington's arm. 'May I talk to you privately for a moment?' he asked. The two men excused themselves and went outside.

'Marcus, I'm confused. I cannot explain the presence of the German soldiers in the grave. I have racked my brain all afternoon. I really can't. It's a complete blank, just like my own survival. There are these gaps in my memory ...' He reached again for the scar on his temple. 'I know I was shot; as for the rest ...'

'I understand,' replied Carrington, trying to reassure him. 'We all blot out certain things we cannot bear to remember.'

Krakowski looked at him and nodded. 'They've found six bodies. One of them has to be David. As for the other five ... must be the soldiers. Apart from the major, there were three guards and two drivers. But why were they killed?' asked Krakowski. 'It doesn't make sense.'

'Executed perhaps – just like you and your brother?' suggested Carrington.

'But why?'

'To silence them? I wonder what was in those crates ...' asked Carrington. 'What do you think happened at the lake that day, Benjamin? What were the Germans doing there?'

'I wish I knew. I wish ... Tell me, Marcus, where's all this heading?' asked Krakowski, a haunted look clouding his face. 'We've found the grave and my brother's remains are most likely in there. David buried with five SS in the same grave; united in death. Extraordinary! In any event, we'll know soon enough. I can lay him to rest then and for that I'm grateful.'

Krakowski paused and took a deep breath. 'I thought very hard about what you said last night,' he continued quietly. Carrington watched him carefully, but said nothing. 'You asked me if I would be prepared to become further involved in the investigation; to testify even, should there be a trial. Frankly, I'm afraid of what's happening here. I sense that a huge tidal wave is forming over there,' he pointed in the direction of the gravesite, 'which will soon come racing towards me. And if I don't step aside it will sweep me away, perhaps even drown me.

Do you understand?' Carrington nodded without saying anything. 'I harbour no feelings of revenge or retribution, only sadness.'

'What about justice?' suggested Carrington.

'At what cost?' Krakowski looked sad.

'That's the one question all of us have to answer for ourselves.'

'I know.'

A journalist spotted Krakowski talking to Carrington outside the hotel. 'Professor Krakowski, has your presence here anything to do with the discovery of the Nazi grave?' he asked, walking up to Krakowski. Several cameramen came running towards them.

'Gentlemen, please,' Krakowski said, holding up his hand, 'you heard Dr Gruber earlier; there will be a statement tomorrow morning. Please be patient. Thank you, no further comment.' He pushed past the journalists and steered Carrington towards the dining room.

Dr Gruber returned to the hotel with Jana before dark. They joined Carrington and Jack at the bar.

'I can see it wasn't easy,' Carrington said, reaching for his scotch.

'These things are never easy,' replied Dr Gruber, ordering a drink for Jana and himself, 'and sometimes full of surprises. The six bodies we found were just the beginning, I'm afraid.'

'What do you mean?' asked Jack.

'We also found this,' replied Dr Gruber, reaching into his pocket. He pushed a shiny gold bar across to Carrington. 'Complete with Reichsbank markings and serial numbers. We found three of them. Can you imagine what this means? The journalists are circling like wolves out there waiting for a statement. Another mass grave from the war is one thing. A mass grave at the Swiss border with Nazi gold in it is something

206

totally different. Professor Krakowski didn't say anything about this, did he?' asked Dr Gruber, looking worried.

'Perhaps he didn't know,' said Jana. Dr Gruber looked at her.

'Why don't we ask him?' suggested Carrington. 'May we borrow the gold for a moment? It would be best if Inspector Gonski and I were to discuss this with Mr Krakowski in private, don't you think?'

'I understand completely. However, the gold is evidence ... Perhaps if Inspector Gonski could sign for it ... we have these rules ...'

'Of course,' said Jana.

Jack took Jana aside. 'May I come along?' he asked.

'Come on, Jack, you know better than that. I'm already risking my neck to have you here. Don't push your luck.'

'I'll go and have another strudel then, shall I?'

'You do that. It might fatten you up a little.' Jack looked hurt. 'And one more thing ...' added Jana.

'What's that?'

'Only little boys sulk.'

Carrington and Jana went straight to Krakowski's room.

'Why didn't you tell us what was in those crates?' demanded Carrington, 'and please don't say you didn't know.' He walked to a small sofa by the window and put the gold bar on the table in front of it. 'What about this?'

'I didn't think it was important after all these years.'

'You–didn't–think–it–was–important? Are you serious?' Carrington tried to stay calm, but didn't quite manage to keep the sarcasm out of his voice.

'I appreciate how you must feel, but if we are to work together you must try to understand me a little better ...'

'What do you mean?' asked Jana.

'I was ashamed to mention it, Jana. Does that make it clearer?'

'Ashamed, why?' Jana looked confused.

'Do you have any idea where this gold comes from?' asked

Krakowski, pointing to the gold on the table. 'It makes my skin creep just looking at it.' Krakowski went to the bar cabinet and poured three cognacs.

'I don't understand.'

'Let me tell you. But here, have a drink first, you'll need it.' Krakowski took a deep breath and handed Carrington and Jana a brandy balloon each. 'This is denture gold, extracted from the corpses of murdered Jews. Do you know what happened to the bodies on the way from the gas chamber to the crematorium? Gold fillings, gold teeth, bridge work and the like was broken out of the jaws with pliers, often with part of the bone still attached. It was then taken to a secret location nearby and processed with typical German efficiency by other Jews. You know, melted down and cast into neat little gold bars, just like this one.' Krakowski drained his cognac and refilled his glass.

'How do you know all this?' asked Carrington softly.

'Not tonight, Marcus, if you don't mind,' replied Krakowski, shaking his head. 'I can't talk about it now ...'

'All right,' Carrington said, reaching for the gold bar. Only, this time, the touch of the cool metal made his skin creep too. 'I'm sorry, Benjamin.'

'So am I,' Krakowski replied and showed Carrington and Jana to the door.

Later that evening Jack received a phone call from Sam Greenberg in Zurich, informing him that a key witness had been located in Argentina and was about to be interviewed. Greenberg suggested that Jack should meet him in Buenos Aires to hear first hand what the witness had to say and hinted that the witness appeared to know a great deal about Newman and his bank. Jack said he would be on the first available plane.

41

It hadn't taken Jack long to convince Carrington and Jana to take the long way home and see what Greenberg's surprise witness in Buenos Aires had to say. After the exhumation, Krakowski had gone back to London for a concert and was waiting for the DNA results.

'That's him over there,' said Jack, pointing to the dance floor. 'I hope I can move like that in my eighties.' Jack winked at Jana, steering her towards an empty table in front of the band. Carrington followed a few steps behind with Sam Greenberg, the American attorney.

All the musicians were old men. The pianist and the harmonica player – both well into their seventies – looked frail, the guitarist had his eyes closed and a cigarette hanging out of the corner of his drooping mouth. The drummer was bald and his dark glasses gave him a comical, almost frog-like appearance. The music, however, was superb.

Anton Hoffmeister loved to dance. Gliding across the dance floor with a young woman in a short black dress, he made the intricate steps of the tango look effortless and easy. He was an imposing man for eighty-six. Tall and slim, with thinning white hair brushed back at the sides and a pencil-thin moustache, he looked like an ageing dance instructor trying to cling to his youth.

In Buenos Aires he was known as Don Antonio and only a

few close friends remembered his German name. He owned several notorious tango clubs and it was rumoured he was a well-connected drug baron and gun runner who enjoyed the protection of the military. Elderly generals with their entourage of young female admirers and high-ranking police officers with their mistresses were frequent visitors to his popular establishments. So were some of the most beautiful women in Buenos Aires.

Since his son's arrest in the US he had begun to gamble again and had fallen on hard times. He had paid off his son's staggering debts to the Colombians and was desperately short of cash. His son was facing trial in Miami for drug smuggling; the US Coast Guard had intercepted his yacht with fifty kilos of cocaine concealed in its fibreglass hull. Envious competitors were circling Don Antonio like vultures waiting for their prey to weaken and were trying to buy his clubs for a pittance.

The music stopped and Don Antonio escorted his stunning dark-skinned partner back to the bar. Turning around, he saw Greenberg talking to a group of people who had just arrived. He walked over to Greenberg and ordered champagne for the whole table.

'This is the Australian lawyer investigating Eric Newman,' explained Greenberg, introducing Carrington. 'And this is Inspector Gonski from the Australian Federal Police, and Jack Rogan the journalist I told you about. Please tell them what we discussed the other day.' Don Antonio smiled at Jana and sat down next to her.

Jack put the photo of the German officer holding the gun to the head of the naked youth in the middle of the table. Don Antonio picked it up and looked at Greenberg sitting opposite.

'We have a deal, remember,' drawled the attorney, waving his finger at him. 'Tell them everything.'

'What would you like to know?' asked Don Antonio, turning to Carrington.

'Do you recognise this man?' Carrington asked.

'Yes, this is Sir Eric Newman, the Australian banker, or SS Sturmbannfuehrer Wolfgang Steinberger as he was known at the time this photo was taken,' replied Don Antonio, pointing to the photograph with the tip of his cigar.

'When did you see him last?'

'About five years ago, right here in Buenos Aires.'

'And before that?'

'We kept in touch after the war. I used to travel regularly to Australia to visit him. About twice a year, I'd say. We had common business interests.'

'You mean the Nazi money in the Swiss bank?' interrupted Greenberg. 'He was investing it for you, isn't that right?' Don Antonio paled, ignoring the question. In his circles, no one would have dared to speak to him like that.

'I'm more interested in the man,' said Carrington, trying to defuse the tension. 'I understand you know who took the photo?' At first there was no reply; Don Antonio looked pensively at his cigar.

'I did.'

'When?'

'Autumn 1944.'

'Where?'

'A lake on the Swiss border ...'

'What was in these crates?' asked Carrington, pointing to the photo. Don Antonio looked uncomfortable, fumbled with a box of matches on the table, and lit another small cigar. He hadn't expected that question.

Interesting, he's playing for time, thought Jack.

Perhaps this is a trap, thought Don Antonio, *and they really have no idea what was in the crates*. He reached for his champagne glass and looked at Carrington through the cigar smoke. He was sizing him up like a poker player. *On the other hand, they may be testing me. If they do know and I don't tell them, they won't believe a word I say about anything and I'll jeopardise the deal with the Americans*. He decided this was not the time to gamble.

'Gold,' he replied.

'You never told us that,' shouted Greenberg, slamming his fist on the table.

'You never asked,' hissed Don Antonio without bothering to look at him.

'Gentlemen, please, calm yourselves.' Carrington spread his hands like a referee trying to separate two prize fighters. 'That explains the three gold bars we found in the grave by the lake,' he said. Greenberg blanched. A barely noticeable smile spread across Don Antonio's face as he realised he had made the right call.

'Do you know what happened to the gold?' Carrington pressed on.

'It was taken across the border by boat to Switzerland.' Don Antonio clicked his fingers to attract the attention of the band. The musicians picked up their instruments and began to play.

'May I tempt you with a tango, Inspector Gonski?' asked Don Antonio, turning towards Jana sitting to his right. As far as he was concerned the interrogation was over – at least for the moment.

'I would only disappoint you I'm afraid, I've never tried it.'

'Then this is your opportunity.' Don Antonio stood up without waiting for Jana's reply and took her by the arm. 'We must talk,' he whispered, pulling her gently towards the dance floor.

'First, we take three small steps together to the right, like this,' he explained, guiding her expertly across the floor. 'Just relax and follow me. Excellent. I knew you would be a natural. Women seem to feel the music so much more intensely; it's instinctive, I think. They anticipate the next move, like you do right now – see?'

'What do you want to talk to me about?' asked Jana. To her surprise, she was enjoying herself. Don Antonio was an excellent teacher and quite an exciting man, even at his age.

'I want to speak to you and Mr Carrington privately, without the American attorney and without the journalist,' began Don Antonio, 'to explain my position and to give you some information I know you will find interesting ...'

'In what way?'

'I have only agreed to cooperate with the Americans for one reason – to save my son. You must understand that at the end of my life he's the only thing of value I have left; he's the only thing that really matters to me.' Don Antonio paused. 'No, that's not quite true. There's another reason ...' he added.

'There is?'

'Yes, Eric Newman and his betrayal ... That's what I want to talk to you about. Now, lean back slowly – just like that. Don't worry, I won't let you go,' he said, holding Jana firmly around the waist. The young woman in the black dress was glaring at them from the bar. 'She doesn't like me dancing with other women,' explained Don Antonio, following Jana's gaze. 'That's Conchita, I could be her grandfather. South American women are so different,' he mused. 'Fiery, possessive and very jealous. Quite a dangerous cocktail, don't you think?' The music stopped and the other couples on the dance floor began to clap.

'Tomorrow morning perhaps?' suggested Don Antonio, walking with Jana back to the table. 'Here, in the club. Please.'

'Well, what do you think?' asked Jack, sitting in the back of the taxi. Greenberg had excused himself earlier. Storming out of the club in a huff, he had mumbled something about having to contact his principals in New York.

'Hoffmeister obviously knows Newman very well and has certainly seen the photograph before – that's obvious. He also knows about the gold. He may even know what actually happened at the lake on that November day in 1944. As for the rest, I'm not sure,' answered Carrington.

'You mean you don't believe he was there? Are you suggesting he didn't take the photo after all?' asked Jana.

'He's a desperate man under a lot of pressure who's made a deal to save his son. To be of value he must have something to offer, to trade. He may be telling us what we want to hear.'

'What about this deal with the Americans?' asked Jana, placing her hand on Jack's shoulder.

'The Americans are only interested in the Holocaust money in the Swiss banks. According to their intelligence, the Nazi money trail is leading from Switzerland to Hoffmeister right here in Argentina, and then – this is still speculation, of course – somehow to Newman's bank in Australia. They can't touch Hoffmeister here, but they have his son in Florida awaiting trial,' explained Jack.

'And?'

'You know the Americans, everything's negotiable and the Jewish lobby – especially in New York – is very powerful. As I understand it, in return for helping them get their hands on the Swiss money, they'll go easy on his son.'

'I see. They get the money and the son gets off lightly, is that it?'

'Something like that.'

'Yankee-dollar-justice; an interesting concept,' said Jana, 'but where do we fit into all this?'

'The Americans believe, if Newman ends up going to trial as a war criminal in Australia and the truth about the Swiss Nazi money trail becomes public, the Swiss banks will come under enormous international pressure to cooperate.'

'That explains why the news of the gold sent Greenberg into such a tizz. I suppose, from his point of view, it was further confirmation that he's on the right track,' observed Jana.

'And Hoffmeister's bargaining power has just gone through the roof,' said Carrington, 'and he knows it.'

'Exactly,' agreed Jack. 'I wonder what Don Antonio wants to talk about tomorrow?'

'You haven't been invited, remember?' interrupted Jana, winking at Jack. 'Don't look so worried, we'll tell you all about it – after. Won't we Marcus?'

'We may,' said Carrington, laughing.

'Ungrateful bastards,' complained Jack, shaking his head. 'I found this guy for you, remember?'

42

Robert Blackburn, the Attorney-General, decided to lie low. Question Time in the Federal Parliament in Canberra was almost over, and he wanted to leave the chamber as soon as possible to meet with his friend, Marcus Carrington.

A well-informed member of the Opposition was grilling the Prime Minister about 'Operation Matchbox' – a secret post-war scheme for the *Employment of Scientific and Technical Enemy Aliens* – code-named ESTEA. He pointed out that ESTEA had been set up by the Labor government of the day shortly after the war. The purpose of ESTEA, he explained, was to facilitate the recruitment of German scientists out of the ruins of the Third Reich to work in Australia on sensitive defence projects. He emphasised the words *sensitive defence projects*. The Prime Minister, Harold Evatt, looked glum as the unexpected broadside found its mark.

'How is it possible,' asked the Honourable Member, holding up a copy of Jack's latest article filed from Buenos Aires, 'that a journalist on the other side of the globe apparently knows more about this woeful affair than the government?' Rob Blackburn realised that he could afford to relax a little as further questions were unlikely to be fired at him at this late stage. It was the Prime Minister's turn to take the heat for a while. He settled back in his green leather seat, put on his reading glasses and discreetly opened Jana's latest report.

Anton Hoffmeister claims that during the last year of the war he was working as an SS undercover agent posing as a representative of the Reichsbank in Switzerland. He was coordinating the flow of vast Nazi gold shipments into the vaults of certain Swiss banks sympathetic to German interests. In return for the gold, the banks agreed to provide the necessary funds to allow an elite group of SS officers to start new lives abroad after the collapse of the Third Reich, read Blackburn, as the Honourable Member – by now in full flight – began making allegations that several of the recruited 'Matchbox' scientists had been active members of the Nazi party.

Hoffmeister is prepared to testify that in November 1944 his friend, Sturmbannfuehrer Wolfgang Steinberger, (according to Hoffmeister, Sir Eric Newman's real name), joined him in Switzerland with the final delivery of Nazi gold. Apparently, some of that gold is still safely locked away in one of the banks in Zurich and is currently the subject of an international investigation.

Blackburn had lost all interest in the parliamentary proceedings and quickly turned the page.

When questioned about the source of the Nazi gold, Hoffmeister – who appeared particularly well informed on the subject – had this to say: 'Prompted by the disasters on the eastern front and the steady retreat of the Wehrmacht, the notorious Special Commando 1005 was formed under the command of SS Colonel Paul Blobel. His secret mission was to dig up the rotting corpses of murdered Jews in the East, strip them of gold rings and other valuables, extract gold teeth from the skeletal remains and burn what was left to obliterate the evidence of the slaughter.'

Blackburn turned the page again, without noticing that his colleagues were leaving the House. *'A large portion of the gold harvested by the exhumation commando – especially out of the Janowska pits at Lvov – was delivered by the SS to a secret camp near Auschwitz and given a new "respectable" identity. There, the gold teeth and jewellery were apparently melted down and cast into small gold bars. Each was stamped with the letters "RB" (for Reichsbank), with the German eagle, the retrospective date 1939, and the exact weight.'*

'Still here, Rob?' asked Evatt, gathering up his papers at the lectern. 'Whatever you're reading must be riveting; you're usually one of the first to storm out of here after Question Time.' Blackburn looked up, surprised to find himself in an almost empty Chamber with the Prime Minister.

'It is. Here, listen to this.' Blackburn walked across to the Prime Minister and began to read aloud. '*Sturmbannfuehrer Wolfgang Steinberger* – according to this, that's our Sir Eric Newman,' explained Blackburn, pointing to the report, '*was responsible for the collection of the dental gold from the exhumation sites and death camps. He was also in charge of the secret workshops and forgery units operated by forced labour in a special "satellite camp" near Auschwitz.*'

'The Newman investigation, I see. Very opportune, wouldn't you say? Are we making progress?' asked Evatt, walking towards the exit. 'We could certainly do with a little assistance after today's debacle, don't you think?'

'Sure, but listen to this,' replied Blackburn, following Evatt to the door. '*In order to avoid capture and annihilation, the SS needed funds, large amounts of ready cash in hard currency – preferably Swiss francs – and new identities for its officers, with the necessary formal papers to give them credibility. Sturmbannfuehrer Steinberger had access to both. The survival plan became known to the initiated as "Operation Walhalla".*' Evatt was shaking his head.

'And you'll love this,' continued Blackburn. '*Hoffmeister* – that's a witness living in Argentina,' he explained, '*who displayed considerable hostility and resentment towards his former friend, volunteered the following on how Newman managed to arrange his entry into Australia in 1946: During the final death-throws of the Reich early in 1945, both Hoffmeister and Newman were enjoying the hospitality of the Swiss banking fraternity in Zurich as "representatives" of the former Reichsbank. Soon after the surrender, Newman went to Rome and spent a year at the Vatican – as the guest of one of the Cardinals. Hoffmeister was unclear about what Newman was actually doing there during that time. However, Newman provided new identification papers and cash to many prominent Nazis looking for somewhere to disappear to. The main destination was South America. Apparently, Hoffmeister himself was one of those who received assistance from Newman in that regard. Newman had access to documentation obtained from recently deceased civilians – birth certificates, passports, diplomas and the like. These documents were then "tailored" by forgers working for him, to provide new, credible identities for the Nazis planning to flee Europe.'* Blackburn paused, adjusted his glasses, and then read on.

'When the time came for Newman to leave the relative safety of the Vatican, he became Dr Erich Neumueller – an aeronautical engineer killed in an air raid in Dresden – who had worked for Messerschmitt on the development of the helicopter. With the support of the Vatican and a Monsignor Brandauer to vouch for him, he managed to have himself included in a secret Australian recruitment program ...'

'Operation Matchbox!' interrupted Evatt. 'Incredible! This is potential dynamite.' The PM snatched the report out of Blackburn's hand. 'If we actually brought this man secretly to Australia in 1946, offered him a job working on sensitive defence projects, allowed him to stay here and become an Australian citizen *and then gave a knighthood* ... to a *Nazi charlatan*; have you any idea what that means six months before an election? I can already see the headlines: "Sir Eric Newman – accused Nazi war criminal, imported by Australian Labor Government at taxpayers' expense – and knighted?" Can you imagine the scandal? The damage? The opposition will crucify us with this.'

'Hold on, aren't we forgetting something here?'

'What?'

'Surely we cannot be held responsible for the actions of another government more than fifty years ago?' suggested Blackburn.

'Don't be naive, Rob. It was a Labor Government, Ben Chifley of all people, a Labor legend. We may be able to somehow distance ourselves from what happened fifty years ago, and that's not our main problem, I agree – but what we do about it now certainly is!' Blackburn couldn't argue with that.

'We have to get in first, Rob, can't you see? We have to take the initiative. We have to prosecute this guy, *this impostor*, throw the book at him before the press gets wind of the full story. How accurate is your source?'

'I'm about to find out. Remember Marcus Carrington, the QC I appointed to investigate the Newman affair?' Evatt nodded. 'He met with this Hoffmeister character in Buenos Aires a few days ago. Carrington is waiting in my office right now with Inspector Gonski to present his report and give me his recommendation.'

'Well then, let's go and hear what he has to say, shall we?'

43

Jana sat next to Carrington in the empty conference room adjoining the Attorney-General's office. She was leafing through her report and was trying to identify the topics most likely to attract questions. She knew the Attorney-General would be well prepared. Carrington finished his second cup of coffee and looked at his watch; he didn't like to be kept waiting. Going over his notes once more, there was something about Hoffmeister that made him feel uneasy. His instincts – honed from many years of dealing with delinquents from all walks of life – told him to be careful. Before making his final recommendation, he would ask for a little more time to cross-check the accuracy of the extraordinary information Hoffmeister had provided.

'This is it, Marcus,' said Jana, straightening her skirt.

'We aren't quite ready.'

'What do you think he'll do?'

'He'll try to pin us down; wait and see.'

Carrington heard footsteps approaching and looked up. His friend swept into the room, followed by the Prime Minister himself.

'You must forgive us, Mr Carrington. You know what politicians are like; they all talk too much and are rarely on time,' joked Evatt, holding out his hand.

'Speak for yourself,' said the Attorney-General. 'I'm only late because of Inspector Gonski's report; I couldn't put it down. Excellent work, Inspector.'

'Thank you, Sir,' said Jana, looking pleased.

Carrington was momentarily taken aback by the Prime Minister's unexpected presence and realised at once that the meeting had taken on an entirely new dimension. Asking for more time would be difficult.

'Can you give us an indication where you are up to with your investigation?' asked Evatt, coming straight to the point. 'The case has now become rather urgent, I'm afraid. In short, Mr Carrington, is there enough evidence to prosecute the man?'

Carrington saw where this was heading and decided to outline some of the key issues instead of giving a yes-or-no answer. He reached for his notes and handed Evatt a copy of the photograph that had started it all.

'We now know who this is,' Carrington said, pointing to the youth hanging from the tree. 'His name is David Krakowski, a Jewish boy from Warsaw. DNA tests have confirmed his identity. We have also located the place where this photo was taken and have found the boy's remains, together with five other bodies, buried in a shallow grave in Austria – right on the Swiss border.'

'Extraordinary. How did you manage all that?' asked Evatt.

'With the help of an eyewitness – Benjamin Krakowski, the boy's brother. He was present when it all happened and is prepared to testify,' explained Carrington. Evatt looked stunned.

'Can he identify the officer in the photo?' asked Blackburn hopefully. 'Is it Newman?'

'No, he can't, but someone else can.'

'Who?'

'Anton Hoffmeister, the man who took the photo.'

'Are you suggesting you found the man who actually took the picture?' asked Blackburn, shaking his head in disbelief.

'Yes, we have. And he, too, is willing to testify.'

'Where on earth did you find him?' asked Evatt.

'Buenos Aires; it's a long story, I'm afraid.' At least the expensive detour to South America had now been explained. Criticism seemed unlikely, but money was always a sensitive issue when dealing with public servants.

'Well then, is the man in the photograph Newman?' Evatt asked impatiently.

'According to Hoffmeister, yes. But please, there's still a lot more work to be done here. We have to cross-check all this information,' Carrington hastened to add, 'before we can begin to rely on it with any confidence. It's all in here.' Carrington reached into his briefcase and put a copy of his *Memorandum of Advice on Evidence* on the table.

'Will it stand up in court?' asked Blackburn, ignoring the document.

'Possibly.'

'Possibly? What do you mean, possibly?' demanded Evatt. Why was it that lawyers never gave a straight answer?

'You must understand, all of this happened more than fifty years ago. Memories fade, evidence disappears, witnesses die,' Carrington said. 'The uncertainties are enormous. In a case like this, anything can happen. We need a little more time ...'

'I do understand, I'm sorry,' Evatt apologised, calming down. 'It's just that this case has suddenly become – how shall I put it – *politically sensitive*. We're under a lot of pressure from the Americans, you see. Rob will explain. Time is a luxury we don't have.'

'If you had to make a decision right now with what you have, what would you do, Marcus?' asked Blackburn. 'Weighing it all up, what would you recommend?' It was a shrewd question; it was the dreaded question Carrington had been expecting. *The fork in the road, decision time*, he thought. *Go ahead, or walk away?* Sooner or later it had to come down to that. Feeling cornered, he took a deep breath, well aware that the Prime Minister and the Attorney-General were watching him carefully. Jana kept staring at the report on her lap and bit her lip, the tension in the room growing by the second.

'On balance,' Carrington replied, taking his time, 'I would prosecute.'

Part III

SECRETS REVEALED

Auschwitz; October 1944

'Heil Hitler,' said the Kommandant, raising his right arm. If he was surprised to see Sturmbannfuehrer Steinberger come marching into his office unannounced, he certainly didn't show it. The major and his trusty Doberman were regular visitors to the camp.

'I want you to find a family deported from Warsaw about eighteen months ago,' replied the major, 'a man with his wife and three children. They were sent here.'

'Eighteen months ... that's a long time in here.'

'I understand,' interrupted the major. 'But there are the selections ...'

'Quite. Do you have a name?'

'Krakowski, a music professor.'

'Krakowski ... Well, we have a Krakowski in the camp orchestra and his two sons are there too. They are Polish I believe.'

'Excellent! Where can I find him?'

'I'll take you to him.'

Wet and covered in soot, the wheezing steam locomotive looked like a one-eyed pre-historic beast crawling into its lair. It came to a stop and a cloud of acrid smoke descended on the platform. When the guards opened the doors of the cattle wagons the bloated bodies of the dead – covered in excrement and blood – fell onto the greasy tracks. The living just stared at the guards from inside, fear and confusion contorting their wan faces. In the background, the camp orchestra played a cheerful medley of Viennese tunes, welcoming the new arrivals to the biggest extermination machine the world had ever seen,

'That's Krakowski over there,' said the Kommandant, pointing to a group of musicians. 'He's the tall one with the violin.'

'Can I talk to him somewhere – alone?'

'Certainly.'

Berenger Krakowski entered the small room and stood to attention. He couldn't see the face of the man leaning against the windowsill – the light near the window was too bright – but the uniform was unmistakable.

He looks much older than fifty-two, thought the major, sizing up the tall, thin man standing in front of him. Despite his threadbare prison uniform, shaved head and multiple bruises, the man had presence. His eyes radiated intelligence, his demeanour defiance.

The major realised at once that a careful approach was needed. He began to walk around Krakowski. 'I have been looking for you for a long time,' he said. 'You weren't an easy man to trace – all that travelling over the years.' The major shook his head. 'Early fame in Paris wasn't enough to keep you there. You went to London for three years and then off to college in America. And finally, Warsaw of all places. An unfortunate choice, was it not?' The prisoner didn't reply.

As a seasoned interrogator, the major knew when to show off for effect. 'I searched Warsaw for months – in vain,' he said. 'And you were right here, next to me, so to speak, every time I visited the camp. Ironic, don't you think?'

Still no reply.

'Often the very thing we seek is right there at our fingertips and all we have to do is to reach out. Correct? Well, it doesn't matter.' The major waved his hand through the air. 'I have found you ...

'Your parents – Olga and Alexander – went down with the Titanic. How tragic. But they were not your real parents, were they?' The major watched Krakowski carefully. 'We know your real father was Berenger Diderot. We know your mother was Francine Bijoux.' Krakowski looked straight ahead. 'Please, feel free to speak.' The prisoner paled, but didn't say anything.

'Very well,' continued the major, 'I will tell you why I'm here. You have something I want.' He lit a cigarette and began to blow smoke rings into the room. 'The housekeeper gave you something when she saw you in Paris, didn't she? Something that had belonged to your real father.' Slowly, the prisoner turned and, for the first time, looked at the major. 'I can see I have your attention. Good.'

There's no way he could know, thought Krakowski.

'She gave you a bundle of old parchments – Templar manuscripts ...' continued the major. The prisoner tried hard not to look relieved, yet a hint of a smile creased his pale face. It didn't escape the major's notice. 'You find this amusing?'

'No, Herr Sturmbannfuehrer, only surprising.'

'You do?'

'Your interest in my past life is most flattering, Herr Sturmbannfuehrer, but I no longer have a life. I'm just a number.' The prisoner held up his arm, showing the major a long number tattooed into the skin. 'In this place, numbers have no future.'

'You have two sons in the camp, I believe. You may think you no longer have a life, but what about them?' the major continued. 'You have survived in here for a year and a half with your boys. That tells me something quite different – that shows ingenuity and adaptability. In short, a will to live, don't you agree?'

'With respect, Herr Sturmbannfuehrer, I don't know what you're talking about,' the prisoner replied curtly. *Madame Colbert had said almost exactly the same words a few months before*, thought the major, and began to smile.

'You have no knowledge of the Templar parchments then?' The prisoner didn't reply. 'I see; that's most regrettable. You may go.'

The prisoner turned around and walked towards the door.

'There is one more thing ...' the major said quietly. The prisoner stopped. 'Just in case you do remember something, perhaps we can come to an arrangement ...'

44

The tinny loudspeakers on the minaret crackled into life, and the singsong of the muezzin called the faithful to prayer; a lonely voice of piety intruding in the bustling commerce of the crowded bazaar. Haddad took off his sunglasses, kicked off his shoes and entered the mosque. He saw a destitute beggar waiting for inspiration from above, but when he looked closer, saw it was Farim in his soiled turban and shabby jalabiya. Haddad walked across the gloomy chamber and squatted down beside him.

'You wanted to see me,' whispered Haddad.

'I have important news,' began Farim, beaming.

'It's about time. Have you made contact?'

'Patience, please.' Farim held up his hands. 'The Defender of the Faith is on the move.'

'Don't tell me to be patient, you miserable cur,' hissed Haddad, bristling with frustration. 'I set you free a week ago and what have you given me in return so far? Nothing!'

'These things take time,' replied Farim, undeterred. He enjoyed having the upper hand.

Haddad was beginning to have second thoughts about Farim's release. Instead of turning into a valuable source of information, Farim appeared to be giving him the run-around.

'You'll be pleased to hear that we won't have to travel all the way to Mecca to find him.' Farim looked around and turned to face Haddad. 'He is coming to Egypt. He's on his way to us,

231

crossing the desert as we speak.'

'Don't lie to me!' hissed Haddad. This was almost too good to be true.

'Why would I do a thing like that?' Shaking his head, Farim continued. 'You have to learn to trust me.'

Haddad almost choked, but managed to control his rising anger. 'Is he coming back here to Cairo?' he asked hopefully.

'No. I hear he's heading for a place near Luxor – Deir el-Medina ...'

This wasn't good news. Haddad knew the ancient tombs of the pharaoh's workmen at Deir el-Medina only too well. The place was notoriously difficult to police and full of smugglers, cut-throats and petty thieves. *It's a clever choice*, thought Haddad. *It won't be easy to corner a resourceful terrorist in that terrain.*

'Do you know the exact location?'

'Not yet, but I will – soon.'

'Are you sure you'll be told?'

'Absolutely. The Jihad is a hungry beast, as this Defender of the Faith has just found out. It devours dollars faster than its enemies. He desperately needs more cash and I've been asked to arrange it for him – again,' Farim explained with a knowing smile. 'That's why he's coming back.'

Greedy turd, thought Haddad, looking at Farim with grudging respect. Farim was never to be trusted, but he shouldn't be underestimated either.

'How will you do that?'

'Same as before. The Australian banker, Mr Newman junior ...'

'Is he interested?'

'He is. I've just spoken to him in London,' explained Farim, looking pleased with himself. 'Now, if you don't mind, I have to pray for our success,' said Farim. He winked and turned to pray.

'Enough! Remember, I'll be watching every move you make.' Haddad couldn't risk doing nothing though he didn't trust

Farim. He hurried back to his office to contact Carrington. He would need his friend's assistance again; this time to help him identify the Defender of the Faith should he really come back to Egypt. Carrington and Jana were the only two people he could trust who actually knew what this elusive man looked like.

45

Jana was waiting for Carrington. Despite the protests of his elderly floor clerk – a retired naval officer named McDougall – she had managed to get into his chambers. But he did warn her not to touch anything.

Jana swiped her fingers along the bookcase crammed with bronze busts, leather-bound law books and an assortment of papyrus scrolls and manuscripts in Hebrew and Latin. Roman emperors and bearded philosophers stared at her – disapprovingly, she thought – from the top shelf. Pressed into service as paperweights, black granite scarabs and an army of small shabtis guarded the mountains of papers covering the desk.

Jana heard the rustle of silk from behind and turned around. Carrington swept into the room and dropped his red bag on the floor. Some books tumbled out.

'How did it go?' he asked, trying to hide his curiosity. He took off his wig and ran his fingers through the sweaty hair plastered to his forehead.

'It's done; he's been charged. Newman hardly said anything,' replied Jana. 'He just looked at me with those ice-blue eyes. Quite unnerving. His solicitor did all the talking. We went through the formalities and Voss wanted to know when his client would be served with all the witness statements. I told him we would write to him shortly.'

'We still have a lot of work to do before that. I really don't like this; it's all a bit back to front. We should have collated all the evidence before he was charged; the devil's always in the detail.' Carrington was still angry about being pressed into prosecuting before he was ready. He pushed the scarabs aside and searched for his notes. 'There are still a lot of loose ends here,' he said pushing papers around the desk. 'To start with, we have to clear up the violin question immediately. Krakowski must see it, touch it, play it. If he recognises it ... well, he has to explain how, and why. We may need expert evidence.'

'What else?' Jana had been warned about the QC's wish lists; always demanding, never-ending and mostly unrealistic.

'I have to meet Dr Rosen and talk to her about Hoffmeister. You know how I feel about Don Antonio. He's too suave; something just isn't right.'

'But he told us so much.'

'Exactly.'

'You don't trust him?'

'I don't know ... too much depends on him; that's what I don't like.' Carrington rummaged through the affidavits on his desk. He had the habit of jotting down ideas on small bits of paper and slipping them under the scarabs. The real challenge was to find them later when he needed them. 'Do you remember what he told us about Newman's betrayal?'

'Sure. Newman syphoned off, oh, millions from the Swiss bank account. How lucky for him those ageing Nazis died in exile, don't you think!'

'Well, he got greedy. Seems he refused to share any with Hoffmeister.'

'Right. Don Antonio obviously wants to get even – that's the worst kind of bias in a witness one can imagine. But we need him.'

Carrington loosened his jabot. 'I want to know what Dr Rosen can tell us about Hoffmeister and his visits to Australia. She needs to see the violin as well. Objects help people remember; objects and voices, it's quite remarkable. I've seen it many times. And Newman's daughter is bound to make an impression on a jury.'

'That shouldn't be too difficult to arrange. She's due in Sydney for a fundraiser soon,' said Jana. 'I've made a note of the date – somewhere. I'm becoming just like you, see?' she joked, searching through her briefcase. 'Incidentally, she's met Krakowski before ... '

'You're kidding, where?'

'At a charity function in New York. A few years ago. Apparently, she knows him – socially and she loves his music, you see. Small world, isn't it?'

'That's amazing. Another coincidence, I wonder?' mused Carrington.

'They should get on quite well then, don't you think?'

'What, Krakowski and the daughter of the man accused of killing his brother? Sure!'

'She was married to a Jew, remember? A Holocaust survivor ...'

'We'll see, won't we?' Carrington looked at Jana. 'I must say, you're very well organised. Barristers are notoriously impractical, you know.'

'You don't say,' teased Jana, ignoring the compliment. 'I'll call Lord Ashburton tonight and talk to him about the violin. I'll try to speak to Krakowski as well – he's giving a concert in New Zealand at the moment, and after that he's here on tour, remember?'

'You'll have to try to pull it all together; we haven't got much time.'

Jana sighed. 'I'll do my best, but it's a bit like herding cats.'

'Just like dealing with lawyers, eh?'

'You said it.'

'This cat is starving,' joked Carrington. 'Come, let me buy you lunch. Let's get out of here!'

The secret of Florentinos' success was not the cuisine but

rather its location – directly next door to the Supreme Court – and its huge selection of keenly priced reds. Lawyers love a bargain; they also love to drink.

Carrington seemed to know everybody in the crowded restaurant. Waving and nodding in all directions, he followed the waiter to their table.

'I wonder who'll be representing Newman,' said Carrington. 'With all the notoriety and media attention this case will attract, every silk in town must be itching to get their hands on it.'

'The best table in the house and an attractive luncheon companion as well; you are a lucky man, Marcus,' boomed a loud voice from across the room. Annoyed, Carrington turned around.

'Hello Archie. I haven't seen you in court for ages. Still practising law?' asked Carrington frostily.

'Oh, I should think so. In fact, we are about to see a lot more of each other – soon,' said Cyril Archibald QC, walking over to Carrington's table, a glass of wine in his hand. Heads turned in their direction. Archibald raised his glass and noisily gulped the wine; he was enjoying himself.

'Don't you want to know why?' asked Archibald, wiping his mouth with the back of his hand.

'I'm sure you're about to tell me.'

'Old war crimes, my dear chap; war crimes,' said Archibald quietly, leaning forward. He handed his empty glass to a passing waiter and walked a little unsteadily back to his table.

'You do have some strange colleagues. Who on earth was that?' asked Jana.

'I think we've just met Newman's barrister – Cyril Archibald. You've heard of him, surely?'

'Isn't he a bit too old for that?'

'Well, many think he should have retired years ago, but he still has quite a reputation. He used to be one of the best,' explained Carrington. 'His cross examinations used to be brilliant. Devastatingly so, actually.'

'Used to be?' asked Jana, raising an eyebrow.

'Well, he's still a cunning old fox, I guess. We mustn't underestimate him.'

'You don't like him, do you?'

'We used to be friends – a long time ago. He was my mentor actually, during my early years at the bar. We were very close.'

'What happened?'

'It's a long story; I'll tell you about it some time.'

Jana knew when to back off. 'May I have a little more wine?' she said.

Carrington pushed his plate aside and reached for the bottle.

46

Jana paid the taxi driver and walked up to the front door of Jack's terrace. She straightened her skirt and pressed the bell. Jack stood in the doorway in a pair of baggy shorts and an apron with a large, smiling garlic clove painted on the front. They hadn't seen each other since Buenos Aires.

'I said seven, not eight. The dinner's almost ruined,' Jack said, hurrying back into the kitchen. 'But ... come in.' Jana noticed he was still limping quite a bit.

'Smells good.'

Jack grinned. 'It should,' he said, 'I used my best brandy. Now, get two plates, please. First we eat, then we talk.'

'I like a man who knows his priorities. No time for, "How are you Jana? It's good to see you" – no Sir, not for this fella,' she joked. '"Get the plates, you're late kid," that's more his style. Must be a shy country boy.'

'Voila! Lobster Cardinale,' announced Jack with a flourish, placing a steaming platter with two large red lobsters cut in half – complete with legs and claws – in the middle of the table. 'Fresh from Tasmania.' He looked pleased with himself and missed Jana's remark completely. 'Tuck in!'

Jana was impressed; lobster was her favourite and she realised Jack had gone to a lot of trouble to get it. 'Not bad for a guy who only flew in this morning. How on earth did you manage all this?' Jana asked, savouring the delicious meat of the tail.

'Delivered by taxi straight from the fish market. I have

connections, you know,' bragged Jack, munching happily.

'Your article about Dr Erich Neumueller, alias Sir Eric Newman, Nazi scientist and secret post-war-Government-import-at-taxpayers'-expense, certainly put a hungry cat among scared pigeons in Canberra, I can tell you. The feathers are still flying. I particularly liked Sir Eric as "the dud match in Operation Matchbox" – brilliant!'

'It was all thanks to you. You gave me the lead – ESTEA, remember?'

'And you found Anton Hoffmeister. Without him, we wouldn't have been able to charge Newman. Hoffmeister was the missing link,' Jana added.

'We make a good team,' said Jack, raising his glass.

'Speaking of charging Newman, you may not have seen the Sydney papers. As soon as the news broke it was all over the front page. His home has been virtually under siege since. TV crews are camped in the park next door. Newman must be furious.'

'He's suing the paper about my last article, that's why I had to come back now. The lawyers want to talk to me urgently,' said Jack. 'They mentioned settlement negotiations; no one wants to go to court.'

'He's obviously fighting back, but that's hardly surprising. Is that a problem for you?'

'Not really. Quite the opposite. The paper wants more and I've got something sensational. That's what I want to talk to you about. We have a deal, remember?'

'You're making me curious,' replied Jana, squeezing Jack's arm. 'So, we're ignoring the Warsaw warning then, are we?'

'You bet; stuff the warning!'

'Just watch your back,' Jana warned, turning serious. 'I mean it. These guys have long arms and sticky fingers ... with claws.'

'So what?' Jack shrugged. 'I'm not walking away from the biggest story I've come across in years just because a fat Polish policeman tries to scare me off. Right now, the Americans are putting a lot of pressure on the Swiss about a hoard of Nazi gold in one of their banks, and I want to be there when the story breaks.'

'What about the Holocaust victims' money?' interjected Jana.

'Yes, that too. I contacted Gruber in Vienna. I don't think he likes me – three days he took, just to get permission to have a peek at the gold bars found in the grave.' Jack rolled his eyes.

'Don't take it personally. They have a department for everything and a different stamp for every document, all of it in triplicate.'

'Tell me about it. Sam Greenberg came with me; we left Buenos Aires together. He was certain those bars from the grave looked just like the gold in the bank in Zurich. You know, same size, weight, same Reichsbank markings, serial numbers, colour and so on. The Swiss have agreed to make one available for tests, actually. Apparently, dental gold has a slightly different composition. If the bars match ... well, you can imagine. There'll be a hullabaloo and Newman will certainly be implicated.'

'Because of the gold found in the grave?' Jana asked. 'If he's convicted ... well ...'

'No, not only because of that; there's more,' Jack explained. He pushed the plunger down and began to pour the coffee. 'Listen to this: The Swiss bank under the spotlight with the gold and the bank with the Nazi trail leading to Buenos Aires and Hoffmeister are one and the same.'

'That's extraordinary, Jack! It all seems to fit. I told you once before, you should have been a detective.'

'No, I'm just a humble newshound – sniff sniff – with a good nose, that's all. A story like this comes along once in a lifetime,' Jack said, grinning, 'and I intend to make the best of it.'

'You deserve it, congratulations.' Jana looked at Jack. 'When are you going back to Europe?' she asked.

'As soon as I'm finished with the lawyers. In two or three days, I expect. But I'll be back, covering the trial of course.'

'Great dinner, Jack. Thanks. Can I have another port?' Jana asked, sinking deeper into the cane chair. It was the first time she had felt totally relaxed in weeks.

'Sure.'

'Do you still have that checked shirt?'

'Why?' Jack frowned, feigning ignorance. 'I didn't think you liked my wardrobe.'

'Because I may need it later,' she purred. Jana kicked off her shoes and began to explore the front of Jack's shorts with the tips of her toes.

'That shirt – eh? I don't think it's been ironed.'

'I can live with that.'

'Are you sure?' Jana nodded. 'But first close your eyes. No cheating, you hear?'

'Okay.'

Jack hurried into the kitchen and returned holding a cupcake with one candle in the middle. 'Now, open your eyes. Many happy returns!'

'Oh, Jack; how sweet of you. You remembered!' Jana stood up and gave Jack a hug. The special lobster dinner suddenly made a lot more sense.

'I remembered the date, but not the number ...' Jack lied. 'That's why you only get one candle.'

'I bet you say that to all the chicks.'

Jack shook his head. 'Only the old ones.'

'Bastard!' Jana burst out laughing. 'Well, forty-three candles on a cupcake wouldn't have worked anyway,' she said with a sigh.

'Forty-three – eh? I'm not that far behind you. Now, blow out the candle and make a wish, but be careful,' Jack warned.

'Why's that?'

'Because wishes can come true – remember?'

47

Newman stared at the email from Hoffmeister. *Damn you, Anton!* he thought. Some people crumble under pressure, but Newman always did his best thinking with his back against the wall. He knew that his most important ally was to learn how to control fear, harness its energy and turn it into positive action. The war had taught him all that.

'You're early,' Newman said. Heinrich closed the study door and walked across to his father's desk.

'I wanted to talk to you before Horst gets here,' replied Heinrich.

Newman smiled; his son was so predictable. 'We'll call off the float. You'll announce it tomorrow,' Newman said calmly.

'But we can't! Not at this crucial stage,' protested Heinrich, agitated.

'We must. We have no choice, do you understand? We have to take the initiative. We make the decision before the market makes it for us. It's called damage control. We'll engage a public relations firm to handle the media.'

Heinrich shrugged. He knew it was pointless to argue with his father. 'What about Horst?' he asked. 'Surely you will not allow him to go through with this latest Farim caper? He's just trying to cover his losses – it's obvious.' Horst had finally come clean about the auction debacle. Surprisingly, he didn't blame Farim for the disaster. On the contrary, he spoke in glowing terms about a new deal proposed by his 'good friend'.

'I'm not so sure about that,' Newman said.

'You can't be serious! First, he's taken in by this Arab trickster and loses a fortune, and now he wants to go back for more and you'll let him? This is madness!'

'We took a risk and things have gone a little sour. So what? That's no reason to give up,' snapped Newman.

'I don't think I need to remind you ... you're facing a criminal trial, a war crimes trial,' Heinrich said. 'The press is hounding us, we're about to call off the float and Horst is going to Egypt to play with mummies? He should be right here doing something useful!'

'Please calm down. He's doing something useful; he's trying to make some money.' Heinrich couldn't remember ever having seen his father so agitated before. He was about to suggest something else when Horst walked into the room.

Horst had prepared himself for a confrontation. Instead, his father greeted him as if nothing had happened. His brother was uncharacteristically subdued. Horst knew immediately that something was wrong. He began to explain what had happened at the auction, and how he'd wanted to make up the losses through another deal involving Farim.

'We can discuss all that later,' said Newman, interrupting Horst impatiently, 'there are more important things right now. I know you have a lot to do, Heinrich,' said Newman, returning to his desk. Heinrich took this as a dismissal and stood up to go. Horst did the same.

'Not you, sit down! I want to talk to you,' said Newman, looking sternly at his son.

Here it comes, thought Horst, steeling himself for the expected tirade. *I knew it was all too easy. At least Heinrich won't be here to gloat.*

'Good luck,' Heinrich hissed sarcastically on his way out. 'You'll need it.'

'Promise me, what I am about to tell you will remain strictly between us,' said Newman, turning to Horst. 'Not a word to anyone, not even your brother, do you understand?'

'I promise,' said Horst gravely, barely able to contain his excitement.

'Come over here and read this,' said Newman, pointing to the computer screen. 'It's from Anton in Argentina.'

Horst read the email. 'What does it mean?' he asked.

'I'll tell you what it means. Someone has found Anton and has persuaded him to testify against me. I don't have to remind you that he knows a great deal about our financial affairs. He also knows a great deal about the past ...' Newman mumbled to himself. 'As you can see, he wants to make a deal. He's in financial trouble as usual and desperately needs cash. He wants me to come to Buenos Aires to discuss it with him. I cannot go of course and Heinrich is needed here. That leaves you.'

'What about Voss? Couldn't he arrange something?'

'Definitely not! We keep the lawyers out of this, do you understand? This is strictly between us.' Horst nodded. 'Now, listen carefully: I will cover your debts – this time – but you'll do something for me in return.'

48

Sheikh Omar hunched low in the saddle and stroked the neck of his camel. 'Allah be praised,' he muttered to himself, 'the storm is easing.' A sandstorm had raged across the Sinai for hours, almost blotting out the relentless sun baking the desert floor.

The Defender of the Faith had realised quickly that it was impossible to wage Jihad from exile. If the Brotherhood was to survive, he had to leave the safety of Mecca behind and return to Egypt. The anonymous pilgrim had to turn into a fierce leader again and show himself to his followers. He also realised that Jihad couldn't function without money – lots of money. The wheels of cooperation and silence had to be oiled with cash; more arms had to be purchased and alliances forged.

Sheikh Omar had arranged to meet Farim in Luxor to discuss the raising of funds – once again through the Australian banker with the baffling interest in Armand de Blanquefort. Why was this wealthy banker interested in an obscure warrior-monk who perished in Egypt seven hundred years ago? Is this experienced businessman offering huge sums of money for an apparently insignificant papyrus because he knows? There was only one way to find out, Sheikh Omar told himself. He had to come face-to-face with the Australian. He would watch his eyes; the truth was always there.

Sheikh Omar squinted through his scarf and looked up. *The cliffs; at last*, he thought, rubbing his burning eyes. The cliffs marked the entrance to a dry wadi which offered a shorter, if more dangerous, route to the Nile. The caravans would always take the longer, safer way. He turned around and waved at his two young bodyguards following behind.

'We'll go that way,' he announced, pointing to a narrow gorge. 'Be careful, the path is treacherous. This wadi belongs to scorpions, vultures and snakes. Make sure you stay directly behind me. Allah be with you.'

Sheikh Omar knew, to stay safe, he had to be unpredictable. He had stayed away from caravans and the ancient pilgrim trails. His spies had warned him that all caravans returning from Mecca were being watched. Informers were everywhere, even among the devout. The danger of travelling alone, without the protection of a caravan, was the price of a safe return to Egypt. The way through the wadi followed a long forgotten trade route to the ancient gold mines of the pharaohs. He remembered travelling this route as a boy with his grandfather – a Bedouin – who knew this part of the desert like no other. The path snaking down into the wadi was dangerous and rarely used in recent times.

Sheikh Omar held up his hand. 'Stop,' he shouted and pulled up his camel. The path was blocked by a large boulder. The only way around it appeared to be across an exposed rock ledge with a sheer drop of several hundred metres into the gorge on one side, and a steep wall of rock rising up on the other. Sheikh Omar's camel refused to step onto the ledge and pressed itself against the rock.

The Defender of the Faith knew how to handle recalcitrant camels. He calmed the frightened animal by whispering soothing passages from the Koran into its ear, and then coaxed it forward – a step at a time.

Suddenly, a king cobra slid out of a crack in the rock directly in front of the camel. The terrified animal stopped in its tracks and began to walk backwards. When the cobra reared up, the camel panicked, lost its footing and began to slide over the edge. Moments before the beast plunged to its death, Sheikh Omar hurled himself backwards out of the saddle.

Dazed by the fall and numbed by pain, he didn't notice the cobra slithering closer until it was almost touching his face. Trembling, he remembered a similar incident as a young boy in his grandfather's tent.

'Lie perfectly still,' he heard his grandfather whisper. 'Do not even blink.' He held his breath and resisted the urge to straighten his injured leg. Instead, he stared motionless at the aroused reptile. The cobra swayed back and forth almost touching his sweating face with its probing tongue. Satisfied that there was no more danger, the snake retreated slowly.

The two boys had observed the terrifying incident from behind.

'Come and help me,' shouted Sheikh Omar, trying in vain to move his stiff leg. The boys jumped off their camels and hurried towards him, their faces aglow.

'You're alive, it's a miracle,' said one of the boys, holding up his hands. 'Allah be praised.'

'The snake spared you, it was the will of God,' said the other.

'At the end of this wadi is a large cave overlooking the Nile, carry me to it,' moaned Sheikh Omar. 'I often stayed there with my grandfather.'

Sheikh Omar, practical above all, realised that his injury had made a safe return to Luxor all but impossible. Instead of melting into the crowd, he would now attract unwelcome attention he couldn't afford. He was searching for a way of turning the unexpected adversity into an advantage.

One good thing, he thought, the cave is quite close to Luxor, difficult to find and easy to defend. There are several escape routes and hiding places. In many ways, it's a much safer location than the workmen's tombs. The snake ... a sign? Perhaps it was meant to be ...

The boys prepared a makeshift stretcher and, following Sheikh Omar's directions, the leg was set and a makeshift splint applied.

'You will be my eyes and ears,' he said to the boys. 'You are the chosen instruments given to me by God. If you faithfully obey my commands, great rewards will await you in Paradise,' he added, pointing gravely towards heaven. 'Now, carry me into the cave.'

49

'What do you mean he's not coming to Deir el-Medina?' growled Haddad. He looked angrily at Farim sitting next to him in the felucca. They had arranged to meet on the boat to avoid being seen together, or worse still, being overheard. In the bazaar, even the walls had eyes and ears.

'He's changed his plans. That's all I know,' Farim replied haughtily. 'He's hiding somewhere in the desert.'

This was bad news. Haddad had carefully surrounded the whole of Deir el-Medina with a small army of sharpshooters. The entire area was under surveillance and could be sealed off at a moment's notice. Agents had been placed in every coffee house and bazaar up and down the Nile. They had even infiltrated the local gangs living in the tombs. But now, it appeared the trap had been set in the wrong place. Haddad would have a lot of explaining to do.

'Do you have any idea what this means? If you are playing games with me, you're finished,' hissed Haddad.

'I have some good news as well,' continued Farim, ignoring the threat. He paused for effect, but Haddad just stared at him without saying a word.

'Remember the Australian financier, Mr Newman junior, who lost a small fortune when your lawyer friend burst into the auction?'

Haddad nodded, recalling Carrington's remarkable performance.

'The Defender of the Faith wants to meet him. I've been asked to arrange it.'

'How will you do that?'

'Mr Newman is arriving tonight.'

'He's coming here, to Luxor?'

'Precisely.' Farim was beginning to enjoy himself again.

'And then what?'

'We'll be taken to the Defender of the Faith in the morning,' Farim announced casually.

Haddad looked at him, dismayed. 'How?' he demanded.

'I've been told to stay in a boarding house in the bazaar. Newman will be staying there too, the lucky chap. Someone will contact us in the morning. That's all I know,' Farim explained. 'For now ...' he added mischievously.

'All right. In that case,' Haddad said, stabbing a finger at Farim's chest, 'you'll do exactly as I tell you. You hear?'

Farim sat in an old wicker chair near the front door and scrutinised everyone entering the boarding house. It was already very hot and the old ceiling fan squeaking lazily overhead did little to cool the fetid air. He tried to look relaxed, but found it difficult to control his unease and kept nervously wiping his face with a handkerchief. Horst sat opposite – glassy-eyed and still half asleep – fighting jetlag by sipping cups of strong, syrupy coffee. He had flown into Cairo from Buenos Aires the night before and had caught the first available flight to Luxor to meet Farim.

Haddad sat, pretending to read the paper, in a dark corner next to two old men playing backgammon. He wasn't taking any chances; the boarding house was surrounded by his agents and everyone approaching it was being watched. The narrow alley outside was teeming with morning shoppers on their way to the market. Suddenly, a shadow appeared in the doorway and a crippled beggar hobbled into the room. Clutching a dirty bowl, he approached Farim's table.

'Follow me,' whispered the wretch, pointing his bowl at Farim. The beggar turned around and moved with surprising agility towards the reception desk.

'Come,' hissed Farim, pulling Horst to his feet. Haddad threw down the paper and was about to get up when one of the servants bumped into him from behind, spilling a pot of boiling coffee into his lap. *A diversion*, thought Haddad, crying out in pain as the steaming liquid soaked into his trousers. *Damn!*

The beggar opened a concealed trapdoor and pointed to a stairway leading down into a tunnel. 'Run that way, quickly! A boat is waiting by the river,' he hissed and secured the door with a large iron bolt from the inside. 'This should slow them down a bit,' he added, before disappearing down another tunnel.

50

Horst felt disorientated and uncomfortable. He was beginning to have second thoughts about the visit. Sitting blindfolded in front of a stranger – an obviously dangerous one – wasn't the ideal way to foster a business relationship. If it hadn't been at his father's insistence that he meet with the Defender of the Faith to arrange to buy the original Blanquefort papyrus, he wouldn't have agreed to come.

'Please forgive the blindfold my friends. It's an unpleasant but necessary precaution, as much for your protection as for mine. I'm sure you understand,' Sheikh Omar apologised, stroking his beard. 'In the unlikely event that you are ever questioned about my whereabouts – however persuasively – you will be able to say with conviction that you don't know where I am.' It was an ominous statement, not a welcome.

'But now that we're here, why the blindfolds?' Farim asked timidly.

'Because I wish it so,' came the curt reply. It was purely a precaution by Sheikh Omar to keep his injury a secret. A disability – however temporary – and leadership, didn't sit well together. He said nothing more.

'Our enemies are expecting me at Deir el-Medina,' Sheikh Omar observed casually. 'Chief Inspector Haddad will be very disappointed, don't you think?' he continued, addressing Farim. 'I'm told you got to know him rather well in prison after your return from London ...' Sheikh Omar was deliberately telling Farim that his extensive network of spies was keeping him well informed. Large beads of perspiration began to form on Farim's forehead and his mouth felt suddenly quite dry.

'I must congratulate you on your remarkable powers of persuasion,' continued Sheikh Omar. 'How did you manage to convince the Chief Inspector to let you go, I asked myself?' An awkward silence followed. Farim realised that his life may depend on the answer to that question.

'I promised him information about you, in return for my freedom,' he replied at last, deciding to gamble. 'I thought that by suggesting such an arrangement I could actually be of assistance to you.'

'Pray, tell me – how?'

'Needless to say, I had no intention of providing the Chief Inspector with accurate intelligence,' Farim assured the Defender of the Faith, 'just information that had the ring of truth, but was in fact quite false.' It was an ingenious reply, meshing truth and fiction into a believable story. Sheikh Omar looked at Farim with grudging respect.

'I'm indebted to you. Your loyalty shall be rewarded – at the appropriate time. But enough of that for now. Please, let's eat. Ah, I can see we'll have to adjust the blindfolds for you,' added Sheikh Omar, laughing. 'I'm sorry.'

'Mr Newman has come a long way to meet you, just as you requested,' began Farim after they had finished the customary meal. 'I have explained your proposal to him and you will be pleased to hear that he has agreed to your terms, subject only to viewing the ...' Farim paused briefly, searching for the right word, '... merchandise.'

'And information about the location of the Blanquefort find,' Horst interjected curtly. He was becoming increasingly annoyed by the charade. Having to negotiate blindfolded with the man he came to see, was clearly absurd. Sheikh Omar could read Horst's body language like a book. He had his visitor exactly where he wanted him to be; uncomfortable, unsure, and completely within his power.

'I'm afraid there's been a slight complication,' Sheikh Omar explained calmly, 'brought about entirely by unexpected circumstances beyond my control.' Farim's stomach began to churn; he didn't like where this was heading.

'What complication?' demanded Horst impatiently. Farim winced. Such directness was considered bad manners, bordering on rudeness.

'My enemies have surrounded the area where the merchandise, as you put it, is hidden. Apparently, they are expecting me to come and collect it. It's a trap of course. There's obviously a traitor in our ranks we'll have to silence. Unfortunately therefore, I cannot show you the merchandise at the moment.'

'In that case, I cannot go ahead with the deal,' Horst snapped and began to get up.

'Please sit down, Mr Newman, I'm not finished yet.'

'But I am. There's nothing more to say. I want to leave – now!' This time, Horst had gone too far. Farim reached across to Horst, trying in vain to silence him.

'Such impatience,' muttered Sheikh Omar in Arabic. 'That will not be possible I'm afraid,' he continued in English. 'You will have to enjoy my hospitality a little bit longer.'

'What do you mean?' demanded Horst, attempting to pull off the blindfold. At a signal from Sheikh Omar one of the guards standing behind Horst hit him in the back with a rifle butt. Horst cried out in pain and fell forward, gasping for air.

'As I was saying, that will not be possible just now,' Sheikh Omar repeated, as if nothing had happened. 'The length of your stay will depend on how cooperative you are, and the generosity of your family.'

'What do you mean?' croaked Horst, rubbing his aching back.

'War is brutal, Mr Newman,' Sheikh Omar explained, 'and whether you realise it or not, you are caught up in a war. As the merchandise I intended to trade with you is presently out of my reach, we'll have to come to an interim arrangement, so to speak. I have responsibilities that cannot wait.'

'What arrangement did you have in mind?' interrupted Farim, sniffing a new opportunity to make some money.

'A sensible question at last,' said Sheikh Omar. Farim was so predictable. 'I'll tell you, but first let's have some more coffee.'

Farim was returned to Luxor by his minders just before sunset. As he began to walk towards the boarding house, he was certain he was being watched. Instead of going inside, he sat down on a stone step and began to contemplate his new role as a double agent. He knew it was only a matter of time before Haddad made contact.

51

Newman was a light sleeper. He could hear someone knocking on his bedroom door and sat up in bed, instantly awake.

'There's a phone call for you, Sir Eric,' said his housekeeper, turning on the light. 'From Egypt. It appears urgent ...'

Newman picked up the phone on his bedside table. 'I apologise for intruding at this hour,' said a silky voice, speaking quite slowly, 'but ...' The voice faded away in mid-sentence.

'I cannot hear you,' shouted Newman, shaking the receiver in frustration. 'Are you there? Speak up!'

'The reception in the desert is always unpredictable – satellite phones, I'm afraid,' came the calm reply. 'As I was saying, the matter is of importance – especially to you.'

'Who is this?' Newman demanded abruptly.

'I am the Defender of the Faith ...'

'How did you get this number?'

'Your son is my guest ...'

'I know that,' Newman snapped. 'I've already agreed to pay the three million you asked – as an advance,' Newman added sarcastically, 'and the five hundred thousand dollars to your Mr Farim. It will reach the designated bank accounts in the morning.'

'Farim has demanded half a million dollars for himself? I see – it is as I suspected. Please cancel the payment to him. He has no further use for the money.' *The traitor has been found,* thought Sheikh Omar. *The snake will be crushed next time it slithers into my cave.*

'I don't understand,' said Newman, trying to make sense of the confusing conversation.

'I'm intrigued by your interest in Armand de Blanquefort,' Sheikh Omar continued, undeterred. 'Your son appears to know very little about the subject – he's obviously only the messenger ...'

'You approached me with an old manuscript and I agreed to buy it, isn't that enough?'

'You've agreed to pay three million American dollars for a seven hundred year old papyrus and a promise – a rather vague one, I would suggest – of more antiquities to come some time in the future – why?'

'Haven't you forgotten something?'

'What might that be?' asked the silky voice.

'My son's release,' Newman snapped angrily. 'I thought that was obvious; Farim made that quite clear ... this is a ransom demand, correct?'

'But you only agreed to do business with us because we offered you the manuscript – right?' Sheikh Omar replied, ignoring the remark. 'And we only approached you, because you were looking for information about the Templars in Egypt – Armand de Blanquefort, to be precise,' he added. Newman didn't reply. Instead, he was trying to figure out where this was heading.

'You don't disagree, that's good. I can therefore only assume that you are fully aware of the manuscript's significance,' Sheikh Omar stated calmly. 'You have nothing to say? I see. There's a further condition ...'

'What condition?' Newman demanded angrily.

'You will have to help me find something ...'

'You speak in riddles – what?'

'Something we are both looking for ...'

'I don't know what you are talking about!'

Sheikh Omar allowed himself a little chuckle. 'Then let me

assist you: Armand de Blanquefort sent one of his most trusted knights back to his native France in October 1305, didn't he? From right here – somewhere in Egypt – with a mission. He gave him something very precious to take back home, something he had to guard with his honour and his life and deliver to the Grand Master of the Templars personally. I'm sure you know what it was. Would you care to tell me?'

Trying to calm himself, Newman reached for the glass of water on his bedside table. Was this enigmatic character testing him, or simply angling for information – which was it? With Horst's life in the stranger's hands, he had to be careful. Yet, to disclose too much could be fatal. He was frantically searching for the right way to answer.

'The consummation of hearts' desire,' Newman replied at last, convinced that if the mysterious stranger was as well informed as he appeared to be, he would understand; if not, he had given nothing away.

'Twelfth century German poetry – Parzival; Wolfram von Eschenbach – an ingenious reply,' Sheikh Omar said after a while. 'I can see we understand each other. We are obviously both searching for the same ... prize.' Newman didn't respond. 'And you must think the Templar manuscript will help you find it – how?'

'The manuscript alone isn't enough,' Newman replied curtly, trying to control his rising anger. He didn't like the rules of this game. 'This is not getting us anywhere!'

'But it is; you are quite mistaken,' Sheikh Omar contradicted him calmly. 'Such impatience! The very fact that you are seeking information about Armand de Blanquefort – here in Egypt – tells me that his trusty knight must have completed his mission and made it safely back to France – and left a trail ... and a few unanswered questions.'

Newman was momentarily taken aback by the compelling clarity of the argument. 'For a man of the desert, you appear to know a lot about this subject,' he said, playing for time.

'For an Australian banker trying to buy an obscure old manuscript for such an exorbitant amount, you must know a lot more,' came the quick retort. 'In fact,' Sheikh Omar continued, 'not only do you obviously know what Armand de Blanquefort sent back to France with his knight, but I believe you also know what was written in the original dispatch that accompanied it. "One is on its way back to France, with a dispatch recording the hiding place of the other",' quoted Sheikh Omar. 'Remember?'

Nothing more was said. All Newman could hear was the desert wind howling on the other end of the line. 'No, I don't!' he said at last.

'I find that difficult to believe ...'

'Don't insult me! You have my son's life in your hands; his life is more precious to me than all of this. I've agreed to your terms, I cannot do any more. Please honour your side of the bargain.'

Sheikh Omar didn't reply. Once again, all Newman could hear was the desert wind in the background. 'In fact, I'm trying to secure the Blanquefort papyrus for one reason alone ...' explained Newman, breaking the nerve-racking silence.

'And what might that be?'

'I am looking for more information,' Newman admitted at last.

'What information?'

'We need to know where it was found!'

'Who is we?'

Newman bit his lip, instantly regretting the careless slip of the tongue. 'The Vatican ...' he replied, coming clean.

Sheikh Omar began to chuckle. 'You are a lucky man, Mr Newman,' he said.

'Oh? Why?'

'Because I believe you. The Church in Rome has tried for centuries to get its bloody hands on the consummation of hearts' desire – and failed. It has tried in vain to find the dispatch Armand de Blanquefort sent to the Grand Master from Egypt in 1305. How disappointing. I thought you knew more.'

'What about the manuscript? The original; we agreed! And the information about ...'

'Where it was found?' Sheikh Omar interrupted. 'That's the key to all this, isn't it?' He began to laugh.

'Without that information the document is useless,' Newman snapped angrily, repeating the words of the black priest.

'And without the information contained in the dispatch Fra. Bernard delivered to the Grand Master, pinpointing the find will not lead you to the consummation of hearts' desire,' came the curt reply. 'You need both!'

'Do not play games with me. What do you want?' Newman almost shrieked, finally venting his pent up frustration.

'I'm the Defender of the Faith,' came the calm reply, 'and your son is my guest. The original manuscript is no longer for sale. And as for where it was found ... Egypt is such a vast country, isn't it? Pity that! Your son will be released as soon as the money has been paid.'

Once again, all Newman could hear was the desert wind. Then the line went dead.

'What happened?' Heinrich demanded anxiously, bursting into his father's study. 'You said it was urgent.' Barefoot and wearing striped pyjamas under his track suit, he looked sleepy and confused. It was three in the morning.

'We have an emergency; Horst has been ... detained,' Newman replied, coming straight to the point. Heinrich just looked at his father dumbfounded, thinking he hadn't heard correctly.

'Where?'

'Our Mr Farim called from Egypt giving me the details – and the demands,' continued Newman calmly.

'Are you serious?'

'I am afraid so.'

'What did he say?'

'Apparently, Horst is being held captive somewhere in the desert near Luxor by the leader of this terrorist group – the Islamic Brotherhood of something or other he went to meet, and Farim is acting as the go-between.'

'What does he want?'

'Three million dollars into a Swiss bank account as an advance, I think he called it. That's all.'

'I knew it! As if the auction disaster wasn't enough, the bloody fool had to go back for more. This is madness!' Heinrich became quite agitated and almost shouted. Newman didn't tell his son that he'd specifically instructed Horst to meet the Defender of the Faith personally to arrange the purchase of the original manuscript. Nor did he tell him about his extraordinary early morning telephone conversation.

'Please, calm yourself; getting upset isn't going to help.'

'What are you going to do – pay?'

'Do you have a better idea?' snapped Newman.

'But, what if they ... you know ...' protested Heinrich moving a finger across his throat.

'We have no choice. We are dealing with desperate men. As long as there's a chance to get him out, we just have to go along with it. But not entirely,' Newman added quietly, a devious smile spreading across his face.

'I don't understand. What do you have in mind?'

'We will pay with money we no longer have.'

'How on earth will we do that?'

'Come over here and I will show you.'

After Heinrich left, Newman rang Joachim Sprungli – his Swiss banker in Zurich – and instructed him to transfer three million dollars out of the Walhalla account into the one nominated by Farim. At first, Sprungli was opposed to the idea, but once he understood the true purpose of the transfer, which couldn't be traced back to Newman, he became quite enthusiastic. It would give the annoying authorities investigating the bank a lovely new red herring to follow. Newman realised of course that the transaction would be closely monitored, the funds traced and most likely frozen once they reached their destination. However, according to Sprungli, that was going to take some time – Swiss bureaucracy; meticulous but slow. It was an ingenious ploy; classic Newman – sting the stinger. The key to its success lay in getting Horst released as quickly as possible. If the Defender of the Faith was true to his word, Horst would be released as soon as the money was paid. If not, Newman reasoned, there was nothing further to be done.

52

Archibald often worked through the night, especially when something challenging landed on his desk. The prosecution had finally served all the depositions, permitting for the first time a complete overview of the entire case against his client.

'Exhibit 1,' scribbled Archibald in his tiny, almost illegible handwriting. 'A photograph, a Nazi ring, a medal, SS uniform insignia and a cigarette case with a swastika, are found in N's holiday home.' Archibald sat back and lit a small cigar.

'Exhibit 2,' he continued to write, 'Krakowski present at lake shooting in November 1944. K. identifies gravesite; 6 bodies found.' Archibald almost broke his pencil in half. 'This is unbelievable! How on earth did Carrington find this guy?' he muttered to himself.

Archibald reached for Krakowski's statement in the pile of papers on his desk and began to read it carefully a second time. This wasn't going to be an easy trial. If the witnesses for the prosecution had any credibility at all and stood up to cross examination, Sir Eric was in deep trouble.

Newman pushed the floor clerk impatiently aside and walked into Archibald's room. Mumbling an apology, his embarrassed solicitor followed close behind.

'Good morning, Mr Archibald,' Newman said, holding out his hand. 'Already working on my case, I see.'

Surprised, Archibald looked up. Clients didn't normally come bursting into his room unannounced. He sensed an aura of new confidence – bordering on arrogance – in his client. This was hardly the demeanour he had expected of a man facing a war crimes trial based on – he had to concede – rather troubling evidence. If he wanted to get out of this, Sir Eric had a lot of explaining to do and Archibald could hardly wait to hear what his client had to say. Newman would first have to convince his counsel, before his counsel could attempt to convince a jury.

'Please forgive my appearance,' apologised Archibald, rubbing the prickly grey stubble sprouting on his chin, 'but I've just spent my first sleepless night on your case. The first of many, I suspect,' he added gravely.

'I appreciate your concern,' Newman said breezily, 'but you've only heard part of the story so far.'

'Quite. And I must say, I'm anxious to hear the rest.'

'Sir Eric has carefully considered all the depositions, just as you asked. He will give us his instructions this morning,' interrupted Voss, fidgeting nervously in his seat.

'I'm encouraged to hear that, Sir Eric, because so far your case is full of surprises, with more twists than a TV soap opera,' said Archibald, unable to keep the sarcasm out of his voice. 'Take this newly discovered grave in Austria, for instance, containing the remains of six bodies. Five of them German soldiers – SS – all showing evidence of bullet wounds. And then we have an eyewitness – a celebrated Jewish composer – who seems to have returned from the dead to tell us about a shooting more than fifty years ago. And here it says DNA tests have confirmed that one of the bodies with a bullet hole through the head is that of his brother.' Archibald took a deep breath and stabbed a finger at the notes in front of him.

'And what about the South American night club proprietor?' he continued. 'Another eyewitness? Apparently providing damaging identification testimony and pointing an accusing finger at you with tales of Nazi gold, collaborating Swiss banks, embezzled money and murder. And finally – as the pièce de résistance – we are presented with something rather romantic: a famous violin. A Stradivarius, allegedly taken from the father of our eyewitness in a German concentration camp. According to the chain of evidence here,' Archibald held up a bundle of papers, 'the violin has somehow turned up in your possession after the war right here in Australia, was given by you to charity and then auctioned in London. And this, I must say, is just the tip of the forensic iceberg waiting to sink you, unless you can ...'

'Explain all that,' Newman interrupted confidently. Smiling, he sat back in his chair and crossed his legs. 'I can!'

'I sincerely hope so – for your sake, Sir Eric, because one thing is already certain. You will go to trial.' Newman nodded briefly without replying.

'I can see we understand each other,' said Archibald, closing his brief.

'Where would you like me to begin?' said Newman.

'Preferably, at the beginning. Please tell us, Sir Eric, who are you?'

53

Carrington was going over his opening address for the last time. It was a tense moment, like the start of a race or the beginning of a final exam. First impressions were important. As an experienced litigator, Carrington always addressed the jury without looking at his notes; a subtle, yet effective, reminder that he was on top of all the facts and legal issues. Preparation and confidence went hand in hand.

'It's almost time to go,' Jana said, looking at her watch. 'I can't believe the moment has finally arrived.' Carrington crossed out a sentence and began to scribble something at the foot of the page. He didn't appear to have heard the reminder. 'Marcus, we really have to go,' urged Jana, closing her briefcase. He nodded absentmindedly and slipped his marking pens into the top pocket of his bar jacket without taking his eyes off the notes. Somehow, there was just never enough time.

Late as usual, Carrington ran up the stairs with his gown flapping annoyingly behind him. He had to hold on to his wig, or risk having it blown off by the stiff morning breeze. The entrance to the court building appeared to be under siege. Clutching furry microphones on long poles like rows of exotic spears in crazy battle formation, a news-hungry crew of excited cameramen was indiscriminately filming everyone who entered the building.

The packed courtroom was throbbing with excited

spectators. Unable to get through, Carrington had to ask the court attendant to clear a passage to the front. Archibald was already sitting at the bar table – waiting.

'Only a very brave man would prosecute a murder case half a century after the event,' observed Archibald. Carrington untied his red bag and began to arrange his books and papers on the bar table. This was classic Archibald – put your opponent off balance as soon as you can.

'Only a man afraid of the evidence would make such a remark,' Carrington replied casually without looking at Archibald. 'I hope your client is going to answer his bail. I cannot see him in court.'

'Oh, he'll be here all right. But be careful Marcus, it will get very hot in the kitchen, don't get burnt.'

'Don't worry, I've got asbestos fingers.'

'All rise,' said the court attendant, pounding the floor with his staff.

The judge entered the hushed courtroom and walked onto the Bench. 'Call the matter,' she instructed her associate. Opening her notebook, she looked with anticipation at the barristers seated at the bar table in front of her and reached for her pen.

All heads turned towards the wood-panelled door at the back of the court. Sir Eric knew how to make an entrance. Dressed in a dark navy, double-breasted suit, white shirt and silver tie, he looked more like an elder statesman than a man accused of murder.

Jack had arrived early to secure a good vantage point in the gallery just above the jury box. *Here he comes*, he thought as he watched Newman walk slowly towards the court attendant waiting for him in front of the dock. With each step the tension grew. It was Jack's first glimpse of the accused. Displaced by reality, the mental picture he had pieced together about Sir Eric evaporated. Carrington the prosecutor sat calmly at the bar table. Jack was wondering what must be going through the barrister's mind. The battle of wits was about to begin.

The judge's associate stood up and faced the accused.

'Eric Newman,' began the associate, reading from the indictment, 'you stand charged with having on the 13th of November 1944, murdered David Krakowski and having, on that day, attempted to murder his brother, Benjamin Krakowski. How do you plead, guilty, or not guilty?'

'Not guilty, Your Honour,' Newman replied calmly, and sat down.

'Ladies and gentlemen of the jury,' Carrington began, rising to his feet after the jury had been sworn in. 'As Her Honour has just told you, it is now my task to open the case for the Crown ...' Newman sat stone-faced in the dock – his back straight as a ramrod – discreetly scrutinising each of the twelve jurors sitting directly opposite. He knew they now held his fate in their hands. 'You have just heard that the accused stands before you charged with murder. The evidence will show that the murder was committed a long time ago – on November 13th, 1944 to be precise – on the distant shores of a lake in Austria.' A ripple of excitement washed over the spellbound spectators hanging on Carrington's every word.

'It isn't often the case, members of the jury,' continued Carrington, looking directly at the jurors, 'that the murderer himself, and the very act of murder, are captured in a photograph with a date written on it.' Carrington paused to let this sink in. 'But that is precisely what happened here. Such a photograph does exist and the circumstances of its discovery are significant.'

Archibald was carefully watching his former pupil work the jury. He was waiting for a mistake. A mistake in the opening address could easily turn into a valuable appeal point later in the trial. Carrington outlined the case for the prosecution with detachment and almost clinical precision. The sober language only added to the drama of his cleverly constructed opening address. The court heard an extraordinary tale of murder, greed and Nazi gold. It was told about heroic survival, famous violins and secret concentration camps. Peppered with fascinating forensic detail, an extraordinary story spanning over fifty years was being pieced together with great eloquence by the unassuming barrister standing at the bar table.

The spellbound spectators in the gallery stared at Newman.

'Thank you Mr Crown,' said the Judge at the conclusion of Carrington's lengthy opening address. Glancing at the clock above the jury box, she noticed it was almost four; the first day of the trial was over. 'The court will now adjourn until 10 am Monday,' Her Honour said, 'bail is continued.'

Carrington felt suddenly very tired. He turned around and looked for Jana. Catching his eye, she winked at him encouragingly.

'I hope for your sake that the evidence can establish all you have just promised the jury,' said Archibald, pointing a warning finger at Carrington. 'Otherwise ...'

'Don't worry, Archie. It's early days ...'

Archibald shrugged and left the court. He found Carrington's confidence annoying. *Cocky bastard*, he thought. *You've got a little surprise coming, mate. That should knock you down to size a bit ...*

Jack caught up with Jana in the corridor just outside the court. 'Marcus had the jury eating out of his hand; impressive,' he said. Jana nodded, but didn't stop to speak to Jack. 'Have you got a moment?' asked Jack, falling in beside her.

'Not really. We are meeting with Hoffmeister.'

'What; now?'

'Yes.'

'Can I come along?'

'What do you think?' Jana replied curtly. 'I shouldn't even be talking to you ... '

THE EMPRESS HOLDS THE KEY

54

Hoffmeister had arrived from Buenos Aires the day before. His solicitor had called in the morning, requesting a meeting with Carrington to go over Hoffmeister's statement.

'Mr Hoffmeister and his lawyers are in reception,' announced the floor clerk over the phone.

'He's here,' Carrington said to Jana, sitting opposite, 'with his entourage. Just as I thought.'

'Entourage?' asked Jana, raising an eyebrow.

'Yes. A high-profile solicitor, and a barrister I know well. Both know how to charge. This will be costing Don Antonio at least four grand a day. Not bad for a guy who's strapped for cash. I think I know who's paying the bills.'

'What do you mean?'

'Wait and see.'

Don Antonio swept into the room and gallantly kissed Jana's hand. Dressed in a blue blazer, white slacks and sneakers, he looked like he had just stepped off his yacht. 'It's good to see you again,' he said. 'How's the tango coming along, Inspector Gonski? You're a natural, trust me. But I should really let my lawyers here do the talking; I'm paying them enough.'

'We have a problem, Marcus,' began the barrister, dropping a copy of Hoffmeister's statement onto the conference table.

Here it comes, Carrington thought, aware of the empty pit in his stomach. *Just as I feared*. 'Oh, in what way?' he said.

'After careful reflection, Mr Hoffmeister is no longer sure ... he can ... identify the accused. You must understand, it was all such a long time ago.'

'I understand perfectly, but your client was very clear about all this when I spoke to him in Buenos Aires. He says here in his statement that he actually took the photo! Does he now maintain that he didn't?'

'It's more complicated than that, Mr Carrington,' the solicitor tried to explain. 'My client was under a lot of pressure at the time he spoke to you. Pressure from the Americans. As you know, his son is on trial in Florida – drugs ...'

'Are you suggesting that what he told me in Buenos Aires was not true?' Looking decidedly uncomfortable, the solicitor began to fidget in his seat.

'I told you what I thought you wanted to hear,' Hoffmeister cut in. 'I'm sorry. The Americans insisted I cooperate. I did it to help my son.'

'You are obviously mistaken. All I wanted to hear was the truth. I thought I made that perfectly clear at the time,' Carrington said frostily.

'There's nothing to be achieved by pointing the finger,' said the barrister. 'We are here in good faith to tell you that my client has reconsidered his position.'

'Good faith! That's a bit rich, isn't it? What you're saying is that your client lied to me then, or he's lying to me now. It has to be one or the other. Do enlighten us, Mr Hoffmeister,' Carrington said caustically, turning towards the suave Don Antonio, 'which one's the lie?'

'Please, Marcus, this isn't getting us anywhere,' pleaded the barrister.

'You're right, it isn't. And thank you for letting me know all this after the opening day of the trial. Perfectly timed, wouldn't you say?' Carrington was bristling with sarcasm.

'What will you do?' the solicitor asked.

'The only thing I can under the circumstances. Your client

will be declared a hostile witness.' Carrington stood up. 'Now, if you will excuse me, I have work to do.'

'I'm sorry it turned out this way,' Hoffmeister said, standing up as well, 'but please remember, I didn't have to come here at all ...'

'You are quite right. I was just wondering about that. Why did you come all the way from Argentina to tell me this, Mr Hoffmeister? Perhaps because everything is for sale, even the truth,' Carrington added as an afterthought, answering his own question.

Hoffmeister stopped at the door, turned around and smiled. 'Welcome to the real world, Mr Carrington,' he said quietly and left the room without closing the door.

'What a performance,' Carrington fumed. 'Do you know what I think? The cunning Don Antonio planned this from the very beginning.'

'What do you mean?'

'He sucked us in. Look at all the information he gave us in Buenos Aires. It was too good to be true.'

'Do you think he was making it all up?'

'No; that's the irony of it. I believe everything he told us was true.'

'I don't understand.'

'He was sending a signal to Newman.'

'You lost me.'

'He knew we would use the information in the case. His evidence is one of the cornerstones of the trial. He also knew this would put huge pressure on Newman. And of course Newman would know exactly where it all came from. Bingo! It was time to make a deal.'

'Isn't that a little far fetched?'

'Is it? No, I don't think so. It's very clever, that's what it is. Hoffmeister knew the whole time he held all the cards. Without him, we couldn't prove any of it,' Carrington conceded. 'I wonder how much Newman had to pay him. Don't forget, Hoffmeister was desperate for cash. You saw him in Buenos Aires. He was manipulating his creditors. He manipulated us as well. We just didn't see it. And now we're paying the price. It just happened, right here in this very room. He just walked out of the case and took the cornerstone with him. We've been had, I'm afraid. You've got to admire the old fox. It's quite brilliant.'

'You really think so?'

'Absolutely! Welcome to the real world – you heard him. That's why he came to Sydney, he wants to give evidence. I'm sure it's all part of the deal. He wants to explain why he's changing his story, can't you see? He wants to assist the defence. And besides, as soon as I attack his credibility, he'll say he was coerced into making the statement in the first place. He'll bring up the deal with the Americans to explain it all. It's very smart. How could I have been so blind? Damn him!' Carrington slammed his fist on the table, making the scarabs duck for cover.

'Temper, temper,' said Jana, surprised by the unexpected outburst. It was a side of Carrington she hadn't seen before.

'Unwittingly, we've handed Archibald his best witness on a plate. We couldn't have subpoenaed Hoffmeister, not in Argentina. We couldn't have compelled him to come. All he really had to do was not turn up at all. But he did. Of his own free will? Come on ... to explain it all? Sure. What a joke! He's here to help Newman!'

'Wouldn't he jeopardise his deal with the Americans by doing all this?'

'Not really. They've got what they wanted. All they needed was for Newman to stand trial. They don't really care what happens after that. The bad publicity genie is out of the bottle and the Swiss banks know it. The pressure's on – conviction or no conviction.'

'But Hoffmeister says on oath he took the photo – he places

himself at the scene of the crime. Doesn't that get him into trouble?' Jana asked.

'He's not the one on trial, don't forget. One of our key witnesses has just changed sides and crossed the floor. Look at the timing. They drop it on us just after my opening address. They let me tell the jury all about Hoffmeister first, before pulling the rug from under my feet. Now I can't just ignore him. He's available. I have to call him as a witness and then try to explain it all. Classic Archie – he'll turn this into a big issue, you'll see.'

Carrington tore up Hoffmeister's statement and threw it in the wastepaper basket under the table. 'What a mess. We walked into a trap with both eyes wide open. Defence one, prosecution nil. This could cost us the trial, you know.' Looking tired, Carrington began to massage his temples.

'What will you do now?' Jana asked, putting her hand on Carrington's arm. She knew her touch would have the desired effect. 'Come on, Marcus, I'm sure you've been in tighter spots before.'

'Regroup. We'll change the order of witnesses. I'll call Benjamin first and deal with Hoffmeister later,' replied Carrington, calming down. 'We might as well start off with the best we have left. The violin has suddenly moved to centre stage.'

'What do you mean?'

'We can still nail Newman with the violin. It's always been the second string to our bow – forgive the pun. It won't be easy, but it can be done. If Benjamin can establish that the violin is his father's Auschwitz Stradivarius and our chain of evidence holds, linking Lord Ashburton's violin to Newman, then ... well, anything can happen in a trial like this.'

'Even without Hoffmeister? I hope you're right.'

'It's a long shot, but we're in too deep. There's only one way to go ...'

'I understand.'

'Has Benjamin arrived?'

'Yes. He flew in last night.'

'Good. I want to talk to him first thing in the morning. It's now all up to him and his beloved violin.'

'A silent witness?'

'Not quite so silent, I hope.'

55

Horst heard screams echoing through the cave. He dismissed the chilling sound at first; part of a bad dream. But, awake now, he rubbed his aching back and stared at the stone-faced guard sitting cross-legged on the floor. The only light came from a torch wedged into a crack in the rock. Apart from a jar filled with turbid water and a straw sleeping mat, the cave was empty.

Then, again, only this time louder, more shrill; a long scream of someone in agony. Horst stood up and walked unsteadily towards the entrance. The young guard blocked the way with his machine gun and, mumbling in Arabic, pointed to the back of the cave with the barrel. The screams grew louder, more urgent. Horst felt sick with fear.

'I want to see your leader,' he shouted hoping the sound of his voice would give him some courage, but the guard turned his back and lit a cigarette.

The next minute, the screams turned into a gurgling whimper – the unmistakeable sound, Horst thought, of someone about to die. He sat down and covered his ears with his hands. The cave entrance darkened and inside came two armed men in dark stained jalabiyas and turbans.

'Get up,' said one, kicking Horst in the back. He handed his machine gun to his friend and pulled a piece of crumpled cloth out of his sleeve.

'Turn around!' he said and grabbed Horst's head, blindfolding him again. Horst was then marched along narrow tunnels from chamber to chamber. He could hear many different voices and smell cooking fires and the pungent odour of unwashed men. After what Horst counted as ten minutes someone grabbed his arm to stop and pushed him down on his knees. Cowering, silent, Horst listened to the hostile murmurs.

'You are a fortunate man, it seems.' Horst recognised Sheikh Omar's voice coming from the far end of the chamber. 'The advance has been paid ...'

Horst's mouth went dry. *Ransom, more likely*, he thought, but wisely held his tongue.

'Your father must be an understanding and generous man. But then, with all things, there is another side. It seems I also have some bad news,' Sheikh Omar continued. 'It has become obvious that we have ... well, let's say we have someone in our midst who has betrayed us. We have been surrounded, and we can't get out.'

The voices in the cave grew louder. 'But, as I said before, things have two sides. So, with this, there is not only darkness; hope has visited us as well – especially where you are concerned.'

Horst sat up, suddenly alert. 'What do you mean?' he croaked.

'Well, we have found the traitor, and with a little persuasion he has confessed. He has told us everything. You may have heard his pathetic confession a while ago. Perhaps you even recognised his voice ...'

'What do you mean? Why would I recognise his voice?' Horst asked, frightened.

'Because you know him.'

'How can that be? I couldn't possibly ...' Horst protested lamely.

'Oh, but you do. We – that is you and I – have both been betrayed by our Mr Farim. He was trying to play one side off against the other, it seems. A dangerous game. But he was rather clumsy, was our Mr Farim. Only yesterday, he brought me some information of rather dubious quality ... It looks as if he was trying to steal from both of us and, at the same time, provide information to our enemies. I can only assume he was bartering for some advantage from them as well.'

Horst's fear rocketed; his only link to the outside world was severed.

'You will therefore be pleased to hear,' continued Sheikh Omar, 'that he has been punished. Punished in the right manner according to the law of Islam.' Horst did not ask what that meant.

'But enough. I have a task for you. I'm sending you out to negotiate with those who are against me. And I am sending you as a free man,' Sheikh Omar explained. 'As a foreigner you have a far better chance of getting through alive, and being heard.'

'You're letting me go?' Horst asked like a frightened child looking for reassurance.

'Precisely,' said Sheik Omar, 'but there is a price to pay for your freedom.'

'What?'

'You will listen to my instructions and obey them, to the letter. You will ask to be taken to the man in charge – his name is Haddad, a chief inspector of police – and you will deliver my terms to him personally. You will take a little present from me, a token of my respect and of my esteem.' Sheikh Omar allowed himself a little chuckle.

'And you must remember, my good man, that my eyes and ears are everywhere. I can reach you in the tent of my enemies just as easily as I can reach you here.'

Horst nodded.

'You leave in the morning.'

Sheikh Omar clapped his hands and with that, the audience was over. The guard standing next to Horst pulled him roughly to his feet.

'This leaves only one more matter,' Horst began. 'The Templar letter – if the money has been paid ... I thought we agreed ... and the information ... the location of the find. It was all part of ... the advance ...'

'The papyrus is no longer for sale,' Sheikh Omar interrupted angrily.

'We paid ... the money ...' Horst continued, his confidence returning. But with that, a guard jabbed him in the back with the rifle butt, and Horst was back on his knees.

'Aah. The one thing you must learn, Mr Newman, is to listen. Now go. You never know when I could change my mind!' Sheikh Omar added, through clenched teeth.

Haddad sipped his coffee sitting at a camp table inside his tent. It was just after sunrise and, with a local guide looking on, he studied a map of the area.

'Someone's coming out of the gorge,' reported Haddad's aide, pushing his head through the open flap of the tent. 'He's waving a white flag.' Haddad reached for his binoculars and stepped outside. As he peered, a tall man riding a donkey came into focus. He was slowly making his way down the steep hillside towards the Nile, leading another donkey by the reins.

'Hold your fire,' Haddad shouted, raising his hand. 'Well, well, this is a surprise,' he mumbled, recognising Horst sitting rather awkwardly on the scrawny beast. 'And what have we here?' Haddad asked, scrutinising the curious sack-like bundle strapped across the back of the second donkey. 'What do you think it is?' He handed the binoculars to the officer standing next to him.

'It looks like a body.'

'Yes, it does.'

'You have a message for me?' asked Haddad, stepping forward.

'Yes, but first I have to give you this,' Horst replied, pointing to the second donkey. He slipped out of the saddle and walked stiffly towards Haddad.

'What is it?'

'It's for you. I wasn't told,' he lied. 'A present from The

Defender of the Faith.'

'Over here,' Haddad said, pointing to the ground in front of him. Two soldiers lifted the heavy bundle off the saddle and dragged it across to the tent. They could clearly make out the shape of a body wrapped tightly in coarse cloth tied with rope at both ends. Haddad noticed the cloth was covered in dark stains.

'Open it,' ordered Haddad. The blood-encrusted face of a man appeared first. Both eyeballs had been gouged out. The mouth was wide open, frozen in extreme terror.

'Farim,' whispered Horst.

'I'm afraid so,' Haddad agreed quietly as further horrors began to appear. Farim's right hand had been chopped off at the wrist, exposing white bone at the stump. The hand itself was tied around his neck with a thin rope. Horst noticed that there was something concealed in the palm of the limp hand. It looked like a flap of skin. 'It's his tongue,' said Haddad, 'the wages of betrayal and theft.' Horst felt suddenly quite dizzy and began to retch.

'Come inside and deliver the rest of your message,' Haddad said, pointing to the tent. Horst looked at him gratefully and followed him inside. Haddad understood the meaning of the mutilated corpse only too well.

'You won't like what I have to tell you,' explained Horst, 'but please, remember I'm only the messenger ...'

Haddad nodded. He had an idea of what was coming.

56

'Sorry, guys,' Carrington apologised, 'late as usual.' He sat down next to Jana and loosened his tie.

'You look rather pleased with yourself,' said Jack, pouring Carrington a glass of wine.

'I just got off the phone; Haddad called from Egypt. Wait till you hear this.' Carrington, now enjoying the suspense, paused until the waitress left the table. 'They've found the Defender of the Faith. He's holed up in a cave near Luxor.'

'We'll drink to that,' Jana interrupted, lifting her glass.

'He's trapped and surrounded by the Egyptian army,' explained Carrington. 'An assault on his stronghold was imminent – until a short while ago, that is,' he added quietly.

'Did you say, was?' asked Jack.

'Yes, was. This guy has balls. He sent an envoy to Haddad to negotiate, and the messenger is even more interesting than the terms.' Carrington paused and reached for his glass, trying to unravel the implications of what he'd just heard.

'Normally you don't shoot the messenger, but in this case you may be tempted ...'

'What do you mean?' Jack asked.

'Who would be the last person you'd expect to turn up in Egypt at this time?' asked Carrington.

Jack shook his head.

'Guess who delivered the demands?'

'No idea,' Jana said.

'Horst Newman.'

'You must be joking, surely!' Jack almost shouted. Some diners turned to glare at him. 'What on earth is he doing in Egypt?'

'Good question. Haddad believes he was negotiating another arms deal with the terrorists.'

'You mean to say, while the father is standing trial for war crimes here in Australia, the son is doing business with Islamic terrorists in Egypt?' Jana said, shaking her head. 'An enterprising family, I must say.'

'I don't get it,' Jack said. 'This doesn't make sense ...'

'The Defender of the Faith made demands?' Jana cut in. 'I thought you said he was surrounded by the Egyptian army. Hardly a position of strength.'

'I know,' Carrington said, lowering his voice, 'but he's asked for safe passage to the airport for himself and fifty of his followers. And a plane to Afghanistan ...'

'In return for what?' Jana asked.

'Three bombs, apparently ready to explode in American embassies somewhere in Africa ...'

'Perhaps he's bluffing,' suggested Jack.

'After Luxor, would you be prepared to find out?'

'Where's Horst Newman now?' Jana asked.

'On his way to a Cairo jail to be interrogated, the lucky chap.'

'What a nice ending to Sir Eric's first day in court. Do you think he knows?

'If he doesn't already, he soon will. I'm sure.'

'And the Defender of the Faith just gets away with it, is that it?' Jack asked. 'They'll never touch him in Afghanistan. Look at Bin Laden.'

'No, not exactly. That's the main reason Haddad called. He has a plan ...'

Jack put down his glass. 'What plan?' he asked, leaning forward.

'The Defender of the Faith and his cohorts won't be allowed

to leave,' Carrington explained. 'The Egyptians are working closely with the Americans on this. No deals for terrorists.'

'What about the bombs?'

'For now, Haddad is playing for time to give the Americans a chance to secure their embassies.'

'How's he doing that?'

'He's pretending to go along with the demands. He's even providing a plane. But that plane won't be allowed to leave Luxor ...'

'You know what that means ...' said Jana. 'Another bloodbath,' she whispered, suddenly feeling very tired. She looked at her watch and reached for her handbag. 'Sorry guys, I've got to go. I've been summoned to Canberra. The Director of Public Prosecutions wants to see me first thing tomorrow morning.'

'On a Saturday? That's very un-public-service-like, wouldn't you say?' Carrington remarked.

Jack paled. He knew there could only be one reason for this meeting; Jana had to be warned. 'Did he ...' Jack began, 'did he say what it was about?'

'The Director called me himself, which is quite unusual,' Jana replied, standing up. 'He said it was urgent, that's all. I guess we'll know in the morning.'

Jack dug his fingernails into the palm of his hand to stop himself blurting anything out. There was the confidentiality agreement, he thought, but realising what she was about to face made him feel quite sick.

Carrington sensed Jack's unease. 'Are you all right?' he asked.

'I'm fine.'

'Hmmm. You look very pale all of a sudden.'

'Marcus is right,' said Jana, pushing in her chair. 'Be good.'

57

The meeting with the Director of Public Prosecutions had been a gut-wrenching blur and Jana felt humiliated and betrayed as she sat in the car on her way back to Canberra airport. When word of this got out – as she knew it almost certainly would – her position would become untenable. She could already hear the sniggering and see the finger-pointing and messages on the computer screens. Her envious colleagues would finally have their day.

Going on leave now – as the Director of Public Prosecutions had strongly suggested – really meant the end of her job. It was certainly an abrupt end to her official involvement in the Newman trial.

At that moment Jana realised just how utterly alone she was. And how much her work meant to her. Independence came at a price.

'Marcus, I've been trying to call you all afternoon, where are you?' Jana asked.

'At the cemetery. I had my phone turned off.'

'I'm so sorry. I didn't mean to intrude.'

'Of course not. You sound upset, where are you?'

'At the airport; just landed.'

'What happened?'

'I'll tell you later. I have to see you – please.'

Jana was waiting for Carrington in the arrivals lounge. She hurried past the crowded baggage carousels and ran towards him with outstretched arms. 'Oh Marcus ...'

'Was Canberra that scary?' Carrington joked, trying to release himself from Jana's grip.

'It's not funny. Let's go for a walk. Somewhere quiet,' Jana suggested, wiping a few tears from her cheek.

The small beach next to the airport was deserted. Listening to the cries of the seagulls and the soothing sound of the waves breaking against the rocks appeared to calm Jana. 'This is why I was called to Canberra,' she said, handing a large envelope to Carrington. 'Open it.' She turned away and watched the seagulls. Carrington opened the envelope and pulled out a photograph. It showed Jana sitting naked on a table with her legs high up in the air, lustily bearing all. Carrington didn't realise that the muscular buttocks of the naked, aroused man standing over her belonged to Jack.

'Where did all this come from?' he asked, shock and disbelief clouding his face as he reached for the next picture. However, as an experienced barrister he knew how to keep his emotions in check.

'Newman is suing the Herald, remember? The photos turned up during settlement negotiation.'

'Jesus! How?' said Carrington. Noticing Jana's distress, he put his arm around her shoulders.

'They were sent to the paper,' whispered Jana, barely able to speak.

'By whom?'

'Anonymously – clever, isn't it? Just look at the timing. It's obvious.'

'Newman?'

'Who else?'

'He's playing dirty. Just like the Hoffmeister caper ...'

'Well, he's been rather successful so far, wouldn't you say?

The paper contacted the police immediately and I have been removed from the case,' Jana said frostily. 'At least now we know who was responsible for the burglary in Jack's house, and that horrible beating. The pictures were taken on the same night, and I'm sure he's behind Warsaw as well. What do you think?'

'It certainly looks that way, but I'm sure he's covered his tracks well.'

'He's toying with us, Marcus. Can't we do something?'

Carrington shrugged. 'I doubt it.'

'Great! And do you know what's particularly infuriating?'

'Tell me.'

'Newman's lawyers used the photos as a bargaining chip and forced a settlement. How humiliating can it get?'

Jana told Carrington everything. About her affair with Jack and her feelings for him. And then, how betrayed she felt. She spared none of the details of the meeting.

'I've been taken off the case; I'm now "on leave",' she said, gesturing the quote marks. 'It's just not done to have the principal investigating officer and the sharp journalist who started it all make whoopee on the kitchen table, is it? For the first time in my life, Marcus, I really don't know what to do. I feel so – so empty, so alone.'

'I know how that feels.'

'I know you do. And I know I can trust you, Marcus,' Jana said, reaching for his hand. Then Jana began to cry; her tears more of disappointment than self pity. 'I thought I could trust Jack as well; I was wrong.'

Carrington reached for his handkerchief and began to wipe away the tears on Jana's cheeks.

'Last night,' she said, looking up at Marcus, 'Jack said nothing. Not a word. He must have known, yet he just let me go ... He said nothing. A true friend could never have done that.'

'Listen, every cloud has a silver lining, especially storm clouds,'

Carrington said after Jana had stopped sobbing.

'Oh really? Please do show me, because right now I can't quite see it,' Jana snapped. 'Don't patronise me!'

'Nothing could be further from my mind. Truly,' Marcus went on and turned to face Jana. 'Listen, I need your help.'

'In what way?'

'Haddad called again this morning. There have been certain developments and he needs my help. Turns out that The Defender of the Faith wants to ride into Luxor with his entourage, horses, camels, the full spectacle, no doubt. We know he likes the theatrical. The faithful and the curious are already flocking to Luxor just to see the show. And one more thing,' added Carrington, lowering his voice.

'What?'

'Farim's been killed. Well, executed would be more accurate. Most horribly, I believe.'

'He had it coming. You said so yourself. But Marcus, I still don't understand how you can help Haddad with all this.'

'You and I are apparently the only two people Haddad can turn to who know what this guy actually looks like. We are the only two who can help him identify the man. Farim's dead, Horst has never actually seen him and those terrorists in jail, or should I say suspected terrorists, cannot be trusted.'

Jana looked at him. 'Go on.'

'I told him we're in the middle of a trial and couldn't possibly come right now. We can't just go and ask the judge to give us a few days off, now, can we? Your Honour, we need a short adjournment while we go to Egypt to hunt down another villain. But don't worry, we'll be back soon, to continue prosecuting this one,' Carrington joked.

'I guess not.' Jana began to laugh.

'Haddad sounded so disappointed. He'd already made the arrangements – flights, tickets, the lot, assuming of course that I'd drop everything and come. He got quite angry, actually. I don't think he can understand that anything might be more important than hunting down my family's killer. You know the mentality – an eye for an eye.'

'Is that why you went to the cemetery?' Jana asked quietly, putting her hand on Carrington's shoulder.

He nodded. 'I was tempted to say yes. I needed a quiet moment to collect my thoughts.'

'So, what's on your mind?'

'I can't go of course, but now ... well, now it turns out you can!'

'Are you serious?'

'Absolutely.'

'I have to think about it.'

'Sure, but don't take too long. Haddad can't stall for much longer.'

'Would you do me a favour?'

'Of course.'

'Could you drop me off at Jack's house? We were going to have dinner tonight. I have to talk to him before I go. To Egypt.'

'Thanks, Jana,' Carrington said, reaching for her hand.

'How did it go?' asked Jack, opening the door with a glass of wine in his hand. Jana walked inside without a word. 'I booked a table for eight. We have to leave straight away.'

'We're not going anywhere, Jack. You knew all along, didn't you?'

'What do you mean?' Jack looked nervous.

'You know exactly what I mean! Photographs, Jack. The ones taken right here.' She pointed to the kitchen table. Jack put down his glass.

'You didn't say anything last night. Not a word – why?' Jack looked at the floor. 'Why didn't you at least warn me? Didn't it occur to you that might have been the decent thing to do? I see, you have nothing to say.'

'Sit down Jana. It's not quite as simple as that.'

'I'm not staying, Jack. Marcus, you know, my friend? He's waiting outside.'

'Let me explain, Jana. Please.'

'What could possibly be an explanation for this, Jack?'

'I was told not to discuss it with anyone. The lawyers were adamant.' Jack knew it sounded stupid the moment he said it.

'Tell me, since when are lawyers' instructions more important than friendship? And trust. You do remember trust? Your words, right here ...' continued Jana bitterly. 'I trusted you, Jack.'

'I didn't want you to get hurt. I thought it would somehow all blow over without you having to know.'

'Oh really? Well, it didn't. The Director showed me the photos this morning. At least he had the tact and decency to let me look at them in private. Can you imagine how I felt? Can you? And I suppose you were the great hero at the paper. Jack the stud at work, fucking his little heart out – all in the line of duty.'

'It wasn't like that at all,' Jack interrupted lamely. 'I had to sign a confidentiality agreement. It's all part of my contract.'

'Don't give me that crap! Do you know how many rules I've broken to pass information to you – to keep you in the loop? Do you? We had a deal, remember? But it turns out you're not a man to keep a deal. You used me!'

'We used each other,' Jack shouted back.

Jana looked at him, turned around and left the house. She did not close the door behind her.

'How did it go?' asked Carrington back in the car.

'Jack is Jack; I should have known better. It's all my own fault, you know.'

'How come?'

'I was stupid. Really bloody stupid. I tried to hold on to something ...'

'What do you mean?'

Jana stared out the car window. 'My youth,' she said quietly.

Carrington had expected quite a different answer.

'Some men just don't grow up,' he said. 'That's their charm and their downfall. Jack is one of those, I'm afraid; that's all. Don't be too harsh on yourself.'

'Thanks, Marcus. Kindness comes naturally to you, but it's true. It's time for me to move on ... I know it is.'

58

Jana pressed the button on her mobile and glanced at the new text message. It was from Jack. Her first reaction was to press delete. Jack had been phoning all day, but Jana refused to take his calls. She re-read the cryptic message: *Must talk. Leaving 2night. Urgent! Professional not personal. Please.*

Trying to suppress her resentment, Jana took a deep breath and dialled Jack's number.

'You said professional, not personal. What do you want?' she demanded brusquely.

'Can't talk right now; I'm at the airport.'

'Running away from something?' Jana asked. 'I thought you were covering the trial.'

'Something urgent has come up. Can you come here?'

'Jack, after all that's happened, why on earth should I?'

'I found something else, something important ... in the ashes ...'

'What did you say?'

'You heard me. Please, Jana. Just meet me at the departure lounge in an hour, I'll explain then.'

Jack was waiting in the club lounge. Jana looked straight at him and sat down on the edge of a chair.

'I don't want to talk about the other night,' Jana said, before Jack could say a word. 'This is strictly professional.'

'Okay. Drink?'

'No, thanks. If I understood you correctly, you said that you found something else ... Well?'

Jack opened his briefcase, pulled out a sheet of paper and put it on the table in front of Jana. 'This is a copy,' he explained, 'the original was taken by the burglar. It was only a small scrap of a badly burnt photo. All that was left of it is what you see here.'

Jana looked at the picture. She recognised the man standing in front of what looked like a castle tower.

'Are you saying you found this in the cottage after the fire and just took it without telling anyone?'

Jack nodded. 'I didn't think much of it at the time; so much was going on. I ...just put it in my pocket.' Jana looked into his eyes without saying anything. 'I found it by accident, Jana. It was poking out of the rubble – right there in front of me. It must have fallen out of that box. What caught my eye was the SS uniform. It's the same man, don't you think?'

'It would appear so.'

'There's something written on the back,' Jack continued. 'Same handwriting, just like the writing on the other photo, I'd say.'

'What?'

'This,' replied Jack, handing Jana another page.

'Montse ...' Jana read aloud. 'One word, obviously incomplete. Is that all?'

'Yes, but it's a significant word.'

'What does it mean?'

'Well, the photo is burnt right up to the "e" here. I'm sure what it said was Montsegur.'

'Come on, Jack, how can you possibly know that?'

'The tower. I remembered the ruins – Montsegur in southern France. A place with a notorious, bloody past.'

'You've lost me, I'm afraid.'

'Here, look, there's a date as well – in German. Februar 1944. It's quite a story.' Jack was interrupted by the boarding call for his L.A. flight. 'I've got to be quick, but, well, a few years ago,' he continued, 'I was commissioned by a London paper to write about a man called Berenger Diderot. The BBC was making a documentary about him at the time and there was quite a lot of interest in this enigmatic abbé and his secrets. I actually went to France to do some research. Diderot lived in a small, remote mountain village near Carcassonne. He went there in 1885 as the new parish priest.'

'So? What's the big mystery?'

'It's a bit complicated but ...'

Jana interrupted. 'What does this have to do with the Nazi in the picture? Where's the connection?'

'I've got to go,' Jack said curtly. 'Keep the copy, it's yours.'

'Come on, Jack. Get to the point. We still have a little time.'

Mollified, Jack continued. 'All right. The Germans were secretly excavating in the area during the War – especially around Montsegur – looking for something ...'

'What?'

'I'm getting to it,' Jack said. 'A few years after his appointment, Diderot began to restore the village church,' Jack continued and leaned to pick up his hand luggage. 'Will you walk with me? Please ...'

Jana stood up and nodded. 'Go on. I'm listening.'

'It won't take long but really, you need to know this. Turns out during the restoration, he came across an old hollow column. It was from the time of the Visigoths and inside he found some old parchments.'

'Was that the great mystery – the parchments?'

'No, not initially – the mystery was Diderot's extraordinary wealth,' Jack replied as they hurried to the departure gate. 'When he discovered the documents in 1891 he was as poor as a church mouse, and then, by 1896 he started spending millions. No one's ever explained the source of that wealth, but it was rumoured he'd discovered a secret of enormous religious significance, something that could rock the Church. There's a lot more of course, a lot of speculation and intrigue ...'

'What about the photo, Jack? Where does that fit into all this?'

'Jana, look, there really isn't much time.' The passengers ahead of them had all gone through. 'Quickly, here, give me the photo,' Jack said and put down his briefcase. 'What do you make of this?' he asked, pointing to a dark shape next to the officer in the picture.

'It looks like a crate of sorts. Two crates actually, one on top of the other.'

'Please sir, you must hurry,' urged the attendant at the gate.

'Exactly. And here on the lid of this one, can you see the markings?'

'There's something there, but it's too small. I can't make it out.'

Jack handed his boarding pass to the attendant, turned around, and put his arms spontaneously around Jana. 'I know what it is,' he whispered into her ear. 'It's a swastika and a cross, a *croix pattée*, the cross of the Templars. The same emblems appear in the other picture. On two of the crates by the lake.'

'You didn't tell me about that!'

Jack kissed Jana on the cheek before she could pull away. 'I also know what the Germans were looking for ...'

'Is that why you were interested in the story in the first place?'

Jack hesitated for a moment. 'Yes,' he replied. 'I'll make it up to you, I promise,' he said, and looked into her eyes for a few seconds. 'I'm sorry.'

'Once broken, some things cannot mend,' Jana replied, lowering her eyes. 'I thought you knew that.'

'You're wrong; you'll see,' said Jack. Picking up his bag, he turned around and hurried through the gate.

Too late, thought Jana, grinding her teeth. Frustration had replaced disillusionment.

59

'I'm beginning to feel a little uneasy about Egypt, you going all by yourself,' Carrington said, linking arms with Jana as they crossed the park in front of his flat. It was their last evening together before Jana's departure. Carrington felt the warmth of her touch; an almost forgotten sensation that sent a ripple of guilt racing across his heart. But he sensed something had changed between them.

'You seem to forget, I'm a big girl. And if I remember correctly, it was your idea.'

'I know it was, and that doesn't help either.'

'Come on, Marcus. It'll be good for me, you said so yourself.'

'You'll miss Benjamin's big day in court tomorrow.'

'I know.' Jana flicked back her hair. 'I'll miss more than that,' she whispered. 'At least I'm doing something useful, something for ...' Carrington put his finger gently on her lips, the intimacy of the gesture surprising them both.

'I know.'

'This is definitely a first,' said Carrington, looking for his Bible on the shelf.

'What do you mean?'

'A lady suggests we should go back to my place after supper to read the Bible? This was supposed to be a farewell dinner, not Sunday school.' Carrington put a leather-bound book on the coffee table. 'Here it is,' he said, pointing to a page, then went into the kitchen to open a bottle of wine. 'Drink first, Bible later.'

'Heathen!'

He sat down next to Jana, and placed the bottle and glasses on the table.

'It's rather intriguing, you must admit,' continued Jana, reaching for her phone. 'Here, look for yourself. This is the text message Jack sent me from New York: "Exodus, 37", that's all it said.' Jana held up her phone. 'Typical Jack; always playing games.'

'Not so sure; I did a little research of my own after you called. There's quite a bit about Diderot on the internet. Jack was right. The Germans were very interested in Montsegur during the War. All very hush-hush. Montsegur was a Cathar fortress in southern France. It was sacked during the Albigensian Crusade in the thirteenth century. The crusaders called it "Satan's Synagogue". After Montsegur fell, hundreds of Cathar heretics and their sympathisers were burnt alive.'

'How awful.'

'In 1944, the Germans were digging up the place – using miners from the Ruhr – searching for something.'

'Do you know what?'

'There's a lot of speculation about this. Some sources speak of old Visigoth treasure, others refer to the Templars and their phenomenal wealth ... and their secrets. But the consensus is that they were looking for some old manuscripts,' Carrington explained, 'and a relic.'

'What kind of manuscripts, do you think, and what relic?'

'The sources are deliberately vague, but whatever it was it must have been hugely important and of particular interest to the Church in Rome. Some religious mystery perhaps or some secret from the past. Something like that. Even the Holy Grail gets a look in. You know how superstitious Hitler was with his astrology. He was obsessed with anything supernatural; knew a lot about the occult.'

'Here it is,' interrupted Jana, 'Exodus 37.'

'Go on ...'

'*And Bezaleel made the Ark of shittim wood*,' Jana began to read, '*two cubits and a half was the length of it and a cubit and a half the breadth of it, and a cubit and a half the height of it*.' Jana paused. 'How big is a cubit?'

'About this long,' Carrington replied, pointing at his elbow, 'from here, to here. And shittim wood is acacia wood.'

'What do you make of all this?'

'Well, this refers to the Ark of the Covenant of course, built to precise specifications by Bezaleel to house the two stone tablets given to Moses on Mount Sinai.'

'You mean, like in *Indiana Jones and the Raiders of the Lost Ark*?'

'The very same.'

'Jack is having us on, surely.'

'I don't think so.' Carrington took the Bible out of Jana's hands. '*And he overlaid it with gold within and without, and made a crown of gold to it round about*,' he read aloud. '*And then here, further down, it says: And he made a mercy seat of pure gold ... and two cherubims of gold, beaten out of one piece made he them, on the two ends of the seat ... and the cherubims spread out their wings on high, and covered with their wings over the mercy seat with their faces one to another*.'

'What does it all mean? You're the learned scholar here.'

'Surely you know the story of Moses and the Exodus – the Israelites leaving Egypt?'

'Sunday school was a long time ago ...'

'You do remember the plagues, the parting of the sea, and the pillar of fire – no?'

Jana shrugged, kicked off her shoes and tucked her feet under her before reaching for her glass. She shook her head and gave Carrington a large smile.

'I see. All right; settle in my dear. It's time for the full story.' Carrington liked this new feeling between them. 'Well, the year is about 1300 BC – no one is quite sure – and the King of Egypt, generally thought to be Ramses II, refuses to let the

Israelites leave Egypt. There's a huge showdown between the Pharaoh – in many ways himself a god – and the god of the Israelites. Many terrible things happen: a plague of locusts devours his crops, the Nile turns blood red and all the first-born males are visited by the angel of death. Finally, Pharoah's had his will broken by inexplicable disasters, and he gives in and lets the Israelites go.'

'That's nice of him,' Jana quipped.

'There was a lot of divine persuasion involved, you must admit. Even a god-king can only take so much.'

'Then what?'

'Well, the children of Israel have Moses. He's their persistent prophet and he's guided by a pillar of fire, and they leave slavery behind them and follow him into the wilderness.'

'I hope it was worth it,' commented Jana, reaching for her glass.

'Funny you should say that; not all of them were happy with the arrangement. Despite being fed by manna from heaven, despite the waters of the Red Sea parting to let them pass ...'

'And then drowning the Pharaoh's charioteers who were chasing after,' interrupted Jana. 'I've seen *The Ten Commandments* you know. Great film.'

'Yes. Well, it wasn't all roses. A lot of them believed Moses had led them into the wilderness only to die ...'

'Not a happy situation.'

'No. So ... remember that and let's get back to the Ark. After three months, the well-travelled refugees reach Sinai and camp in front of a mountain.'

'Ah, the famous mountain.'

'Quite. There, the voice of God speaks directly to the Israelites and offers them the terms of the Covenant – the Ten Commandments, which they will have to obey as a nation.'

Jana laughed. 'They all begin with, Thou shalt not ... isn't that right?'

'More or less. Moses is then summoned to the top of the

mountain and given the famous tablets ...'

'... inscribed by the finger of God.' Jana completed the sentence. 'How exciting.'

'This was the first set,' Carrington explained.

'What do you mean, there were more?' Jana asked, looking confused.

'Patience; all will be revealed. After handing the Tablets of the Law to the prophet on the mountain, God also gave Moses certain instructions – precise and very detailed – for how to construct an amazing object.' Carrington paused and reached for the Bible on the table in front of him.

'*Build an ark of acacia wood, two cubits and a half shall be its length* ... You heard the rest. Moses stayed up on that mountain for forty days and forty nights.'

'I suppose the instructions were rather complicated,' observed Jana, 'but still, forty days is quite a long time, even for something so special, don't you think?'

'Spot on, as usual. That's what the Israelites thought too. They got a bit anxious, you see, frightened of being lost and abandoned in the wilderness and decided to turn to the old, more familiar gods for help.'

'I can understand that. Maybe the old jobs back in Egypt didn't look so bad after all,' Jana suggested, enjoying the story. 'Even bondage can look rather attractive after wandering around in the wilderness for a while.'

'They approached Aaron, the brother of Moses, and asked him to build them images of the old gods they could worship. When the prophet finally came down from the mountain with the tablets, he was met by a most horrible sight. The Chosen People were dancing around the image of a golden calf. Understandably, Moses lost his temper, smashed the Tablets of the Law in an act of fury and put three thousand offenders to the sword.'

'A man with a mission, not to be crossed, I see.'

'Prophets are notoriously dangerous and unpredictable,'

Carrington joked. 'So, he's silenced the idol worshippers by considerably reducing his unruly flock, and then climbed the mountain again to ask God's forgiveness.'

'Surely not another forty days and nights ...'

'Absolutely. These things take time. Not only did he succeed in placating the angry God, he came back with new tablets.'

'A replacement set.'

'Quite. Compliments of a merciful and forgiving God.'

Jana began to clap slowly in mock applause. 'Bravo, Marcus, you certainly know your scriptures, I'm impressed. But surely this is just a wonderful old story, right? It's been told and retold through the millennia.'

'Most likely, yes ... yet ...' Carrington looked at the glass in his hand.

'Yet ... what?'

'Let me answer you this way: You've heard of Heinrich Schliemann, I hope?'

'I remember seeing something interesting about him on the Discovery Channel not long ago. He found Troy, didn't he?'

'That's the man. But do you know how he found it?'

'He dug it up, I suppose.'

'Yes. But you have to know where to dig. Right?'

'Sure.'

'Unlike all the mainstream scholars of his day, he followed his instincts and took Homer's Iliad quite literally, you see. And he located the site.'

'A lateral thinker.'

'An original thinker, not afraid of being different.'

'Are you suggesting there could be something factual about the story of the Ark and the Ten Commandments? Are you seriously suggesting the Ark and the tablets could exist?'

'All I'm saying is, yes, it's possible. Most myths and legends have some factual foundation that's embroidered through the ages. However, the kernel of truth is always there. Funny thing about truth ...'

301

'What?'

'It doesn't change. It doesn't go away. All you have to do is find it.'

'And how do you do that, Marcus Aurelius?'

Carrington leant across to Jana and tapped her gently on the tip of her nose with his finger. 'By keeping an open mind.'

60

'What do you mean you can't find him?' Carrington demanded. His junior looked flustered. 'Do you have any idea what this means? We're due back in court. Lord Ashburton was supposed to be here at noon with the violin. Go and find him. Now!'

It was Carrington's first day in court without Jana, and he was missing her already. Dreadfully. To his surprise, he found it difficult to concentrate. *She'd be half way there by now*, he thought, *all by herself.*

'You are still under oath,' the judge reminded Krakowski waiting in the witness box. 'Yes, Mr Crown,' she continued, nodding towards Carrington at the bar table in front of her.

'Mr Krakowski, just before the luncheon adjournment you told the court about your father's violin,' Carrington began, rising to his feet. 'I think you referred to it as precious. Why was it precious?'

'My father was a child prodigy. At the age of ten he was already giving concerts all over Europe. Count Esterhazy heard him play Paganini in Vienna. Apparently the count was so impressed by the boy's performance that he presented him with a violin after the concert. The violin was a Stradivarius. It also had a name ...'

'A name you say? What name?'

'It was called *The Empress*. It was named after the Empress

Elisabeth of Austria – the Kaiserin.'

Carrington glanced over his shoulder; Lord Ashburton had still not arrived.

'You said in your evidence this morning,' Carrington continued, trying to buy time, 'that you and your family were deported from Warsaw after the ghetto uprising in April 1943, and sent by train to Auschwitz. Is that correct?'

'Yes, that's right.'

'You also told the jury that your father took one item with him, his violin, because it was his most treasured possession. Is that right?'

'Yes, he couldn't bear to leave it behind. It was part of him.'

'What happened when you arrived at Auschwitz?'

Krakowski paled. Trying to calm himself, he reached for the glass of water in front of him.

'Your Honour,' protested Archibald, rising to his feet. 'I must object. This evidence is hardly relevant.' Archibald realised that Krakowski had the jury eating out of his hand and hoped an objection now would break the spell of Krakowski's carefully chosen words and restrained, spellbinding delivery. Any account from him of the enormous human tragedy in which the accused was implicated would be disastrous for Archibald's client. Krakowski sounded truthful, accurate and honest; a devastating combination in a witness giving evidence against one's client. *Just as one would expect from a seasoned performer,* Archibald thought.

'Mr Crown?' asked Her Honour. 'What do you say about that?'

'The relevance of this evidence will become apparent shortly, Your Honour,' Carrington explained calmly. The judge accepted the assurance.

'Please continue, Mr Krakowski. What happened next?' Carrington asked, turning towards his witness.

'A German officer came over to us, pointed to the violin case under my father's arm and asked if he was a musician. My father explained who he was and told the officer that we, that is my brother and I, were also accomplished musicians. We were ordered to stand aside. In the confusion my mother and sister were ... swept along by the crowd ... they were all moving away from the train. It was the ...' Krakowski's voice became almost inaudible.

'You have to speak up, Mr Krakowski,' said the judge, 'we cannot hear you.'

'It was the last time I saw them ... alive.' Krakowski covered his face with his hands and sat down.

'Your Honour, I think a short adjournment would be in order,' Carrington said quietly.

A clever performance or a truthful witness? Archibald asked himself. He jotted down the last answer and underlined the word 'alive'. Krakowski's pause struck Archibald as odd and he made a note to cross examine Krakowski about this. It was always the little things – a word, a gesture, an intonation, a pause – that provided the clues. Those were the real gems pointing to the things hidden behind the words and occasionally, with luck, even to the truth.

After the adjournment, a more composed Krakowski told the jury how his father had been put in charge of the camp orchestra, which had to perform at the railway station every time a death-train rolled into the camp. The guards thought that music would calm the new arrivals, he explained, and make them easier to control.

The Kommandant was passionate about classical music, Krakowski recalled, and was taking violin lessons from Krakowski's father. It was during one of those lessons that the Kommandant discovered that the violin was a Stradivarius.

'Curiously enough, instead of confiscating the precious instrument,' Krakowski testified, 'not only did the Kommandant let my father keep it, but whenever he entertained visitors he would ask my father to play for his guests. They ... my father and his quite famous instrument, were a curiosity that became the favourite topic of after-dinner conversation at the Kommandant's table, because ...'

A commotion at the back of the court interrupted Krakowski's evidence. Annoyed, the judge looked up. Turning around, Carrington recognised Lord Ashburton brandishing a violin case above his head.

'I think I can explain, Your Honour,' Carrington said calmly, 'a piece of evidence has just arrived.' Lord Ashburton followed the court attendant to the bar table and handed the violin to Carrington. 'You're cutting it fine,' hissed Carrington, opening the violin case, 'what happened?'

'I only flew in this morning,' replied Lord Ashburton. 'The Stradivarius was on a concert tour in Japan; I had to come via Tokyo ...'

'Thanks, any longer and it would have been sayonara ...'

'Bravo Marcus!' whispered Archibald, leaning towards his opponent. He began clapping his hands together in mock applause. 'What a performance; this is turning more and more into a circus.'

'In that case, you must make sure that your client doesn't turn into a clown, or the last laugh could well be on him,' Carrington retorted calmly. *Right on cue*, he thought to himself. *I'm sure everyone thinks we have carefully orchestrated this. If only they knew! Well, here it comes* ... Slowly, Carrington took the violin out of its case.

'We are waiting, Mr Crown ...' said the judge impatiently, pointing with her pen to Carrington.

'I apologise, Your Honour.' Carrington turned to Krakowski in the witness box. 'Please, have a look at this instrument, Mr Krakowski,' he said, handing the violin to the court officer.

At first, Krakowski explored the beautiful instrument with the tips of his fingers. Then, holding it up against the light, he began to examine it carefully from all sides. Letting the tension mount around him, Carrington took his time before asking the next question.

'Is this the violin your father took with him to Auschwitz?'

'I object, Your Honour!' Archibald barked. 'My friend is leading the witness.' Archibald was not going to make it easy for Carrington.

'I reject the question in that form, Mr Crown,' ruled the judge.

'To put it another way,' Carrington continued unperturbed, 'do you recognise this instrument?'

'Yes, I do.'

'What can you tell the court about it?'

'I believe it's my father's violin ...' Krakowski paused in mid-sentence.

That's not good enough! Carrington thought, pressing his knuckles against the bar table until they turned white. *Think man, think!*

'But to be absolutely sure, Your Honour,' Krakowski continued, turning towards the judge, 'I would have to play it. Is that possible?'

'Your Honour, may the witness ...?' Carrington asked.

'Any objection, Mr Archibald?'

'No, Your Honour.' Looking annoyed, Archibald glanced at Carrington. 'Act one, scene two, the witness fiddles in the box. Bravo Marcus,' Archibald mumbled under his breath and sat down. 'What next?'

'Relax, Archie, and enjoy the tune.'

'If it helps you, Mr Krakowski, you may play the instrument,' Carrington said, handing the bow to the court attendant to take across to the witness. Krakowski stood up, lifted the violin to his chin and closed his eyes. This moment of total concentration was how he focused before every performance. Courtroom or concert hall, an audience was an audience.

A hush fell over the spectators in the gallery. All eyes were on the man standing motionless in the witness box. Slowly, the bow touched the strings and the first notes of a Mozart Adagio drifted eerily across the spellbound court.

How strange, Carrington thought, *the violin is giving evidence.*

Krakowski played a short passage and then stopped.

'Has this assisted you?' Carrington asked. For a while, Krakowski didn't respond, almost as if he hadn't heard the question at all. Then, opening his eyes, he looked directly at Newman sitting motionless in the dock opposite.

'You have to answer,' the judge prompted quietly.

'There is absolutely no doubt in my mind, Your Honour, that this is the violin my father took with him to Auschwitz,' came the clear and precise answer. 'This is the Empress.'

'I tender the violin, Your Honour,' Carrington said. When he sat down, he noticed that the palm of his hand was bleeding where he had dug his fingernails in while waiting for Krakowski's answer.

61

Haddad showed his ID to the flight attendant and pushed past the passengers leaving the plane. Looking down the aisle, he saw Jana lifting her hand luggage out of the overhead locker and hurried towards her.

'I cannot tell you how much I appreciate this,' Haddad said, helping Jana with the luggage. 'It must have been a very long flight.' Jana thought he looked tired and a little embarrassed. He was, she thought, an old fashioned man, and rather shy.

'It's the least I can do after all you've done for me,' she replied, putting her hand reassuringly on his arm. Jana knew how to put men at ease. 'Marcus sends his regards.'

'I'm sorry we have to meet again under difficult circumstances,' Haddad apologised, 'but the situation is both urgent and serious, I'm afraid. We have to fly to Luxor straight away; he's already on the move,' Haddad explained, lowering his voice. 'There's little time.'

The dry, searing heat rising out of the desert made Jana's eyes water. 'What do you mean he's on the move?' she shouted, trying to make herself heard; the roar of the rotor blades was deafening.

'Come, I'll show you,' Haddad replied, helping her into the chopper.

Before turning south towards Luxor, the pilot flew over the Pyramids. Jana looked in awe at the monumental structures shimmering like pieces of a geometric puzzle assembled by the hands of giants on a carpet of sand. A tribute to humanity's quest for immortality.

They followed the silvery band of the Nile and reached Luxor just before nightfall. 'There,' Haddad shouted, pointing to a small cloud of dust, 'the road, next to the river.' Haddad told the pilot to make another pass and handed Jana his binoculars. 'Can you see them?' he asked. Jana nodded.

'Looks like something out of *Lawrence of Arabia*,' she said, training the binoculars on the procession of camels and horses snaking along the riverbank. The riders, their faces hidden behind scarves, were heavily armed. Some carried large green banners with crescent moons and quotations from the Koran embroidered into the coarse fabric, others were beating kettle drums tied to the saddles of their camels. Four riders holding burning torches led the column. Jana noticed a curved sword strapped across each of their chests. She looked down at the familiar ruins of the Luxor temple and shivered.

'Where are they going?' Jana asked.

'To the airport. The Defender of the Faith has demanded a plane – to Afghanistan. The procession is to show his followers that he's in control.'

'But he's trying to leave the country, isn't he?'

'Well, yes. But how does it look to you? He knows these people; he also knows how to manipulate crowds. These are simple folk, you see. They want to believe and they love a spectacle. And he's giving them one.'

'Clever man.'

'Yes, and a dangerous one.'

'And one of the riders down there is the elusive Defender of the Faith, I suppose,' observed Jana, handing the binoculars back to Haddad.

'Yes, but which one? That's where I need your help, Jana. You're the only one I can trust who actually knows what he looks like.'

'What's the plan?'

'I'll explain everything later ...' Haddad pointed to the pilot and shook his head. They landed next to an Egypt Air plane parked in the middle of the runway.

'That's the Phoenix that'll take them to Afghanistan, I presume,' Jana said, pointing to the plane.

'You could say that, but this Phoenix won't be rising out of the ashes. The Defender of the Faith and his men will not leave this place alive,' Haddad replied, lowering his voice.

'Another bloodbath?'

'Not necessarily.'

'Surrender?'

'Perhaps.'

Jana wasn't convinced. 'What about the Americans and the bomb threats?' she asked.

'The Brotherhood has made one fatal tactical error – procrastination,' Haddad explained, 'and it's given the Americans time to organise. They've evacuated all the embassies and moved in the marines. There will be no deal with the terrorists!' he added.

Jana noticed tanks and armoured personnel carriers surrounding the runway. 'Surely, the Defender of the Faith must know what's going to happen here,' she said, pointing to the tanks and soldiers, 'or is he that sure of himself? Or that arrogant?'

'He has no choice, Jana. It's destiny after all. Rather than dying in a remote mountain cave as an outlaw or, worse still, being captured, he will now have his moment of glory.'

'Is that what you want?'

'No, but it's the faster, safer option,' Haddad said quietly.

'What do you want me to do? Identify the body, is that it?'

'If it comes to it, frankly, yes.'

'What if he surrenders and you take him alive, what then?'

'He will go to trial.'

'You don't really want that, do you?'

Haddad didn't answer. He bit his lip and looked away. Just as the silence was becoming embarrassing, one of his men approached and reported to him excitedly in Arabic.

'They'll be here shortly,' Haddad said. 'You'd better come with me.'

The soldiers guarding the airport opened the barbed wire gates. Barking orders into the phone, Haddad demanded reinforcements to control the cheering crowd pushing against the barricades. It was almost dark by now.

The riders ignored the soldiers and passed slowly through the gates. They stopped in the middle of the runway, dismounted and took off their shoes.

'What are they doing?' asked Jana.

'Look, they're facing towards Mecca. I think they're going to pray,' said Haddad.

Suddenly, the crowd behind the wire fence fell silent. The rebel fighters knelt down together and began to pray. At the end of the prayer the outlaws stood up as one and, leaving their camels and horses behind, began to walk slowly towards the waiting plane.

Jana gripped Haddad's hand.

'I know,' Haddad said quietly. 'You don't have to watch. This is for you, Marcus; I promised,' he whispered, reaching for the microphone. 'It is written.'

'Lay down your weapons and put up your hands,' Haddad's voice boomed through the loudspeakers. The airport floodlights came on, illuminating the tarmac like a stage. Momentarily blinded, the surprised warriors tried to shield their eyes. 'Lay down your arms, now!' urged the voice again. Armoured personnel carriers – headlights trained on the confused combatants – were closing in from all sides. Some of the fighters began to run towards the plane, others turned back, trying to reach their frightened camels and horses. Not a single warrior threw down his gun. Looking in vain for cover, the men began to fire their automatic weapons at the approaching vehicles.

'Fire at will,' Haddad ordered. Machine gun fire erupted from all sides. Three men almost reached the plane only to be mowed down by gunfire from the open doors of the aircraft. Several camels were hit in the crossfire. The animals collapsed spectacularly onto the tarmac, blood gushing from huge wounds.

A few horses managed to get away; all the others lay dead or wounded on the runway, shrouded in clouds of cordite. Gradually, the guns fell silent. It was over in minutes.

Jana stared at the carnage. 'This is obscene,' she whispered, barely able to speak.

'Violent death is never beautiful,' Haddad replied.

'I know.'

Soldiers swooped in from all sides. They cleaned up the bloody mess, gathered the bodies and took them to an empty hangar. There, laid out in neat rows, they were available for Jana to view. First, Haddad took Jana to the eight seriously wounded survivors. She looked carefully at each face; all young men. The Defender of the Faith was not among them.

'We don't have to do this right now,' Haddad said, noticing Jana's distress. 'Many have been horribly ...'

'Please, I would rather get it over with,' Jana insisted, pressing a handkerchief against her nose. Walking slowly along the silent rows, Jana stopped in front of each body and shook her head. When they came to the last row, Haddad became agitated.

'Jana, please; he must be here,' pleaded Haddad. 'None of them got away.' When they approached the last body, Jana looked at it for a long time before shaking her head.

'I'm sorry, he's not here,' she said at last.

'Are you certain?'

'Absolutely.'

62

Carrington glanced at his notes on the bar table. There was only one topic left to cross out.

'And finally, Mr Krakowski,' Carrington said, coming to his last question, 'were you present during the exhumation of the bodies found at the lake?'

'Yes, I was there until the remains of the first body were located. I left after that.'

'Thank you, Mr Krakowski. I have no further questions.'

Archibald felt suddenly quite calm. The ordeal of waiting over, his cross examination could begin. Holding the top of his gown with both hands, he rose to his feet and looked at Krakowski. Creating tension was a favoured technique of his and this time would be no different.

'Mr Krakowski, when did you see your mother and sister for the last time?' he asked at last. Surprised, Krakowski looked up. It wasn't the question he had expected. Archibald saw the flash of fear in the witness' eyes and smiled.

'Just after we arrived at Auschwitz, at the railway station. They were walking towards the camp with the others ... that was the last time I saw them.'

'In your evidence yesterday I believe you said it was the last time you saw them – alive,' Archibald said, pointedly referring to his notes. 'Isn't that right?'

'That's correct,' Krakowski replied, turning pale.

'What did you mean by this?'

'I don't understand.'

'What I'm asking you is this ...' Archibald explained. '... did you see them again – later perhaps – when they were no longer alive?'

'I object,' Carrington interrupted. 'This is hardly relevant.'

'It goes directly to credit,' Archibald snapped.

'I allow the question,' ruled the judge. Krakowski reached for the glass of water in front of him and just sat there.

'Would you like to hear the question again?' the judge asked quietly. Krakowski shook his head and took a sip of water.

'Yes, I did see them again,' he whispered.

'When?'

'A few days later.'

'Where?'

'In the camp.'

'Where in the camp?'

'Do I have to answer this?' Krakowski asked, looking distressed.

'Yes, you do,' said the judge.

'After the bodies were taken out of the gas chamber ... before they were taken to the ... crematoria ...'

'Yes?'

'They were processed.'

'What do you mean they were processed?' Archibald pressed on.

'The hair of the dead women was shaved off and collected in large cardboard boxes. It was made into socks for U-boat crews. Rings – mainly gold wedding bands – were pulled off the fingers and the bodies were searched ...'

'I cannot hear you,' Archibald said.

'The bodies were searched for valuables, mainly gold and jewellery which was sometimes hidden inside ... you know in ...'

Archibald noticed expressions of horror on the faces of the jurors and decided not to explore this answer any further. 'Is that where you saw your mother and sister again?' he asked instead.

'Yes.'

'What were you doing there?' barked Archibald.

'I was ...' Krakowski stopped in mid-sentence, covering his face with his hands.

'Please, you must answer,' said the judge.

'Breaking gold teeth out of the mouths of the corpses – with pliers,' Krakowski whispered.

'That was your job, was it?'

'Yes.'

'As I recall it, you told us yesterday that you were playing in the camp orchestra with your father and brother.'

'That was a privilege, not a job. It had to be earned.'

'A privilege to be earned. I see. How?'

'By performing special duties for the Germans.'

'Such as you just described, I take it?'

'Yes.'

'Let me get this right: In return for the privilege of playing in the camp orchestra, you performed special duties for the Germans, such as processing the corpses of your recently murdered fellow inmates, including your dead mother and sister – is this correct?'

'It wasn't like that!' Krakowski shouted.

'Please answer the question, yes or no,' thundered Archibald.

'Yes,' came the faint reply.

'And the answer you gave earlier that you saw your mother and sister for the last time as they walked away from the train was false wasn't it?'

'Yes.'

'It was not true, was it?'

'It was an incomplete answer.'

'It wasn't the truth, was it?' Archibald pressed on.

'I object, Your Honour,' interjected Carrington. 'My friend is harassing the witness. The question has been answered.'

'You have your answer, Mr Archibald,' the judge agreed. 'Ask your next question.'

'As Your Honour pleases. And you volunteered for these special duties, I take it?' Archibald asked, glaring contemptuously at Krakowski.

'No, not exactly.'

'What do you mean, not exactly?'

'It was very difficult for the Germans to get people to perform these tasks,' Krakowski explained, regaining his composure. 'It was made clear to us as soon as we arrived that if we – that is my brother and I – did not volunteer, as you put it, our father would be sent to the gas chamber. We did what we had to do, to keep him alive.'

'I notice the time, Mr Archibald,' interrupted the judge. 'The court will adjourn until 10 am tomorrow.'

'One question too many, Archie,' Carrington said, leaning across to Archibald. 'Don't you think?'

Archibald did not reply.

63

Jana stepped into the tiny whitewashed room and closed the door. She didn't want the guard placed outside on Haddad's insistence, to overhear her conversation.

He'll be back in his flat by now, Jana thought, dialling Carrington's home number, *poring over the daily transcript*. Remembering Carrington's familiar routine brought a smile to her weary face. The full horror of the previous night had finally caught up with her; Jana felt shaky and very alone.

'God, I miss him', she mumbled, listening to the dial tone race across the globe.

'You sound tired,' Jana said, noticing the fatigue in Carrington's voice.

'You sound frightened,' he replied.

'I am.'

'Where are you?'

'In a police station in Luxor – under guard.'

'What's the charge?'

'Very funny. I'm one of the good guys, remember? Most of the rebels are either dead or dying – except one.'

'I saw it on the news. The Egyptians are claiming a big victory against terrorism. But let me guess – the Defender of the Faith wasn't among them, right?'

'Good guess. Perhaps he really is the Chosen One. Haddad is beside himself.'

'I can imagine. What will you do now?'

'Haddad is convinced the Defender of the Faith didn't leave the cave with the others, but somehow managed to slip away. He's going back tomorrow morning to search the area again. I'm going with him.'

'Be careful, please. This is a dangerous game. The Chosen One is a desperate man and Haddad's a proud one; that's a lethal cocktail. Haddad has lost face, and that's bad, especially for an Arab. Listen to me; he will not rest until he has tracked down his man. And to do that,' Carrington added seriously, 'he needs you. Don't get caught in the crossfire.'

'Don't worry, I know how to keep my head down,' Jana reassured him, trying to sound confident. Carrington was unconvinced. He already regretted having encouraged her to go to Egypt in his place.

'How's the case going?'

'Benjamin had a hard day. Bearing your soul in public isn't easy. Blowtorch-Archie was in great form and Benjamin got a little bit singed, I'm afraid. And besides, your replacement is woeful.'

'You don't know what you're missing until it's gone, see?' Jana joked.

'Spot on. But seriously, Jana, I think you should come back. You've done enough already. Leave it to Haddad.'

'I can't.'

'Why not?'

'Because I made a promise. I promised to help him find your family's killer.'

'You're starting to sound just like him.'

'Tell me, would you hesitate if you could be here instead of me?'

'No – but ... I ...'

'But what? You can't but I can, that's the only difference,' Jana argued, her voice sounding hoarse. 'I was there too, remember? Elizabeth and Isabella died right there, next to me ... You even went to the cemetery to tell them you couldn't go,' she reminded him quietly.

'Jana, please ... Why are you doing all this? For Haddad? Come on, you've done more than enough already.'

'Can't you see? I'm not doing it for him.'

'What do you mean?'

'I'm doing it for you!'

'But why?' Carrington asked, instantly regretting the foolish question.

'Why? Because ... I ...' Jana's voice trailed off and the line went dead. All of Carrington's attempts to call her back failed.

64

Carrington burst into the robing room. 'You look rather chirpy this morning,' observed Archibald, glancing at his former pupil. Carrington had been awake all night. Yet, despite the lack of sleep, he felt remarkably refreshed. He tried to complete Jana's sentence in his mind, over and over. And, frustrated but cheered and with complete licence to fill in the gap, he kept coming back to one interpretation. *What if I'm wrong?* he thought, checking himself. *There's no fool like an old fool.*

'How much longer will you be with Krakowski?' Carrington asked, ignoring the remark. 'Our expert is standing by; I would like to give him an indication ...'

'Not too long, I should think. By the time I'm finished with your virtuoso you won't need the expert anymore. This evidence isn't going anywhere and you know it,' Archibald added, trying to intimidate his opponent.

'That's for the jury to decide.'

'Well, today's violin day,' Archibald said, putting on his wig. 'Let's go and fiddle a little, shall we?'

'Mr Krakowski,' Archibald began, a little louder than the day before. 'You told us yesterday that there was absolutely no doubt in your mind that the violin shown to you by my friend was the Stradivarius your father took with him to Auschwitz.'

'Correct.'

'And you came to that conclusion by simply touching it,

playing it, listening to it. That's right, isn't it?'

'Yes.'

'Would you please look at this violin here,' Archibald said, reaching into the red bag under the bar table. He pulled out a violin case, opened it and handed the instrument to the court attendant. 'Please take your time. You may play it if you wish.'

'What am I looking for?'

'I would like you to compare it with the violin you say belonged to your father, and tell the jury how the two instruments differ from each other.'

Krakowski held the violin up against the light and examined it carefully from all sides. Then he played a short Mozart passage, just as he had done before.

Archibald was enjoying himself. He had borrowed the violin from the Conservatorium; it was an original Stradivarius.

'This is a splendid instrument, there's no doubt about that.'

'That's not what I asked you. The question was: How does this violin differ from the one you played here in court yesterday? Would you like to see it again?'

'Yes, please.'

'Could the witness be shown Exhibit D, I think it was?' The court attendant handed the violin to Krakowski.

'It feels different, it sounds different,' Krakowski said after a while, looking at the two instruments in front of him.

'It feels different, it sounds different, you say,' Archibald repeated. 'Would you agree with me that these are entirely subjective considerations?'

'I suppose they are.'

'Would you also agree with me that the two instruments look virtually the same?'

'Yes, they are remarkably similar,' Krakowski agreed, 'right down to the colour of the varnish.'

'Assume for the moment that the violin I handed to you earlier is a genuine Stradivarius. Would that in any way alter your evidence?' Carrington glanced at Archibald standing at the lectern next to him. He had to admire the old fox's ploy and it was obvious that the jury thought it impressive too. So did the judge.

'No, it would not.'

'Why not?'

'Violins are individuals. No two instruments are ever completely alike, even if made by the same craftsman. There are always differences.'

'You are referring to the different sound or the different feel, I take it – the subjective matters we touched upon earlier?'

'Yes.'

'But you do agree with me that the two instruments look virtually the same, isn't that so?'

'Yes.'

'Objectively speaking therefore, would it be correct to say that you cannot point to a single concrete difference between them?'

'You mean different size, shape, colour; a distinguishing mark perhaps – things like that?'

'Precisely.'

For a moment, Krakowski looked pensively at Newman sitting stoically in the dock opposite.

'What's your answer?' Archibald demanded, certain that he had finally closed the last gate and cornered his witness.

'No, it would not be correct to say that.'

'Are you seriously suggesting that you can objectively point to a real difference between these two instruments?'

Carrington began to smile. His opponent had just walked into a fatal trap.

'Yes, that's right,' Krakowski answered calmly. Alarm bells should have been ringing loudly by now but Archibald appeared not to hear them. Oblivious to the enormous risk he was taking, he continued the pursuit.

'Please, Mr Krakowski, do show us this difference. I'm sure the jury would like to see it,' Archibald said, unable to keep the sarcasm out of his voice.

'I can't, it's hidden from view.'

'It cannot be seen; how convenient. Pray tell us then, what is this mysterious difference?'

You'll be sorry, thought Carrington, glancing sideways at his opponent. *Never ask a question if you don't know the answer.*

'One morning, as we were waiting for another train to arrive,' Krakowski began quietly, 'my father dropped his violin. It was very cold and his fingers were stiff, you see. When he picked it up, he noticed that the sound post inside the violin had been dislodged.' Krakowski held up the violin and pointed to the bridge in the centre of the instrument. 'The sound post is a small piece of wood just below here,' he explained. 'Every note played on the instrument travels through the sound post. It's the soul of the violin,' Krakowski said, looking directly at Archibald. 'We took the violin to one of the workshops in the camp to repair it. My father had repaired violins before and knew exactly what to do,' Krakowski explained. 'First, he removed the sound post through the f-hole here. But before inserting it again and wedging it into place, I remember he did something quite unusual, something completely out of character. I think it was a small act of defiance.' Krakowski paused, pointing to the violin in front of him.

'What did he do?' Archibald asked impatiently. 'Please do not keep us in suspense any longer.'

'He scratched something into the sound post with the tip of a fountain pen. Four things actually: a small Star of David, the words Roha and Parzifal and the number of our family's Swiss bank account. It was a very long number. My brother and I could never remember it, I'm afraid. That way, our father said, at least we would always know where to find it.' Archibald paled. 'It was a silly little prank,' Krakowski continued. 'If we were to remove the sound post I could actually show you,' Krakowski explained calmly, resting his finger on top of the violin. 'I hope that's objective enough for you, Mr Archibald.'

It was a rare moment. Archibald was speechless and rendered so at the hands of the unassuming, softly spoken musician. He swallowed several times without making a sound. Instead of cornering the witness, he found himself with his back against the wall and nowhere to go.

'We can help you remove the little post, if you like,' mumbled Carrington, enjoying his opponent's dilemma.

'Where to from here, Mr Archibald?' asked the judge. Archibald didn't respond. 'Mr Archibald?' the judge asked again.

'Perhaps I can assist, Your Honour,' Carrington interjected, rising to his feet.

'This violin is obviously a very valuable instrument. One would ordinarily be most reluctant to interfere with it. However, these are extraordinary circumstances and we will ask the current owner – the trustee, that is – for permission to remove the sound post. The Crown intends to call an expert witness in any event. I'm sure he could attend to the task without damaging the violin. I can also indicate to Your Honour,' Carrington added, looking directly at the jury, 'that we will seek leave to re-examine Mr Krakowski on this topic and tender the sound post once it has been removed – to corroborate his evidence.'

'What do you say to that, Mr Archibald?' asked the judge.

'No further questions, Your Honour,' Archibald growled and sat down.

'Coward!' shouted a voice from the gallery.

65

Out of breath and perspiring, Haddad followed Jana up the steep escarpment. 'My men have searched every corner of the cave again this morning,' he said, wiping his flushed face with a handkerchief. 'Nothing!'

'Even the Defender of the Faith cannot just disappear without a trace,' Jana replied. 'Unless he has a flying carpet there must be a simple explanation for all this. There has to be another exit somewhere.'

'That's what I thought all along,' Haddad agreed. 'Let's go inside and have another look.'

They moved from chamber to chamber, but found nothing. It appeared that the cave could only be entered from the side facing the Nile.

'The whole area was sealed off as soon we knew he was inside. A fly couldn't have crawled out without being noticed,' Haddad said.

'Why don't we go up in the helicopter and have a look from above – who knows?' Jana suggested.

'Good idea.'

As the pilot made a low pass over the mouth of the cave, Jana noticed a gorge on the other side of the escarpment.

'The pilot wants to know what we're looking for,' shouted Haddad. Jana shrugged. Just as the helicopter was turning away from the gorge, something shiny caught her eye.

'There, what's that?' Jana pointed to the shaft of light rising from the ground. The pilot circled the spot and descended into the gorge.

'It's a camel,' Haddad shouted back, handing his binoculars to Jana. 'A dead one – have a look.' The shattered carcass of a camel came into view, the silver studs on the back of the broken saddle reflecting the sunlight. When the helicopter roared past, three vultures gorging on the rotting carcass took flight.

'It hasn't been there long. It must have fallen from somewhere up here. There,' Jana said, pointing excitedly to the side of the cliff directly above the dead camel, 'a path, along the ridge.' The pilot followed the narrow track carved into the rock ledge until it suddenly disappeared into the mountain.

'The elusive back door to the cave, you think?' asked Haddad. Jana nodded.

'Look over there, Bedouins!' Haddad pointed to a campsite at the entry to the gorge. The pilot put the helicopter down in the sand next to a cluster of black tents. Several tall men, their long robes flapping furiously in the draught of the rotor blades, came running towards them.

'You stay here,' Haddad said, unfastening his seatbelt. 'Look, they're all armed. If there's any trouble we take off at once, understand?' Jana nodded. Haddad followed the men to one of the tents and disappeared inside.

Jana was getting anxious; Haddad was taking his time. The pilot, too, was getting nervous. He was reaching for the machine gun under his seat when Haddad came out of the tent.

'I think we have our answer,' Haddad said.

'What took so long? I was getting worried.'

'The usual thing; no one wanted to talk.'

'But you changed their mind, how?'

'With a mixture of baksheesh and threats. Mainly baksheesh, I'm afraid,' Haddad joked, rubbing his fingers together. 'This is

Egypt, remember?'

'I see. You used sophisticated methods of interrogation then,' teased Jana.

'Sophisticated? Well, let's say, effective.'

'Who are these people?'

'Traders, on their way to Luxor.'

'Can you trust them?'

'Not really.'

'Well?'

'Apparently, three men came out of the gorge late last night, on foot. They bought camels from the Bedouins and left at first light. That way,' Haddad pointed west, towards the Nile. 'They were in a great hurry.'

'The Defender of the Faith?'

'Must be.' Haddad shook his head in frustration. 'This is a major trade route leading directly to Luxor. The man has nine lives! Not only did he dupe us all, his followers included, he had no trouble sacrificing his men it seems. Anything to get away.'

'And the old man over there with the beard is the tribal elder, I suppose,' Jana said, pointing to a group of men watching the chopper take off.

'No, their leader's inside. He can't walk; the women were bandaging his injured leg.'

'What now?'

'What do you suggest?'

'If your baksheesh was generous enough and they actually told the truth, we should be able to spot these men from the air. Don't you think? They couldn't have gone very far. We'll follow the trade route and, hopefully, we'll find them.'

'Exactly.'

Sheikh Omar pushed the leather flap of the tent a little to one side with his stick, and watched the helicopter disappear behind the escarpment.

'Allah will reward you, and so will I,' he said to the old man with the beard. 'You did well telling them what they wanted to hear. Your story of three men coming out of the gorge last night was very convincing. They've gone away – for now. But they'll be back. We must leave immediately.'

The helicopter followed an ancient wadi – a gateway to the Nile – used by countless caravans bringing their wares to the markets of Egypt. Within minutes of their finding the wadi, a sand storm rose out of the desert from the east. It was now too dangerous to fly low and the pilot had to turn back.

Haddad was furious. He radioed ahead and ordered his agents to seal off all approaches to Luxor from the east. Every man riding a camel in the vicinity was to be detained.

'We questioned two of the wounded about their leader,' reported one of Haddad's officers at the airport.

'Did you find out anything new?' asked Haddad, hurrying to his jeep.

'There was something odd. Apparently none of them actually saw the Chosen One, but there was a rumour going round the cave ...'

'What rumour?'

'That he was injured. Incapacitated, something like that. I know it sounds vague,' apologised the officer, 'but they both mentioned a broken leg.'

'What did you say?' Haddad shouted, clenching his fist.

'A bad leg,' repeated the officer timidly.

'Did you hear that?' Haddad turned to Jana. 'The Defender of the Faith has an injured leg!'

'The man in the tent ... do you think?'

'Yes, it all fits. Bedouins always stick together. He was playing with me. Damn his soul!' fumed Haddad. 'He mocked me. At least now I know what he looks like. Let's go back and this time let's have a platoon of sharpshooters with us.'

The helicopters circled the entry to the gorge several times. Just before sunset, the sandstorm calmed, permitting a clear view of the terrain below. Haddad swore loudly, and then immediately asked for Allah's forgiveness. As he had feared, the tents had gone and the Bedouins had disappeared into the desert without a trace.

66

'Professor Bernadini, you are currently a director of the American Federation of Violin and Bow Makers Inc. Is that correct?' Carrington asked, introducing his expert witness to a hushed court.

'Yes, that is so.'

'Do you specialise in any particular field?'

'I do – the history and development of musical instruments, especially the violin. I have written several books on the subject.'

'And one of those books is this one, I believe,' Carrington continued, reaching for a slim, leather-bound volume on the bar table. '*The Violin Makers of Cremona*,' he read out aloud.

'Yes, it was published last year. It deals with the great Italian violin makers – or luthiers, is the correct term. It begins with Andrea Amati, who founded the Cremonese School and culminates with the great Stradivari himself.'

'And in your book you investigate their various techniques, I understand? Constructing their instruments, and the special woods they used, the varnishes they invented and so on – right?'

'That's correct. In order to follow the development of the violin, reaching its pinnacle with Stradivari,' Bernadini went on, thrilled to have another opportunity to show the depth of his knowledge. He failed, however, to notice, when he went on and on, that the judge was starting to shuffle in her seat.

'One has to understand the evolution of this extraordinary craftsmanship. For example, Stradivari's methods of building a violin didn't stand still. They improved all the time, especially between 1684 and 1700,' Bernadini continued, hardly drawing breath. Carrington resisted stopping the lecture. There was a point to all this and Bernadini would serve them well.

'Then, the Long Stradivarius emerged in about 1700, giving us the magnificent, unsurpassed instrument we know as the Stradivarius today.'

Archibald appeared disinterested and sat, playing with his pencil. He didn't object once.

Carrington, however, thought there was nothing quite as compelling as a true expert's passion. 'And would it be correct to say,' he continued, 'that from time to time you have been called upon to authenticate violins attributed to the famous Cremonese violin makers?'

'Yes, I have acted as a consultant on numerous occasions, especially for auctioneers and insurers.'

'Would you please take a look at this instrument?' Carrington handed Exhibit D to the court attendant. 'What can you tell us about it?' Bernadini took a pair of horn-rimmed glasses from a silver case and began to polish the thick lenses with his handkerchief. The glasses made his eyes appear huge and distorted, like those of a curious fish staring through a glass bowl. He reached for the violin and began.

'It is my considered opinion, that this is an authentic Stradivarius – a Long Stradivarius in fact – manufactured by the maestro between 1700 and 1710. It is a superb example of his craft, which reached its peak during his more mature years.'

'You state in your book, Professor, that many violins were given names, which helps to establish their provenance?'

'Yes, that's correct. Many have names, you see. Individuals. Like people.'

'In that context, does the name, *Empress*, mean anything to you?'

Bernadini looked up, surprised. 'Oh yes. The Empress – die Kaiserin, as it is known in German – was a very famous violin. It was named after Kaiser Franz Josef's wife, Elisabeth, in 1867, the year of her coronation in Hungary. She was a great beauty – very popular indeed and much loved by her subjects. The violin belonged to a Hungarian noble family, the Esterhazys.'

'Do you know what happened to it?'

'Yes, it's quite a story.'

'Please tell us.'

'Well, there was this young virtuoso, a boy from France, giving a concert in Vienna in 1905. Apparently, his violin was stolen the day before the concert at the railway station – the gypsies they said, of course. Count Esterhazy, a great music lover, heard about it and came to the rescue. He lent the boy a violin for the concert – the famous Empress. However, there was a condition ...'

'What condition?'

'The boy had to play Paganini – the Count's favourite. Of course the boy obliged and his performance was a sensation. At the end of the concert, the Count stood up in his box and announced that the young man should keep the violin because there was no one else in the Empire who could play like him. Well, of course the whole of Vienna was talking about the magnanimous gesture. Pity we don't have patrons like that anymore,' lamented Bernadini.

'Can you tell us the boy's name?'

'Unfortunately there appears to be no record of it. But the papers referred to him as Little Sparrow.'

'Do you know what became of the Empress?'

Bernadini shrugged, apologetic and looked towards the judge. 'The boy took the violin back to Paris. And after that ... it just disappeared. Turbulent times they were ... wars ... revolutions ... the world changed. That was the last ...' Bernadini stopped mid-sentence and turned to look at

Carrington.

'You are not suggesting,' whispered Bernadini, 'that this violin is ... the Empress?'

He sat straighter in his chair. 'Of course! How stupid of me ... it is, isn't it? You must tell me!' Bernadini was almost shouting. He reached for the violin and cradled it to his chest.

'Professor Bernadini, please,' interrupted the judge, looking sternly at the witness. 'Calm down and answer Mr Carrington's questions. This is no time for questions of your own.'

'Sorry, Your Honour, it's just that this is ... once in a lifetime ...' Bernadini voice trailed off.

Carrington deliberately rearranged his papers on the bar table and took his time asking the next question. *The jury needs time to fully appreciate the significance of the Professor's evidence*, he thought. And Bernadini did, indeed, need to calm down.

'Is it the case, Professor, that you are also a restorer of musical instruments?' Carrington asked, introducing his next topic.

'Yes. Over the years, it has become a natural extension of my field. It helps me understand the true character of the instruments,' the professor explained. 'A bit like dissecting a body during an anatomy lesson.' Archibald stopped playing with his pencil and sat up.

'In that case, Professor, may I take it you wouldn't have any difficulty removing a sound post?'

'No, it's not that difficult, if you have the right tools that is.'

'How would you do it?'

'I would use this,' answered the professor, reaching for a leather tool pouch inside his pocket. 'I have this always with me,' he explained. 'My tools.'

Bernadini held up a small, curved, S-shaped tool made of brass. 'This is a sound post setter,' Bernadini explained. 'The name says it all.'

'Could you remove the sound post without damaging this instrument here?' Carrington asked, coming to the question everyone had been waiting for.

'Yes, I suppose I could – but why? Touching this Strad would be ... well, vandalism!' Bernadini slipped the sound post setter back into the pouch and looked pleadingly at the judge.

'Please remove it,' Carrington said calmly, ignoring the question. Bernadini began to fidget nervously in his seat.

'Professor ... please,' said the judge quietly. Bernadini reached into his coat pocket again and slowly pulled out the small leather pouch.

Bernadini mumbled something in Italian, sounding to Carrington like an expletive, and loosened the four strings. Then he picked up the sound post setter and inserted it skilfully through the f-hole. Like a surgeon in a delicate operation, he began to probe the inside of the violin. Suddenly, a smile began.

'Bene, bene,' he mumbled to himself, trying to dislodge the little piece of wood. 'Here it is,' he announced as he pulled the sound post through the eye of the f-hole and held it up for all to see.'

'May I approach, Your Honour?' Carrington asked the judge.

'Please do.'

Carrington walked slowly across to the witness box and looked at the violin in Bernadini's lap. The journalists in the gallery stopped scribbling; the jurors leant forward to get a better view. All eyes were on Carrington.

'Please, take a closer look at the sound post here,' Carrington said. 'Can you see anything unusual?' Bernadini leant forward.

'There is something,' Bernadini said after a while, adjusting his glasses. 'It's hard to see. Some writing and ... how curious.'

'Can you tell us what it is?'

'It looks like ...' Bernadini hesitated and lifted the piece of wood closer to his face until it almost touched his nose.

'What is it?'

'It looks like ...'

'Yes?'

'A star?'

The judge had to call for order several times before the excited journalists in the gallery settled down.

'Anything else?'

'Two words.'

'Can you read them?'

'Yes; the first one here says R–o–h–a ...'

'And the second?'

'Parzival.'

Once again, the judge had to call for order.

'Anything else?'

'Over here, on the other side ...'

'What is it, Professor?'

'Numbers: 8241 ...'

'Thank you, Professor,' interrupted Carrington, 'there's no need to read out all the digits.' Carrington realised that the case had reached a high point. There was only one more important piece of evidence he needed.

'Finally, Professor, are you able to tell us when all this may have been inscribed into the wood?'

Professor Bernadini ran the tips of his fingers several times over the surface of the little post. Holding it up towards the light, he began to examine it carefully with a magnifying glass.

'It's impossible to be absolutely accurate, you must understand, but judging from the discolouration of the inscribed area and the faded residue of ink, I would say it has been there for quite a long time.'

'Are we talking months, years, decades perhaps?'

'I'm certainly not talking in terms of months.' Bernadini paused, and traced the outline of the star with his index finger. 'What I can say with confidence, however, is that it has been there for a long time; several years, I'd say. I'm sorry, that's the best I can do.'

'And the sound post itself? Would you say it was the original, or a later replacement?'

'Oh, no, this is no replacement! This is an authentic

Stradivarius sound post.'

'Thank you, Professor Bernadini, I have no further questions,' Carrington said, adjusting his gown, which had almost slipped off his shoulders. 'I tender the sound post, Your Honour.'

When he sat down, Carrington noticed that Archibald had broken his pencil in half. 'He's all yours,' Carrington said, turning to his opponent.

'I have no questions,' Archibald told a stunned court without even looking at Bernadini in the witness box.

'Brave step,' Carrington whispered. Archibald ignored him.

'You are excused, Professor Bernadini,' Her Honour said, smiling encouragingly at the man in the box.

'We will now turn to ...' A strange, gurgling noise from the dock below interrupted her. When she looked down, Newman was getting to his feet and, as he tried to loosen his tie with both hands, he knocked over the glass of water in front of him. Staring at the judge with bulging eyes, he opened his mouth like a dying fish at the end of the hook. Before the court attendant could reach him, Newman collapsed, hitting his head against the wooden bench with a thud that resonated through the courtroom.

Part IV

TABOT MUSA

Egypt; October 1305

The Nubian porters waded ashore first, their naked, muscular bodies glistening like polished ebony in the glare of the desert sun. They ignored the crocodiles basking in the mud close by, tied the boat to the trunk of a palm tree and watched the five tall white men tinker with a large wooden chest strapped to the mast. The bearded, red-faced men were dressed in body armour that, to the Nubians, was both awe-inspiring and frightening. Two curious hippos circled the boat, waiting for the right moment to attack the unwelcome intruders. Despite the large spray of murky Nile water from their flared nostrils each time they surfaced, no one gave them a second glance.

As a seasoned commander, Fra. Armand knew exactly just how vulnerable he and his men were. Fra. Armand suspected the Abyssinians had somehow made contact with the porters who seemed, suddenly, suspicious and hostile. He realised there was little time; five knights, no matter how well armed and experienced, couldn't defeat an army. Moreover, they'd had little food for days and some of them had had a raging fever since leaving Axum.

Their attempt to reach the Gulf of Aqaba, sailing north along the African coast, had been put to an end by a storm in the Red Sea. Shipwrecked, and with only meagre provisions, they had travelled inland across the desert to reach the Nile. Two knights had perished along the way.

'We'll take the boat and leave the porters behind,' said Fra. Armand, reaching for his sword. He knew surprise was their best weapon. 'We must do it now, when they least expect it. Look, they're all on shore, just waiting for the right moment to finish us off.' The other knights nodded.

'Now!' Fra. Armand shouted and cut the rope. Carried along

by the strong current, the boat left the shore. The Nubians plunged into the river to swim after it. Surprised by the commotion, the hippos took a dive. The knights hoisted the triangular sail and pointed the vessel towards the middle of the Nile. As Fra. Armand hacked off the hand of the first Nubian climbing on board, the others behind him turned away in horror. Fra. Armand smiled; the boat was theirs – at least for the moment. If the Greek trader they had met the day before was right, they should reach Thebes by nightfall.

'There, look,' shouted Fra. Armand, pointing to the shore. 'The portals of Thebes.' Partially buried under drifts of sand, the ruins of a mighty temple-city came into view. The knights pulled into a small cove and covered the boat with dry palm fronds. Fra. Armand was certain the Abyssinians had followed.

'This is as far as we go. I think we've reached the end of our journey, my friends,' he said. 'Hurry, please. They'll be here by daybreak, if not sooner.

'What's your plan?' asked Fra. Bernard, following his commander through the tall stone arch into the temple.

'I'm looking for the right place, before it gets too dark.'

'For what?'

'To hide something ...'

'You don't mean ...? The chest's far too big to bury in here,' protested Fra. Bernard. 'Anyway, they would find it in no time.'

'Quite so. But that's not what I have in mind.'

'What then?' Fra. Bernard looked puzzled.

Fra. Armand put his arm around the tall knight's shoulder. 'You are the youngest and strongest among us,' he replied. 'I believe, with God's help, you can make it to Alexandria ... alone. We'll stay here and face our enemies in the morning – but not you. You must slip away after dark tonight. I have asked the Good Lord for guidance and he has answered me. Yours will be a sacred mission, Bernard. If you succeed, we'll not have died in vain.' Fra. Armand's face lit up. 'Tomorrow we shall surely die; but we shall not be defeated,' he added, placing his hand on the hilt of his sword.

'What mission?' asked another knight.

'We'll give Bernard something to take back to France so powerful and precious that the Pope will tremble and the king will pale with envy, when they hear about it,' explained Fra. Armand.

'Bernard, you will only take one. You cannot possibly conceal two. And so, we mustn't tempt fate, we must shape it,' he said quietly to himself. 'The other will be hidden – right here.'

The knights lifted the Ark of the Covenant out of the chest and placed it on a slab of broken granite. Stepping back from the relic, they stood in awe, watching the moonlight caress the two golden angels protecting the mercy seat with outstretched wings. The mercy seat began to glow, illuminated by a moonbeam. The knights fell to their knees, bowing their heads in prayer.

'If we have offended Thee, O Lord, forgive us,' Fra. Armand began to pray. 'If we have failed Thee, O Lord, forgive us. Protect our brother Bernard on his journey. Guide him safely back to France and give us strength to die with honour, as true knights serving Thee.'

'Amen,' came the chorus.

When, later that night, the Abyssinians found the empty boat hidden under the palm fronds, they burnt it. Without the boat, their foe was trapped. They surrounded the ruins with armed torch bearers and made ready to attack at first light.

Just before dawn, the knights embraced for the last time. Preparing their weapons for combat, they watched the sun rise slowly out of the desert. As the sun rose, the Abyssinian battle drums began to beat, like the heartbeat of a thousand warriors longing for glory. The Abyssinians entered the temple from all sides at once, searching for their elusive enemy. When they reached the great hall of the temple with its rows of gigantic columns soaring towards heaven, they could see the Ark in front of them on a makeshift altar of broken stone. At each of its four corners stood a knight in full body armour – splendid, motionless and silent. Emperor Wedem Ara'ad's warriors stood still, paralysed by superstition and fear.

Slowly, the silent knights began to move. First, they raised their shields, then their swords and began to beat the shields with the blades – an unmistakable reply to the bellicose drums beating all around them. The spell was broken.

The first wave of attackers was hacked to pieces before it could reach the Ark. The second climbed over the writhing bodies of the dying and met the same fate. The disciplined defence of the warrior monks seemed impregnable. The Abyssinians continued to attack, but made little progress until a carefully aimed lance pierced Fra. Armand's left eye, killing him instantly. The dead knight fell backwards, his bleeding head crashing against the Ark. A trail of blood ran down the white tunic that covered his armour and merged with the red cross of the Templars on his chest. The knights' defence was no longer unassailable.

Stripped naked by the jubilant victors, the blood-encrusted bodies of the four knights were carried on shields to the river. There, the corpses were decapitated and thrown into the Nile, fodder for the waiting crocodiles. Intoxicated by victory and blood, the Abyssinians did not notice one of the knights they had followed to the temple the day before, was missing.

67

Heinrich Newman sat in the empty hospital waiting room with his eyes closed. It was 10 pm; seven hours after his father's dramatic collapse.

'Wake up,' said Dr Oberndorfer – Newman's personal physician – tapping Heinrich on the shoulder.

'How is he?' Heinrich asked.

'Not too well, I'm afraid,' the doctor replied. 'He had a massive stroke.'

'Can he talk?'

'Come, he wants to see you.'

Newman lay propped up in the bed. Staring vacantly into space, with his mouth partially open, he was breathing heavily. A nurse was dabbing his forehead with a sponge. Newman had aged a decade in a few hours and looked vulnerable and frail.

'How are you?' Heinrich asked quietly, reaching for his father's hand. It felt limp and cold. Newman turned his head slowly towards his son.

'He can hear you,' Dr Oberndorfer said, 'but you must speak up.' Newman began to move his lips, but there was no sound.

'It takes a little while before he can say anything,' the doctor explained. 'Lean over a bit more.'

'Sorry, I can't hear you,' Heinrich said, squeezing his father's hand.

'Get Habakkuk,' whispered Newman, slurring the words, his

345

weak voice barely audible.

'What did you say?'

'Habakkuk; get him – now!' Newman looked pleadingly at his son. 'Now,' he repeated.

'Habakkuk?'

Newman nodded.

'As you wish,' said Heinrich. 'I'll call him.'

'Hurry!'

'What's the prognosis?' Heinrich asked, following Dr Oberndorfer out of the room.

'Impossible to say at this stage. As you can see, he's very agitated and wants to talk. He shouldn't really, but we both know what he's like; there's obviously some urgency.'

By the time Father Habakkuk arrived, Newman had recovered somewhat. He appeared lucid and composed and, when Heinrich finally realised his father would not talk in his presence, he brushed past Habakkuk, gave him a disapproving look and left the room.

'We're running out of time,' Newman began, trying to focus on the black priest sitting by his bedside. 'You know what happened in court?'

Habakkuk nodded. 'I was there ...'

'Of course; then you heard it all. A Swiss bank account, would you believe, after all these years. With the number, right there, under our very noses.' Newman began to breathe heavily. 'It's suddenly all so clear. He's still taunting us, even from the grave. What we've been looking for is in a bank vault in Switzerland – it must be. We suspected this, remember? He even quoted from die Dokumente in der Schweiz; now we know!'

'And Krakowski now has it all within reach. We handed it to him! How ironic,' Habakkuk interrupted.

'Well, yes, that. And fortuitous.'

'What do you mean?'

'If only we could ... Perhaps there's a way after all. Perhaps one last chance ... one last throw of the dice ...' Newman's voice trailed off.

'What's your plan?' Habakkuk asked, pulling his chair closer to the bed. For a moment, as Newman's gaunt face grew a smile, Habakkuk saw a hint of the old, arrogant man once more.

'Listen carefully,' Newman whispered, 'this is what we should do ... and I know just the man to help us.'

68

When his master class at the Sydney Conservatorium was over, Krakowski closed his violin case, took a bow and hurried to the exit to meet Dr Rosen. She had sounded upset when she phoned him earlier from the hospital and pleaded with him to meet her after the class.

'I'm sorry, Benjamin. I know it's your last night, but this is urgent,' Dr Rosen apologised. Krakowski shrugged and steered her towards a side entrance to escape the waiting press, the autograph hunters and the curious.

'I'd rather see you anytime than face these wolves,' he joked. 'You look exhausted. How's your father?'

'Not good; the stroke was severe. Can we go somewhere private please? I need to talk to you about him.'

'Sure. How about my hotel?' Krakowski suggested. 'We can walk.'

Krakowski pointed to an empty table at the back of the piano bar, turned to the waiter and ordered two cognacs.

'I don't want to sound melodramatic, but I do believe this is a wish – quite possibly the last – of a dying man,' she said. Krakowski put his hand reassuringly on hers. 'My father wants to talk to you.'

'What? But he's on trial. I couldn't possibly ... it wouldn't be right!' Krakowski withdrew his hand and almost knocked over his glass.

'Benjamin, please listen. I know how you must feel, but there won't be any more trial.'

'Why on earth would he want to talk to me?'

'Because he wants to give you something.'

'Give me something? You can't be serious. What?'

'Something that belonged to your father,' Dr Rosen said quietly.

Krakowski turned to look out the window. He reached for his glass as, slowly, the implications began to sink in. The harbour lights receded and all he could see was his father standing alone under the Arbeit-macht-frei-gates of Auschwitz. Krakowski made himself blink, hoping the disturbing vision would disappear. When he opened them again, all he could see was the pain in Dr Rosen's expression.

'Do you realise what you just said?' Krakowski asked, his voice cracked. Dr Rosen nodded.

'So, it's him after all. He's admitting it. But why? I don't understand!'

'Benjamin, please. There isn't much time,' pleaded Dr Rosen. 'You must see him.'

'When?'

'Now.'

The man propped in the hospital bed barely resembled the man Krakowski had confronted in court just days before. Gone was the arrogance, the almost regal bearing. What remained was a shadow of approaching death. Krakowski felt ill at ease and, for an instant, he saw that the patient's eyes – ice blue and crystal clear – hadn't changed at all.

'Please leave us, Bettany,' Newman said, watching Krakowski carefully.

'The circle is almost complete,' Newman began, as soon as they were alone. 'We meet again. Do you believe in destiny, Mr Krakowski? Your father certainly did.'

349

'What do you want from me?'

'I want to close the circle.'

'You speak in riddles. What circle, what destiny?'

'Please, sit down. We don't have much time and I have a lot to tell you,' Newman said, ignoring the question.

The door to Newman's hospital room remained closed for a long time. Dr Oberndorfer sat next to Dr Rosen dropping his eyes anxiously to his watch almost every five minutes. *The patient should be resting,* he thought. But this patient, he realised, would not take kindly to being interrupted. However, after an hour, he stood up, knocked on the door and opened it. Dr Rosen could hear her father's voice; he was almost shouting.

'But you must! You have no choice. You owe it to history, you owe it to mankind, you owe it to ... Diderot, your ...'

Almost colliding with the doctor, Krakowski stormed out of the room. All colour had drained from his face. Dr Rosen noticed he clutched a bundle of papers to his chest. She stood up and hurried towards him.

'Benjamin, what happened?' she asked. Krakowski didn't reply. He walked to the water cooler and poured himself a cup.

'Let's get out of here,' he whispered and gulped down the water. When they reached the elevator, neither of them noticed the black man sitting in the far corner of the waiting room, quietly reading his breviary.

Krakowski looked at his reflection in the window of the speeding taxi. What he saw frightened him. Dr Rosen sensed his unease and reached for his hand.

'You are a fortunate man, Benjamin,' she said.

'Oh? Why's that?'

'Because you haven't lost your compassion. Despite everything you've been through, your humanity, your capacity to love, has remained intact. Thank you for seeing my father. I know you didn't do it for him, or for yourself for that matter.

I think you did it for me,' she whispered.

'What makes you say that?'

'It's all in your music. All one has to do is listen. An angry man, a bitter man, could never have created such beauty. Your music touches the soul. My husband was the same, only he did it through healing. He wasn't a religious man as such, but he was very spiritual.' Remembering her husband brought a smile to Dr Rosen's pale face. 'He used to reprimand me ...'

'In what way?'

'"If we don't believe in something greater than ourselves," he used to say, "we are destined to remain forever small." Not everyone can see that.'

'Few know where to look.' Krakowski squeezed her hand.

'Well, what was it that my father wanted to tell you, Benjamin?' Dr Rosen asked, curiosity getting the better of her.

'He kept talking about destiny, about forces beyond our control, forces that shape our lives. At first he didn't make sense at all; I thought he was hallucinating.'

'But?'

'But then he started to explain and it all came together in a strange kind of way.'

'Do you want to tell me about it?'

'He solved one of the great puzzles that has haunted me since Auschwitz.'

'Are you serious?'

Krakowski kept staring out the window. 'Absolutely,' he whispered.

'What puzzle?'

'Why my brother and I were taken out of the camp by the SS.'

'You didn't know?'

'No, everything happened so fast. You must understand, we – that is my father, my brother and I – were all in different dormitories. The camp was huge. We only saw each other when we played in the orchestra, and then only for a short time. All

351

I remember – and I have been over this a thousand times before – is this ...'

'Your hotel, sir,' interrupted the taxi driver, pulling up in front of the entrance.

Krakowski paid the fare. 'Night cap?' he asked, turning to Dr Rosen.

'Yes, please. I think we can both do with one.'

'Déjà vu,' Krakowski said, walking into the piano bar they had left just a few hours before.

'You were saying ...'

'A new train had just arrived and we were playing as usual. I still don't know how we did it. All around us was chaos; guards shouting, women screaming ... children. Then the Kommandant came over to us with an SS officer – a tall man with a dog – and ordered my father to go with him; no explanation. I didn't see my father again until the next morning. Apparently, and this of course I didn't know, the officer had been looking for my father for a long time.'

'Why?'

'Because of who he was; or more accurately, because of what he had.'

'You've lost me, I'm afraid.'

'During the night, the German officer and my father made some kind of pact, a deal as they say. They agreed to make an exchange.'

'An exchange? What on earth do you mean?'

'My father had hidden some old manuscripts inside the lining of his violin case. My brother and I didn't know anything about that. In return for those documents, the officer promised to take us out of the camp and smuggle us into Switzerland.'

'How extraordinary. My father told you all this?'

'Yes. He claims that the SS officer in the camp was ...'

'Him?'

Krakowski nodded.

'Do you believe it?'

Krakowski pointed to the leather pouch on the table in front of him, shrugged, and continued. 'I saw my father only once more after that – the next morning at the railway sidings – just before he handed his violin to the officer and we were marched out of the camp by the SS. That was the last time I saw him. He had to stay behind of course. We couldn't really talk, everything happened so fast. However, he did make me promise him something.'

'What?'

'My father had this deposit box in a Swiss bank. It had a long account number and two passwords,' explained Krakowski. 'I knew the number and the passwords were inscribed in the sound post; just as I explained the other day. I saw him do it; we thought it was all a joke. I also knew the name of the bank; we had spoken about it often at home. The whole thing had to do with some old documents in safekeeping, something like that. No money, no diamond necklace, no title deeds to the family estates, only old papers. We used to laugh about it. Father never really explained, yet, he made me promise ...'

'Promise what?'

'To go to the bank and retrieve the deposit box. In fact, he pleaded with me.'

'Did you ask why?'

'I tried, but there wasn't time. He did say, however, that once I opened the box I would understand ... because it was my destiny. And then,' Krakowski recalled, pointing his finger at Dr Rosen, 'he reminded me about the hidden number inside the violin. *The Empress holds the key* – remember?'

'But I thought you said the violin was handed to the officer ...'

'True, but apparently it was supposed to be given to me ... in Switzerland. You know, something of value ... for the future.'

'After the officer had taken the manuscripts out of the case lining, I suppose? That's what he was really after – right?'

'Something like that. But it didn't quite turn out that way, did it?'

'My father told you all this?' Dr Rosen asked, peering at Krakowski.

'Yes, he was brutally frank.'

'How odd. That's just not like him; not like him at all.'

'I had almost forgotten about all this, you see,' explained Krakowski. 'I couldn't remember the account number in any event and the whole violin thing didn't seem important after all these years – until now that is.'

'And now you know the number.'

'Yes, now I know. Thanks to the Empress giving up its secrets in court the other day. It does look a bit like destiny, don't you think?'

'Destiny? Perhaps. Did you have any idea the violin was that famous?'

'Yes, father was very proud of it and often spoke about the Empress – his Sissi, as he affectionately used to call it.'

'Sissi?'

'Yes. Sissi was Empress Elisabeth's nickname.'

'How extraordinary.'

'Initially, the violin had a quite different name, you know.'

'Oh?'

'It was called the Gypsy Queen.'

'How come?'

'Well, before the violin passed to the Esterhazys it belonged to the gypsies.'

'How did the Esterhazys get it?'

'Apparently, the Count often invited the gypsies to play for him on his estate; Hungarian gypsies' prowess with the violin is legendary. Then one day the gypsies got into trouble; big trouble. The Count intervened on their behalf. On his next birthday the gypsies presented him with the violin.'

'What a story! How do you know all this?'

'It's quite well documented, actually; father researched it all. And when Elizabeth became Empress,' Krakowski continued,

'Count Esterhazy renamed the violin in her honour. The Gypsy Queen became The Empress.'

'Fantastic!'

'Sure. And sad. Kaiserin Elizabeth was the Princess Diana of her time. Estranged from her husband – the Emperor Franz Josef – she travelled through Europe; alone. In the end ...'

'What?'

'A tragic end; she was assassinated. An anarchist stabbed her through the heart with a file.'

'Oh that's dreadful.'

'Yes, and where do you think it happened?'

'Where?'

'In Geneva; on the shores of a Swiss lake.'

'Another lake – that's scary.' A cold shiver raced down Dr Rosen's spine.

'Yes, and quite close to the other one ... spooky, isn't it?'

'Threads of destiny?'

'Perhaps.'

'But what about this elusive deposit box? Is it still there, do you think?'

'I'm not sure, but you know the Swiss. Precise and thorough to the end.'

'And what about these mysterious documents?'

'Well, here they are. This is what your father gave me,' Krakowski explained. He pulled a small bundle of papers out of a leather pouch and placed them on the glass table in front of him. 'He said, if I studied them carefully, all would become clear. And, that there would be a few surprises.'

'These look really old,' said Dr Rosen, pointing to the faded parchments on the table.

Krakowski hadn't recounted everything Newman had told him. Not because he didn't trust Dr Rosen, but because he still found it difficult to come to terms with it. He didn't tell her about Diderot. Neither did she question him about the argument she'd overheard in the hospital.

'How do you feel about all this?' asked Krakowski.

'Relieved.'

'Oh? In what way?'

'The uncertainty is finally over.'

'Uncertainty?'

'I suspected all along that the man in that horrible photo was my father,' she said quietly. 'I tried to put it out of my mind, you see; denial. I refused to accept it. But, as soon as I saw the violin case in the picture Jana showed me in New Guinea ... well, I knew then. I think my mother knew the moment she first laid eyes on the photo; that's what destroyed her in the end.'

'Closure then at last, you think?'

'I hope so. But what about you?'

'Deep down, I also knew it was him. I sensed it – when I saw him in court the first time. His eyes; it was all in his eyes.'

Krakowski gathered up the documents on the table in front of him. 'At first it was intuitive. Nothing specific, just a feeling. But then came the violin and now these ... The past is really catching up with me, don't you think?'

'What will you do now?'

'I have to see Marcus in the morning before I leave – I really must try to explain all this. I owe him that.'

'Why such a hurry?'

'The fate of the travelling musician, I'm afraid. Insatiable concert-goers, fickle press, relentless schedules,' Krakowski joked, winking at her. 'You know how it is. I've paid for it with two divorces ...'

'But you married opera singers ... surely they understood?'

'Ships passing in the musical night ... I'm afraid I hit an iceberg on both occasions,' Krakowski said, laughing. 'But seriously, I have to go to Warsaw. I promised, you see – I'm dedicating my second concerto to the city and its Holocaust victims. Poland has claimed me ...'

'A famous son.'

'Something like that. But first, I'm going to Zurich ...'

'I thought you might. I'm leaving too. A fundraising dinner in Vienna and then off to Rome for a charity do.'

'The whole of Europe seems to have claimed you.'

'Not quite. I'm shamelessly raising money,' Dr Rosen explained, shrugging off the compliment. 'Touting for eyesight – pennies.'

'In that case, why don't we meet in Rome, say, after your Viennese-penny-collection and my Warsaw-concerto-dedication? I have an Eternal City apartment overlooking the Piazza Navona.'

'Very tempting. I'll think about it, but on one condition: You must promise to tell me all about this mysterious deposit box ...'

'I promise,' Krakowski said, holding out his hand.

Dr Rosen raised an eyebrow. 'Another promise? Benjamin, are you sure?'

'Absolutely.'

69

'Don't you think it was perhaps just a little bit reckless to go and see Newman on your own – just like that?' Carrington reprimanded Krakowski.

'Possibly,' Krakowski answered. He was annoyed at having to justify himself. 'So what would you have done? The man appears to be close to death, he wants to give me something that had belonged to my father. And, aren't we forgetting something else here?'

'What do you mean?'

'He admitted it all and handed me the proof!'

'I do understand Benjamin, but this could have compromised the entire trial.' Carrington ran his fingers through his hair. 'Then again, it probably doesn't matter anymore.'

'What do you mean?'

'The Director of Public Prosecutions is reviewing the case as we speak. You know, looking at the medical evidence, the legal angles and all that. I agree with you, I can't see the trial continuing if he's really that ill. And besides, it would seem that the political objective has already been achieved.

'The important thing was to put him on trial. I think the Attorney-General would be quite happy to drop the whole case now without having to face the uncertainties of a long jury trial. Justice has very little to do with all this,' Carrington lamented. 'In the end, it all comes down to politics and expediency.'

'What now?'

'Well, if we're right, it's all over.'

'Not quite, Marcus. Not quite. In some ways, this is just the beginning.'

'What makes you say that – what else did he tell you? It's those documents he gave you last night, right?'

'That's certainly part of it, but there's more, much more. It's all linked together like some complex riddle reaching out of the past with clues left along the way. We're all ensnared, you know. It's far from over.'

'Come on, Benjamin, not the fickle finger of fate again – please?'

'Newman told me something you should know. Something about the Defender of the Faith.'

When Carrington heard this, he sat down. This was going to be a longer conversation than he'd originally thought.

'Apparently, the only reason Newman agreed to do business with him was this.' Krakowski opened his briefcase and took out a sheaf of papers. 'This is a copy with a translation. It's an old papyrus written in French dating back to the fourteenth century. It's only recently surfaced in Egypt and Newman's been looking for it for years. You know, through dealers in all the right circles; that means the black market too. The terrorists offered it to him for sale, provided he was prepared to do business with them. It would appear that my father had been looking for it as well.'

'What is it?'

'I'm not sure yet, but, according to Newman, it's some kind of missing link. I haven't had a chance to read any of the papers yet. I'll do it on the plane.'

'You're going to Switzerland?'

'Yes.'

'The deposit box?'

Krakowski shrugged. 'I rang the bank and explained the situation. They're expecting me.'

'They must have been mighty pleased to hear from you. The international spotlight's on them right now, you know. So many allegations of Nazi gold and misappropriated Jewish fortunes in their coffers.'

'You can never tell with the Swiss – inscrutable, yes, but always proper and polite. What about you?' Krakowski asked, changing the subject.

'If the trial is over, I'm going to Egypt.'

'Jana?'

'Yes. Jana and the terrorists.'

'And you question destiny?' Krakowski shook his head. 'Really, Marcus, you should listen to yourself.'

'You're right,' Carrington conceded, laughing.

'You're going after the Defender of the Faith,' Krakowski said, more a statement than a question.

'Well, we've at least cornered one villain; we can't just let the other one go free, can we?'

'No, no. We certainly can't. So, I have to get going. This didn't quite turn out the way we thought it would, did it?'

'It rarely does. But before you go, there's something I want to show you. Jack Rogan gave this to Jana just before she left for Egypt.' Carrington pushed a copy of a photograph across his desk.

Krakowski looked at the faded image of the German officer standing in front of the castle tower. 'Newman?'

'It would appear so. Jack found it in Newman's mountain cottage after the fire. He only just told us about it. Be that as it may, he did quite a bit of research; clever chap. Apparently it was taken somewhere in France, a place called Montsegur. It's written on the back – well, partially.'

'What did you say?' Krakowski asked, his voice sounding hoarse.

'Montsegur, the ruins of a Cathar fortress in southern France. The Germans did some excavations there during the War. All very hush-hush. Does the place mean something to you?'

'More than you can possibly imagine. May I keep this?'

'Sure. But you should really speak to Jack. He did a story on a French priest called Diderot a few years ago. Diderot lived somewhere near Montsegur at the turn of the century, I believe. There was some sort of controversy involving the Church. Jack seems to know a lot about it.'

Krakowski paled. 'He mentioned Diderot?'

'Yes, he spoke to Jana about him the other day. Why?'

'My God, it all fits! Everything Newman said ...'

'What do you mean?' Carrington asked, surprised by Krakowski's reaction.

'Diderot was ... oh, nothing; another time perhaps. I really have to go, Marcus. Thanks for everything.'

'Sure, Ben, another time,' Carrington said, holding out his hand, 'until then.'

This wasn't the time to ask for an explanation.

70

Jana noticed her door was ajar as soon as she opened her eyes. Propping herself up on her elbows, she saw something lying in the doorway. The guard, she thought. Looking up, she noticed a dark shape – utterly still – next to her bed. The shape began to move slowly towards her.

'If you scream, I'll have to kill you,' a voice whispered. Jana could see something glinting in the half-light. A blade, she thought, wide and curved; a sword.

'Get up!' hissed the shape, leaning over her then speaking some words in Arabic. Jana didn't move. A sweaty hand was placed over her mouth from behind. Jana could hardly breathe. The sheet she was clutching to her breasts was ripped away and strong hands lifted her off the bed.

'One sound, you die. Understand?' said a voice from above. Jana nodded. The hand let go of her mouth. She gasped for air, but had the presence of mind not to struggle. A blanket was wrapped tightly around her. Someone in the corridor outside switched on a torch and pointed it to the floor. Jana followed the beam of light out of the corner of her eye and almost threw up. A severed head – glassy eyes wide open – lay in a pool of blood in the doorway. Then everything went dark as a pillowcase was pulled over her head. *The executioner's hood*, she thought, *blindfolding the condemned*.

The man carrying Jana over his shoulders like a rolled-up

carpet, moved like a cat; fast and silent. Staying in the shadows, he threaded his way through the dark alleys towards the Nile.

Jana could hear the splashing of running water. *The river*, she thought. The man stopped. She was lifted off his shoulders and could feel strong hands holding her from below. The sound of water came closer, so did the smell of mud and rotting fish. The hands supporting her let go and dropped her onto something hard. Rolling helplessly from side to side, she cried out in pain. *A boat*, she thought, *we're on a boat*. She tried to move her arms to steady herself, but couldn't. The blanket was too tight, so was the pillowcase covering her head. Breathing heavily, Jana noticed a new sound – sharp and whip-like – canvas flapping against a mast.

71

As soon as the plane began to taxi towards the runway, Krakowski relaxed. Sitting back in his comfortable first class seat, he finished his drink, reached into his pocket and pulled out the photograph. *Newman, at Montsegur*, he thought, looking wistfully at the young German officer smiling at him out of the past. Who would have believed it?

'Another gin and tonic, sir?' asked the stewardess. Krakowski nodded. He slipped the photo into his briefcase, closed it and placed it on the empty seat next to him. After a while he opened it again and pulled out the bundle of papers Newman had given him at the hospital. It was the first opportunity he'd had to examine them properly. He looked for Abbé Diderot's letter to Madame Colbert – just as Newman had suggested – and began to read:

By the time you read this, my dearest, I will be in the Lord's hands ... you know of my son. You know where to find him ... My letter will explain everything ... one day he will understand ...

Krakowski's head began to spin. He felt suddenly drowsy and closed his eyes. Had his father really been adopted? Were the Krakowskis – Alexander and Olga – not his real grandparents, he asked himself. And what about this mysterious French priest – Berenger Diderot – and Francine Bijoux; what did it all mean? Did Newman really know that much about his family? Why?

Dozing off, Krakowski saw his father sitting in front of the fireplace in his Warsaw study. 'Do you know who Parzifal was?' he heard him ask. 'You're named after him.'

'He was a knight who went searching for the Holy Grail.'

'Quite so. Everyone thinks the Holy Grail is a cup, but they are wrong ... all wrong. Wolfram von Eschenbach knew it wasn't a cup; he knew it was ... a stone ... he called it the consummation of hearts' desire ...'

Krakowski opened his eyes and looked at the piece of paper in his hand. He hadn't seen his father's handwriting in years, yet he recognised it at once – small and precise. 'The Grail is not a cup, but a stone,' he read, and began to arrange his father's notes into some kind of chronological order. He kept coming back to one particular page. Titled *The Journey of the Ark – Conclusions* it was pinned to a thick wad of faded notepaper tied together with string. The page was covered in his father's handwriting, with many quotations and references scribbled into the margin.

The Puzzle

King Solomon (970–931 BC) builds the magnificent First Temple in Jerusalem as 'a house of rest for the Ark of the Covenant of the Lord'.

The Ark disappears well before Jerusalem is sacked by Nebuchadnezzar in 587 BC and the Temple is burnt to the ground.

Where did the Ark go?

When the Jews return from exile in Babylon in 538 BC and build the Second Temple on the site of the first, the Ark is not mentioned. How can that be? How can the most precious object in the Old Testament suddenly vanish without a trace?

What happened to the Ark?

Kebra Nagast (Glory of Kings) – the answers?

The story of King Solomon and the Queen of Sheba in this thirteenth century Ethiopian manuscript records a widespread oral tradition, which states that:

The Queen of Sheba travelled to Jerusalem to meet King Solomon. He was smitten by her beauty and charm, she by his wisdom. They became lovers. By the time she left Jerusalem she was with child. After she returned to her homeland, Ethiopia, a boy, Menelik, was born. At the age of twenty, Menelik journeyed to Jerusalem to look for his father, the king. King Solomon acknowledged him as his son.

The elders became resentful of all the honours bestowed on this stranger from a distant foreign land and, after a year, convinced the king to send him back to his mother, the mysterious black queen. Menelik left Jerusalem accompanied by the first-born sons of all the elders. One of them was Azarius, son of Zadoc, the High Priest of Israel. Without Menelik's knowledge, Azarius stole the Ark of the Covenant from the Holy of the Holies in the Temple and convinced Menelik — after they had journeyed such a long distance it was impossible to turn back — that this was the will of God. The Ark had arrived in Ethiopia.

Krakowski's eyes began to burn; the lines became a blur. Exhausted, he took off his reading glasses and closed his eyes. He ran his fingers over the crumpled pages of his father's notes; perhaps touching them would help make sense of what he had just read. So much of it was incomplete, almost deliberately vague.

Despite all that, holding the very documents his father had hidden in the violin case – the trade for the lives of his sons – was profoundly moving. His father was speaking to him, guiding him.

The cryptic references to *Dokumente in der Schweiz* – documents in Switzerland – could only mean 'the deposit box,' he mumbled to himself. *That's the promise. It has to be! And, the Empress holds the key. Of course; it all fits,* he thought. Krakowski pushed the papers carefully back into his briefcase. *Tomorrow,* he thought and let out a deep sigh. *Tomorrow I will know.*

72

'This way please,' the receptionist said and showed Krakowski to a private waiting room. 'Dr Ulrich will be with you in a moment.' Krakowski noted how the paintings and antiques gave an air of understated opulence; more like the Fifth Avenue apartment of a wealthy American industrialist than a waiting room in a Swiss bank.

'We've been expecting you, Professor,' said the director extending his hand. 'You have a truly extraordinary story. Needless to say, we have followed the trial in the press with great interest.' He motioned for Krakowski to sit again. 'And thank you for keeping Ulrich Privatbank out of the papers. Our confidentiality is something we prize very highly,' he added. 'May I offer you some coffee?'

'No, thank you. As you might understand ... I'm anxious to find out if my father's deposit box is still here after all this time.'

'No reason it shouldn't be.' The director's tone changed. 'My family has offered our valued clients world-class security and discretion for over two hundred years.'

Krakowski looked straight at the director. 'Indeed. I appreciate that. As I understand it, my father's account was opened before the War.'

'We have of course made enquiries since you called. You will be pleased to hear that your understanding is correct. There is a deposit box and your access steps are, as you know, very specific.'

Krakowski looked up, unable to hide his excitement. 'It's here?'

'Yes,' said the director. 'I assure you, we always honour our obligations. The passage of time is not an issue.'

'So ... where to from here?'

'Your father's instructions, according to our records, contain several ...'

'Two passwords and an identification number,' interrupted Krakowski.

'Quite. We have the latest technology here to facilitate those checks. If you would care to follow me.'

Moving quickly and silently through three stories of concrete and steel, the express elevator took only moments to reach the vault. 'Through there,' said the director, pointing to a massive, round steel door at the end of a brightly lit corridor.

'As you can see, everything is computerised. Much more secure than people, don't you think? All the information has to be entered on the keyboard here. Let me show you.'

After the director had left, Krakowski took off his jacket, hung it over the back of the chair and sat down in front of the computer. He carefully punched in the letters R, O, H and A and pressed 'Enter'. A button labelled 'Next' appeared and, still holding his breath, he entered 'PARZIFAL'. A red flashing 'error' appeared on the screen, followed by 'Try again'.

Krakowski stared at the screen, his heart racing. He was sure his middle name was the second password. Yet, something was obviously wrong. But what? Krakowski loosened his tie. 'Think, man, think!' He, tried to calm himself. *The spelling*, he thought, taking a deep breath, *it has to be the spelling. Parzifal, Parzifal,* he read over and over.

Then he remembered he'd read something on the plane. He opened his briefcase and searched for the copy of Wolfram von Eschenbach's epic he had bought in Sydney. *Of course*, he thought, *PARZIVAL, the original spelling's different!* He punched in 'PARZIVAL', pausing before he typed the 'v', and held his breath. 'Next' said the screen.

Krakowski sat back, looked to the heavens and nodded. *Thank you, thank you,* he was saying to himself. *Only the number to go.*

He opened his wallet and took out a small piece of paper with the number noted on the violin's sound post. He slowly typed in the long number. Before pressing 'Enter', he compared it several times with the number on the paper.

'Access granted' said the screen.

Krakowski was exhausted, but now all he had to do was wait. His thoughts drifted back and the first image was of his father looking at him with love and with pain as they stood together at Auschwitz. He remembered the promise he made to the man he'd loved so dearly, but known so little. And here, now, something momentous was coming towards him from the past, something that had been waiting for him for a long time. A loud beep broke the silence. The black glass door in the wall slid open and a steel box appeared on a conveyer belt.

This whole procedure, thought Krakowski, *is exactly like a cremation, only in reverse.* This coffin was not leaving the world through the furnace, it was being returned from deep within the earth.

Krakowski lifted the box and found it surprisingly heavy. He placed it on the table and noted a keypad on the top right hand corner. He punched in the access code, the indicator light flashed green and the lid clicked open. Inside another, smaller, metal container sat his father's original deposit box. The lock, the final obstruction, had been removed.

Krakowski, hand shaking, applied a little gentle pressure and prised it open.

The contents have been methodically arranged, he thought, *just like Father would have done.* On top was a bundle of neatly folded letters tied with ribbon. Then came several larger documents with tissue paper in between; old parchments looking brittle and faded. At the bottom – taking up most of the box – was a long, rectangular object wrapped tightly in linen, like a shroud.

Krakowski untied the ribbon and reached for the top letter. The documents were assembled as a trail to the past; the most recent on top, the oldest at the bottom. He sat down, trying to calm himself, and began to read. The first letter, written in French, was dated January 1917.

My beloved son, what you are about to read will no doubt cause some anguish and pain. Yet, I hope and trust that once you learn the truth, you will understand ...

Diderot's letter to his son – my father, Krakowski thought. *How extraordinary. This is the one referred to in the note to Madame Colbert – 'my letter will explain everything'.*

Krakowski read for several hours. He was only interrupted by a phone call from Dr Ulrich, politely offering refreshments.

73

Carrington put on his wig, adjusted his gown and was headed for the door when his mobile rang.

'Marcus, it's me, Benjamin.'

'Where are you?'

'In a bank vault in Zurich.'

'How did it go? What did you find?'

'Are you near a fax? I want to send you something.'

'Send it here to my chambers, I'm late for court. Newman had another stroke; he's in a bad way.'

'Just as we thought. Please, call me back as soon as you can, but read what I'm about to send you first. I know you'll find it difficult to believe ...'

'Sounds intriguing.'

'It is. More than you can possibly imagine. I'll wait here for your call.'

'I've got to go.' Carrington hung up, grabbed his brief and hurried out of the room.

Archibald advised the court that the Accused had suffered another stroke during the night, leaving him paralysed and unable to speak. The trial was over and Newman, albeit severely disabled, even close to death, was a free man.

Archibald walked over to Carrington and held out his hand. 'We'll call it a draw, Marcus, what do you think?'

'I didn't realise this was a contest,' Carrington replied, closing his brief. 'You know better than I, who, or shall I say, what, your client really is.'

'Come on, Marcus, you know that's not our job. Without Hoffmeister's evidence you wouldn't have got a conviction, admit it.'

'Someone once told me there's nothing quite as unpredictable as a jury trial. I've never forgotten that, Archie.'

Carrington hurried back to his chambers and went straight to the fax machine. The green light was on, with several pages waiting in the tray.

Across the top of the first page, Krakowski had scrawled: 'Marcus, please read this and phone me. I need your counsel. I will stay here and wait for your call. Ben.' Carrington cleared the law books off his leather chair, turned on the lamp and began to read.

The first page was barely legible – a copy of a papyrus in French, with a paragraph in Latin towards the end. The letter from a Fra. Armand de Blanquefort to Fra. Jacques de Molay, Grand Master of the Templars, was dated October 1305. The second page was a typed translation:

We quit Axum with the Holy Relic some three months past and have now reached the Nile. Regrettably, what follows is not good news.

Our number has been reduced to five. Two of our brothers perished during the most arduous of journeys. We have endured great hardships and deprivation and have encountered many dangers. We can trust no one and the Abyssinians have pursued us all the way. Our Nubian servants have turned hostile and we cannot go on without them. We are weak and in poor health. I fear for our future and the safety of the precious treasure in our care.

Carrington took off his glasses and looked at the small ibis-headed statue of Thoth standing on his desk.

I have asked the Good Lord for guidance and devised the following plan: I believe it is only a matter of hours before the Abyssinians find us. I am sending Fra. Bernard, who is strongest and youngest among us, ahead to

Alexandria in the hope that he can elude our enemies and make the journey safely back to France.

After much deliberation, we have decided to send you one of the _____ in case we fail to _____ and the Holy _____ lost _____ hope _____ approval.

Carrington held the fax up towards the light. He followed the text with his finger until he reached the missing parts. *Lacuna,* he thought, *missing bits in the manuscript; what a pity.* Then he continued to read:

The other _____ has been well hidden in the place recorded below and is out of our enemies' reach _____

The next part in Latin contained elaborate directions to a hiding place. Returning to French again, the letter concluded:

I know this is a desperate measure, but we have become desperate men near the end of our strength. We entrust our fate to God.

Your obedient servant,
Armand de Blanquefort

October 1305. Interesting, Carrington thought. That's two years before the Templars were arrested by King Philip the Fair. That particular mass arrest was sanctioned by the Pope himself, he noted. He reached for the phone and dialled.

Krakowski sat up with a jolt. 'Are you really telling me that you're sitting somewhere underground in a Swiss bank vault?' Carrington joked. 'Reading old manuscripts? Too much schnapps, more like.'

'Have you read my fax? What do you think?'

'Calm down, Benjamin. Very interesting, but ...'

'But you don't know half of it,' Krakowski interjected. 'Have you noticed the missing parts? I think I know what that's about.'

'You do?'

'Yes, I have Diderot's letter to his son that explains it all. I know you'll find this hard to believe – part of me still can't –

but Diderot's son was my father ...' Krakowski said quietly.

'Come on, Ben, are you seriously suggesting Diderot was your grandfather? You are joking, surely.'

'I haven't been more serious in my life, Marcus. That's what I couldn't tell you the other day – I had to come to terms with it myself first,' Krakowski explained. 'It's all in my father's papers; it all fits. There's proof.'

'Go on.'

'Marcus, I don't know how else to put it. This is ... a matter of monumental importance. And it's all here, right in front of me.'

Carrington said nothing.

'Marcus, you're still there, right? I know, it sounds ... well ... let me convince you.'

'Please do.'

'The Holy Relic, the one in the Blanquefort letter is the Ark of the Covenant. The Templars, removed – no, stole – it from Axum in Ethiopia in 1305.'

'Come on, Ben. That's a tall one.'

'You must believe me! Wait, it gets better. This is what is here: *We have decided to send you one of the* _____ Krakowski quoted. 'Do you know what Blanquefort sent to the Grand Master, in France, from Egypt, in an act of final desperation?' Krakowski asked, his voice sounding shrill.

'Tell me.'

'One of the two ...' whispered Krakowski.

'Yes? I can hardly hear you.'

'One of the two Tablets of Moses – the Tablets of the Law!'

'Benjamin, come on ...'

'I'm serious, Marcus, I really am.'

'How can you say that? How can you be so sure?'

'Why? Because ... because it's right here in front of me!'

'What do you mean?'

'I mean, right here in front of me on the table.'

'What does it look like?' Carrington asked, turning serious.

'Describe it to me.'

'I've never seen anything quite like it. It's very strange, not at all what you would expect,' Krakowski replied.

'In what way?'

'Well, to begin with, it's very heavy. Like stone, only heavier.'

'What do you mean?'

'The material looks like stone, but isn't, if you know what I mean. It's bluish, sapphire-like. Like stone, I guess, but different.'

'How big is the tablet?'

'About half-a-metre-or-so long and very heavy. But, when I lifted it, it started to bend; it's flexible. I know this sounds weird, but that's the best I can do.'

'Is anything written on it?'

'Yes, it's covered in writing.'

Carrington's mouth went dry. He had to swallow several times before he could ask the next question. 'What does the writing look like? Describe it to me,' he whispered.

'Well, it looks ... like ...'

'Yes,' Carrington said, impatient. 'What?'

'Just like, you know, hieroglyphs, I suppose. Beautifully carved, mind you,' Krakowski explained.

'The finger of God laying down the Law in Egyptian hieroglyphs?' Carrington asked himself. 'It couldn't be, surely! But then again, why not?'

'Are you still there?' Krakowski asked.

'You know, Ben, the account you just gave me,' Carrington said after a while, 'is identical to the clearest description we have of the Tablets of the Law in the Scriptures. There's only one difference; the writing. Apart from that, it really is the same.'

74

'You look good on television,' Dr Rosen said. She walked across the polished parquetry floor and sat down next to the open window overlooking the piazza. 'How did the commentator put it? He plays with the passion of Rachmaninoff and the virtuosity of Paganini – the melancholy mood of Eastern Europe meets the sunny sparkle of Italy. The Warsaw concert was obviously a great success.'

'You're making me blush. It was very emotional and brought back many memories – most vividly,' Krakowski explained. 'Drink?' He opened a bottle of Chianti and sat down next to her. 'Salute.' They touched glasses. 'And Doktor Bettany charmed the Viennese and loosened their purse strings, I hear.'

'Where did you hear that?' asked Dr Rosen, laughing.

'I read it in *The Times*, actually.'

'Well? Here I am.' Dr Rosen looked expectantly at Krakowski. 'We had a deal, remember?'

'You too? That Swiss deposit box certainly appears to have aroused a great deal of interest lately,' Krakowski observed quietly. 'In many different circles, it would appear.'

'What do you mean?'

'I think I'm being followed – since my visit to the bank in Zurich.'

'Really?'

'Well, at first it was just a hunch. Then, well ... I kept noticing familiar faces – a reflection in a shop window, a face in the audience, at the next table in a restaurant, at the hotel reception. Always young men with Slavic features, in need of a shave. I'm good with faces. I notice such things. Then, in a crowded lift in Warsaw the other day, I overheard a conversation between two of them – in Russian. They clearly assumed I couldn't understand. They mentioned a priest they called the Black Dominican. They were joking about having to report to him twice a day about the crazy musician – me, I assume – standing next to them in the lift. Strange, isn't it? I wish I could tell you more, but ...'

'Perhaps I can help,' Dr Rosen interrupted.

'You can? How?'

'After you left, my father sent for me – urgently, just before his second stroke. I thought – hoped rather – he wanted to make peace with me,' Dr Rosen explained, her eyes turning misty.

'Go on.'

'Instead, he said he wanted to tell me things about his past; things I had to know before it was too late. It was really more like a confession, a rather surprising one, I must say.'

'A confession?' Krakowski raised an eyebrow.

'Yes, I know. Well, at first he was quite rational. He spoke about the War and coming to Australia ... even mentioned my mother, which was really out of character. But then, he got quite agitated and started rambling. I thought he was hallucinating, but now, I'm no longer so sure.'

'In what way?'

'He said some strange things; nothing made sense. For instance, he said that the Cardinal and – his black priest – would stop at nothing to get their hands on ...' Dr Rosen paused mid-sentence. Her attention was taken by a small batch of children running around Bernini's fountain in the busy square below. One jumped into the fountain and began splashing water at the others.

'On what?' said Krakowski, a little annoyed at the break in

the story. 'He mentioned a black priest and a Cardinal?' he went on, turning to look at what had distracted the doctor.

'Yes, and I'm sure I heard him say ... the ark. No, he used the words Holy Ark and the missing ... something; he didn't say what. I didn't take him seriously of course; I thought, you know, he's lost it. But he was adamant, wouldn't let go and kept returning to this weird topic. He said the Ark was on the move – whatever that means – and that even if it were actually found, it couldn't be taken anywhere against its will because it had a will of its own – a divine will.' Dr Rosen became quite animated by her recollection, and kept staring down into the piazza. Krakowski followed her to the window and put his hand on her shoulder.

'This is very strange, my father's notes refer to the very same thing. He even quotes various ancient texts supporting this extraordinary view,' he explained. 'An object with a will of its own, a conduit to the Divine that can influence events, shape history ...'

'And how is it supposed to accomplish all this? What do those ancient texts say about that, Ben?'

'By appealing to – no, guiding,' Krakowski corrected himself, 'something rare and precious.'

'What?'

'The hearts of worthy men.'

Dr Rosen put her hand on Krakowski's arm and turned around to face him. 'And then he said,' she continued, 'that he realised at last that the Cardinal was the wrong man ... that the Ark would not reveal itself to the Church ... that it was now all so clear. He explained that you, you were the chosen one, that you had the missing link within your grasp and that you had been saved for that specific purpose. He also said that the time had arrived – for the Ark to guide you and all you had to do was to listen. These were his exact words.'

'Amazing. The ravings of a confused old man – you think – close to the end? Or something more, perhaps?'

'I don't know what to think, Ben, but I do believe that in a round about way this was as close as he could get to ... some kind of reconciliation. He was trying to, well to justify himself, I guess,' Dr Rosen added quietly. 'He knows he doesn't have much time left. In the end, we all have to come to terms with our life, have to face our ghosts, don't you think?'

Krakowski nodded, and said nothing.

'And then, he did something surprising,' explained Dr Rosen, 'he actually took my hand ...' She stopped in mid-sentence, choking with emotion. 'And told me that he admired my work,' she continued haltingly, 'and that he was proud ...' She reached for her handbag, took out a handkerchief and wiped away tears. 'And just before I left Sydney, I found out from our family solicitor that my father has made a large bequest to the Rosen Foundation,' she said, a faint smile lighting up her troubled face. 'Founded by a Jew!'

'But that's marvellous,' said Krakowski. 'Better late than never. We should drink to that.' He reached for the bottle and refilled their glasses. Dr Rosen looked at Krakowski, a melancholy look casting a shadow across her face, and lifted her glass.

'So, what about this Cardinal and his black priest? How do they fit into all this?' asked Krakowski.

'My father never spoke about the War when I was a child. We, my mother and I that is, didn't really know anything about his life before he came to Australia. Apparently he was actually in Switzerland when Germany surrendered and then travelled to Italy. Right here to Rome. The Vatican to be precise.'

'Interesting ...'

'He stayed in the Vatican for almost a year, he said.'

'Did he tell you what he was doing there?'

'He was – how did he put it now – reinventing himself.'

'How?'

'By helping the Church. He had something the Church wanted – desperately ...'

'Montsegur,' whispered Krakowski, turning pale.

'What did you say?'

'Nothing, please go on.'

'Apparently, during the War, the Germans had found what the Church had been searching for in vain for centuries,' Dr Rosen continued. 'Do you want to know what it was?'

'Tell me.'

'A cache of old manuscripts. The secret archives of the Templars.'

'Hidden by the last Grand Master, Jacques de Molay, in the ruins of a Cathar fortress – Montsegur – just before the mass arrest of the Templars in 1307,' Krakowski added quietly.

Dr Rosen looked stunned. 'You never cease to amaze me, Ben. How do you know all this?'

'From the documents in the safe deposit box,' Krakowski replied. 'There are forces at work here, Bettany, I don't really understand, yet they are real, powerful, primeval.'

Krakowski went on, softly. 'At times I feel like a pawn, a puppet on a string, tied to something reaching out of the distant past I can't understand, pulled along by someone I don't know ... You asked about the deposit box,' Krakowski continued, changing the subject. 'Well, let me show you something.' He walked into the next room, lifted a mirror off the wall and began to open a large wall safe, turning the dials with speed.

'Perhaps you have the heart of a worthy man,' Dr Rosen suggested, following him.

Krakowski opened the safe and carefully lifted out a heavy, rectangular object wrapped in linen. 'Tell me about the Cardinal,' he said.

'Apparently, there was a young Monsignor at the Vatican in 1945, a close friend of my father's. They both came from the same Bavarian mountain village – Berchtesgaden – you see, and had grown up together. The Nazis had smuggled the Templar archives into Switzerland for safekeeping just before the end of the War. My father gave the whole collection to the Church in return for a new identity and passage to Australia. The Monsignor is now a Cardinal; Brand ... – something, in charge of the Office of the Doctrine of the Faith ...'

'The direct successor of the Inquisition. New name, similar methods, same purpose. How neat,' Krakowski interrupted.

'It would appear that my father and the good Cardinal have been collaborating – you know, working together all these years on a ... my father called it a quest. Trying to find something – a relic of enormous importance to the Church in Rome.'

'Did he say what it was?' Krakowski interrupted, holding his breath.

'Unfortunately, he didn't. He was very weak by then and could barely speak. I don't know what he was talking about.'

'But I do.'

'You do?'

'Yes.' Krakowski motioned to the package on the table. 'This, here.'

'Are you serious? What is it?'

'It is ... arguably ...' began Krakowski haltingly, 'the most significant, the most precious artefact on earth, something that belongs to humanity, to all generations still to come ... I can't find the right words, I'm sorry.' Krakowski shook his head in frustration and placed his hand on the parcel. 'Let me put it this way: If I could use music instead of words to describe it, it would have to be the most moving, the most inspired, uplifting piece I could ever hope to compose and I would need the combined genius of a Beethoven, a Mahler and a Mozart to do it justice.'

'What is it, Benjamin?' Dr Rosen asked again. 'Please, tell me.'

'No – I'll show you.' Krakowski started unwrapping the package, carefully untying the knots binding the leather thongs. 'Here it is,' he said, his voice hoarse. Dr Rosen noticed tears in his eyes.

381

'What is this?' she asked again, mesmerised by the object on the table.

'According to the Templar chronicles, it's one of the two Tablets of Moses – the Luchot HaBrit – the Tablets of the Covenant,' Krakowski explained. 'Inscribed with the Ten Commandments, the covenant between man and his Creator.' Dr Rosen looked stunned.

'But these look like Egyptian hieroglyphs,' she said after a while.

'I know ...'

'Is it authentic?'

'I'm not sure, but my father was convinced it was the real thing. It's all in his papers. He believed, you see.'

'May I touch it?'

'Of course, please ...'

Dr Rosen ran the tips of her fingers gently over the smooth, stone-like surface and closed her eyes. She was exploring the tablet with the precision of the gifted surgeon, combining intuition with experience, as only a healer knows how.

'What do you feel?'

At first, Dr Rosen didn't answer. After a while, however, she opened her eyes and looked at Krakowski sitting opposite. 'What I feel, Benjamin, is ... love. It radiates, it flows. I've felt it before in some patients, mainly in extreme situations, close to death. A concentration of grace.'

Krakowski reached for Dr Rosen's hand and kissed it spontaneously. 'You put it so eloquently, Bettany,' he said. 'Do you know what my father wrote about the tablet in his notes?'

'Tell me.'

'He observed that it appears to exude – love. He felt it too, you see, just like you.'

'Is this the missing link then?' Dr Rosen asked, pointing to the tablet.

'No. This is.' Krakowski held up a scroll he had also taken out of the safe.

'Oh, what is it?

'An original letter – a dispatch, sent from Egypt by Armand de Blanquefort, a knight, to the Grand Master of the Templars in 1305,' he answered quietly. 'Which, I believe, will lead us to the other tablet, and, quite possibly, the Ark itself.'

'This brittle old papyrus?' Dr Rosen asked. 'Is that all you need?'

Krakowski smiled. 'No, we do need a little more than that.'

'What?'

'Faith and a bit of luck.'

75

Avoiding the early morning traffic choking the Eternal City wasn't easy. However, that was precisely what the car sent by the Cardinal was trying to do by following the narrow Rome back streets. Father Habakkuk was to be brought as quickly as possible from the airport to the Vatican. The Cardinal didn't like to be kept waiting.

The Swiss Guard saluted, and escorted Habakkuk up the wide marble staircase to the Cardinal's private apartment; an honour reserved for the privileged few.

'I have sad news, Eminence; Sir Eric had another stroke,' Habakkuk reported.

'Bad?'

'Yes, I'm afraid. The trial is over.' The Cardinal stood up and walked across to the tall window overlooking the dome of St. Peter's. His thoughts raced back to his early school days more than seventy years ago. To two inseparable friends skiing down icy slopes to school in the valley below. It was a lifetime ago but it felt like yesterday.

'He asked me to give you this.' Habakkuk opened his briefcase.

'Oh, what is it?'

'He called it his final contribution to the quest; a curious document. A single page. Armand de Blanquefort wrote it just before he was killed in Egypt in 1305.'

'Is it authentic?' the Cardinal demanded impatiently.

'Yes, I believe so. I've translated the text; it makes for interesting reading.' He handed the translation to the Cardinal.

These are, I believe, the last words I will be able to record before our enemies overwhelm us. We are surrounded, escape is impossible ...

The Cardinal read the short document several times and then paused, running his finger slowly along the lines. 'It reads like a prayer,' he said at last.

'That's what Sir Eric thought. We actually named it the Blanquefort Prayer.'

How extraordinary; the pieces of the puzzle are finally falling into place, thought the Cardinal, taking off his reading glasses. He reached for the remote control on the table in front of him and turned down the music.

'Krakowski's violin concerto?' Habakkuk asked.

'Yes. A most remarkable piece. It tells me a great deal about the man.' Coming from a connoisseur like the Cardinal, this was a serious compliment.

'What do you make of this?' asked the Cardinal, holding up the page. 'After all, you're the expert here.' A smile crept across Habakkuk's shiny black face; praise from the Cardinal was rare.

'When we place this new document next to Blanquefort's earlier dispatch ...'

'The one he sent with Fra. Bernard to the Grand Master in France?' interjected the Cardinal.

'Yes, the Bernard Dispatch. If we consider them together, with all the other information we have: legend, the Scriptures and well-documented historical facts, they all seem to converge – and fit perfectly.'

'Explain.'

'Assume for the moment that the Kebra Nagast, the Glory of Kings, is historically accurate and the Ark of the Covenant was brought to Ethiopia by King Solomon's son Menelik. Let's use that as our starting point,' Habakkuk said.

'That's quite a leap,' said the Cardinal. 'Most historians would disagree with you; they think it's all just romantic nonsense.'

'Perhaps so, Eminence, but we now have certain evidence – contemporaneous records – to back it up.'

'Go on.'

'Well, it goes like this: Prince Lalibela returns from exile in Jerusalem and wrests the throne from his half-brother, Harbay, with the help of the Templars he's befriended during his stay in the Holy Land. In return, the Templars are granted privileges and actually get to see the Ark. The Templars remain in Ethiopia even after Lalibela's reign – biding their time. Unlike Lalibela, his successor, the new king, is uneasy about the presence of these threatening strangers.' Habakkuk paused before continuing. He knew he had to choose his words carefully.

'He doesn't trust them, and with good reason. The Templars have only one aim, only one reason for staying in Ethiopia – to steal the Ark and take it back to France. And that's precisely what they do in 1305. Proof? Here.' Habakkuk took a sheaf of papers from his briefcase.

'*We quit Axum with the Holy Relic some three months past,*' he quoted from Blanquefort's Bernard Dispatch, '*and have now reached the Nile.*' Habakkuk glanced at the Cardinal. '*... I have devised the following plan ...*'

'We've known about the Bernard Dispatch since '45,' the Cardinal interrupted again. 'It was referred to in Berenger Krakowski's writings.'

'You're right, Eminence, Krakowski mentions it; he even quotes some parts. We also knew about its existence from material purchased from Diderot.'

'Yes, I remember,' the Cardinal agreed.

'But for the first time, Eminence, we have the full text of another contemporaneous document also written by Armand de Blanquefort a short time later – the Prayer – right here.'

Habakkuk held it up like a trophy, 'Actually referring to the Bernard Dispatch. We have corroboration!' he added, excited. 'And then we have this: *The Holy Relic we leave behind is but a shell – empty, its very essence gone,*' Habakkuk read aloud. '*The* _____ *of the Prophet are out of our enemies' reach; one is on its way to France with a dispatch recording the hiding place of the other ...*'

'Well?' asked the Cardinal, 'what does it all mean?'

'This is all new material, Eminence, 'but it does accord with our oral traditions in Ethiopia ... even the secret ones ...'

'The legend about the Templars' theft of the Ark and its glorious return to Axum, handed down from Guardian to Guardian?'

'Precisely. Except, I don't believe it's a legend at all. I believe it's historical fact. And the proof, Eminence, is once again right here ... here in these documents.' Habakkuk tapped the sheaf of papers.

The Cardinal looked at Habakkuk for a few minutes. Though Habakkuk was very bright and undoubtedly an expert, perhaps the best-informed scholar on the subject, he was still unconvinced. Of course, the Cardinal thought, Habakkuk's loyalty to the Church was beyond question, but he was Ethiopian. He'd grown up there; his cultural and emotional ties to it were strong. *All this would have to taint his objectivity*, thought the Cardinal, yet ... Habakkuk could read the doubt in the Cardinal's demeanour, but pressed on.

'Your Eminence, I think we both know what Armand de Blanquefort sent back to France with Fra. Bernard in an act of final desperation. It fully supports Diderot's extraordinary claim regarding an ancient sacred relic in his ...'

'No! We don't know,' the Cardinal interrupted. 'We *think* we know, is perhaps more accurate.'

'Up to a point perhaps, Eminence, but we must consider this,' Habakkuk replied diplomatically. To contradict the Cardinal was never easy. 'The jealously guarded secret handed down by each Guardian of the Ark to his successor since the Ark's return to Axum in 1305, does have a direct bearing on this subject. It cannot be ignored. However ...'

The Cardinal held up his hand. Habakkuk stopped mid-sentence, afraid that he had gone too far. 'There is someone else who would like to hear about this secret,' said the Cardinal, looking at his watch. 'Mass has just finished; if we hurry we might just catch him before the audiences begin ...'

'Someone else?' Habakkuk asked, puzzled. 'Who?'

'The Holy Father. Come.' The Cardinal stood up and hurried towards the door.

76

Pope Julius finished saying morning mass in the Sistine Chapel and was slowly shuffling down the aisle with the help of Sister Bernadette, his minder. At ninety-one, the Pontiff's body was worn out and frail; his mind, however, was as sharp as a rapier.

'Father Habakkuk has arrived, Holiness,' said the Cardinal as the Pope walked past. Sister Bernadette glared at him. Pope Julius stopped and turned.

'Are we getting closer?' he asked, his voice sounding faint.

'I believe so, Holiness. You wanted to know about the theft of the Ark. Father Habakkuk can enlighten us.' Placing his hand on Habakkuk's shoulder, the Cardinal pushed him gently forward like a headmaster showing off his star pupil.

'Come, give me your arm,' said the Pope. 'Walk with me.' Towering over the Pontiff, Habakkuk held out his arm. 'Look, angels and demons; up there.' The Pope pointed to the ceiling. 'So it is down here ... Now, did they really steal the Ark?'

'Yes Holiness, they did.'

'What happened to it?'

'Well, at first, the priests tried to conceal the theft, but it was a catastrophe too big to hide. The Black Emperor sent out his bravest warriors who, as we now know, caught up with the Templars and the Ark in Egypt. The Ark was recovered and returned to Axum; the treacherous knights were killed ...'

'Please tell His Holiness about the secret ...' interjected the Cardinal, realising there wasn't much time.

'Only certain priests were allowed to approach the Ark. After it was returned to Axum and opened for the first time since its removal by the Templars, they found that the tablets were missing. This has been a well-guarded secret ... only the initiated few knew. The Ethiopian clergy's been searching for the tablets ever since – hoping, no, longing, for their return.'

The Pope stopped walking. 'You will find them, my son,' he announced, looking up at Habakkuk with watery eyes, 'but be careful. Remember, angels and demons ...' The Pope's tiny hand, extended to mark the end of the discussion, looked like crushed parchment, wrinkled and almost translucent. *The Ring of the Fisherman*, thought Habakkuk, bending down to kiss the ring.

'I didn't know the Holy Father took a personal interest in this,' Habakkuk said, after the Pope had left the chapel.

'Oh ... more than you can imagine,' replied the Cardinal. The 'chance meeting' with the Pontiff had turned out better than he had expected. He'd just moved his best pawn into a strategic position on the chessboard of his long career.

'If your interpretation is correct, the Templars removed the tablets just before the Ark was recaptured by the Abyssinians.'

'Yes, and actually managed to send one of them back to France with Fra. Bernard – that's the tablet Diderot claims to have discovered in France in the 1880s.' The Cardinal nodded. 'One is on its way to France with a dispatch recording the hiding place of the other,' Habakkuk quoted from the Blanquefort Prayer.

'Leaving an empty, meaningless Ark for the Emperor's men. Ingenious! The Templars had the last laugh, as usual,' said the Cardinal. 'If this is right, the other tablet is most probably still in its original hiding place somewhere in Egypt – waiting,' he added pensively, 'to explode!'

'And we have good reason to believe that Professor Krakowski now has sufficient information to find it,'

Habakkuk pressed on.

'Is that what Sir Eric thought?'

'Yes, Eminence, he was sure. His last words on it were: "My only regret is to be so close, and yet so far ... My punishment has already begun."'

'He said that?'

'Yes. But he also said that, ironically, it was now all up to Krakowski to lead us to the tablet and quite possibly the Ark itself.'

'Oh? And how exactly would he do that? He's a musician, not a biblical scholar!'

Habakkuk smiled. 'Sir Eric met with Krakowski at the hospital and returned the Auschwitz violin papers to him. He had nothing to fear, you see. The trial was practically over by then and he was very ill. But he had a plan ...'

'Oh?' The Cardinal looked bemused.

'He planted an idea ... no, he ignited something in Krakowski – Sir Eric called it the flame of destiny. He challenged Krakowski to complete what his father had begun. A stroke of brilliance, don't you think?' said Habakkuk, carefully watching the Cardinal. 'Sir Eric told me that he had handed the torch leading to the final stage of the quest to Krakowski, convinced he'd carry it all the way because it was his destiny. And all we have to do is follow it.'

'Typically Erich,' the Cardinal said, shaking his head. 'Plotting to the end.'

'Krakowski now appears to have all the necessary information required to complete the task.'

'Assuming of course that Blanquefort's original Bernard Dispatch is among the documents.'

'Quite so,' Habakkuk agreed, 'but Sir Eric was certain the original parchment would be in the Swiss bank.'

'*Die Dokumente in der Schweiz*,' said the Cardinal. 'The treasure we've been looking for since the War. Just waiting in a safe deposit box in Switzerland!'

'To be collected by Professor Krakowski. Precisely!'

'How ironic!' said the Cardinal. Then, carefully watching Habakkuk out of the corner of his eye, he said, 'And what do you think about all this? Have you formed a view?'

'I believe Sir Eric is right, Eminence.'

'And what do you suggest we do next?'

'We'll let Krakowski take us where we cannot go.'

'And how, pray tell me, will you accomplish this?'

'I've arranged for Krakowski to be watched. He's under surveillance, around the clock. Every move, all his conversations; we're following his associates, too.'

The Cardinal was impressed. There was obviously a lot more to Habakkuk than he'd thought. 'How have you managed all that?' he asked.

'Sir Eric introduced me to one of his old and trusted contacts – a Colonel Sorokin, a very resourceful Russian ...'

The Cardinal held up his hand, stopping Habakkuk. 'I don't need to know the detail.'

'I fully understand, Eminence.' Habakkuk was aware his methods were somewhat unorthodox. And the Cardinal was a practical man only interested in results, and prepared to turn a blind eye as long as he and the Church were not compromised.

'If we're right and Blanquefort's original Bernard Dispatch is in fact in the Swiss bank, I'm sure Krakowski will go to Egypt to look for the tablet himself. Sir Eric gave him all the clues ... Krakowski wouldn't be able to resist.'

'And what'll we do? Wait? Hope for the best?' asked the Cardinal.

'Not quite.'

'Oh?'

'I'm going to Egypt to find out more about this,' Habakkuk said, holding up the copy of the Blanquefort Prayer. 'I want to be a step ahead of Maestro Krakowski when he finally comes looking.'

Habakkuk did not elaborate, nor did he mention the

Defender of the Faith or the Brotherhood. Occasionally, even the Church had to deal with the devil – history was full of examples. And besides, he was certain the Cardinal would rather not know.

'And you have all the necessary contacts to do that, I take it?' the Cardinal asked.

Habakkuk nodded. 'Colonel Sorokin is well connected in Egypt.'

'Speaking of Egypt, what about Sir Eric's son? Isn't he in jail there, awaiting trial?'

'Yes, Sir Eric's trying to negotiate his release. And, well, there was something else Sir Eric asked of me, Eminence. In fact, he's asking for a favour.'

'What favour?'

'He wants to make a bequest to the Vatican Museum.'

Surprised, the Cardinal looked up. 'How odd, did he say what it was?'

'No, but he did say that it was something very precious and that you would recognise its significance. He was hoping you would become its champion; that's all I know. Apparently his lawyers will contact you soon.'

'Intriguing,' said the Cardinal, shaking his head. 'Incidentally, Brother Frumentius has been asking after you – repeatedly. He appears to be exceptionally well informed. You will have to deal with him ... he could become a problem. Do I make myself clear?'

'Absolutely, Eminence,' replied Habakkuk, taking a bow.

77

'The ways of Allah – blessing be upon his name – are often difficult to fathom, Ms Gonski,' Jana heard a voice address her in English, 'but always full of wisdom and purpose.' The silky voice sounded vaguely familiar.

Momentarily blinded by the light, as the pillowcase was pulled off her head, Jana squeezed her eyes closed and slowly opened them. She instantly recognised the bearded face looking at her.

'We meet again,' Sheikh Omar continued, 'but regrettably you are still going the wrong way.' The lantern hanging from the centre post cast intricate shadows against the canvas walls of the spacious tent. Fingers of sand reached across the carpets and pointed, accusingly, she thought, at her. Sheikh Omar sat on the floor. Leaning comfortably against a large, colourful cushion, he looked more like a desert prince than a terrorist at the top of the most wanted list. 'Welcome to my humble home. Please sit.' He clapped twice and a dark-skinned youth materialised carrying a large beaten copper platter piled high with fragrant fruit. The boy placed it on the carpet next to Jana. 'Please eat; you are my guest.' Sheikh Omar pointed to the fruit platter.

He speaks with an English accent, Jana thought. *Educated at Oxford or Cambridge, I'd say.*

'Prisoner would be more accurate, don't you think?' she replied curtly, slowly moving her aching limbs. The boat trip had been uncomfortable enough but the wild camel ride into the desert left her stiff and exhausted. Anger had replaced fear.

'I prefer guest,' Sheikh Omar replied calmly. Western women were so ill mannered, he thought, their men were not to be envied. Jana sensed his irritation; smiling wanly, she reached for an orange. She looked up at him and began to peel it.

Clever woman, thought Sheikh Omar, noticing the change in her demeanour.

'If you treat your guests like this,' Jana said, holding up a corner of the dirty blanket draped around her, 'then I must pity your enemies.'

'Our paths cross again,' continued Sheikh Omar, ignoring the remark. He washed his hands in a small silver basin and dried them with a linen cloth handed to him by the boy.

He has beautiful hands, Jana thought, *and manicured nails.*

'Why am I here? What do you want from me?' she demanded. Sheikh Omar winced. He wasn't accustomed to being questioned like this – especially not by a woman, and certainly not in his own tent.

'Why are you here? That's a good question. Why have you come back to Egypt, Ms Gonski? Please tell me.' Jana didn't reply.

'I see. Let me answer for you: you came to assist my enemies – you were looking for me among the dead martyrs at the airport, hoping to identify me – isn't that so?' Sheikh Omar said frostily. 'As you can see, I'm still very much alive – disappointed?' Jana began to eat her orange in silence. 'You have nothing to say?'

Jana swallowed. 'You killed innocent people,' she snapped. 'Friends of mine died that day ...'

'That is regrettable – war is brutal.'

'Yes. Yes it is. And brutal is something you know about.'

'But the man with you – Mr Carrington, I believe; he will arrive tomorrow from Australia?' Sheikh Omar continued, ignoring her question. 'I wonder why he's coming to Egypt – do you know?'

'I'm sure your spies will be able to tell you, but you still haven't told me why you brought me here.'

Sheikh Omar chuckled. 'You will help me send a message to my enemies – a very memorable one, I hope; impossible to ignore and hard to forget ...'

'What do you mean?'

'Such impatience. You will find out soon enough,' Sheikh Omar replied. 'But for now ...' Loud shouting coming from outside interrupted him. A man burst into the tent, tore down the lantern and extinguished the candle. The shouting stopped and Jana could hear engine noise – coming closer. *A helicopter,* she thought, *a search party?*

'But for now,' Sheikh Omar continued in the darkness, 'I'm afraid I will have to send you on another little journey.'

78

Brother Frumentius stood behind the column, watching. Once Habakkuk had walked past, he stepped out of the shadows. 'Are you avoiding me?' he whispered, linking arms with Habakkuk. 'Keep walking, we're being watched.'

'No, I've only just now returned from Sydney. I had to speak to the Cardinal first, and ...'

'I know; angels and demons ...'

Habakkuk paled and shook his head. 'There, you've done it again; in the Sistine Chapel ... a few minutes ago. How?'

'There are no secrets in this place, you know that.'

'Perhaps not, but ...'

'Did you speak to the Cardinal about Diderot? The archives?'

'He won't give his permission.'

'Aah, perhaps it no longer matters.'

'Oh?'

'Come on, we know you're getting close.'

'You may be right.'

'You know the Ark and the tablets ... belong together,' Frumentius reminded Habakkuk. 'I know you do. The tablets must be returned!'

'I don't agree. We've been down this path before; it's no use.'

Frumentius looked at Habakkuk. 'Can you at least tell me what you've found out? You promised. We know about the Krakowski connection and the new Templar papyrus. We know about the Defender of the Faith ... angels and demons ...'

'Well then ...' Habakkuk shrugged. Unnerved by Frumentius' obvious network of spies, he was stalling to work out how to deal with this new threat. He glanced at the elderly man – Frumentius was not only well connected in Rome, but a master of intrigue, even by Vatican standards. Habakkuk knew how dangerous that could be.

'All right. Yes, I believe we are very close.'

'Egypt is the key?'

'Yes. Armand de Blanquefort and his knights; it's quite complicated.'

'Try me.'

'No, not here!' Habakkuk looked around. Being seen with Frumentius like this could turn into a problem. 'Why don't you come with me to Egypt and see for yourself? I'm leaving tomorrow.'

'Are you serious?' Frumentius said, surprised.

'Yes. I promised, remember?' replied Habakkuk, a smile spreading. It was safer to have Frumentius by his side, he thought, than to have his obviously well informed agents poke around in Egypt – or worse still – interfere at this critical time. 'You must deal with Frumentius,' he heard the Cardinal say.

He would do just that. This way, he could keep an eye on Frumentius and bide his time. He was certain the Cardinal would approve.

79

The tiny flame flickered restlessly in the terracotta oil lamp left behind by the guards; crazy shadows danced on the stone walls of the chamber like dragon tongues. At first, Jana couldn't see beyond the bright halo surrounding the flame. When her eyes became accustomed to the gloom, strange objects appeared to float towards her out of the shadows.

To her left, a pair of large statues carved from black granite guarded the entrance to the tomb. One had the slim, shapely body of a woman and the head of a lioness; the other, the head of a hawk and the body of a man. A wooden sarcophagus, its lid half open, was wedged against the wall behind the statues. Jana didn't have the courage to see if the mummy was still inside. Crouching on the floor on her right, a jackal-headed creature was protecting four translucent alabaster Canopic jars. In each were the organs of another deceased, placed near the mummified bodies in the hope of being reunited in the afterlife.

Precious loot from countless graves, thought Jana, looking in awe at the burial treasures surrounding her. *No doubt the work of callous tomb-robbers, oblivious to the dreams of the dead.* When she lifted the lamp higher, Jana noticed fresco-like paintings on the walls. They were huge but one in particular caught her eye: an ibis-headed god, seated on a throne, an ankh in his left hand, a sceptre in his right.

Thoth, thought Jana, remembering Carrington's lecture. *Oh*

Marcus! What am I doing here?

Jana's hand began to shake, making the flame splutter and then go out. The god receded into the darkness. Fear was no stranger to Jana, yet it took all of her willpower and training to resist screaming. All sense of time disappeared.

When darkness is added to silence, even the faintest sound can appear deafening. Jana heard a scraping noise in the distance. A shaft of light crept slowly down the stairs and something very cold appeared to kiss Jana on the back of the neck. 'It's just a draft,' she reassured herself, watching the light. Suddenly, a key turned reluctantly in a lock, a chain fell to the stone floor and the gate squeaked open.

'Ah, there you are. I see, your lamp's gone out,' said a familiar voice, coming closer. Shielding her face with her hand, Jana lifted her head. Sheikh Omar, flanked by two bodyguards with machine guns, stood in front of her; an executioner sizing up his next victim.

'It's you again,' Jana said, trying to sound confident. 'Your hospitality leaves much to be desired.'

The woman has courage, thought Sheikh Omar, looking down at the creature at his feet. 'How do you like our little treasury? Impressive, wouldn't you say? You are one of the few allowed to see it.' Cowering on the floor, Jana felt small and vulnerable. 'Do you know why?' Jana shook her head. 'Because you are part of it,' Sheikh Omar told her, laughing. 'I may let you live,' she heard him say, 'but only if you do exactly as I tell you. Get up.' Jana stood up. 'Now, take off the chador.' Jana didn't understand. 'The robe,' repeated Sheikh Omar impatiently, 'take it off!'

80

The curfew in force meant that security in Luxor was tight. The army was everywhere and Carrington was taken by jeep to the temporary command centre next to the airport.

At first, he didn't recognise Haddad, standing in front of a whiteboard in the crowded, smoke-filled room. The chief inspector appeared to have aged a decade. His thinning hair was long, unkempt and plastered into place with shiny pomade. His crumpled shirt – unbuttoned at the top – looked like it had been slept in for a week, with a limp tie, dangling annoyingly from a sagging knot half way down his chest. But most disturbing of all, was the look in his eyes: haunted, feverish, desperate. Just like the mood in the room.

Haddad concluded his briefing and walked back to his desk as the officers filed out of the room. Carrington took off his hat and stared at the whiteboard. Several large photos, surrounded by arrows and Arabic writing, were pinned to the middle of the board.

One in particular caught his eye. The image, fuzzy and quite blurred, was of a woman kneeling in front of two men dressed in battle fatigues, their faces hidden behind hound's-tooth patterned scarfs. The men were pointing their machine guns to her head, like game hunters with one foot on their trophy.

The woman didn't look at the camera. Trying in vain to cover her naked breasts with her hands, she kept staring at the floor. Fear began to claw at Carrington's insides.

Haddad looked up from his desk. Recognising his friend, he raised his arms. Their eyes met; the look in Haddad's said it all.

'Jana?' Carrington asked hoarsely. Haddad didn't reply. Instead, he got up awkwardly, walked across to his friend and embraced him without saying anything.

'When?'

'Last night, while you were in the air.'

'How?'

'It shames me to have to say this; it was an inside job. One of our men let the fanatics into the building through a side entrance in the cellar. Several guards were killed – decapitated.' Haddad pointed to one of the photos pinned to the board; headless corpses in pools of blood. 'I insisted she stay at the police station to guarantee her safety. I failed Marcus, I am deeply sorry.'

'It's not your fault.' Carrington regained his composure and put his arm around his friend's shoulder.

'It's very generous of you to say that, but we both know it is. She was my responsibility. I asked for her help, she trusted me, and I failed. That's all there's to it.'

'Self-recriminations will not get her back. But we will – you and I, together; I know it,' Carrington said.

'I would gladly trade my life for hers,' he said, grateful.

'I know you would.' Carrington walked over to the whiteboard. 'How did you get this?' he asked, changing the subject. He pointed to the large photo pinned to the board.

'It was sent to Al Jazeera an hour ago through the internet.'

'Any demands?'

'Unfortunately, no. There was only one line of text: "We have the shameless woman who desecrated our glorious dead".'

'What do you make of that?'

'She was looking at all the bodies after the shooting; she was trying to identify the elusive Defender of the Faith who wasn't there. I'm sure they're referring to that.'

'What do you think they'll do with her?'

'Well, one good thing, I suppose, is the fact that she's still alive. If they wanted to kill her, they would have done so by now. I expect some kind of demand – soon. It fits the pattern.'

'I hope you're right,' Carrington said, taking a closer look at the photo. 'Have you analysed this? Can you get a clearer image?'

'Not yet. It's with Forensics in Cairo. They are working on it.'

'Look, there's something in the background – here.' Carrington pointed to a spot on the wall behind the two gunmen.

'Yes, I can see it,' Haddad agreed, putting on his glasses. 'What do you think it is?'

'It's very blurred of course, but to me it looks like hieroglyphs. Writing on the wall – literally speaking.' Carrington remembered Jack Rogan's remarkable success with dissecting photographs, especially innocuous features lurking in the background.

Haddad looked at his friend. 'Now that you mention it ... yes, you're right. I will call Cairo straight away.'

'Let's see what your lab boys can come up with. Who knows, it might just give us a little clue ...'

'What's wrong?' Carrington asked, walking past the guard into Haddad's office early the next morning. Haddad sat at his desk. He was staring intently ahead.

'This was delivered here just after midnight,' Haddad said, holding up a crumpled piece of paper.

'By whom?'

'A little urchin, running an errand for a stranger in return for a few coins. Anonymous and safe.'

'What is it, a ransom demand?' Carrington asked hopefully.

'See for yourself.'

Carrington read the note. 'What does this mean? The woman

will be executed in three days for having desecrated our glorious dead. What does he want?' Haddad couldn't look at his friend. Instead, he covered his face with his hands.

'Withdraw your forces from Luxor and expel all foreigners or others will share her fate,' Carrington read on. 'It's addressed to you.' He kept staring at the paper in his hand.

'Not exactly what we expected, is it?' Haddad said at last.

'Three days! My God, this is madness. What is he going to do – just kill her?'

'I'm doing all I can, Marcus, believe me, but we're dealing with a fanatic – at least no longer an anonymous one.'

'What do you mean?'

'We did make some progress here last night – significant progress.'

'Oh?'

'Remember, I told you the Americans were following a promising lead about this self-proclaimed Defender of the Faith who appeared out of nowhere. Well, they've come up with this ...'

Haddad walked over to the whiteboard and pointed to a new piece of paper pinned to it. 'The Defender of the Faith has a name – Dr Mamoud Halef Omar, eminent Egyptologist and former director of the Egyptian Museum in Cairo. We even have a photo from his old employment records – right here.'

'Could this really be the man?' muttered Carrington. The man in the photo – handsome, young, in a smart Western suit – looked vaguely familiar.

'Well, here's his profile – straight from the CIA: Mamoud Halef Omar was educated at an exclusive French boarding school in Alexandria and then studied in Paris and Cambridge where he obtained his PhD. He returned to Egypt and commenced work at the Egyptian Antiquities Organisation in Cairo. He rose rapidly to prominence and became Deputy Director of the Egyptian Museum in Cairo at an early age,' Haddad read.

'Now here's the really interesting bit: In 1992, he became embroiled in a much publicised scandal involving an important find in Luxor. According to the records of the investigation by his Department, Omar refused to acknowledge the discovery of an old papyrus found by one of his colleagues and tried to suppress the find. The manuscript itself vanished. At the same time, a number of valuable antiquities were stolen from the museum and various excavation sites throughout Egypt and it was widely rumoured that Omar was somehow involved. Omar disappeared before the enquiry was completed and charges could be laid. The file was closed. According to the colleague who found the papyrus the document was an important fourteenth century letter written in French by one of the Knights Templar – Armand de Blanquefort.'

'Could you repeat that?' Carrington interrupted excitedly. Haddad handed him the report.

Carrington read the passage again and smiled. He reached into his coat pocket, pulled out a single sheet of paper and pinned it to the whiteboard.

'What's this?' Haddad asked, putting on his glasses.

'This, my friend, is a copy of the papyrus found by Dr Omar's colleague.' Haddad opened his mouth to say something but was, momentarily, speechless. 'Well, what are you going to do – sit there?' Carrington asked, reprimanding his friend.

'No, of course not! Where on earth did you get this?' Carrington just shrugged. 'I'm trying to find out as much as I can about Dr Mamoud Omar – know your enemy, remember, Marcus Aurelius? I've already arranged for Professor Khalil to come here this morning – all the way from Cairo.'

'Who is Professor Khalil?'

'The Director of the Egyptian Museum in Cairo; Omar's former assistant who found the papyrus. I'm sure the good professor would be most interested to know how you got your hands on that.' Haddad pointed to the whiteboard.

'I'm sorry. I'm just anxious – the relentless sand in the hour glass ...' said Carrington, regretting the earlier curt remark.

'I know.'

'What's he like?'

'She, not he,' Haddad corrected, looking out the window. 'You'll find out in a moment; she's just getting out of the car. But, how ... did you?' asked Haddad, pointing to the piece of paper Carrington had just pinned to the whiteboard.

'I'll tell you when she gets here.'

81

'You are full of surprises, Chief Inspector,' Fatima Khalil said, holding out her hand. 'A phone call at dawn, an Army jeep with a military escort and an Air Force jet, all just for me. How exciting.'

She lit a cigarette and inhaled deeply, enjoying the nicotine rush. 'Well, here I am. Surely you didn't bring me all this way to discuss the inundation level of the Nile?'

Carrington couldn't help but admire the confidence of the elegant woman leaning casually against Haddad's desk. She reminded him instantly of Dr Rosen – same aura, same spark, same vintage. For a Muslim woman to succeed in Egypt and reach high office as she had obviously done, was remarkable in itself. Haddad introduced Carrington.

'What you told me on the phone was intriguing enough, to say the least. I'm used to mysteries, it goes with my job,' Professor Khalil said, laughing, 'but there's obviously more to all this.'

'I'll let Marcus explain the rest,' Haddad said. 'This part should really come from a scholar, not a policeman.'

Carrington walked across to the whiteboard, removed the sheet of paper he had pinned there earlier and handed it to Professor Khalil. The expression on her face changed abruptly. She stubbed her cigarette out in the ashtray on Haddad's desk and held up the paper with both hands.

'Where did you get this?' she asked quietly. Her voice

sounded hoarse and had lost its earlier confidence.

'It was offered for sale.'

'By whom?'

'This man, we believe.' Haddad handed Omar's personnel photo to Professor Khalil.

'Omar?' The professor paled.

'It would appear so.' Carrington nodded.

'What do you want from me?'

'Your help, Professor. A woman's life may depend on it.' Carrington handed the photo of Jana kneeling half naked in front of her captors to Professor Khalil.

'You knew Omar very well. You worked with him for years, you were colleagues. We need to find out all we can about him. Quickly,' Carrington continued.

'Yes, but that was years ago.' Professor Khalil fumbled nervously with her handbag and lit another cigarette.

'You found the Templar papyrus. It was your discovery, a significant one, I believe,' interrupted Haddad.

'Yes it was,' Professor Khalil agreed, 'but the scandal, the investigation, the ruined careers and the innuendos that followed – is a chapter in my life I would rather forget.'

'I completely understand,' Carrington said, 'but – and please forgive me for saying this – that's a luxury we just cannot afford in this case.' Professor Khalil glanced again at the photo in her hand and nodded.

'Omar is one of the most brilliant men I have ever come across. He's a gifted linguist with a phenomenal memory. He's charming, witty, the proverbial walking lexicon; a genius,' Professor Khalil explained quietly, 'especially with ancient languages. We called him our petit Champollion – after the decipherer of the hieroglyphs – I think he rather liked that.'

'Who wouldn't?' said Carrington.

'Quite. Anyway, he had it all: career, international acclaim, and a beautiful French wife. He was very ambitious and extremely jealous. When his wife left him, it all changed. He became a different man.'

'In what way?' Carrington asked.

'She had an affair with one of his colleagues – a French archaeologist – and ran off to France with him. And Omar became a virtual recluse, introverted, a loner. And, while religion had never played a major part in his life, he turned to Islam – in a most radical way ...' Haddad locked eyes with Carrington. 'He took a dislike to all foreigners, especially tourists visiting ancient sites,' continued Professor Khalil. 'He called them infidels, unwelcome intruders. It was as if ...' she paused, searching for the right words, 'he had declared war on the world – the Western world, if you know what I mean. He grew a beard and discarded Western clothes, preferring sandals and the simple jalabiya. We actually used to tease him about it.' Professor Khalil's face held a faint smile as she remembered her former colleague dressed like a cleric.

'And then, he became obsessed with something he'd discovered during his research; it had to do with the holy places of Islam. I remember, he was writing a paper on it. He was always writing papers, translating old texts and publishing articles. He was doing some work on the Temple Mount in Jerusalem, the Al-Aqsa Mosque and the Dome of the Rock, to be precise. Inside the Dome there's an outcropping of the bedrock of Mount Moriah with an indentation, a mark in the rock, believed to be the footprint left by the prophet Mohammed as he leapt into heaven. This is also the site of the original temple of Solomon which, as you know, was built to house the Ark of the Covenant.' Professor Khalil sensed a growing impatience in her audience.

'There's a reason I'm telling you all this,' she explained. 'You want information about the man I knew. This is all part of it – an essential part.'

'Please do go on,' Haddad said, encouraging her.

'He was fascinated by the Knights Templar ... they occupied the Al-Aqsa Mosque for seven years during the Crusades ... I'm not sure if you knew that. Anyway, he was convinced they'd come to Jerusalem with a secret mission – looking for something.'

'What exactly?' asked Carrington. Professor Khalil looked wistfully at him and reached for the ashtray; she was obviously playing for time.

'The Ark of the Covenant,' she replied quietly at last.

'And this obsession, you mentioned,' Carrington asked, 'can you tell us more about that?'

'The Ark of the Covenant, well ... more accurately its contents were at the very centre of his mania. Omar was sure that if he discovered the legendary Tablets of Moses – assuming of course they did in fact exist – it would be the ultimate prize; enormous religious and political ramifications. He called them the Holy Grail of Archaeology. And I suppose, in a way, they would be just that. What he had come across in his research was an ancient Ethiopian text – the Kebra Nagast. Are you familiar with it?' Professor Khalil asked, looking at Carrington.

'I am. Please go on.'

'And the Ethiopian legend about the disappearance of the tabotat – the theft of the Ark by the Templars?' Carrington nodded. 'Omar firmly believed the legend was based on fact. We had many arguments about that. On this subject he appeared totally inflexible; completely convinced, without any objectivity. He had the certainty of a somnambulist.'

'I'm afraid you're losing me here,' Haddad interrupted.

'I'll be brief,' promised Professor Khalil. 'This is the connection: the discovery of the Templar letter – a simple papyrus wrapped around a dagger with the Blanquefort family crest engraved on the blade, was the first, well, no, it was the only tangible piece of evidence to suggest that the Ethiopian legend may be fact. It became an obsession. This led to the scandal I mentioned, the investigation and his ultimate dismissal and subsequent disappearance. But you know all about that.'

'Do you think Omar still feels the same way about finding that elusive Holy Grail of Archaeology? After all these years?'

'An obsession like Omar's doesn't go away; it only becomes stronger and more compelling.'

'Then why would he have offered the letter for sale – just recently? How do we explain that? Doesn't that suggest the opposite?' Carrington probed.

'Not necessarily. Without knowing the circumstances, it's difficult for me to say, but just prior to the scandal, he wanted to do just that.'

'What? Sell the papyrus – but why?'

'No – not actually sell it, but offer it for sale, to find out who might be interested. The idea behind it was simple: anyone showing interest in such an obscure document had to know a great deal about the subject and could therefore ...'

'Have some information concerning the whereabouts of the hidden tablet – information about the hiding place ...' interjected Carrington.

'Precisely. Offer the papyrus for sale to flush out what others might know.'

'Ingenious.'

'Classic Omar.'

'If Omar were to be offered that information now, what do you think he would do?' Carrington asked, watching Professor Khalil carefully.

'What are you suggesting – information concerning the hiding place referred to in the papyrus?' Carrington nodded. 'He would do anything to get his hands on it,' Professor Khalil replied without hesitation.

'Do you think he would trade the life of a woman – an infidel – in return?'

'He would trade his own soul.'

'I was hoping you would say that.'

'Don't look so glum, he'll call back, you'll see,' said Haddad, slapping Carrington encouragingly on the back.

'I've tried all morning. His mobile is switched off,' Carrington complained.

'But you spoke to his housekeeper in London ...'

'She wasn't much help. All she said was that Krakowski is giving a charity concert in Rome.'

'When?'

'Tonight. We're running out of time!'

'Well, why don't you go to Rome and talk to him? At least you know he'll be there; it may be the only way.'

'Are you serious? Do you think I could get there in time?' Carrington asked hopefully.

'Sure. You can go back to Cairo with Professor Khalil – her plane is leaving shortly. I'll make sure you're on a connecting flight to Rome.'

'And you'll make contact with Omar as we agreed?' fussed Carrington, pacing nervously up and down in front of Haddad's desk.

'Keep calm. Just leave that to me,' Haddad said. Carrington smiled at him gratefully.

Carrington sat next to Professor Khalil in the Air Force jet returning to Cairo. Apart from some military personnel chatting in the back, they were alone in the cabin.

'I would value your opinion on this,' said Carrington, taking the enhanced image of the hostage photo out of his pocket. 'What do you make of it?' Carrington pointed to the wall in the background behind the armed guards in the picture. 'Something about it looks vaguely familiar to me. I think I've seen this before – somewhere.'

Professor Khalil held the photo close to her face. 'Here, this might help,' said Carrington, handing her a magnifying glass.

'That's better. Well, this is rather interesting. Firstly, here on the right – it's a classic composition: Thoth on a throne with an ankh in his left hand and a staff in his right. You can just see the ibis head here,' said the professor, pointing to the curved beak behind the guard on the right. 'And on the left we have a man, the deceased I'd say, paying homage to the god. The portion of text here, reading from left to right, is from the Book of the Dead, Chapter 94,' came the precise answer. 'This is a tomb and what's particularly noteworthy is the exceptional quality of the painting; pity this isn't in colour. I agree with you, there's something rather familiar about the composition ... I wonder ...'

'What's on your mind?'

'Just a hunch. I'd prefer to look it up in our library first ... this is too serious for speculation.'

'Sure. Would you?' Carrington realised there was no point in pressing the professor for more.

'Certainly.' She put her hand reassuringly on his arm, enjoying the closeness of this interesting man sitting next to her. 'I'm terribly sorry about your family; Naguib told me. Regrettably, we live in violent times. If Omar is really behind all this, I will certainly do all I can to help, you can count on it. I too have a score to settle, remember?'

'We have two days,' Carrington reminded her.

'I'm well aware of that.'

'If you find anything, anything at all, please call me, day or night.'

'I will. And if you should really get your hands on Blanquefort's dispatch with the instructions ...'

'You don't think I can, do you?'

'I doubt it.' Professor Khalil shook her head.

'Trust me, I will,' Carrington said confidently. 'Do you want to know why?'

'Tell me.'

'Because I know where it is.'

82

First, the jumbo circled the Eternal City, and then lined up to land. Carrington turned on his mobile and glanced at the screen. *At last*, he thought and began to press the buttons. *Concert starts 8 pm – Colosseum. Ticket at entrance. Ben.* Carrington looked at his watch; he would be cutting it fine.

The taxi driver ignored the blaring horns of the cars stalling behind him, and pulled up next to a double-parked stretch limo. Carrington paid the fare and ran towards the entrance. It was five minutes to eight.

Carrington felt like an intruder in his crumpled tweed jacket and khaki slacks; everyone around him was dressed in dinner suits and evening gowns. Using his few words of Italian, Carrington tried to explain to the security guard at the gate that a ticket was supposed to be waiting for him. At first, the guard just eyed him suspiciously. However, as soon as Carrington mentioned Krakowski's name, a ticket materialised and he was shown to his row. *The power of fame*, he thought and settled gratefully into his seat. Slowly, the excited voices around him fell silent as the lights went out.

Suddenly, out of the darkness below, came a strange sound – the unmistakable roar of a lion – followed by steel clashing against steel. Conjuring up images of swords, shields and battle axes, the eerie sound effects spoke of combat, blood and death; a cruel cacophony of suffering long past. Carrington looked up.

Fingers of coloured light parted the darkness and began to explore the top of the open arena. Illuminating an arch here, a column there, the light beams spiralled slowly downwards.

When the light reached the stage at the bottom of the arena, the orchestra began to play Handel's Entry of the Queen of Sheba. A tall woman wearing a black evening gown stepped into the pool of light. Leaning forward, Carrington recognised Dr Rosen.

'Welcome,' said the lady in black, speaking English. An Italian translation appeared on two large TV screens mounted on the crumbling stone walls behind the stage. 'I'm sure most of you would have wondered why the Colosseum – such a notorious venue – was chosen for this occasion. A venue famous for its violent past, where life was cheap and countless people died in the most barbaric circumstances to entertain the bloodthirsty citizens of Imperial Rome. The choice, ladies and gentlemen, was quite deliberate. What brings you here tonight is a noble cause.' Dr Rosen paused, letting her voice echo through the ancient edifice, and slowly raised her arms in a gesture of embrace.

'We can rise above the cruel and the callous; we can turn a place like this into an arena of compassion and generosity ...' The audience responded with enthusiastic applause.

She's a natural, marvelled Carrington, *no wonder they call her the Pied Piper of the Chequebook.* Swept along by the adoring crowd, he stood up and began to clap as well.

'I have a little surprise for you,' Dr Rosen announced. 'There will be a small addition to our program tonight. We are privileged to have as our special guest an artist who, I am sure, is well known to you all and whose music has inspired and delighted us with its extraordinary beauty. Ladies and gentlemen, Maestro Benjamin Krakowski has agreed to open our concert by playing for us the first movement of his Second Violin Concerto.'

Krakowski acknowledged the applause and the cheers by

holding up his violin, and walked on stage. He kissed Dr Rosen gallantly on the cheek, bowed towards the audience and then turned around to face the orchestra seated behind him.

A short distance away – in the Vatican – Cardinal Brandauer turned up the volume on his TV and pressed the record button. The camera zoomed in on Krakowski leading the orchestra through the stirring opening bars of his concerto. *So, this is the man who will lead us to our elusive destination*, mused the cardinal, concentrating on a close-up of Krakowski's expressive face. *I wonder* ... The white hair – a little too long – the closed eyes, the prominent nose and the strong, almost chiselled chin, all looked the part. *Krakowski is a lucky man*, thought the Cardinal, *not only is he a brilliant performer, he looks like one too.*

An usher tapped Carrington on the shoulder during the intermission, mentioned Krakowski's name and pointed to a set of stairs. Threading their way through the noisy crowd lining up for free champagne, they descended into the Colosseum's labyrinthine underworld.

'Salve Caesar, morituri te salutant,' Krakowksi joked, recognising Carrington in the archway. 'According to Signore Cavalli here, this is where the gladiators used to enter the arena. He should know, he's the mayor of Rome,' continued Krakowski, laughing. He introduced Carrington to the smiling gentleman standing next to him. 'You look like you need a drink – here.' Krakowski handed Carrington a glass of champagne. 'What's all this about Jana? Your messages were rather cryptic and my housekeeper is a woman of few words.'

'Can we go somewhere a little more ... you know, private?'

'Sure, how about the lion's den, over there.'

'I thought we were in it,' Carrington replied, pointing to the raucous crowd. Krakowski steered Carrington through another archway. When he turned around, a tall man wearing an ill-fitting tuxedo bumped into him. Apologising profusely in broken Italian, the man walked away. *Another one*, thought Krakowski, *even here.*

'Jana's been abducted – by the terrorists.' Carrington handed a copy of the hostage photo to Krakowski.

Shocked, Krakowski stared at the picture. 'It just goes on, and on, doesn't it? Will it ever stop?'

'When will what stop?' Dr Rosen asked, butting in from behind. 'Benjamin told me you would come. All this way just for our little fund-raiser, I'm impressed.' She kissed Carrington on the cheek. 'It's nice to see you.'

'He didn't come here for that,' Krakowski explained sadly. 'Here, look at this.' When he handed her the hostage photo, a loud gong signalled the end of the intermission.

'We have to go,' said Dr Rosen, returning the photo. 'I'm so sorry, Marcus, this is awful! How can we help?' The gong boomed again, this time more urgently.

Carrington thrust the note announcing Jana's imminent execution into Krakowski's hand. 'Here, read this, Benjamin. I would like to offer the Defender of the Faith something in return for Jana's life,' he said, 'something he has coveted for years ...'

'Oh? What?' Krakowski asked, walking towards the stairs.

Carrington swallowed hard. 'The original Blanquefort letter you found in the deposit box ...'

'You can't be serious!'

'I need your help, Benjamin ...'

'Not now. Please ... after the concert ...'

'It'll be all right, Marcus,' said Dr Rosen, squeezing Carrington's arm. 'Trust me,' she added and hurried after Krakowski.

Instead of returning to his seat, Carrington remained in the gloomy domain of the gladiators and wild beasts. The music sounded different down there; more distant, filtered somehow, by stone and time. Carrington felt suddenly very tired and closed his eyes. When he opened them again, he thought he could see shadows floating up the stairs from below, and hear footsteps. He felt something brushing against his chest, but it was only the mobile vibrating in his shirt pocket.

'I've been trying to ring you all evening,' an excited voice said on the other end. 'I have ...' The reception was poor and the voice trailed off.

'Fatima, I can barely hear you,' Carrington shouted, suddenly wide awake. 'Have you found something?'

'Yes!'

83

Professor Khalil told her driver to wait at the exit and hurried into the Cairo airport terminal. Carrington's plane had just landed.

'Your hunch was right,' Professor Khalil said excitedly, 'not bad for an amateur.' She linked arms with Carrington and guided him to her waiting car. 'We've both seen the tomb painting before – or to put it more accurately – we've seen something very similar before.'

'Similar? That's hardly good news.'

'Patience.' The driver opened the car door and they climbed into the back seat.

'What appeared so familiar to us was this here. It's from another tomb, a famous one – this one.' Professor Khalil handed Carrington a coloured photo showing an almost identical composition. The only difference was the figure facing the god and the text itself. Instead of a man, it was Queen Nefertari who was paying homage to Thoth.

'Queen Nefertari's House of Eternity,' said Carrington, 'of course! Obviously Jana isn't held in there; Nefertari's tomb is open to the public. But the paintings are so similar, one could be forgiven for thinking,' Carrington speculated, 'that they were perhaps painted by the same artist. How strange.'

'That's exactly what we thought at the museum. Fortunately, one of my colleagues remembered this,' Professor Khalil said, handing Carrington a journal – an American university publication. 'Try page 12.'

The article, entitled *The Master Painter of Deir el-Medina – A Workman's Tomb*, was by Dr Reuben Hudson of Chicago. Under the heading was a picture. Carrington pulled the creased copy of the enhanced abduction photo out of his coat pocket and placed it next to the article. The wall scenes were identical.

'The hieroglyphic texts here, and here, are the same. Both are from Chapter 94 of the Book of the Dead. The text in Nefertari's tomb is different,' Professor Khalil said.

Carrington began to read the article. Dr Hudson compared the similarities between the paintings in Queen Nefertari's sumptuous tomb and the tomb of Uni, the humble painter. He concluded that they appeared to be the work of the same artist. Artisans living in the pharaoh's workmen's village often decorated their own tombs with extraordinary artwork. They had access to all the necessary materials and craftsmen. They had both the skills and the opportunity. Moreover, the pharaoh's priests not only permitted, but actually encouraged them to do it.

'Dr Hudson was excavating with his team from Chicago at Deir el-Medina a few years ago when he made an extraordinary discovery,' Professor Khalil explained. 'He opened the tomb of a lowly artisan decorated with the most exquisite paintings normally only found in royal tombs. He noticed how similar the decorations were to those in Nefertari's tomb in the Valley of the Queens which, as you know, is very close to Deir el-Medina. We know for a fact that all the artists who worked on Nefertari's tomb came from Deir el-Medina.'

'Do we know where Uni's tomb is?' Carrington asked hopefully.

'That's the bad news; unfortunately, no. We don't appear to have a record of its exact location. As soon as the excavation project was completed, the tomb was closed up again to preserve it. This is normal practice.'

'Well, someone has to know where it is, surely.'

'Yes, someone obviously does.'

'Who?'

'Omar, of course, and Dr Hudson. Omar knows this area like the back of his hand. He was working for the Supreme Council of Antiquities at the time. Not a single stone moved without his permission.'

'Would the museum know where to reach Dr Hudson?'

'I knew you'd ask that. His address was on his excavation permit. I have written it down for you. Here it is.' Carrington leant across to Professor Khalil and kissed her spontaneously on the cheek.

Professor Khalil's office was on the top floor of the Egyptian Museum. To avoid the tourist crush, they entered the large neoclassical building through a side entrance reserved for staff.

'This is one of my favourite places in the whole world,' Carrington said, following Professor Khalil up the stairs past a pair of gigantic stone effigies of Horus. 'I could just lose myself in here for a while, say, for a year or two ...'

'You mean just move in and sleep in a sarcophagus, for instance?'

'Exactly. I used to dream of something just like that as a boy.'

'I know what you mean. My favourite time is the evening, after all the visitors have gone.'

'A night at the museum?' joked Carrington.

'Something like that, but not up here. In our storage area in the basement, that's the place where everything comes alive ... Down there, we probably have more in storage than on display. I like to explore. I like the surprises, the unexpected, the mystery, the wonder of it all. It's extraordinary what's in there. Come in.' Professor Khalil opened the door to her office, walked across to the large desk in front of a window overlooking the entrance and began to rummage through the mountain of papers.

421

'Any luck with the ...?' she asked casually. Expecting a no, she raised an eyebrow and looked a little mockingly at Carrington.

'This must be your I-told-you-so, look,' joked Carrington, reaching into his pocket. He pulled out an envelope and placed it carefully on top of the desk. 'Open it.'

Professor Khalil opened the envelope and peered inside, disbelief and wonder transforming her face. 'It couldn't be ...' she whispered, running her fingertips along the lines.

'We quit Axum with the Holy Relic some three months past and have now reached the Nile,' she read breathlessly.

Carrington reached for her hand and squeezed it. 'It is. The description of the hiding place is in Latin – quite detailed and precise – down here,' he said, pointing to the bottom of the page. Professor Khalil reached for a notepad and pen and began to translate.

'I've already done it,' Carrington said, laughing, 'but let's see what you come up with.' Professor Khalil appeared not to have heard him and continued to scribble furiously on her pad.

'My Latin is a little rusty, but ...'

'While you engage in linguistic acrobatics, could I please engage in something a little more mundane – like a phone call?' Carrington asked.

'Through there,' said, Professor Khalil. She pointed with her chin to the left, but didn't take her eyes off the page.

To track down Dr Hudson quickly turned into a telecommunications nightmare. After a dozen or so calls to universities, non-English speaking housemaids and polite answering machines, Carrington had finally established that Dr Hudson was holidaying somewhere in New Zealand. His last hope was Hudson's daughter. The reception was bad – crackling annoyingly – and Carrington had to shout to make himself understood. At the end of the confusing conversation he had only written down two things: trout fishing and Huka Lodge.

84

Jack paid the fare and helped the taxi driver with the luggage. He picked up the crumpled envelopes lying under the letterbox bulging with junk mail and walked up the stairs to his front door. *A bath and a beer*, he thought, stretching his stiff limbs. The Nazi money trail investigation had hit a serious obstacle after the abortion of the Newman trial. The Swiss banks had hired a raft of the best lawyers money could buy to muddy the waters. The strategy was simple: Obstruct and delay, the public has a short memory. Jack's paper was losing interest; the dream of the big story was turning sour. Feeling exhausted after the long flight from Los Angeles, Jack went into the kitchen, took a cold can of beer out of the fridge and looked at it longingly. He was about to open it, when Waltzing Matilda chimed cheerfully out of his coat pocket. He put the beer on the kitchen table and answered the call.

'Jack, where are you? It's Marcus.'

'At home. Sydney.'

'I thought you were in the States.'

'Just walked in.'

'Thank God!'

'What do you mean? Where are you?'

'Cairo. Jana's been kidnapped. We need your help.'

Jack knew that Jana had gone to Egypt to assist Haddad in capturing the Defender of the Faith. He also knew that

Carrington had followed her there after the collapse of the trial. However, since he hadn't spoken to either of them since leaving Sydney, the news of Jana's abduction had taken him by complete surprise.

Carrington's request came at a good time: Jack needed a distraction, and the best distraction was a new story. Replacing dejection with anticipation, the excitement churning in his empty stomach told him that Jana's abduction had all the hallmarks of a good story: danger and adventure. Still feeling bad about the photographs and their tiff, Jack was eager to redeem himself. *This could be the opportunity to do just that, he thought.*

Jack left the unopened tinny on the kitchen table and rang for a cab. *I could have just asked him to wait. Well, at least I'm packed,* he thought, looking at his suitcase in the corner. *With a bit of luck, I should just make it.* The Air New Zealand flight to Auckland was due to leave in less than three hours.

'Dr Hudson isn't here, I'm afraid,' said the receptionist politely, eying the handsome stranger with interest. 'He's camping out tonight with his guide. Secret men's fishing business,' she added conspiratorially. The exclusive lodge on the Huka River near Lake Taupo on the North Island of New Zealand was very popular with well-heeled angling enthusiasts from all over the world. The disappointment on Jack's face said it all.

'Can't it wait until tomorrow?' she asked. Jack shook his head sadly. 'Well, let me see ... if it's really that urgent, perhaps one of our boys could take you to the camp if you like,' suggested the hostess, taking pity on the mysterious visitor from Sydney.

Jack was tempted to kiss her. 'Your blood's worth bottling, as we say on the other side of the ditch,' he told her instead. 'Thanks. And a room as well, please?'

'We only have a suite left ... '

'Do I have to mortgage my house?'

'Quite possibly.'

It was already dark when Jack walked into the remote camp by the river with his guide. A small fire was burning in front of a neat tent and the mouth-watering aroma of roasting venison drifted across on the evening breeze.

Dr Hudson sat in a canvas chair facing the river. Surprised, he looked up when the two men walked into the circle of light. Instead of being annoyed by the intrusion, the exuberant American welcomed Jack like an old friend and appeared flattered to have been tracked down so far away from home.

'That's Uni's tomb, no doubt about it,' announced Dr Hudson, pointing to Thoth sitting on his throne. Carrington had faxed a copy of the abduction photo to Jack in Sydney. 'Poor girl. What are these guys doing in the tomb?'

'They're using it as some kind of hiding place.'

'As a hiding place it's certainly a good choice,' Dr Hudson said, refilling Jack's tumbler for the third time. He didn't believe in nips. Jack's head began to spin; he had only eaten airline food for the past three days.

'Is there any way you can help us find the tomb?' Jack asked, trying to concentrate.

'Without actually going there myself, not really. Even then, it wouldn't be easy. We closed it up after we finished the dig. That was years ago. You'd barely notice anything from the outside now,' the American explained. 'I really couldn't show it to you on a map either, or accurately describe its location. The landscape is barren, monotonous and desert-like, if you know what I mean. There are no obvious landmarks or orientation points.' The two guides had finished setting the table and were opening the wine. Dinner was about to be served.

'But ... wait a minute,' the American said, getting a little unsteadily up from his chair. 'I have an idea.' Jack looked at him expectantly. 'There's someone who knows the terrain better than anyone; someone who could find the tomb without difficulty, I'm sure.'

'Who?'

'Ahmad Babar.'

'Who's he?'

'Here, have another scotch,' Dr Hudson said, putting his arm affectionately around Jack's shoulder. 'Come, let's eat and I'll tell you all about him.'

85

Carrington hurried up the stairs – taking two at a time – stormed past the dozing guard and burst into Haddad's Luxor command centre. It was the afternoon of the third day.

'Well, has he agreed?' he demanded breathlessly. He took off his hat and began to massage his neck. Glancing at the whiteboard, he noticed it was covered with new material – photos, arrows and tight columns of Arabic writing. He also noticed that Haddad was still wearing the same limp clothes.

'The scout returns,' Haddad said, waving his assistant impatiently aside. 'We have finally established a reliable channel of communication with Omar – it took some time I'm afraid. Very high-tech and sophisticated, you should know.'

'I see. How does it work?'

'We leave notes for each other in a coffee house – in the bazaar.'

'That's it? Are you serious? Is it reliable?'

'Absolutely. This is Egypt, remember? You must try to understand where you are and who you're dealing with.'

'Did he respond to the proposal?' Carrington ran his fingers nervously through his hair, a haunted look clouding his face. He had spoken to Haddad just before leaving Cairo a few hours before. At that stage, Omar still hadn't replied.

'Here.' Haddad handed Carrington a smooth piece of limestone with Arabic writing on it – in charcoal. 'This was thrown through one of our windows here just before you arrived.'

'From Omar?' Haddad nodded. 'An ostracon; nice touch. What does it say?'

'You have until sunset.'

'Thank God! He has agreed then.'

'It would appear so, but it doesn't give us much time. How did you go?'

'If you had left me some space here, I could add my bit,' Carrington said, pointing to the whiteboard.

'Here.' Haddad tore two pieces of paper off the board. 'Be my guest.'

Carrington took several pages out of his pocket and began to rearrange the board. He removed the copy of the Blanquefort Prayer he had pinned to the board two days before and attached it to the top left hand corner. Then he stuck the hostage photo next to it, followed by Omar's execution note. 'The woman will be executed in three days,' Carrington read out loud. Holding up the ostracon he said: 'You have until sunset. This is the third day. Well, here it is.' He pinned the original Templar dispatch – delivered by Fra. Bernard to the Grand Master in France – to the board and stepped back.

'How did you get it?'

'Krakowski found it among his father's papers in a Swiss bank vault.' Haddad shook his head in disbelief. 'Fortunately, Krakowski had the original with him; in his Rome apartment, in a wall safe. And to his everlasting credit, he didn't hesitate for a moment before handing it over.'

'Is it authentic?' Haddad asked sceptically.

'Absolutely. Here's the proof.' Carrington pinned another page next to the Bernard Dispatch.

'What's that?'

'A translation of the Latin part; detailed instructions to guide us to the exact place where the knights hid the tablet before they were killed by the Emperor's men in 1305.'

Haddad walked across to the board and read the translation.

'This is it?' he asked. 'This could be anywhere.'

'True. You have to know where the knights were killed to make sense of it. In other words, you have to know where Omar's manuscript was found.'

'How would you ... but of course; it was Professor Khalil who found it,' Haddad said excitedly, slapping Carrington on the back. 'She must know.'

'She does.'

'Well?'

'Right here in Luxor.'

Haddad was drumming his fingers impatiently against the desktop. 'But where?'

'You really want to know?'

'Why are scholars always so longwinded?'

'Why are policemen always so impatient?'

'We don't like dead bodies, that's why.'

'We like to get it right.'

'Okay, okay.'

'Professor Khalil believes the tablet is hidden in the Karnak temple complex; all the available evidence appears to suggest this.'

'Great. That's one of the largest archaeological sites in the world. Good luck!'

'But she knows exactly where.'

'She does? What, from these instructions?'

'Yes. Remember she worked in the temple with Omar for several years. They were restoring inscriptions.'

'Of course ... then Omar must know as well ... As soon as he reads this ...'

'Yes, but none of this really matters right now,' Carrington interrupted impatiently. 'We must hand over the original papyrus – we're running out of time! How do we give it to him? What about Jana? Will there be an exchange, what about ... how ... when?'

'Calm down, please ...' Haddad held up his hand. 'Until you

walked in here we had nothing to hand over – right? You have to let me handle this my way. We're in a difficult position here; we have to be very careful.' Haddad scribbled something on a piece of notepaper and then rang the bell on his desk. An old man in a white turban entered almost immediately. Haddad folded the note in half and handed it to him. 'You know what to do. Hurry!'

'What was all that?' Carrington asked.

'I'm arranging the handover. Try to relax – please?'

Carrington took a deep breath. 'You're right of course, it's just the ...'

'Relentless sand in the hourglass,' Haddad interrupted. 'I know.'

Carrington looked gratefully at his friend. 'What do we do now?'

'We wait – this is Egypt. Trust me.'

'Don't you want to know about Dr Hudson and the elusive tomb of the master painter of Deir el-Medina?' Carrington asked. 'Don't tell me you've forgotten already.'

Haddad could barely keep his eyes open. 'Are you telling me you've tracked him down as well?' he asked, rubbing his tired eyes.

'I didn't, but Jack Rogan did; at the Huka Lodge.'

'Another mystery location, what's that?'

'A fishing retreat in New Zealand.'

Haddad shook his head in disbelief. 'And?'

'Dr Hudson remembered the tomb well. It was closed up a few years ago, just as Professor Khalil said. Difficult to find and all that, but there's one ray of hope ...'

'Oh?'

'Ahmad Babar.'

'Who's that?'

'The foreman who was in charge of all the local workers during the dig. He lives somewhere right here in a village near Luxor and apparently knows exactly where to find the tomb.'

Carrington looked at his friend and raised an eyebrow. 'I suppose it's now all up to you, Chief Inspector. This is your turf. I've done my bit, wouldn't you agree?'

Haddad looked stunned. 'Would the position of assistant chief inspector be of any interest to you?' he asked casually. 'We could use resourceful chaps like you.' Carrington shook his head. 'You'd be out of your depth, I suppose, is that it?'

'I'm a scholar, not a policeman, remember?'

Haddad picked up the phone and said something quickly in Arabic. 'Well then, the local chief of police is on his way; he'll take us to Babar.' Haddad said. 'We might as well do something useful while we wait for the handover, don't you think? This is my bit; happy?

'Not bad. That's why you are the chief inspector, see?'

86

Ahmad Babar straightened his aching back and wiped his neck with a wet rag. He was irrigating the family's fields with the shadoof by raising precious Nile water from the river into the channels running between the plots. It was backbreaking work. His donkey was patiently waiting in the shade for his evening trot back to the village. Reaching for his water bottle, Babar noticed a plume of dust drifting through the palm trees.

A jeep skidded along the rutted track and came to a halt next to the donkey. Three men got out; Babar recognised one of them – the local police chief. *This could be trouble*, he thought, watching the men apprehensively.

'Greetings from Dr Hudson,' said the police chief, walking over to his cousin. Carrington and Haddad stayed behind, letting the two men talk in private. The police chief showed something to his cousin, who looked at it for a long time. After much gesticulation and hand wringing, Babar nodded and the two men approached the jeep.

'He knows where it is,' the police chief said in English. 'He thinks he can find it. But we have to be careful. He's really scared.'

'Do you think he knows something ... about ...?' Carrington asked, looking anxious.

'We'll take him back to the station,' Haddad said, frowning at his watch. The sun was rapidly sinking lower, approaching the top of the rugged cliffs to the west. He knew there would be no room for error.

When they walked into the Luxor police station, they were greeted by chaos. A car bomb had just exploded at Sharm el-Sheik – a popular tourist resort on the Red Sea – killing at least eighty. Moments after the bomb went off – detonated by a suicide bomber driving a truck into a crowded restaurant – the Brotherhood for the Liberation of Holy Places had claimed responsibility by sending a taped message to Al Jazeera, the Arabic TV station. Apparently, the attack was in retaliation for the Luxor airport massacre. The message ended with a demand for all foreigners to leave Egypt.

'This is all we need,' fumed Haddad, trying to fend off the pack of excited officers attempting to speak to him all at once.

'Don't let anyone pass unless I say so,' he instructed the guard at the door. 'Come.' He took Carrington by the arm and steered him along the crowded corridor. 'We don't have much time. Close the door.' Haddad walked to his desk and unfolded a large map of Deir el-Medina.

'Show me, where is it?' Haddad demanded, pointing to the map. The police chief pushed his frightened cousin towards the desk. Carrington looked anxiously out the window; he was watching the shadows in the square below grow longer by the minute.

Babar stared at the map for a long time. 'It's approximately here, Sir,' he said finally, pointing with a dirty fingernail to a spot on the map.

Haddad looked at him sceptically. 'You don't seem very certain.'

'I'm sure I can take you to it. But here ... on the map ...' Babar shrugged apologetically.

'Could you find it at night, in the dark?'

'I think so.'

Haddad was about to ask something else when the door opened and the old man with the white turban appeared in the

433

doorway. 'I thought I told you ...' Haddad barked, looking up. He stopped in mid-sentence. 'Come in.'

The man hurried across the room and handed Haddad a note. 'We have a reply! Take him outside,' Haddad said, pointing to Babar. Turning to the whiteboard, he pinned up the note. 'Omar wants the original dispatch first – to authenticate it. If it's authentic, Jana will be released. There will be no exchange.'

'That's it?' Carrington asked, his voice sounding shrill. Haddad shrugged.

'We can't just give him what he wants and then hope for the best without anything to bargain with,' Carrington protested, 'surely!'

'Do you have a better idea?' Haddad snapped back, looking pale and exhausted. 'He's holding a life in his hands; we only have an old papyrus. At least it will buy us a little time.'

'Of course, I'm sorry, it's just that ...'

Haddad slapped Carrington encouragingly on the back. 'I understand – tick tock. But this is the time to stay calm and outfox the fox; and you and I will do just that.' Carrington looked at him sadly, admiring his friend's energy and optimism.

'Please, give it to me ...' Carrington handed him the papyrus. Haddad scribbled something on a piece of paper, folded it in half, attached it to the papyrus and gave it to the old man standing at his desk. 'Go – hurry!' The man left the room.

'Now, come over here and listen.' said Haddad, turning to Carrington. 'How do you catch a desert fox?' Haddad asked rhetorically. 'You become like him; you try to think like he thinks, feel what he feels, want what he wants,' Haddad answered his own question. 'I believe I know how Omar thinks and what he wants.'

'You do?' Carrington asked.

'This attack at Sharm el-Sheik changes everything. We have very little time. I've been ordered by Cairo to take over the investigation; I should really be on my way right now,' Haddad explained. 'I think this is all related. Just look at the timing ...

Rule number one – don't believe in coincidences.'

'Are you suggesting he wants to draw us away from here?' asked the police chief.

'Absolutely, and distract us. Obviously the planning for this attack has been going on for a long time – so why now, at this very moment? Coincidence? Hardly.' Carrington was following the exchange with interest. 'What do you think?' Haddad asked, turning to his friend.

'The way I see it, we're dealing with a man here with two separate agendas, with two quite separate personalities, if you like. On the one hand, we have Omar the terrorist, the leader of the Brotherhood who has just escaped certain death by trying to assert himself as the true Defender of the Faith.' Carrington paused, collecting his thoughts. 'On the other, we have Omar the scholar, obsessed with the notion of finding the – how did Professor Khalil put it – the ultimate prize of archaeology, the tablet, which as of right now, may almost be within his grasp.'

'Very good, go on ...' Haddad encouraged Carrington.

'If I were that hypothetical desert fox, I would translate the letter immediately – that goes without saying – and then try to find the location before it's too late, for whatever reason. In short, I wouldn't hesitate, I wouldn't wait. I would go for it – now.'

'I agree. Omar knows this whole area – the Karnak temple in particular – like no other. He worked here for years, charting the temple, restoring it. Professor Khalil seems convinced that the tablet is hidden somewhere in the temple precinct,' Haddad said, developing Carrington's thoughts further. 'If she's right, we have the perfect trap, with the bait already waiting.'

'Irresistibly – for the last seven hundred years or so,' Carrington pointed out.

Haddad turned to the police chief. 'We'll put the entire temple under surveillance – at once, but discreetly. Forgive me for saying this, but I cannot trust the local officers here, not after what happened. Use the commando unit we brought up from Alexandria.' The police chief looked glum. 'You know I'd trust you with my life, Ali, but please ... understand.'

'You're right of course; I'll take care of it at once.'

'And leave all the beggars and other riff-raff who spend the nights there undisturbed. Everything must look normal. Use them as cover,' Haddad suggested. 'We don't want to scare our fox away, now, do we? Be careful! If Omar gets wind of this ...'

'The men will melt into the stone, I assure you; no one will know they're there.'

'I hope so.' Haddad took a deep breath after the police chief had rushed out of the room. 'Now, let's get down to the important bit.'

'What do you mean?' Carrington asked.

'Finding Uni's tomb, of course. What else?'

87

Omar couldn't control his rising excitement. Drifting slowly across the Nile towards him was a felucca, its large, triangular sail trapping the evening breeze. The moment he'd dreamt about for so many years was coming closer; the arduous journey was nearing its end. He unrolled the original Blanquefort Prayer – the very papyrus his assistant had found in the Karnak temple – and, brushing small pieces of sand off the carpet, he placed it carefully in front of him.

'The Holy Relic we leave behind is but a shell – empty, its very essence gone,' he began to read. 'The ... of the Prophet are out of our enemies' reach; one is on its way to France with a dispatch recording the hiding place of the other ...' he repeated quietly.

The dispatch recording the hiding place of the other was within his grasp. Finally coming towards him, now, on the felucca approaching the jetty.

'What if it's a fake?' he asked himself for the hundredth time. He tried to dismiss the doubt, but knew there was only one way to banish it forever.

The vessel drifted into the reeds and came to a stop. One of Omar's young bodyguards jumped ashore, waved at Omar sitting in front of his tent and came running up the embankment.

'Do you have it, my son?' whispered Omar, barely able to

speak.

'I do.' The eager young man knelt down beside him and pulled a scroll out of the sleeve of his jalabiya. It was almost dark and a blood-red moon rose slowly out of the eastern desert like the angry eye of a waking Cyclops; ominous.

'Blanquefort's dispatch to the Grand Master,' Omar exclaimed, 'it is!' He held the manuscript close to the lantern. Then he placed it next to the Blanquefort Prayer on the carpet in front of him. Identical: same brittle papyrus, same handwriting, same discolouration. Feeling calmer now, he pulled pencil and paper out of a large pocket in his robe and began to translate the Latin part of the text.

Omar moved camp every day to reduce the risk of detection or, worse still, betrayal. By always keeping close to the Nile he was able to travel by boat, which not only greatly improved his mobility but added to his cover. Omar travelled with a small entourage – two young bodyguards who would gladly lay down their lives for him. He communicated with his mullahs by messenger or satellite phone to make certain no one really knew where he was.

'Allah be praised!' Omar said at last, putting down his pencil. 'It's all here!' In the approaching darkness, the full moon had transformed the river into a band of molten silver – a path leading all the way to the temple looming large in the distance. It was irresistible, drawing him closer with the alluring siren call only he could hear.

Omar looked at the original text for a long time. It was all so simple, so obvious. Only one small uncertainty remained: what if someone had accidentally found the hiding place? It had been there for seven hundred years. With so much mindless plunder in earlier times and, more recently, so much restoration, one could never be sure.

And to have been able to barter this priceless document for

one mere useless infidel, a woman at that, made the success even sweeter. Westerners were so sentimental, such gullible fools. And as for holding her pitiful life in his hands, the mere thought made him tremble with excitement. Her execution would be the final act, giving his reputation a much needed lift.

'We'll break camp tonight,' Omar announced, standing up, 'and leave by boat.' The full moon was an auspicious sign, he thought. The night and the moon – darkness for cover and the full moon to show the way; all the light they'd need.

'The moment has arrived, my sons,' Omar said, pointing towards Luxor. To the two impressionable young men watching him in awe, Omar looked, and sounded, very much like The Chosen One.

88

Carrington followed Haddad up the barren hill from the Nile, careful not to lose his footing in the dark. Babar and two marksmen led the way.

'Our camp was right there,' Babar explained pointing to a narrow ledge overlooking the ancient village of the pharaoh's tomb builders.

'Not so loud!' Haddad said, mindful that any noise would travel far in the exposed cemetery, especially at night. The full moon helped Babar orientate himself, but made the group more conspicuous in the open rugged terrain.

Carrington felt awkward in his dark jalabiya and kept adjusting his turban. He would have preferred his trusty hat. They stopped at the ledge and sat down, realising that nothing attracts the eye more than motion. To the marksmen, their night vision gear strapped on, all appeared quiet and deserted. The whole area was pockmarked with excavated shafts leading into the tombs of the pharaoh's workmen; most were no more than small holes in the ground, often filled with sand and rubble.

'From the camp over here, we walked along the ridge – there – then we got to the tomb,' Babar whispered excitedly.

'Show me,' Haddad said, before turning to the sharpshooters. 'You stay here and watch the hill; report anything that moves.' Haddad adjusted his radio and followed Babar up the slope with Carrington. When they reached the spot Babar remembered, there was no trace of the tomb.

'We did close it up,' he explained, 'but there was a rock and some steps ... we left them ... outside. Somewhere here, between these.' He pointed to two small holes in the ground roughly thirty metres apart.

'Where exactly, can you remember?' Haddad asked quietly, trying to encourage him.

'All this rubble here is new – different. We didn't leave it like this, I'm sure.'

Haddad put his hand reassuringly on Babar's shoulder. 'All right, calm down. Take a good look at what's here now and try to remember the tomb after it was closed. Doing your best, where would you say it was? Here, use this.' Haddad handed Babar a shovel to mark the spot. 'Take your time.'

Babar reached for the handle and walked across to the small tomb on the far side of the slope. He stopped in front of it, turned around and began to retrace his steps.

'Here,' he said, thrusting the shovel into the ground. 'It should be right here,' he repeated, gaining confidence.

'All right, start digging,' Haddad said. 'Carefully, please ... as little noise as possible.'

Jana had no idea how long she had been in there. After the humiliating photo shoot she had only received two more visits – both from a toothless old woman who hastily placed a plate of food and a jug of water near her.

Sitting on the stone floor, she heard a faint noise at the far end of the chamber. It was persistent – a repetitive scraping. Jana looked across to the sarcophagus; the sound was coming from that direction. The wooden coffin – like some strange instrument of the netherworld – amplified the sound and it became more urgent. Goose pimples began to march down her spine like an army of tiny spiders sensing danger. *There's something inside*, Jana thought, trying not to panic. *Wanting to get out!* Steeling herself, Jana picked up the lamp and crawled slowly across to the sarcophagus.

Pressing her ear against the wood, she listened: the sound came from behind it and not within. This was no ghost; someone was out there! To give herself courage, she punched at the side with her fists, tears of frustration running down her wan cheeks. The scraping didn't stop. Something louder was needed.

The stone jar, she thought, reaching for one of the alabaster jars next to the crouching Anubis. Sitting back on her heels, she lifted up the heavy jar with both hands and let it drop to the stone floor. It landed with a thud. 'That's better,' she mumbled, lifting the jar again.

'This is hopeless,' Carrington said, watching Babar scrape away more rubble and soil without success. Just then, the radio strapped to his friend's belt began to crackle. Holding his hand over his mouth, Haddad said something in Arabic and then switched the radio off.

'Stop!' he hissed, tugging at Babar's sleeve. 'Someone's coming.'

They lay down and carefully peered over the edge. Two people – one tall, the other short and bent – were slowly climbing the hill from the opposite direction.

Carrington, who was lying next to the hole Babar had just dug, heard a dull sound coming from the opening.

'Did you hear that?' he whispered to Haddad.

'What?'

'There it is again. Listen. Someone's in there ... knocking!'

'Nonsense! You are imagi ...' The next thump – this time louder – couldn't be ignored.

'I think you're right,' hissed Haddad, putting his ear to the ground. The two dark shapes came closer. Haddad pulled his pistol out of the shoulder holster and placed it within easy reach in front of him.

'Look. They've stopped – over there, next to the other tomb.'

The tall one turned around, bent down and pulled something heavy out of the ground. Moments later, both disappeared into the side of the hill.

89

Omar stared ahead as the vessel sliced through the moonlit waters of the Nile. When the familiar pylons of the Karnak temple materialised out of the dark, he began to smile. The prize he had coveted for so long was waiting for him somewhere inside the ruins of the ancient temple. The mere thought of the tablet – now almost within his grasp – made him tremble. This tablet was a source of immense power; much greater than anything even a pious Muslim leader like himself could hope to attain through terror or war. With the suicide bombing at Sharm el-Sheik already sending ripples of fear around the globe, the stage was set for the Brotherhood to claim a victory of a different kind – a spiritual one: one of the Tablets of Moses in *Muslim hands! This should teach the arrogant crusaders a lesson,* he thought. God was on his side!

Omar was confident that apart from the usual beggars, the temple would by now be deserted. Moreover, the bombing had its desired effect: the troops stationed in Luxor were already flying out. *Chief Inspector Haddad will have his hands full,* thought Omar, and smiled. *He'll be waiting in vain for the release of the wretched woman.*

His felucca was a floating arsenal; he had enough explosives on board to blow up a skyscraper. Omar's two young bodyguards carried machine guns under their jalabiyas. Omar's small automatic however, was strapped to his body, along with a number of hand grenades.

'We'll go through here,' Omar explained, 'and enter the temple one by one.' He pointed to an abandoned underground passage leading from the river to the temple. 'I'll go first and you'll cover me. Stay close and keep visual contact at all times, understood?' The boys nodded. 'Remember, follow the shadows and move slowly; try to look just like the beggars. Where are the tools?' One of the boys showed him a sack slung over his shoulders. 'Allah be with you, let's go.'

The police chief surveyed the forecourt through his binoculars, satisfied that the commandos were in position on top of the pylon and along the roof. The usual groups of beggars, squatting around a small fire near the temple entrance, were fighting over cigarettes scrounged from visitors during the day. They occasionally looked up to see the usual tourist coaches arrive for the last Sound and Light Show of the day. Things were normal.

No one paid any attention to the bearded man limping slowly towards the pylon. While Omar hobbled through the entry to the temple wall, his two young bodyguards stayed in the shadows and followed one by one.

Once inside the vestibule, Omar took a deep breath and leant against the cool stone. As his eyes adjusted to the gloom, he could see the gigantic columns of the Hypostyle Hall through the archway on his right.

His approach had been carefully timed. Using the show as his cover, he could do all his searching as the inside of the temple was usually deserted and in total darkness during the performance. No one was allowed to enter the temple at night. Any noise he made would not be noticeable, and the inevitable chaos at the end of the performance was perfect for a getaway.

The meticulous and cautious Omar had thought of everything. Except, in his eagerness to reach the prize he'd coveted for so long, he'd broken one of his own cardinal rules: he had failed to allow for the unexpected.

90

'What do these tombs look like inside?' Haddad asked, training his binoculars on the spot where the two strangers had disappeared into the ground. 'Could they be connected in some way, say, by a tunnel?' He remembered the earlier intelligence about Omar and his possible hiding place somewhere in this area.

'Most tombs have a short, narrow passage and a single chamber at the end,' Babar explained, 'but if a tunnel were to be dug ... well, one could easily join them.'

'What are you going to do?' Carrington asked, hoping for another signal.

'Wait. We can't risk a confrontation. Not in there, we have no idea what ...' The radio crackled into life again, alarmingly loud in the stillness of the night. The police chief was reporting in. The commandos were in position, all was quiet. Haddad repeated his instructions to not engage Omar under any circumstances. Meanwhile, the two sharpshooters, like a pair of strange birds with their beak-like night vision gear, had silently crept up the hill and were patiently waiting for their quarry to reappear.

'There, look,' whispered Carrington, 'someone's coming out.' The two marksmen lifted their rifles.

'What do you see?' hissed Haddad.

'It looks like ... it is ...'

'Well?'

'An old woman carrying ... a bucket,' answered one of the soldiers, lowering his rifle. The old woman emptied the bucket and disappeared. Haddad looked at Carrington.

'Are you thinking ...?'

'A prisoner?'

Haddad nodded. Moments later, the old woman reappeared, followed by a tall young man holding a torch.

'He has a gun,' said one of the marksmen, the green cross in his scope following the man's head.

'If he fires, shoot,' Haddad said to the soldier on his left before propping himself up on his elbows.

'Drop your weapon – now!' Haddad shouted in Arabic. His voice cut through the silence and echoed ominously across the barren hillside. Taken completely by surprise, the young man froze. Then, everything happened very fast. He pushed the old woman aside, lifted his gun and fired in their direction. One of the marksmen shot him through the head. The young man was dead before he hit the ground and rolled down the steep hill like a rag doll.

Jana could hear rapid gunfire directly above. Instinctively, she extinguished the oil lamp, but immediately regretted it; anything was better than total darkness. What should she do: shout, or stay still? Who was out there? Friend? Foe? She felt light-headed and dizzy and could not stop the tears rolling down her cheeks.

Then she remembered the scraping noise she'd heard and knelt down on the stone floor to feel her way in the darkness with her outstretched hands. She was searching for the alabaster jar and, when she found it, took a deep breath, wiped away her tears and began to pound the floor again. It took all the strength she could muster.

The old woman was hysterical. Haddad slapped her face, but was unable to get any sense out of her. Carrington, searching

447

the ground where she'd fallen, found loose rubble covering a wooden trapdoor. Using bare hands, he scraped away the debris and opened the door and, as he stared into a narrow shaft, he heard the first thump.

They followed the noise – down to one small empty chamber and, further along, to another. The passage narrowed and Carrington had to squeeze through, moving sideways. The thumping grew louder. 'Jana, over here,' he shouted. Trying to move faster, he dropped the torch and as he bent to pick it up, wedged his chest against the wall and got stuck.

'Jana,' he whispered, barely able to breathe. Haddad had to push hard from behind to free him. Carrington stumbled forward and ran into an iron gate blocking the way. The thumping came from somewhere out of the dark close by. Haddad reached over Carrington's shoulder from behind and held up his torch. Carrington pressed his aching forehead against the iron bars and gasped.

Covered head to toe in a black robe, was Jana. She was kneeling on the stone floor directly in front of him.

Momentarily blinded by the light, she was facing in his direction with her eyes firmly shut. She held an elaborate alabaster jar above her head, and was about to pound the floor again. To her left, stood a life-sized statue of Sekhmet; the bellicose goddess was guarding the entry to the burial chamber. To her right – in dark black granite – was the god Horus, watching over her. But on the wall behind her, painted in brilliant colour, was the god who saved her – Thoth, staring all-knowingly into eternity.

91

Haddad led them out. He retraced his steps through the narrow tunnel, with Carrington, supporting Jana, close behind. Babar and his two commandos were guarding the entrance. As Haddad stepped out into the open, the light on his radio began to flash.

'I think we may have something here,' whispered the police chief.

'Speak up. What is it?'

'Two men inside the temple – there's something suspicious about them.'

'What do you mean?'

'They're working on something; a breach in the temple walls ... We can see them clearly from up here. Sounds like they're using some tools – metal on stone ...'

'Where?'

'In the Hypostyle Hall – near the spot the professor mentioned ...'

Haddad's mouth went dry. *This could be it*, he thought. 'Don't let them out of your sight. Seal off the area, but do absolutely nothing else until I get there. Do you hear?' Haddad almost shouted. 'This is an order!' He added for good measure.

'Yes, Sir.'

'We've found the woman. She's safe. But keep this to yourself.'

'I understand. Congratulations.'

449

Squatting on his heels in the far corner of the Hypostyle Hall, Omar watched his boys trying to loosen a small chunk of stone wedged between two larger blocks. *This*, thought Omar, *was most likely the spot described by Blanquefort.* He'd memorised the critical passage from the Latin and was going over it time and again to make sure he hadn't missed anything.

The tablet was hidden in the Hypostyle Hall, that much was clear, and it narrowed the possibilities considerably. The southern wall it referred to 'has to be the Binding of the Two Lands,' Omar reassured himself. 'There's nothing quite like it anywhere else in the entire temple precinct.' The Binding of the Two Lands – a large relief cut into the massive stone blocks – depicted the god Horus holding a lotus in his hand. Horus was facing the ibis-headed god Thoth holding a papyrus. Between them, the pharaoh was kneeling before the gods. The lotus and the papyrus represented the two lands – Upper and Lower Egypt, being joined together under the pharaoh's feet.

'Three stone blocks below the right foot of the bird-headed creature with the long beak, is a gap in the wall, as wide as the arm of a man. The gap has been sealed with a chunk of stone ...' Omar quoted by heart from Blanquefort's instructions. 'The tablet is concealed deep within the cavity behind the stone.' It sounded simple enough. But it was difficult for the boys to loosen the stone wedged into the wall. Omar stood up and walked across to them. 'Use the crowbar here,' he whispered impatiently, 'but wait for the show to begin,' he added, 'before you make any noise.'

Haddad stood on the deck of the police launch crossing the Nile, his fingers drumming the side of his legs.

'It can't go any faster,' said Carrington, trying to stanch Haddad's impatience. 'We're almost there.'

'You're right. Yes ... and we found Jana, didn't we? That's truly amazing! How is she?'

'She's resting.' Carrington put his hand on Haddad's

shoulder. 'Fate, my friend. Do you think it's him?'

'I know it is.'

The police chief was waiting for them at the jetty. 'They're still working on the wall,' he reported. 'Come, quickly, I'll show you.'

'What about the tourists watching the show?' Haddad asked, looking at his watch. 'It's going to start any moment.'

'They should all be seated by now ...'

'I was afraid of that.' Haddad was feeling very uneasy; images of the *Aida* massacre still fresh in his mind.

'I don't like it, but there's nothing we can do.' He shrugged, 'Inshallah; let's go!' They left Jana in the police launch under guard and hurried towards the temple.

'We have to climb up here, I'm afraid,' the police chief explained, pointing to an elaborate rope ladder the commandos had rigged up. Carrington climbed up first, followed by Haddad and the police chief. Towards the top, Carrington almost lost his footing and was grabbed by the strong hand of a soldier reaching down from above. The stone roof of the Hypostyle Hall had collapsed long before; all that remained were massive slabs of stone connecting some of the capitals of the gigantic columns. Following one of the soldiers crawling along the top, they reached a ledge and lay down flat.

Suddenly, a shaft of eerie green light crept along the pylon and came to rest on the lotus-shaped capitals of the columns. The haunting sound of reed pipes, cymbals and drums, amplified by microphones at strategic spots throughout the temple, echoed across the forecourt. The famous Karnak Sound and Light Show had begun.

'A long, long time ago,' began the narrator, 'man was created out of the tears of the sun god ...' Haddad winced, annoyed by the unwelcome distraction.

The police chief pointed down into the hall below. Slowly,

they lifted their heads and peered over the edge. Carrington could see two men pushing their shoulders against an iron rod wedged into the wall. When they extracted the rod, a chunk of stone fell out and hit the ground with a thud. The two men stopped working and looked anxiously around.

'There, look,' said Carrington, pointing to a third man emerging from the gloom. The man limped across to the hole in the wall left by the stone and peered inside.

'Omar?' whispered Haddad.

'Must be, but I can't see his face, he's too far away,' Carrington replied. The man reached into the hole and, standing on the tips of his toes, pushed part of his shoulder into the cavity. He was breathing heavily and, withdrawing his arm, stepped back. Something dark and angular emerged from the hole, but got stuck.

One of the soldiers kneeling on top of the ledge adjusted his rifle. A small screw fell out of his night vision gear and fell over the edge, making a sharp pinging sound as it hit the stone floor. The three men below froze. Haddad waved his finger from left to right. No one moved.

'There's someone there,' hissed Omar, looking up. The two boys reached for their machine guns and disappeared into the shadows. Instead of ducking for cover, Omar grabbed the crowbar and tried to loosen the object stuck in the hole.

Omar freed the object, lifted it carefully out of the hole and placed it on the ground. Kneeling down, he ran his trembling hands over the cool surface of the tablet and closed his eyes. It was so different from what he had imagined. The tips of his fingers could feel grooves and shapes – writing. 'Tabot Musa,' Omar muttered to himself over and over.

Haddad stared at the man kneeling in the pool of moonlight on the ground below. He wanted to savour the moment a little longer, but something inside him told him to act. He glanced at Carrington lying next to him, reached across and squeezed his hand. 'An eye for an eye,' he whispered. 'Watch.'

'It's over, Omar, put your hands above your head,' Haddad shouted from above, his voice chilling and strong. At first, Omar remained perfectly still, then he rolled to one side with surprising agility and disappeared from view. 'The temple is surrounded, there's no way out,' Haddad continued. Two machine guns began to fire from below, trying to find the voice. Haddad turned towards the police chief. 'Take them out, but I want Omar alive.'

92

Habakkuk was trying to distract Father Frumentius by chatting quietly about Ethiopia and their early days at the Vatican. Their flight into Luxor had been harrowing and Sorokin suddenly appeared reluctant to make contact with the Defender of the Faith.

Sorokin walked across the hotel terrace, ordered some tea from a passing waiter and watched the two black priests out of the corner of his eye. He had misgivings about coming to Egypt at such short notice and Habakkuk made him feel uneasy. If it hadn't been for his old friend's hospital bed plea, he would not have accepted the assignment. And in any case, Newman's request had come at an awkward time. Dealing with terrorists in a country like Egypt was always dangerous, but making contact with the Defender of the Faith when the entire Egyptian security forces were trying to hunt him down, was reckless. Sorokin knew he had to be very careful.

Sorokin reached into his pocket, and pulled out his mobile; one of his agents was reporting in. Still on the phone, he hurried across to the priests at one of the tables.

'There's gunfire at the temple,' he said, pointing towards Karnak, lit up like a beacon in the distance.

'The Brotherhood?' Frumentius asked.

'Could be. No one really knows what's going on, but shooting in the middle of the night during the Sound and Light Show, with all those tourists ...'

'What do you suggest we do?'

'We go and have a look. Come.'

Sorokin's agent was waiting in front of the hotel. They piled into his small Fiat and raced towards the temple.

'My men are already there,' the agent said, trying to distract Sorokin from his maniacal driving. 'They'll meet us in the car park.' He had covered the short distance in minutes and pulled up behind the tourist coaches.

'Please stay here,' said Sorokin, turning to the two priests in the back. 'I'll find out what's happening.'

Frumentius stared at the temple in front of him and watched the beams of light glide and come to rest on a tall obelisk; its point facing the night sky like a gigantic transmitter sending prayers to the gods. His hands began to sweat: the obelisk reminded him of Axum. Closing his eyes, he began to pray. He could hear his brother whisper in his ear, 'You will know when you are getting close; you will feel it in your soul ...' Frumentius was trembling.

'Are you alright?' Habakkuk asked, looking anxiously at the priest in the seat next to him. Frumentius didn't appear to have heard him.

Sorokin hurried back to the car. 'What's going on?' Habakkuk asked, impatiently winding down the window.

'There's a lot of confusion, but we do have a gun battle – right there. You can hear it,' Sorokin explained, pointing towards the temple. 'The word is, the Defender of the Faith is trapped inside ...' he added calmly. 'That's all I know – for now.'

'That's enough!' Frumentius cried out and opened the car door.

'Where are you going?' Habakkuk asked, trying to stop him. 'Wait!'

Frumentius did not seem to hear him and ran past the seated spectators towards the illumined temple wall.

The enthralled spectators, who had thought the gunfire was part of the show, realised something was wrong when the forecourt was suddenly lit up from above. The panic began in earnest when heavily armed men in black combat fatigues and balaclavas started darting from cover to cover along the temple wall.

There was screaming and the exchange of gunfire almost drowned out the voice booming from the loudspeakers.

'Tabot Musa,' Frumentius repeated to himself over and over, 'I know you are here,' as he kept running towards the light, seemingly oblivious to the chaos around him.

93

Omar's bodyguards had been well trained. Using every bit of available cover, they moved quickly and without fear firing at targets they couldn't see, relying on instinct and lightning reflexes. Despite their precarious position, trapped inside the temple, they were pinning down their invisible attackers and had wounded two commandos, one seriously.

'Where's Omar?' Carrington asked, trying to keep his head down.

'I don't know, but he can't get far,' Haddad replied. The furious shooting continued until one of the two machine guns fell silent. The soldier lying on the ledge opposite turned around and gave Haddad the thumbs up.

'One down, one to go,' muttered Haddad, 'That's more like it.'

Omar moved on all fours towards a small gap in the wall; he knew the temple layout intimately and had managed to crawl away. *Now to somehow make it back to the tunnel*, he thought. He could see dark shapes moving towards him from all directions and pressed himself flat against the face of Amun-Ra carved into the temple wall behind him.

'When the pharaoh died,' boomed the narrator, 'his body was prepared for its journey into eternity ...' The lights changed colour, illuminating a different part of the temple. 'The spells were important and would ensure a safe passage into the afterlife ...'

Carrington climbed carefully down the rope ladder and hurried after Haddad.

'They've spotted him on the other side,' explained the police chief, pointing excitedly to the southern end of the temple. 'Come, this way!'

For a moment, Omar watched as the bright finger of blue light moved slowly down the stone wall. Holding his breath, he pressed the precious tablet to his chest. The accusing beam stopped a few metres above his head, crept a little to the left and then changed colour.

'Before he was allowed to enter the world of Osiris,' the narrator's voice continued, 'the pharaoh had to pass one final test: the weighing of his heart ...' Omar stared at the light quivering above him and stood perfectly still. The light – this time red – began to follow the outline of the giant effigy of Osiris, god of the underworld, carved into the temple wall behind him. Omar crouched next to the open jaws of the monster Anmut – another part of the judgement scene – waiting to devour the treacherous heart of the impure. Omar wanted to move, but his legs wouldn't obey. As the light came closer, so did the jaws of the monster.

'To pass the ultimate test, the king's heart had to be placed on a pair of scales held by the god Anubis. The heart was to be weighed against Ma'at, the feather of truth ...'

As the beam of light reached the feet of the god, a second beam – white and blinding – exploded out of the darkness. There, caught in brilliant white light, was Omar's face.

'This is the end of the road, Omar!' Haddad roared. 'Raise your hands above your head.' Omar stood motionless and shielded his eyes from the glare with one hand. The other clutched the tablet tightly against his chest. He couldn't see the gun barrels pointing at his heart, nor could he see Haddad, but he could hear the words from the man in the forecourt with a megaphone in his hand.

Machine gun fire erupted from above. Omar's second bodyguard, still alive, had managed to climb to the top of the temple wall just above Omar. The commandos responded instantly, blowing away the gunman's face and the back of his head. He fell from the wall – robes flapping like a prayer flag – and hit the ground at Omar's feet. Horrified, the crowd began to scream.

Haddad felt a jab of searing pain and reached for his shoulder where one of the stray bullets had ripped away part of his sleeve.

'You've been shot,' Carrington yelled, pulling out his handkerchief. 'Give me that.' He tried to wrench the megaphone out of Haddad's hand.

'It's nothing,' Haddad shouted, not letting go. 'It's just a scratch.'

'At least let me ...' Carrington attempted to stem the flow of blood with his handkerchief.

'You will not see the woman alive, unless you do as I say,' Omar shouted back, playing his last card.

'Get Jana, now!' ordered Haddad, turning to the police chief standing behind him. 'Hurry!'

'You are wrong again,' Haddad replied, playing for time. 'I've just seen her – buried alive in a tomb ...'

A flicker of doubt flashed across Omar's face. *It can't be. He's bluffing,* he thought, *yet ... he knows!*

'I don't believe you,' he thundered. 'She will die unless you do as I say. I am the Defender of the Faith.' Omar raised his right hand, trying to hold back the inevitable.

'Just look at this pretend prophet in his blood-splattered jalabiya' said the police chief, as he stared at Omar, the tablet pressed against his chest and the bullet-riddled body of a young martyr at his feet.

Haddad smiled, turned around and pointed over his shoulder towards the river.

'If you don't believe me, then see for yourself,' he said. 'Here she comes now.'

Omar stared towards the river. He saw someone walking slowly towards him, head to toe in a black chador.

'This is a trick,' he said to himself, without taking his eyes off the tall, dark figure approaching. 'It must be!'

Haddad hurried towards Jana and took her by the hand.

'For the last time, Omar – here, look!'

'Thank you, Jana,' whispered Haddad, folding back her headscarf to expose Jana's face. 'This is for Elizabeth and Isabella,' he called out, turning towards Carrington standing next to him.

'You're bleeding,' Jana said.

'It's nothing.'

Haddad turned towards Omar. 'It's over!' he shouted. 'You've failed!'

Omar stared at the woman standing next to Haddad in the circle of bright light. Recognition brought despair. Surrender was unthinkable, so was defeat.

Still clutching the tablet with his left hand, Omar reached under his robe with his right. A commando, thinking he was going for a weapon, shot him through the hand; Omar fell to his knees. The tablet crashed to the floor beside him. He was bleeding profusely, but still tried to get up. He almost managed to stagger to his feet, but lost his balance and fell back on his knees. Then, almost in slow motion, Haddad thought, Omar reached into the folds of his jalabiya with his shattered right hand and pulled out a black, egg-shaped object.

'It's a grenade,' Haddad warned. 'Get down!'

Omar lowered his head and pulled the pin with his teeth. Staring longingly at the tablet in front of him, he mustered all of his remaining strength, spat out the pin and shouted: 'Allah akbar'. Moments later, a hail of bullets ripped his chest apart.

'No-o-o-o-o-o!' cried Frumentius waving his arms as he jumped over the barricades and ran to Omar. Caught in the crossfire several times in the back, he staggered forward and collapsed.

With his last strength he crawled forward. 'Tabot Musa,' he groaned, his eyes turning glassy. As the tips of his fingers touched the tablet, the grenade exploded, blowing away his trembling hand.

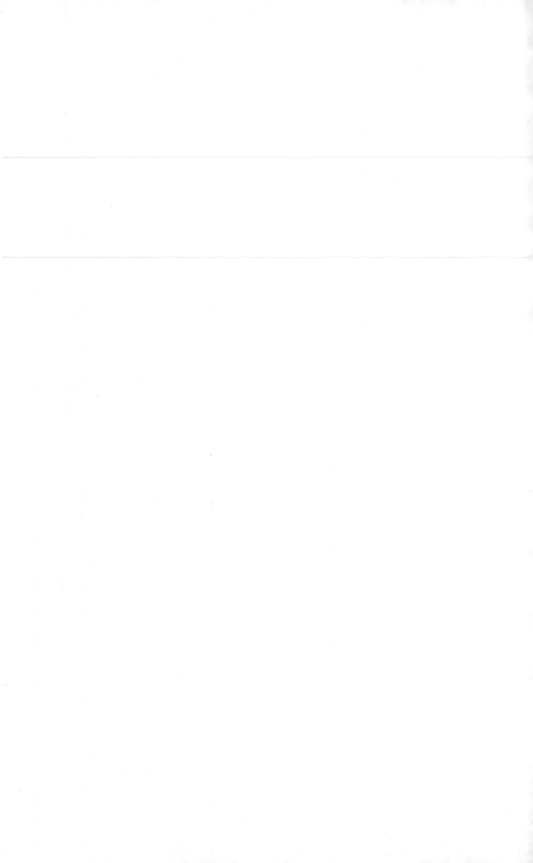

Part V

'THE CONSUMMATION OF HEARTS' DESIRE ...'

Wolfram von Eschenbach – Parzival

Paris; 17 March 1314

With a candle in his right hand, the Dominican followed the gaoler into the dungeons. This would be his last opportunity to question the prisoner before sentencing in the morning.

Jacques de Molay, last Grand Master of The Poor Knights of Christ and the Temple of Solomon, was lying on the floor of his dark cell. The rats scurrying through the rotting straw of his bedding foiled his attempts to pray when the iron-studded oak door creaked open. Fra. Jacques sat up, awkwardly moving his chains and trying to shield his eyes from the bright light.

'Jacques de Molay, his Holiness wants more answers,' announced the Dominican and stepped into the cone of light creeping across the wet floor. 'He has my confession; what more does he want?' asked the prisoner.

'We're not interested in your confession. I have a quite different subject in mind.'

'What?'

'The Black Emperor and his holy relic,' whispered the Dominican. 'You know all about it, don't you?' he said. 'And now,' he continued, leaning over the prisoner, 'you will tell me all you know.'

'I have nothing to tell you. Leave me in peace.' Fra. Jacques slumped back into the filthy straw.

'You know I cannot do that,' answered the Dominican.

Fra. Jacques did not reply.

'Persuasion again – so be it. Take him!' shouted the Dominican. Two men, their faces concealed under black

465

hoods, stepped out of the shadows, unshackled the prisoner and dragged him out of the cell.

The chamber, dark and musty, was lit by torches wedged into iron rings along the massive stone walls. Droplets of water glistened on the high, vaulted ceiling like tears of futile compassion unable to soften the hearts of brutal men. Two men in leather aprons stoked the flames of the fire in a large stone fireplace. And a monk sat at a wooden table in the corner, ready to record the questions and the answers. He reached for his quill and began to sharpen the tip with a knife.

The Dominican pointed to the rack. Fra. Jacques was stripped naked and strapped face down to an iron frame on four legs standing in the middle of the chamber.

'Let us begin.' The Dominican's shaved pate glistened with sweat.

'Your knights accompanied Prince Lalibela from Jerusalem to his homeland in 1185 – is that right?'

Fra. Jacques did not respond.

'I see you are already familiar with our little wedges,' the Dominican said, noting the prisoner's deformed nails and fingertips. Driving small wooden wedges under the fingernails had been one of his more persuasive interrogation tools but he knew memory of pain was often far more effective than singed flesh; it could be as powerful as pain itself. He had broken teeth out of the jaw and prodded the exposed nerve with a hot iron to some effect, but this time the Dominican had something quite different in mind. He pointed to the fire.

A hooded man pulled an iron poker from the flames, its yellow-red tip angry in the gloom. The torture master placed the glowing tip near the prisoner's face, allowing the savage heat to deliver its warning. Slowly, the Dominican repeated the question. Once again, there was no answer. Walking towards the spreadeagled prisoner, he pointed to his lower back. With the poker held firmly in gloved hands, the torture master let the glowing tip almost touch the prisoner's back; the exposed skin blistered in silent reply.

'What's your answer?' whispered the Dominican. Fra. Jacques still did not respond. The Dominican nodded. The torture master allowed the glowing tip of the poker to rest against the prisoner's skin. Slowly he applied pressure. The prisoner screamed as the sickly-sweet stench of burning flesh filled the air. The Dominican nodded again and the poker was removed. 'Answer me!'

'Yes,' groaned the prisoner.

'You see, we begin to understand each other. Now, helping Prince Lalibela to the throne was not the main reason the knights accompanied him to his homeland – yes?'

The prisoner nodded.

'I take it you agree.'

The prisoner nodded again.

'What was the real purpose of their mission?' There was no reply. The Dominican nodded at the torture master. The glowing iron was applied again and held until the prisoner's eyes rolled back and his screams turned into a choking gurgle.

'We both know where this is heading,' said the Dominican, leaning over the prisoner. 'It is ultimately pointless to resist.'

'Lalibela ...' Fra. Jacques whispered, 'he was many years in exile in the Holy Land.' Tears ran down his face. 'He befriended the knights stationed there.'

'Go on.'

'He wanted their help to depose his brother, the king.' Fra. Jacques began to choke.

'There's no stopping now!' the Dominican shouted. 'Go on!'

'He ... he told them a secret.'

'What secret?' asked the Dominican.

'Lalibela told the knights that ...' The prisoner choked again. 'Water,' he groaned and a sip of putrid water was poured down his throat, on which he almost choked again.

'What was the secret?'

'The most sacred relic in the world ... from Jerusalem ... it was taken to his country a long time ago and ...'

'And?' demanded the Dominican.

'And ... was ... still ... there!'

'What relic?'

'The Ark ... the Holy Ark ... of ... the Covenant.'

The Dominican walked across to the scribe to check the last answer had been recorded perfectly.

'Then? Then what happened to those knights? They stayed on after Lalibela, is that right?' The prisoner nodded. 'And over the years there were new arrivals from the Holy Land, is that right?' he asked, coming closer to the topic of real interest.

Again, the prisoner nodded.

'They stayed because there was a plan,' the Dominican continued, raising his voice, 'a plan implemented during your stewardship. That's correct, isn't it?' Once again, the prisoner did not reply. 'I didn't hear your answer.'

'I don't know what you speak of,' croaked Fra. Jacques.

'Bring the brazier,' shouted the Dominican, becoming agitated. The torture master began to shovel burning charcoal into an iron brazier while his assistant poured oil over the prisoner's feet and rubbed it into the skin with a rag.

'Let it begin,' ordered the Dominican. Leaning forward, the torture master positioned the brazier. The flesh of the prisoner's feet began to sizzle like a spit roast. This was one of the most devilish of all the Inquisition's tortures. Many had gone mad through this so the Dominican had to choose the fine line between ultimate pain and death. He also knew it was his last chance to get the answers he needed. 'The plan, tell me about the plan,' he raged as the oil drips from Fra. Jacques' feet fanned the flames.

'The plan,' screamed the prisoner, 'was ...' He stopped mid-sentence and was suddenly quite still.

The Dominican pulled the brazier away, afraid he had gone too far. 'Water,' he shouted. A bucket of water was poured over the prisoner's head.

'The plan, you wretch, what was it?'

'To bring the Ark back to France,' moaned the prisoner.

'And you mean to steal away with it, don't you? And that's precisely what happened.'

The prisoner nodded.

'Where is it now?' asked the Dominican, though he knew the answer. *Surprising how many still lie under these circumstances*, he thought.

'The Ark was left behind ... the knights were killed ... by the Emperor's men.'

'Where?' asked the Dominican, wiping his hot face with his sleeve.

'Egypt.'

The Dominican smiled; the Grand Master was telling the truth.

'But before they were killed the knights removed something from the Ark – yes?'

The prisoner nodded and then screamed again.

'Let me help you,' the Dominican said, relieved to see the prisoner was still conscious. 'The knights removed the tablets,' he whispered into the prisoner's ear, 'before they were put to the sword, isn't that so?'

'Yes,' groaned the prisoner. The Dominican took a deep breath; he was almost there.

'Where are the tablets now?' he whispered suggestively into the prisoner's ear. 'Tell me and the pain will stop.' There was no answer. 'Where are they?' roared the Dominican, pushing the brazier back under the prisoner's feet.

'You will never know!' shouted the Grand Master. The Dominican pulled the prisoner's head towards him by the hair.

'Tell me, you wretch.'

'They are safe.'

'Where? Tell me!'

'Never! All has been recorded for those who come after us;

for those who are worthy. The tablets will decide when to show themselves. But your filthy Pope and your corrupt king will never find them. Never! I curse them both; may they appear before the Good Lord for judgement – soon!' For an instant, a smile illuminated the Grand Master's wan face, then his body went limp.

The interrogation over, the Dominican let go of the prisoner's hair.

The next morning, Fra. Jacques de Molay – last Grand Master of the Templars – unexpectedly recanted his earlier confession and was burnt alive on an island in the Seine. Within a month, Pope Clement V was dead and King Philip of France followed him by autumn. Philip's three sons all died young. Fra. Jacques' curse had become reality.

94

'I knew I'd find you here,' Carrington said, walking past the dozing guards into Haddad's command centre. 'I couldn't sleep either.' He took off his hat and threw it on the table.

'Omar's been positively identified; it's definitely him. The Defender of the Faith is dead!' announced an elated Haddad. 'We've done it, my friend. But look at this, Marcus, you'll find it interesting.'

'What's that?'

'The passport we found on the mysterious black man who tried to stop Omar.'

Carrington instantly recognised the crest. 'A Vatican passport?'

'We don't see too many around here I can tell you, but it is. It belongs to a Monsignor Frumentius Mariam Selassie ... born in – Axum, Ethiopia,' Haddad explained, leafing through the document. 'Are you sure you haven't seen him before?'

'What on earth do you mean?'

'According to this boarding pass here, he flew into Cairo from Rome the same day you did. He was actually on your flight.'

'Where does he fit into all this?'

'I don't know yet, but I intend to find out. We'll advise the Vatican later today.'

Carrington looked glum. Haddad put his arm affectionately around his friend's shoulder. 'If you want to be successful in the Orient, Marcus, you have to learn to hide your true feelings a little better. I can read you like the proverbial book,' Haddad joked.

'You can?'

'You're itching to ask about the tablet, right?'

'Is it that obvious?'

'Plain.'

'Since you appear to know my innermost thoughts, can you put this pathetically transparent Westerner out of his misery and just tell me?' Carrington sighed. 'Is there anything left, anything at all?'

'Yes. The artefact broke into several pieces during the explosion. The forensics guys have retrieved them ...'

'Could I ...'

'Perhaps later, Marcus. I've already notified Professor Khalil; it's technically her jurisdiction.'

Carrington's face sank. 'What did she say?'

'I got the impression she would have gladly swum up river all the way from Cairo, dodging hippos and crocodiles just for a glimpse ...'

'I bet.'

'But the Air Force came to the rescue once again. She'll be here later today. You'll get your chance then, I promise.'

'You always have the right answer, don't you,' Carrington said, massaging his temples. He was trying to ease the dull headache that had kept him awake all night.

'There's someone here who wants to say hello,' Haddad said casually.

'Who?'

'See for yourself.' Haddad pointed to the door behind his desk. 'In there.'

Carrington opened the door and peered inside. The room seemed empty apart from a sofa and a wooden chair. In the gloom, Carrington could just make out the shape of a man lying on the sofa, with his long legs folded over the armrest and his head propped up on a duffel bag. Carrington walked into the room and almost fell over a pair of boots. The man on the sofa stirred, turned his head towards the door and opened his eyes.

'Jack?' asked Carrington, looking stunned. 'Is that you? What are you doing here?'

'I got sick of trout fishing, mate.' Jack rubbed his stiff neck and sat up.

Carrington walked over to the window and opened the blinds. 'I don't believe it. How on earth did you get here so fast?'

'It wasn't by camel express, I can tell you. Baksheesh, me boy,' replied Jack, rubbing his fingers together. 'Lots of it. I hopped on the last plane out of Cairo and got myself almost arrested at the airport here, asking for you. If it hadn't been for your mate over there, I'd be in jail for sure.' Jack pointed to Haddad standing in the doorway. 'I hope there's a good story in all this, Marcus, that's all I can say. I've spent my last advance just getting here, not to mention risking my neck ...'

'How are you?'

'Right now, between fortunes, I'd say.'

'How come? I thought the Swiss Holocaust gold story would keep you going for a while ...'

'No such luck. With so much at stake, the big boys are digging in; the whole thing is getting bogged down. And with the Newman trial up in smoke, the papers are losing interest. That's freelance journalism for you.'

'Never mind. Perhaps there's a new story for you right here.' Carrington sat down next to Jack and slapped him on the back. 'You bloody rascal; you saved Jana's life, you know.'

Jack grinned at Carrington. 'She's all right then. Well, that's something, I suppose. Do you reckon I'm back in the good books?'

'Why don't you ask her?'

'She's here?'

'Follow me.'

Carrington led Jack down a narrow flight of stairs to a room at the back of the police station. 'In there,' he said, knocking on the door.

'Come in,' replied a faint voice from inside.

'She's still a little weak,' said Carrington opening the door. 'Been through a lot,' he added quietly. 'There's someone here to see you, Jana.'

'Oh? Who?' asked Jana, squinting at Carrington standing in the doorway.

'A white knight from New Zealand.' Carrington stepped aside to let Jack enter. Then he moved outside and closed the door behind Jack.

The tiny, white-washed room looked like a prison cell with heavy iron bars on the window. Apart from a mattress on the wooden floor and a cane chair, the room was empty save for Jana and the insects circling the dusty light bulb dangling from the ceiling. Jana was sitting in the chair facing the window, still wearing the black robe given to her by her captors. *She looks like a nun, uncertain whether to take her vows or walk away from God,* Jack thought. She appeared to have aged; her cheekbones, more prominent than usual, gave her a haunted look.

'Planning to join a monastery?' asked Jack, shaking his head, 'I thought this was a Muslim country. And you keep complaining about my wardrobe; really. You should look at yourself.'

'Jack?' Jana began to struggle out of her chair, a crooked smile lighting up her pale face, 'is that really you?' She held out her arms. 'Help me?'

'You need fattening up, kiddo. Desert tucker must be crap,' said Jack, running his hand down Jana's back. 'You're skin and bones.'

'Thanks, Jack,' whispered Jana, thrilled to have Jack's familiar humour and comforting embrace. 'You really know how to cheer a girl up.'

'One of my many talents. What on earth happened?' Jack wiped away the tears streaming down Jana's face with the tips of his fingers. 'That bad – eh?'

'You really do want to know, don't you! Got a hanky?'

Jack pulled a crumpled blue checked handkerchief out of his pocket. 'It's done a few miles, I'm afraid,' he said, handing it to Jana. Jana blew her nose.

'Am I forgiven?'

Jana looked at Jack with teary eyes. 'Yes, but you definitely need a new hanky.'

95

As the Cardinal finished addressing the deputation from Argentina his secretary discreetly handed him a note. *Frumentius is dead.* The Cardinal slipped the note into his pocket and excused himself. Two reports from Egypt were waiting for him in his study. The official one was from the Egyptian authorities in Luxor, informing the Vatican that Monsignor Frumentius Mariam Selassie had been killed in a terrorist attack. The other, from Father Habakkuk, was a more candid and detailed account. It concluded: *The tablet was obliterated in the explosion; Rome is not implicated.*

How fortuitous, thought the Cardinal, *the long search is finally over; the danger has passed.* He opened the bottom drawer of his desk and took out a bundle of papers tied in purple ribbon. He had painstakingly assembled this collection over years. All came from the secret archives of the Inquisition and on top was one he knew almost by heart – the confession of Jacques de Molay. Smiling, the Cardinal pushed it aside and began leafing through for the paper – a rubbing of the Diderot Tablet, as it was known in the Vatican – purchased from Abbé Diderot in 1896.

For centuries, the Church knew about the possible existence of the legendary Ark of the Covenant and the lost Tablets of Moses. But more recently, thanks to the enterprising Diderot, it had also been aware of what was written on one of the tablets ... and the devastating consequences should that knowledge ever find its way into the public domain.

'There is only one God.' read the Cardinal. 'His name ...' The faded lines had him staring until his eyes watered. Did it really all begin with the Egyptians? Was the whole idea of one, all powerful god an inspired Egyptian invention? What if Moses was an Egyptian priest – a sorcerer even – worshipping an Egyptian god? How could the Church ever explain that, or try to reconcile it with the Old Testament? It was up to men like him to ensure that it never came to that – whatever the cost.

With Krakowski's *Second Violin Concerto* booming out of the stereo, the Cardinal walked over to the window overlooking the dome of St Peter's. To him, this music would somehow always epitomise the quest for the missing tablets.

But the Diderot Tablet itself had never surfaced. Diderot's mysterious death before he could finally hand it over to the Vatican, meant any knowledge of its whereabouts went with him to his grave. He went to that grave as a man unshriven; the priest refused him absolution on his deathbed. The tablet had simply vanished. And the Vatican secured the documents; money had bought silence.

The search by the Germans during the War – secretly encouraged by the Holy See – had located the remaining Templar archives buried in the ruins of Montsegur, but not the Diderot Tablet. Historians had generally believed that the Templar archives had escaped the net of Pope Clement V with the Templar fleet which slipped out of La Rochelle in 1307, never to be heard of again. In fact, the archives had been hidden by the last Grand Master – Jacques du Molay – in Montsegur before the seneschals of King Philip threw him in irons on Friday 13 October 1307 – the original Black Friday. Thanks to the Cardinal's close friendship with Newman, those records were now safely locked away in the secret archives of the Office of the Doctrine of the Faith.

The Templar Tablet, as the Cardinal liked to call it, had now been destroyed. Frumentius, the only other person in Vatican circles apart from Habakkuk and himself who knew all the facts, was dead.

While Frumentius' uncompromising allegiance to the interests of Ethiopia had been a problem for decades, Habakkuk's loyalty to the Church was beyond question. The claim by the Ethiopian clergy that the original Ark of the Covenant was in Axum had never been taken seriously by historians. In any event, without the tablets, the Ark – even if it did exist – thought the Cardinal, was not a threat. He was satisfied that the Church's position was safe again at last. The Cardinal smiled; the difficult task begun by his predecessors so long ago had been completed. The Pontiff would be pleased.

When the last note of the concerto sounded, the Cardinal gathered the documents and sorted them – arranging them carefully in chronological order. He tied the purple ribbon tightly around the parcel and rang for his secretary.

'Return this to our archives immediately,' said the Cardinal, placing the bundle into a leather pouch. 'An important chapter in the history of Mother Church has been closed today.'

'Jahwohl, Eminenz,' replied the secretary and left the room.

96

'You two amaze me,' said Professor Khalil, storming into Haddad's office. She lit a cigarette and pulled up a chair next to Carrington. 'This puzzle has been around for seven hundred years and in walks a pair of self-appointed "Ark-eologists" and it's solved in a few days. So much for scholarship; I desperately need guys like you on my staff. Interested?'

'In that case, you should offer him a job as well,' said Carrington, pointing to Jack leaning against the windowsill.

'Oh? Who's that?' asked Professor Khalil, raising an eyebrow.

'I'm Jack Rogan, the journalist who tracked down your Dr Hudson in the wilds of New Zealand ...' replied Jack. He stepped forward and extended his hand.

'You make quite a team, you three,' Professor Khalil said, laughing, and shook Jack's hand.

'It's official; Omar is dead,' Haddad explained.

Professor Khalil looked at him silently for a few moments. 'And the relic?' she asked quietly after a while.

'Broken into seven pieces, I believe.'

'No one touched them? No eager little police fingers tampering with the evidence?'

'No, we did just as you asked,' Haddad reassured her. 'We tried to piece them together to make sure we had all the bits before the bodies were taken away, that's all.'

The professor raised an eyebrow. 'And?'

'See for yourself. They're bringing it all up now.'

Professor Khalil exhaled noisily and, obviously relieved, smiled at the man who had just entered the room bearing a large wooden tray covered with coarse sackcloth. Haddad pointed to his desk. 'There.'

'Well, gentlemen, this appears to be it,' announced the professor. 'Marcus, would you please do the honours and lift the veil, so to speak?'

'As you wish.' Carrington walked over to the desk and carefully folded back the cloth. Illuminated by the morning sun shining into the room, the fragments on the tray began to glow. *The rays of Aten*, thought Carrington, staring at the relic in awe, reaching out of the past like a celestial spotlight. The fragments on Haddad's desk looked just as Krakowski had described them in his strange telephone conversation with Carrington – bluish, sapphire-like and covered in exquisite hieroglyphs.

The forgotten cigarette between Professor Khalil's fingers turned into a column of ash and dropped unnoticed to the floor.

'Gentlemen, this is history,' she said quietly, her voice hoarse. She bent over the fragments and pointed to the first hieroglyph – a tiny owl – in the top left hand corner.

'What does it say?' Jack asked.

'There is only one God,' Professor Khalil began haltingly, running her trembling fingertips along the beautiful inscription. Then she paused, staring intently at the next group of characters. 'His name is ...' Pausing again, she bent down lower for a closer look. 'His name is ...'

'Yes?' Carrington's voice was tense.

'ATEN.' The professor lit another cigarette and glanced at Carrington. 'This is obviously from the Amarna period – but one of the Tablets of Moses? Come on! It doesn't fit, admit it.'

'Doesn't it?'

'What do you mean?'

'The timeframe is okay – within a hundred years or so, possibly less, right? Akhenaten died in 1334 BC. We know that.

Moses is supposed to have left Egypt sometime during the thirteenth century BC – close enough. Agreed?'

'So?'

'Let's go back to the eighteenth dynasty – fourteenth century BC, shall we?' Carrington said, and looking around realised how many details he would need to fill in.

'Fact: Akhenaten, the "Heretic King", has just abolished all the gods and elevated Aten to the supreme position – Aten becomes the one and only true god. This is the first time we have monotheism,' continued Carrington, 'and there's turmoil ... especially among the powerful priesthood that depends for its very existence and livelihood on serving a whole pantheon of gods. To make things worse, Akhenaten abandons Thebes, and builds a new capital – Akhetaten – 150 kilometres downstream. And this idea of one supreme god, this radical idea of the cult of the Aten, is only accepted by some of the well-educated elite. General population? They're lost, confused and they're desperate for old, familiar gods. As for the priests? They're outright hostile and bide their time ...'

'Thank you, Marcus, excellent lecture,' said Khalil, showing her impatience, 'but where is this going?'

'Please, professor, bear with me ... there is a point.' Carrington spoke more quickly now. 'Once Akhenaten dies in 1334 BC, the abolished gods are reinstated, the priesthood is powerful again and the new pharaoh returns to Thebes. Aten is consigned to the dustbin of history – or is he?'

'What are you suggesting?' asked Khalil, drawing deeply on her cigarette.

'What if the cult of the Aten went underground, monotheism survived, and it stayed, in secret among the elite. But the priests, who need to guard their privileges, destroy all images of Aten; any memory of Akhenaten's erased.'

Professor Khalil looked at Marcus. 'And then?'

'Enter Moses, just a few decades later,' Carrington continued. 'What if Moses was a well-educated Egyptian, a priest perhaps,

481

who believed in monotheism and was a secret follower of Aten? Monotheism is embraced by the Jews in captivity in Egypt – Moses becomes their spokesman, their champion.'

'Why?'

'It's ... well it's a win-win. He's been exposed as a follower of Aten and made lots of enemies; even his friend, the pharaoh, turns against him and he cannot oppose the priests alone. So he sides with the Jews and takes up their cause – he'll lead them out of bondage and out of Egypt. But he has to unite them, control their thinking, and he has to persuade the pharaoh to let them go. You know the rest. We've all read it in the Bible; the plagues, the Exodus.'

'That's quite a story,' Professor Khalil said after a while. 'Nothing but speculation, wouldn't you say?'

'Any more than other stories in the Old Testament?' Jack interjected.

'He does have a point,' Haddad cut in.

'Where's the evidence?' demanded the professor.

'Right here in front of us,' Carrington explained, pointing to the broken tablet.

'Come on, Marcus, really ...'

'What if,' continued Carrington undeterred, 'this tablet is authentic? What if it is one of the two original tablets of Moses? The fact it's inscribed with hieroglyphs makes perfect sense. The Jews lived in Egypt for a very long time. They were familiar with the language and the writing.'

'But weren't the tablets supposed to have been inscribed by the finger of God? What, using hieroglyphs? Come on, Marcus!'

'This is the second set, remember? The first set, the original, was inscribed by the finger of God; the Bible is quite clear about that. And I'm sure you know what happened to that.'

'Well, the naked dancing round the idol you mean ... yes, so he smashed the tablets to pieces.'

'Worshipping the Golden Calf, precisely! And then?'

'Remind me.'

'He was given a second set, remember? And he had to inscribe it himself.'

'In hieroglyphs?'

'Of course he would have used hieroglyphs – the obvious choice of a well-educated Egyptian like Moses!' argued Carrington.

'Not bad, go on.'

'Then we have the Ark itself. What do those detailed instructions about its construction remind you of? A classic Egyptian shrine, wouldn't you say? Like the ones in your museum. Moses had all the craftsmen with the necessary skills ...' Carrington paused and walked across to the window. 'Gods in shrines being carried around by priests with long poles resting on their shoulders is nothing new either ... get the picture?'

'The Opet festival of ancient Thebes, right here in Luxor; the Amun procession between the two temples,' said Professor Khalil quietly. 'The god inside the portable shrine.'

'Exactly. The idea was already there.'

'But the evidence, Marcus, where's the evidence?' she said.

'Why don't you read on?' Carrington suggested, pointing to the tray. 'I can tell you exactly what the rest of the inscription says.'

'You've seen it before!'

'No, I haven't; Naguib here can vouch for that.'

Haddad shook his head. 'He hasn't seen it.'

'I don't understand,' said Khalil, 'but tell me anyway, what does it say?'

'It recites five of the Ten Commandments. Then, it ends with a short hymn to Aten.'

Professor Khalil walked to the desk and ran the tips of her fingers across the hieroglyphs. This time, she said nothing for a long time and then turned slowly around.

'How did you know?' she asked quietly.

Carrington took a crumpled piece of paper out of his back pocket, smoothed out the wrinkles and put it on the desk next to the tray. 'I knew, because of this.'

'What's that?'

'Please, read it.'

The professor picked up the paper and turned towards the light.

'I know I'm only the dumb policeman here,' Haddad said, 'but would someone please tell me what's going on?'

'I'm with you, Naguib,' said Jack, shaking his head. 'I'm confused.'

'What Fatima has just read,' Carrington explained quietly, 'is a rubbing, a copy you could say, of the other Tablet of Moses ...' Haddad shook his head. 'It begins with: There is only one God, his name is Aten, then goes on to recite the first five Commandments and concludes with a hymn to Aten – just like this one here ...'

'Where is it?' asked Professor Khalil, her voice barely audible.

'Until quite recently, it was in a bank vault in Switzerland. However, right now it's in Rome with Krakowski ...'

'How did you. ...' She was interrupted by the phone ringing on Haddad's desk. Haddad excused himself.

'You were right, this is quite a story,' said Jack, turning to Carrington. 'I'd better ring my editor.'

'You see, Jack, right place ... right time.'

'Tell me about it. I'm usually a step or two behind; it's the story of my life.'

'Perhaps your luck is changing.'

'It's about bloody time!'

'The day is full of surprises,' announced Haddad, putting down the receiver. 'Someone is downstairs trying to claim the body of Monsignor Frumentius.'

'Who?' Carrington asked.

'His brother.'

97

Something about the old man in the simple, coarse woollen robe and little pillbox hat made Haddad want to stand to attention. It was an aura, a certain dignity that the others in the room sensed as well.

A holy man, thought Jack, looking at the lined face gleaming like polished ebony. Leaning on the arm of a younger man, the old man limped into the room with his prayer stick. Jack had felt something like this before; his first encounter with the Dalai Lama some years back. He pulled his notepad out of his pocket and watched as the two black men bowed and the younger stepped forward.

'This is Father Athanasius Mariam Selassie, brother of Monsignor Frumentius Mariam Selassie who was killed yesterday,' he announced in English, pointing to the old man behind him. 'He arrived this morning from Addis Ababa. As he only speaks Tigrigna, he has asked me to interpret for him.'

'And you are?' Haddad asked.

'Forgive me, I'm Father Habakkuk,' he continued, handing his passport to Haddad.

Vatican. Two in one day, how extraordinary, thought Haddad, searching for the date of entry into Egypt. 'How can I help you?'

'Father Athanasius has come to claim his brother's body. He wants to take him back home to Axum for burial. He has a plane standing by ...'

'I see. Can you tell me what Monsignor Frumentius was doing here in Luxor? He only arrived from Rome the other day, with you, I believe,' added Haddad, watching the black priest carefully. 'A sightseeing trip, perhaps?'

'You are well informed, Chief Inspector.'

'Goes with my job.'

'Not exactly sightseeing,' Habakkuk replied.

'Can you enlighten us?'

'We came here on Church business.'

'What kind of Church business?'

Habakkuk smiled benignly. 'I'm not at liberty to say ...' The Vatican passport in Haddad's hand suddenly made sense. Immunity.

'I see. Well, unfortunately, the body cannot be released just now. Our investigations have not been completed, I'm afraid. However, I will see what I can do ...'

While Habakkuk translated, Jack noticed that the old man kept staring at the fragments on Haddad's desk and was tugging at Habakkuk's sleeve from behind. When Habakkuk turned around, the old man said something to him in a strange sounding tongue.

Habakkuk pointed to the desk. 'Father Athanasius asks if those pieces over there belonged to the man who blew himself up at the temple last night.'

'For a man who arrived from Addis Ababa only this morning, Father Athanasius appears to be exceptionally well informed,' replied Haddad frostily.

'It goes with his job,' Habakkuk replied.

'His job, you say? And what might that be?'

'Father Athanasius is the Guardian of the Ark of the Covenant at the Church of Saint Mary of Zion at Axum.' Carrington raised an eyebrow and glanced at Professor Khalil.

'Yes, these are the pieces we found. Please have a look,' interjected the professor, inviting the old man to come closer. The old man shuffled across to the desk and stared at the fragments on the tray.

'Tabot Musa, Tabot Musa,' he repeated over and over and his hands began to shake. For a moment it looked as if he were about to collapse, but Habakkuk managed to reach under his arm to steady him. The old man sank to his knees, dropped his stick and folded his hands in prayer.

'What is he saying?' Professor Khalil asked, reluctant to intrude into the old man's meditation.

'The Tablet of Moses,' answered Habakkuk quietly.

'How does he know that?' Professor Khalil asked.

'He's the Guardian, he knows ...'

Still on his knees, the old man turned towards Haddad and said something in a shrill voice.

'Father Athanasius humbles himself before you. He beseeches you, no, he begs you,' translated Habakkuk, 'to return this sacred relic to where it belongs.'

'And where does it belong?'

'It belongs ...' Habakkuk paused, searching for the right way to express himself, 'where it was removed from ... a long time ago. It belongs to its true home – inside the Ark of the Covenant.'

'Is Father Athanasius referring to the original Ark of the Covenant mentioned in the Old Testament?' probed Carrington. 'Made according to instructions given by God to Moses?'

'Of course.'

'And where is the Ark today?' Professor Khalil asked, watching Habakkuk carefully.

He looked at her for a while, uncertainty clouding his face. He appeared to hesitate before answering this time. 'It is safe,' he replied evasively. 'You must understand, our country is a troubled land ... civil war, famine, poverty,' Habakkuk explained. It was obvious that he was no longer just translating, but adding comments of his own.

'But is Father Athanasius suggesting he knows where the

original Ark is?' Professor Khalil pressed on regardless.

'Yes.'

'It's not up to me to make that decision,' interrupted Haddad. 'I will have to ask my superiors in Cairo.' The old man looked at him sadly after the reply had been translated, picked up his prayer stick and got awkwardly to his feet. Lowering his head, he walked slowly towards the door. He stopped halfway, turned around and faced the desk once more. Raising his right hand in a blessing-like gesture, he said something quietly that Habakkuk did not translate.

'What did he say?' Jack asked.

'The Guardian said the Ark will decide ... not Cairo,' Habakkuk replied and followed the old man slowly out of the room.

'I don't like this guy,' said Haddad, pointing to the door. 'He gives me the creeps.'

98

Carrington looked up at the colossal Ramses II statue guarding the Luxor temple. The shadows were getting longer and the last of the tourists were leaving.

'Naguib was right,' Jana said softly, approaching Carrington from behind. The two bodyguards Haddad had insisted must accompany her at all times stayed discreetly in the background, watching. 'He was certain I would find you here.' Startled, Carrington looked up. 'I didn't mean to intrude.'

'You are no intruder,' Carrington replied. 'Where's Jack? I thought he was with you.'

'We went shopping. New clothes, from the bazaar – see?' Jana spun around, showing off her ill-fitting long skirt and blouse. 'This is all we could find. Jack called it desert Armani.'

'Most becoming.'

'Liar.'

'Did you make up?'

'In a way we did. He saved my life, you said so yourself. However ...'

'However, what?'

'Nothing stands still, we've all changed. And besides, once something is broken you can never piece it together again without the cracks showing. Yes, we've made up, but the cracks are there; forever.'

'Where's Jack now?' asked Carrington, changing direction.

'Trying to contact his editor; he's been on the phone all

morning.'

Carrington shrugged. 'You were right here, remember?' he said, pointing to a spot on the ground. 'Here with us, sitting next to Isabella ... You know, I could see it all again just now: the procession, the elephants, the torches, the carnage ... I heard the cheers, the drums ... the flying shrapnel,' he continued haltingly. 'Yet, in ancient times, these very walls witnessed another procession, a much happier one. This place was the symbolic heart of a great Theban religious festival,' explained Carrington, 'the Opet festival. Have you heard of it?' Jana shook her head. 'The Beautiful Feast of Opet, as it was called, celebrated the rebirth of divine kingship,' continued Carrington. 'Come, let me show you.' Carrington took Jana by the hand and guided her towards the great colonnade of Amenhotep III.

'Was this what you wanted to show us before the *Aida* performance when we ran into ...?' Jana asked.

'Balthazar with the biblical face,' replied Carrington, pointing to a narrow breach in the temple wall. 'Correct. The Defender of the Faith stood right there and refused to let us pass, remember? Now we know why.' A wave of fear washed over Jana as she recalled Omar's face encounter.

'Here, look,' said Carrington, pointing to the intricate carving in the temple wall. 'During the festival, the god Amun was taken on a journey. He left his home in the Karnak temple sanctuary and came over here to Luxor.'

'What, he went on a little holiday?' Jana joked.

'Not quite. The image of the god was first bathed by the priests, dressed in fine linen, adorned with magnificent jewellery and placed into a shrine. The shrine was then carried by the priests on a ceremonial barque, right here to Luxor. Imagine, crowded avenues filled with cheering spectators watching the procession. And then came the highlight – the pharaoh himself, in all his splendour, waiting to greet the god.'

'The priests walked?'

'Sure, the two temples are quite close.' Carrington pointed to the western wall. 'This shows the journey of Amun from the Karnak temple to the temple sanctuary right here at Luxor. The return journey's on the eastern wall.' Jana admired Carrington's enthusiasm and depth of knowledge, but found it difficult to keep up with him as he darted from one scene to the next. She stumbled and if it hadn't been for Carrington's strong arm catching her, she would have fallen.

'You should be resting,' he said sternly.

'I wanted to see you ...'

Carrington squeezed her hand gratefully. 'We had a strange visitor this afternoon,' he explained.

'I heard. The Guardian – of the Ark? Come on.' Jana raised an eyebrow. 'What did you make of him?'

'The old man was all right, but there was a black priest with him, Father Habakkuk ...'

'What about him?'

'Haddad didn't like him. Policeman's instinct, I suppose.'

'And you?'

'Not sure, but it was an extraordinary encounter to say the least.' Carrington smiled. 'Benjamin would have called it destiny.'

'And you, what would you call it?'

'I'd agree. Just look at what's happened to us. To you, to me, to Benjamin, even Jack. It's as if we're all somehow linked – in some kind of shared dream, some kind of strange quest. I no longer feel in control ... I want to wake up!'

Jana stroked his hand. 'But you are awake, Marcus,' she reminded him.

'I know, and that's the really scary bit. There will be no waking up, nothing goes away – the quest has become reality and it hasn't finished yet.' Holding hands, they strolled along the dromos, the avenue of human-headed sphinxes leading to the other great temple – Karnak – a short distance away.

'Omar is dead, the man who ordered the murder of your

family is no more,' Jana said. 'That's ... well, that's about as final as it gets, wouldn't you say?'

'I was hoping so. More than you can imagine. But now it's happened, I'm no longer so sure ...'

'What do you mean?'

'It's difficult to explain. It doesn't feel final, it's not over yet, there's more to come, more to be done – I can sense it.'

'The tablets?' Jana asked quietly.

'Perceptive as usual. Yes, until that's resolved, there can be no closure.'

'What's on your mind?

'I believe the tablets should be returned ... to Ethiopia.'

Glancing at Carrington, Jana stopped. 'Do you really think the Ark exists?' she asked. 'Silly question,' she corrected herself, 'I still remember your keep-an-open-mind-lecture, vividly!'

Carrington laughed. 'At least now I know you're paying attention.'

'I hang on every word.'

'It's possible,' Carrington said seriously. 'I have no doubt that the Guardian actually believes the relic in his charge is the real thing ... but ...'

'And the passionate archaeologist in you would happily give his right arm – and the rest – to find out,' interrupted Jana, '... if the holy grail of archaeology does in fact exist. Right?' She turned spontaneously towards Carrington and gave him a peck on the cheek.

'As I have obviously become rather predictable lately, there's little point in saying anything further on the topic,' Carrington joked. 'However, even if the original Ark does not exist, I do think the tablets should be returned.'

'Why?'

'Consider the alternative. Can you imagine what would happen if this went public? A single line written in hieroglyphs – *There is only one God, his name is Aten* – and the whole of Western theology's rocked to the core.'

'I hadn't quite appreciated all that,' conceded Jana.

'Can you imagine the furore, the fierce denial by the Vatican, the endless scientific tests, the theological debates by armies of ecclesiastical spin doctors manipulating the faithful; the secret agendas, the cover-ups, the accusations, the pain? Can you imagine the damage to the Ethiopians, their church, their faith, their culture? It's just too controversial, too emotional a topic for rational thought,' Carrington explained passionately. 'This is a matter of faith.'

He stopped, and looked back towards the temple brooding in the half-light behind them. 'Omar was so keen to get his hands on this artefact,' Carrington continued. 'He recognised what it meant; he knew how much power and prestige it would give him, the political influence it would provide. In the hands of a fanatic, a terrorist like Omar, this would have been the most potent political and ideological weapon of our time. This tablet is capable of smashing the very pillars of Christianity. Can you imagine that? Far more effective than suicide bombs and maimed bodies, don't you think? Nations have gone to war for much less than this.'

Jana nodded.

'Of course, all of this involves Benjamin as well. I've already spoken to him about the Guardian and his request.'

'What did he say?'

'He has some serious reservations about the idea as you'd expect. He wants to make up his own mind and meet the Guardian first. But he has agreed, in principle. We just have to work out a way to bring them together.'

'Why do you think he's agreed?'

'Apparently there's a specific reference – a request, an entreaty if you like – in his father's papers about this very point.'

'What kind of request?'

'There's a letter written by his grandfather, Abbé Diderot, to his son, Benjamin's father, expressing a wish. No, more than that, beseeching him that one day when the time was right and both tablets have been found, they should be returned to where they belong. And we know of course what that means. As the Guardian rightly pointed out, the tablets belong to the Ark. And then, there was one more rather curious plea,' added Carrington.

'What?'

'Diderot was adamant that the tablets should be kept away from the Church in Rome – at all cost! Strange, isn't it?'

'Why?'

'Remember, Diderot knew what was written on the tablet he had found. He was a scholar and a priest; the implications could not have escaped him. I think he realised that the Church would suppress all this. He must have known that the tablets would be lost forever if the zealous Cardinals in the Vatican got their hands on it.'

'Incredible! And all this because of two small slabs of stone.'

'The written word ... yes, it's powerful.'

'But you wouldn't just hand them over now,' asked Jana. 'Surely ... you wouldn't miss the opportunity to complete what the Templars, and the Church for that matter, have struggled to achieve for centuries? You want to find the – how did your Wolfram put it in *Parzival* – the consummation of ...'

'... hearts' desire. But remember, it will only reveal itself to us if we are worthy. Are we worthy? Are we worthy to make history – perhaps even change it?'

'There's only one way to find out,' Jana said, a mischievous sparkle in her eyes. She leant across to Carrington and quickly kissed him again on the cheek. 'Why don't we?'

'I thought the devil's advocate was a man,' Carrington joked. 'I was obviously wrong.'

'I don't mean to taunt you, but wouldn't you have to ask yourself for the rest of your days, what if ...? Especially you, Marcus, especially you!'

'That's precisely what I was wrestling with just now, before you came,' Carrington replied.

'And?'

'I think I've found a way to do both.'

'What on earth do you mean?'

'Return the tablets to where they belong and find out – without starting a Holy War.'

'And how will you accomplish all that, Marcus Aurelius?'

Carrington took off his hat and pointed to his cheek. 'One more of those little kisses and I'll tell you,' he answered.

99

With his hand firmly planted on the horn, the driver of the police car wove his way through the narrow lanes of the crowded bazaar.

The Guardian, staying at the house of a Copt merchant was due to meet Carrington that evening. And Jack, eager to find out more about the mysterious Ethiopians, had pleaded for permission to come along.

'I hope this won't ruin your career,' Carrington said to Haddad, sitting next to him in the back of the jeep.

'With Omar dead they will forgive me anything,' Haddad reassured him, 'especially the disappearance of a few pieces of useless stone.'

'Useless stones you call them? I see, that's brave. What about Professor Khalil?'

Haddad winked at his friend. 'Leave her to me. I think she will find your offer irresistible.'

'And the body?' asked Jack, turning around to face Haddad sitting behind him.

'Releasing the body is up to me. What more can we hope to find out anyway? A foolish tourist ran into the crossfire and got shot. Regrettable, sure, but there you have it. In the overall scheme of things, not such an important matter, but please keep this to yourself,' said Haddad, placing his hand on Jack's shoulder. Jack nodded.

'That's going to be the official line,' continued Haddad. 'I'll try to keep the Vatican out of it. Something tells me the Cardinals in Rome would appreciate that. And besides, with Sharm el-Sheikh ... let's say my superiors in Cairo have other things on their minds.'

'I hope you're right,' said Carrington.

Haddad patted Carrington encouragingly on the arm. 'Don't worry, my friend, this is the least I can do for you. Here we are.'

The outside of the tall, narrow building looked derelict, belying the spacious and comfortable internal courtyard. One face to the world outside and another to family and guests inside. As they walked in, they saw Habakkuk sitting next to the Guardian on a bench by the fountain.

'I bring good news,' Haddad announced. 'The body can be released tomorrow.'

'The Guardian thanks you,' Habakkuk translated, 'for having acted so quickly. He knows how busy you must be. He also thanks you for the courtesy of coming here to inform him personally.'

Haddad bowed politely. 'We can make arrangements to have the body taken to your aircraft tomorrow morning if you wish.'

'That would be most helpful. Thank you, Chief Inspector.'

'As for the matter of the broken tablet ... Mr Carrington here would like to suggest something to you.' Jack had discreetly remained in the background, watching. He pulled out his notebook and jotted notes about the exchange.

The Guardian lifted his head slowly and looked at Carrington with myopic, watery eyes. Carrington, though slightly unnerved, held his gaze, a sense of awe radiating towards him from the old man. He could smell frankincense.

'As I recall it,' began Carrington, 'the Guardian said the tablet should be returned to where it belongs ... inside the Ark. The Ark as in the original from the Old Testament – correct? And am I correct also, in saying that he was its guardian and knew where it was?'

'Your recollection is accurate,' Habakkuk replied.

'In that case, we agree – in principle – that the proper course would be to return the tablet to the Ark.'

'In principle?' asked Habakkuk. 'What do you mean by that?'

Carrington smiled. His hint at more to come had been picked up. 'We have a proposal, a simple request.' Carrington paused, letting the words find their mark. 'We would like to accompany the tablet and witness its return to the Ark.' If the old man was in any way surprised by this suggestion, he certainly didn't show it. His face remained composed; his eyes unblinking.

'When you say we, who are you referring to?' Habakkuk translated.

'Three women and three men who have been closely involved in ... how shall I put this? The journey, yes, the journey of the tablets.'

'You said tablets just now, Mr Carrington. Did you mean more than one, or was that a slip of the tongue?' Habakkuk enquired, asking for clarification.

'I am speaking about two tablets ...'

Habakkuk translated.

The Guardian appeared to have difficulty breathing and dropped his prayer stick.

Habakkuk looked thunderstruck. 'Would one of the men you were referring to be Maestro Krakowski?' he asked quietly. It was now Carrington's turn to look nonplussed.

'I must say, Father, this is surprising, one could almost be tempted to say – psychic.' Jack took a step forward to hear better.

'I think I should explain ...' Habakkuk said.

'Please do.'

'The Guardian and his late brother have made it their life's work to find the lost tablets and return them to the Ark. As you know, the tablets have been missing since the Templars removed them ... sometime in the fourteenth century. When he joined the Dominicans as a young man the Guardian was sent to Rome and worked there for decades ... he was a valued member of the Office of the Doctrine of the Faith ...'

'Ah, yes, also known as the Inquisition,' Carrington cut in.

The Guardian looked away.

Habakkuk, however, ignored the remark and continued. 'Father Athanasius remained in Ethiopia and became the next Guardian after his uncle's death twenty years ago.'

'And you, Father, what's your part in all this?'

'I'm the Guardian's assistant. We believed that the Diderot Tablet, as it is known in Rome, had been lost. But you now tell us otherwise ...' he continued.

'The Diderot Tablet, as you call it, was recently located in a bank vault in Switzerland,' Carrington explained.

Habakkuk paled. 'And Maestro Krakowski is prepared to return it as you suggest?'

'Yes – in principle.'

'May I ask why?'

'To honour his grandfather's wish, I believe ...' Carrington replied, 'but he wants to meet the Guardian first and make up his own mind.'

Sir Eric was right, thought Habakkuk, trying to suppress his elation. Then he turned to the Guardian and translated. Carrington noticed a slight smile as he spoke.

The Guardian closed his eyes and, clutching his prayer stick, lifted his head towards heaven. His body began to tremble and his eyes rolled back in his head; he seemed to have entered a trance.

'Please, Mr Carrington. Do not be alarmed,' said Habakkuk, noticing Carrington's worried face, 'the Guardian is only seeking guidance.'

Within minutes, the shaking stopped and the Guardian opened his eyes. He looked surprisingly refreshed, and stood up slowly. He walked up to Carrington, placed his right hand gently on Carrington's shoulder, and spoke a few words in a high-pitched voice.

'It is agreed, my son. God will reward you, in this life and the next,' said Habakkuk, eager to translate the Guardian's blessing.

100

As he walked towards the dilapidated DC3 parked at the far end of Luxor airport, Carrington began to have second thoughts about the journey.

'Not exactly a Lear Jet is it, mate?' observed Jack, struggling with his camera gear. 'Do you think it can fly? I must say, travelling with you guys is a journalist's dream; a new story every day. Now this one ... it's a corker!' Jack winked at Jana.

'You've earned it, Jack. You're part of it,' Jana said. 'The big story at last, eh?' Turning to Carrington she asked, 'Where's the tablet, Marcus?' Carrington shrugged. 'I don't know. I left that up to Naguib ...' Carrington pointed to Haddad waiting for them at the gangway.

Jack glanced at Jana walking along beside him. *She's changed,* he thought, noticing the different tone in her voice. The intimacy, the warmth was no longer there. Not for Jack. But for Carrington ...

'Everything's ready,' said Haddad. 'Here are your papers.' He took Carrington aside. 'Listen, Marcus, I feel uneasy about all this ...'

'What, the trip?'

Haddad nodded. 'Why?'

'Gut feeling. Something isn't right here. I just can't put my finger on it.'

'Come on, you're just tired.' Carrington squeezed Haddad

encouragingly on the shoulder. 'We made the right decision, you told me so yourself.'

Haddad shrugged. 'Inshallah,' he said. 'The coffin is already on the plane, you're all travelling in the same cabin ...'

Carrington looked alarmed. 'What – the coffin as well?'

'I'm afraid so. This is really just an old cargo plane, if you know what I mean ...'

'And Professor Khalil?' Carrington asked anxiously.

'Ah, here she comes now,' Haddad replied. 'I told you – irresistible offer, remember?'

'And the rest, I bet.' Carrington watched her hurry towards the plane, a duffel bag casually slung over one shoulder. He noticed she was also carrying a wooden box.

'Once I showed her Omar's treasures from Uni's tomb, she was ready to agree to anything,' Haddad joked. 'You should have seen her, I could hardly drag her away from it. And when I mentioned your plan with the Ark and the Guardian, well, she practically ran back to her room to start packing. She called it the archaeologist's dream trip. I've done my part, don't you agree?'

'Here we go again!'

'Marcus, I can't believe I'm doing this. Part of me says I must be out of my mind,' said Professor Khalil, trying to catch her breath. 'Are you seriously suggesting we should all get into this jalopy here and fly to Ethiopia with an old man who claims to be the Guardian of the Ark of the Covenant? And all that just to return what may be one of the Tablets of Moses to where it belongs?'

'Yep. Do you have a better idea? Would you rather bury it in one of those dungeons under your museum until the so-called experts are finished with it?' Carrington joked. 'You want to know, just like me, don't you? Not one day, but right now,' he added quietly, helping her with her duffel bag. 'What if the Ark really does exist? Have you thought of that? What if the tablet is authentic?'

'I can't stop thinking about it. We've become accomplices, you know.'

'You mean partners in the archaeological crime of the century? How exciting.'

'Archaeological crime of the century?' Jack butted in. 'Can I quote you?'

'Not unless you fancy twenty years in a Cairo jail,' replied Carrington, his tone suddenly serious. 'We are in this together; all of us. Remember that.'

'Seriously, Marcus, here, take it before I change my mind.' Professor Khalil thrust the wooden box towards Carrington. 'I never thought I would do this.'

'The tablet?'

'Yes. And is this your Indiana Jones hat – raider?' she joked, pointing to Carrington's much loved Akubra.

'Something like that. This is the Aussie version.'

'Most becoming – for a delinquent of your stature.'

'I can already see where this story is heading,' interrupted Jack, frowning.

'What do you mean?' asked Jana.

'Most of it will have to remain off the record. What do you reckon, Marcus?'

'Quite possibly.'

'That's just great,' lamented Jack, shaking his head.

The engines of the old plane coughed into life, and slowly the propellers began to turn. 'Thanks for everything, Naguib,' said Carrington, embracing his friend. 'I'll take good care of your useless stones, you can count on it.'

'Useless stones? I see, that's brave,' Haddad replied, laughing. 'Officially, the tablet was destroyed in the blast. Pulverised, gone forever. It doesn't exist.' Haddad winked at Carrington. 'There's one more thing you should know,' he said, lowering his voice. 'I just had word from Cairo. Horst Newman is about to be released.'

'What? Are you serious? Why?'

'Politics and money. Quickly, listen, I'll tell you why.'

The engine noise inside the plane was deafening. The few seats in the sparse cabin were held together with duct tape and from the ceiling, wires and cables dangled like cold spaghetti. The Guardian sat in the back next to his brother's simple coffin. Secured to the floor with cargo nets, the coffin looked like a dead spider caught inside its own web. Jack was wedged between Jana and Professor Khalil in the front and Carrington squeezed into the seat behind them. The flight to Axum would take several hours, announced the pilot, and they would follow a flight path across the Arabian and Nubian Deserts.

'You said yesterday, Father, that you're the Guardian's assistant,' Carrington said to Habakkuk sitting next to him, 'yet you travel on a Vatican passport?'

'I worked in Rome for many years, just like the Guardian's brother, before returning to Ethiopia,' explained Habakkuk. 'I continued my research there.'

'Into the disappearance of the tablets, I take it?'

'Quite. I've written a book about the Kebra Nagast ...'

'The Glory of Kings,' interjected Carrington, 'I'm familiar with it.'

'And several articles on King Lalibela and the Templars,' added Habakkuk.

'Legend or fact, what do you think?' asked Carrington.

'Well, with all that has happened recently, the scales of probability have tipped considerably in favour of fact, wouldn't you say?'

'The Church in Rome has of course been very interested in all this for quite a long time,' interrupted Jack, turning around. 'Certainly from the thirteenth century onwards, but especially since the discovery of the Diderot manuscripts ...'

'And understandably so,' added Carrington. 'It's ... well, it's dramatic isn't it, if one considers those hieroglyphs and what's actually written on the tablets ... almost unthinkable consequences.' Carrington watched Habakkuk intently.

'Don't you think the Vatican would be desperate to get its hands on what we appear to have right here – and make that box disappear?' asked Jack.

Habakkuk did not reply. Jack and Carrington had, unwittingly, he thought, come too close to the truth.

'Something puzzles me,' continued Carrington, looking out the window. 'Do you mind if I ask you a personal question, Father?'

'I think I know where this is heading,' Habakkuk interrupted quietly. 'Let me pre-empt your question and tell you something about myself.'

'Please do.'

'As a young man, I spent several years with the Guardian's brother in Rome. We were cataloguing the archives of the Inquisition. Both of us worked for Cardinal Brandauer, who was – still is – particularly passionate about this subject. We were convinced that the key to the whereabouts of the tablets – should they still exist – rested with the Templars. And as it turned out, we were certainly looking in the right place, don't you agree? But things became very complicated.'

'In what way?'

'Let's just say we had differences of opinion. We could no longer work together and I returned to Ethiopia. That was many years ago.'

'May I ask why?'

Habakkuk stared out the window. Searching for the right answer, he was watching the endlessly shifting patterns in the sea of sand below. 'I disapproved of his methods ... Brother Frumentius and the Cardinal believed that the end justified the means. One should not speak ill of the dead, but Brother Frumentius seemed to have forgotten why we had embarked on the search in the first place. And, most importantly, his loyalties appeared to have changed ...'

'Oh?'

Habakkuk began to fidget in his seat. 'He had lost sight of ...'

'Yes?'

'The Ark, what it stands for, what it means to our culture, our country, our people.'

'In what way?' asked Carrington.

'He abandoned his allegiance to his brother, the Guardian, and transferred it to the interests of the Church in Rome,' Habakkuk explained. He knew that the best lie was always the one closest to the truth. By simply reversing roles and putting Frumentius' position as his own, Habakkuk had come up with a plausible explanation.

'But you arrived together from Rome just the other day, did you not? How ...?' Carrington asked.

'Does that fit? interrupted Habakkuk. 'The Guardian sent me there – to talk to his brother.'

'Oh – may I ask about what?'

'I was sent to remind him ...' Habakkuk stopped in mid-sentence.

'Remind him of what?' pressed Carrington.

'Of his duty. I tried to turn him back ...'

'Did he listen to you?'

'I'm not sure. But it no longer matters, does it?'

'And your loyalties, Father, where do they stand? I need to know.'

Habakkuk turned around and pointed to the old man sitting at the back. 'With that man over there,' he lied, 'and what he stands for.' Carrington wasn't convinced. He could hear Haddad's warning ringing in his ears: 'Be careful, Marcus, watch the black priest ...'

'I have a surprise for you,' announced Habakkuk, walking down the aisle. 'The Guardian has asked the pilot to make a little detour. If you look out of the widows on the port side –

the left here – you will soon see something very interesting.' The sound of the engines changed and the plane began to descend.

'What are we looking for?' Jana asked, turning towards her window.

'Mount Sinai ...' answered Habakkuk. 'Over there,' he said, pointing to a forbidding peak, 'is Mount Saint Catherine, the highest mountain in Egypt. We are now getting very close.'

The high-pitched voice of the Guardian interrupted Habakkuk. The only words Carrington could understand were Gebel Musa, the mountain of Moses, and it all sounded like a cry for help.

'The Guardian asks if you would permit him to hold the tablet,' translated Habakkuk, leaning across to Carrington, 'just for a moment, while we fly over the sacred mountain.' Carrington handed him the box and Habakkuk carried it carefully to the back. The plane made a sharp turn to port. 'We are now directly above Mount Sinai,' Habakkuk pointed out, 'there – you can see the stone chapel next to the small mosque on the top, and the monastery of St Catherine in the valley below.'

Everyone, except the Guardian, looked out the windows as the plane circled the famous mountain. Carrington glanced towards the back. The Guardian sat motionless in his seat. He held the wooden box resting on his lap with one hand, and his brother's coffin with the other. Only his lips moved in silent prayer.

'Look – there,' Carrington said, tapping Jana on the shoulder, 'a true mystic communicating with his God and the dead – amazing.'

When they landed in Axum it was already dark. Monks from the monastery were waiting at the airstrip and took them to their lodgings – a drab breeze-block building next to the Cathedral of St Mary of Zion.

'I'm sure you will be comfortable here,' said Habakkuk, showing them into simple, whitewashed rooms. 'About tomorrow ... Maestro Krakowski and Dr Rosen are due to arrive from Addis Ababa in the afternoon, I believe,' Habakkuk explained, 'and the Guardian would like to meet you all in the Cathedral tomorrow evening after dark.

101

'What's that?' asked Haddad, pointing to the parcel on his desk.

'The airport CCTV tapes,' answered his assistant. 'Just arrived from Cairo by courier.'

'Late as usual.' Haddad broke open the parcel and walked across to the TV. 'Let's have a look.' The tapes showed new arrivals going through passport control, clearing customs and collecting luggage at Cairo airport. Haddad had requisitioned the tapes of Carrington's return flight from Rome. He reached for the passenger list, and pressed the fast forward button. A blur of shapes and faces raced across the screen like confused genies trying to get back into the bottle. The passenger list confirmed that Monsignor Frumentius and Father Habakkuk had both been on Carrington's flight.

Each time he saw a black face, Haddad stopped the recorder. *Here they are*, he thought, winding back the tape: *Two black men in suits presenting their passports at the counter.* Haddad recognised Frumentius, and Habakkuk, who appeared to be talking to a tall man standing behind him in the queue. At first, Haddad didn't pay any attention to this, but when the same tall man was standing next to Habakkuk at the baggage carousel later, Haddad sensed something worth watching. As he played the tape frame by frame, a snapshot captured the face of the tall stranger front on. Haddad froze. 'It can't be!' he cried out, staring at the screen. Then, taking a deep breath to calm himself, he reached for the phone.

102

Splashing muddy water in all directions every time one of its wheels hit a pothole, the vintage DC3 shuddered to an abrupt halt. A small boy ran past Carrington and pushed wooden chocks under the wheels.

Krakowski looked like a movie star in his white linen suit, dark glasses and Panama hat. *He could have stepped straight out of an Agatha Christie thriller*, thought Marcus, and the only thing missing was the bow tie.

'This is one of those, Dr-Livingstone-I-presume moments,' Krakowski joked, embracing Carrington. 'We do meet in the strangest places.'

'And I almost called you Hercule,' Carrington replied, laughing.

'You're right, he does remind you of Poirot,' Dr Rosen cut in, kissing Carrington on the cheek. 'A slightly slimmer version, but only just.'

'Good to see you both,' Carrington said.

'Without Bettany we wouldn't be here, I can tell you,' explained Krakowski.

'What do you mean?'

'Have you been to Addis Ababa lately?' Krakowski sighed. 'Lucky for us, Bettany here got a celebrity welcome and the authorities cut through all the red tape; didn't even open our luggage. I just sailed through next to her. Without that ... I really wonder. Most of the other passengers are still being interrogated by the military.'

'Celebrity reception? How come?'

'Apparently half the population here owes her ...'

'Owes her? What?'

'Eyesight.'

'Of course! You've been here before,' Carrington remembered, helping them with their luggage.

'Take good care of that, Marcus,' Krakowski said, handing Carrington a leather portmanteau, 'there's something rather precious in there.'

'I can't wait to see it,' Carrington said excitedly, running his hand over the smooth leather.

'Where are we going, Marcus?' asked Dr Rosen.

'We're staying in a monastery,' Carrington replied, 'with working monks. It's quite an experience, I warn you, but very original. The others are waiting for you there; we couldn't all fit in the limousine, you see.' Carrington pointed to a dusty Land Rover with no doors.

'What's that?' asked Krakowski, looking confused.

'Your taxi. Cheer up, Ben. When was the last time you were picked up at a remote airstrip and driven to an old monastery to stay the night, eh?'

'What about the Ark, Marcus?' enquired Dr Rosen, handing her bag to one of the waiting monks. 'Have you found out anything more about it?'

Carrington shook his head. 'The Guardian will meet us in the cathedral tonight. I expect we'll hear it all then.'

'Good. I can only spare a day or two. I have a concert in London on Saturday, I'm afraid,' Krakowski said, wiping his neck with a handkerchief. 'Full house.'

'Relax, Ben. You're not turning into a musical conveyer belt, now, are you?' Carrington joked, winking at Dr Rosen.

Patting Krakowski affectionately on the arm, Dr Rosen said, 'Remember what you told me in Rome the other day?'

'What did I say?' Krakowski asked, feigning ignorance.

'There are more important things in life than scalpels and fiddles ...'

'I said that?'

'It's almost time,' Habakkuk announced, hurrying towards them. 'Please, come.'

'It's built like a fortress,' Jana observed, pointing to the massive stone walls of the cathedral. 'It looks more like a medieval castle than a house of God. I suppose, if the Ark is really in there, well ...'

'It used to be, but not anymore,' Jack said. 'Emperor Haile Selassie built a small sanctuary just behind it in the sixties, which is supposed to house the Ark – isn't that right, Father?'

'This is the holiest site in Ethiopia,' Habakkuk explained, sidestepping the question, 'it has quite a history. The original church was built in the fourth century by the Emperors Shezana and Ezana. They were brothers, the first Christian co-rulers of our country.'

'And wasn't it Emperor Ezana who, according to legend, brought the Ark of the Covenant from the island of Tana Kirkos to Axum?' Krakowski asked.

'You are well versed in our history, Mr Krakowski,' Habakkuk replied. 'The Ark was kept on that island for over eight hundred years.'

'So you're planning to become a tour guide here when you retire,' Jana joked. 'Are you also learning to speak ...um ...?'

'Tigrigna,' interjected Habakkuk, coming to her assistance.

'Not quite. I've read it all just recently in my father's papers,' Krakowski said. 'He was fascinated by this place.'

'Because of the Ark?' enquired Professor Khalil.

'Yes ...'

'Have you ever actually seen the Ark, Father?' Krakowski asked, turning to Habakkuk.

'It is forbidden!' Habakkuk knew instantly that he shouldn't have said it, but it was too late. Everyone looked stunned.

'Where does that leave us then?' Carrington asked, breaking the awkward silence.

'The Guardian will explain everything. Please, follow me.'

The flames from hundreds of candles lit up the lofty interior of the cathedral. The Guardian was waiting for them in front of the altar, his hands folded in prayer. The pungent scent of frankincense filled the air and apart from two monks holding the incense burners, the church was empty.

This is the moment, Krakowski thought, remembering his grandfather's wish. He tightened his grip on the leather portmanteau containing the tablet. All the twisted threads of his life were coming together with surprising clarity. For an instant, Krakowski imagined he could see his parents walk hand-in-hand down the aisle beside him, but it was only the shadows of the flickering candles dancing along the walls of the nave.

Habakkuk asked them to line up in front of the altar and face the Guardian, who then addressed them in Tigrigna. His high-pitched voice sounded unfamiliar and strange.

'The Guardian requests that you place the tablets here in front of him. He would like to bless them,' Habakkuk translated, pointing to a pair of cushions. Krakowski lifted his tablet out of the portmanteau. Placing it carefully on one of the cushions, he bowed towards the Guardian and stepped back. The tablet began to glow in the candlelight. *It's waiting for its twin*, thought Krakowski.

'Tabot Musa,' whispered the Guardian, lifting his hands in prayer. Habakkuk motioned to Carrington to step forward. Carrington opened the wooden box and placed it on the second cushion. The fragments had been carefully pieced together by Professor Khalil; the tablet looked almost whole again as if it had healed itself. It too appeared to glow.

'I welcome you,' the Guardian continued. 'My entire life has been devoted to finding the tablets. That search is now over. They have been found and for that we must thank the Lord.' The Guardian pointed to the cushions in front of him. 'You have been chosen by the Almighty to return the tablets to where they belong. I am grateful to you – Ethiopia is grateful.' The Guardian lifted his eyes to the skies, and then paused. 'For hundreds of years, the Ark stood on this very spot just behind me,' he said. 'It survived invasions, fire, wars, and the greed of men. It was only removed on a few occasions – to protect it. However, before I can continue, it is my solemn duty to ask you to swear an oath that you will not reveal what you are about to learn to anyone ...'

Just what I need, thought Jack, biting his lip.

'The Guardian will now approach each of you,' Habakkuk said. 'If you are prepared to take the oath, please say "I swear" when he places his hand on your shoulder. If you cannot, you will be asked to leave.'

Jana was first in line. The Guardian, a short man, came over and looked up at her. Jana remembered looking into the eyes of another old man not that long ago – ice blue, crystal clear and cruel. But these eyes were hooded, almost transparent and gentle, radiating kindness and compassion. As the old man placed his hand on her shoulder, she felt a warmth that seemed to flow into her whole being.

'I swear,' she whispered, barely able to speak, and then smiled at the old man through tears in her eyes. *That feeling*, thought Jana – it was the same she'd experienced waking up in old Mrs Gonski's bed as a young teenager on the brink of self-destruction. It was love. When the Guardian moved on, she reached for Carrington's hand and squeezed it hard. He too could feel the powerful aura radiating from the old man.

How extraordinary, Krakowski thought, watching the Guardian move slowly from Christian to Jew to Muslim. *We've all just taken an oath of silence to protect two sacred artefacts belonging to humanity; we can rise above ourselves after all.* Benjamin knew then, beyond any doubt, that in honouring his grandfather's wish he had chosen the right path.

The Guardian returned to the altar. 'I thank you, one and all,' he said quietly. Then, after a pause, added, 'The Ark you seek is not here in Axum.'

'We've been had!' whispered Jack.

'Shush!' Carrington silenced him.

'The relic in the Sanctuary Chapel behind the cathedral is an old replica,' said the Guardian. 'The original Ark is safe – elsewhere. I'm only its Guardian. The Ark is in the care of the Keeper who is not allowed to leave it. He is expecting you. You will be taken to him tomorrow.'

103

Sorokin had only one thing on his mind: getting out of Egypt as quickly as possible. Years of working undercover had taught him how to blend into crowds. He adjusted his dark glasses, and kept watching the departure gate. *Ten more minutes,* he thought, *and I'm through.* While he had every confidence in his forged papers, he knew that airports were dangerous places for a man like himself. Very dangerous.

'Going to London, Colonel Sorokin, or would you prefer Gregory Molotov?' asked Haddad, placing a hand on Sorokin's shoulder from behind. 'Another auction, perhaps?' Sorokin didn't flinch.

'You are mistaken, sir,' he said, turning slowly around. 'I'm not a colonel, and my name isn't Sorokin nor is it Molotov.'

'Perhaps not today,' replied Haddad. 'Today you are George Kovacs from Budapest, I believe. How interesting.' Sorokin raced through his options. He could easily take out Haddad, a small man, and dash for the exit. Then he noticed the two soldiers with machine guns standing behind Haddad. He would have to negotiate.

'And you are?' asked Sorokin, casually taking off his glasses.

'I'm Chief Inspector Haddad. You are under arrest.'

104

The Guardian's plane was refuelled and ready to leave. It was just after sunrise.

'Where are you taking us, Father?' Carrington asked.

The black priest shrugged. 'Only the Guardian knows.' Habakkuk looked annoyed; he'd been unable to contact the Cardinal the night before. Overtaken by events, he hadn't spoken to His Eminence since Frumentius' death.

'But he's staying here to bury his brother ...'

'Gebra Christos will take us to the Keeper,' snapped Habakkuk.

'Who is Gebra Christos?'

'That's him over there.' Habakkuk pointed to a priest with long white hair walking towards the plane. 'He's the Protector of Secrets ...'

Professor Khalil had spent the entire night examining Krakowski's tablet with Carrington, lamenting the fact that she wasn't able to take a plaster cast of it. Krakowski on the other hand, looked refreshed and was busily scribbling something on notepaper.

'You look rather chirpy this morning, Ben, what are you doing?' Dr Rosen asked, glancing over his shoulder.

'Jotting down a few ideas – they came to me in the cathedral. I couldn't get them out of my head.'

'Ideas? But these are clefs and staffs ... notes.'

'Yes, musical ideas; melodies, phrases, whole brass sections, the violins here and then the oboe and the flute – it's quite extraordinary. There was music everywhere last night. I've never experienced such a feeling before.'

'You're composing?'

'I suppose I am. Look, I'm just writing down what I hear – no corrections!'

'Just like the Mozart manuscripts you told me about,' continued Dr Rosen. 'How did you put it – a flawless flow of musical genius written down by someone taking dictation from God.'

'I wouldn't go quite that far,' Krakowski said, laughing, 'but there's certainly something about this place.'

'Funny you should say that, I had a strange dream.'

'Oh? What about?'

'Surgery. I think I've finally worked out a safer and cheaper way to do these operations. It actually came to me in the cathedral last night ... I must come back here soon to do some more work. You know my husband ... he ... '

Krakowski squeezed her hand. 'I know.'

'Don't look so glum,' Jana said, linking arms with Jack. 'What's wrong?'

'Nothing much. It's just that one of the greatest stories of all time appears to be unfolding in front of my very eyes, and I'm told to leave my camera gear behind and swear an oath of silence, that's all. And guess what?'

'What?'

'Silly me has already promised ...'

'What?'

'A great story with great photos!'

'Wasn't that a little hasty?'

'I needed the advance ...'

'Oh Jack; not again ...' Jana shook her head. 'You'll just have to come up with something, won't you? But don't forget your oath,' she reminded him, wagging her finger.

'I'm working on it.'

Jana turned to face Jack full on. 'I'm so happy, Jack, I can't explain it ...' she said.

'You are glowing, Jana, you know, like ...' A sadness washed over him. 'Like what?'

'Like a woman in love,' he replied quietly. Jana blushed deeply and she let go of his arm. Carrington watched her from behind; he too had noticed the glow. For the first time since the Luxor horror he felt at peace. The grieving had somehow eased, even stopped in the cathedral the night before.

Grieving is love without a home, thought Carrington. *Perhaps I've come home*. Remembering the Guardian's words – *God will reward you, in this life and the next* – he began to smile.

The plane climbed slowly, circled Axum, and then turned north. 'This feels like a pilgrimage. I wonder where we're heading,' said Professor Khalil, looking tired.

'The Protector of Secrets will take us into his confidence in due course I expect,' replied Carrington. 'I only hope it isn't Mount Sinai; there was nowhere to land and I can't see any parachutes,' he quipped. 'Seriously, what did you think of Ben's tablet?'

'Well, both have been crafted from the same material, so much is clear, but it isn't stone. I haven't seen anything quite like it before. It's a strange, stone-like substance, yet quite different. Alien. Extra-terrestrial perhaps.'

'You mean, like – not of this world?'

'Exactly.'

'What do you think it is?'

'You'll laugh.'

'Try me.'

'A meteorite.'

'Star dust?'

'Yes. I saw a small stele carved from a meteorite in South

America once; it reminded me of that.'

'And the writing, the hieroglyphs?'

'That's easy; classic New Kingdom. Eighteenth dynasty I'd say, close to the reign of Akhenaten. Amarna period or shortly thereafter.'

'The biblical time of Moses – close enough. That fits.'

'It does.'

Gebra Christos, the Protector of Secrets, leaned over to Habakkuk, whispered and pointed to the others. Habakkuk unbuckled his seatbelt and stood up.

'I can now tell you where we are heading ...' said Habakkuk, slowly. This was enjoyable, he thought.

'Drum roll please, Maestro,' Carrington joked, leaning across to Krakowski.

'We are going to Lalibela,' Habakkuk announced.

'The Eighth Wonder of the world – according to UNESCO, that is,' blurted Krakowski.

'What do you mean?' Carrington asked.

'There are these extraordinary rock-hewn churches from the thirteenth century –King Lalibela built them but, to this day no one really knows how it was done.'

'The locals believe they were built by angels,' said Khalil. 'Perhaps they're right.'

'It was the capital of the Ethiopian Empire during the Zagwe dynasty. It used to be called Roha,' Habakkuk explained.

Roha! Of course, thought Krakowski. *Father's second password; he knew!*

'You are a well-informed lot,' Jack cut in, furiously taking notes. 'I must confess, I haven't even heard of the place.'

'I've always wanted to see them,' said Professor Khalil, 'they're supposed to be amazing. Whole churches – some completely freestanding monoliths – carved out of solid rock from the top down, with windows and altars and large open spaces. Quite unbelievable, really.'

'My late husband visited the churches just before he ...' said Dr Rosen quietly, '... his plane crashed in the mountains not far from here. I've wanted to visit them ever since.'

'I had no idea this is where it happened,' Jana said, reaching for Dr Rosen's hand.

'His body has never been found. He's still out there,' whispered Dr Rosen. 'Perhaps waiting for me.'

'Well, Doctor, you are about to see the churches,' Habakkuk said, looking out the window. 'We are almost there. Here they come – look.' The plane had commenced its descent and was losing altitude fast.

'Those long trenches over there – can you see them – are all part of the churches we're going to visit,' Habakkuk explained. 'And here, just below us, is the River Jordan and the village itself.' The plane made a wide turn to slow its descent, giving them a splendid view of the ancient site below. As they drew closer, the deep trenches revealed themselves as massive walls of pink tuff protecting the churches from the world outside.

'That's Beite Medane Alem down there.' Habakkuk pointed to a huge free-standing rectangular structure in the centre of a walled courtyard. From above, it looked like a Greek temple. 'The largest of the rock-hewn churches in Lalibela. And there, in the next enclosure, are the Beite Mariam churches,' he continued excitedly, 'and down here, the twin church Golgota – Debre Sina. Can you all see it? This is the holiest shrine in Lalibela.'

'What's that strange-looking structure in front of it?' Jana asked.

'The Tomb of Adam ...'

'What? The Tomb of Adam? And I haven't got my camera,' cried Jack, nose pressed against the window. 'Can you believe it?'

'This is the best way to see them – an angel's view from above. You really get an idea of the scale. A whole mountain had to be chiselled away by hand to create all this,' observed

Habakkuk.

'Look at all these people,' Krakowski interjected. 'Is there a festival?'

'No. These are pilgrims ...'

The pilot put the plane down on the short, rutted runway with great skill and turned off the engines. Carrington looked out the window. A contingent of bearded monks stood in front of a contraption without windows, seats or doors. Usually pressed into service to deliver livestock and farm produce to market, the old bus looked more like an open sardine can on wheels than a vehicle capable of locomotion.

One by one, they climbed down the wooden ladder leaning against the plane and walked across to the waiting monks. 'Please, get in,' said Habakkuk, pointing to the bus. 'The Keeper sends his greetings. He will meet us in the Selassie Chapel tonight,' Habakkuk announced, 'after all the pilgrims have left. He is preparing the way.'

105

'We are both practical men, Chief Inspector,' said Sorokin, watching Haddad carefully. 'I can help you, if you help me.'

'The way I see it, Colonel,' replied Haddad, spreading his fingers, 'you are the one very much in need of help, not me.'

'Actually, the ones really needing help – urgently, I might add – are your friends you sent into Ethiopia with Father Habakkuk this morning.' Judging by the expression on Haddad's face, Sorokin knew he had chosen the right approach.

'How so?'

'Father Habakkuk is a very dangerous man. He's a zealot with a mission, and we both know how dangerous that can be.'

'I'm listening.'

'He's not what he seems. He's not helping the old Guardian recover the tablets; he's working for the Vatican. He wants to destroy the tablets and all those involved. No witnesses, you see.'

'How do I know you're not just making all this up?'

'Chief Inspector ... please ... This is insulting to both of us and there isn't much time.'

'How do you know all this?'

'I overheard things ... you know how it works ...'

'What's on your mind?'

Sorokin began to smile. 'Here's the deal, but it doesn't only involve me.'

'Oh? Who else then?'

'Horst Newman.'

'You lead a charmed life, Mr Newman,' said Haddad, stepping into the tiny cell. Shackled to the wall, Horst sat on a stool in the corner.

'From where I sit, it doesn't quite look like that,' replied Horst, lifting the chains cutting into his chafed wrists.

'As your lawyer would have told you yesterday, negotiations for your release are well advanced. However, certain obstacles remain. Quite tricky ones, I might add.'

Horst sat up as if poked with a hot iron from behind. 'What obstacles?' he demanded.

'I understand that you are well connected in Ethiopia; to both the rebels and the military ...' Haddad continued, ignoring the question. 'Wasn't it only last year that you supplied weapons to both sides?' Horst did not reply. 'This is not a trick question, Mr Newman. If you are prepared to help us, we could perhaps remove the tricky obstacles standing in the way of your release ...'

'How can I possibly help you, Chief Inspector?' asked Horst, looking suddenly interested.

'Through your Ethiopian contacts. And besides, your sister appears to be in serious danger. She's in Ethiopia as we speak and needs your help.'

'This is a bad joke, surely,' replied Horst, shaking his head.

'Far from it. But there's someone who can explain all this much better than I,' said Haddad, walking to the door.

'Who?'

The cell door creaked open and a prison guard appeared in the doorway. 'Bring him in!' barked Haddad. 'I think you already know this man.'

Horst gasped. 'You?' Bumping his head against the low doorframe, Sorokin stepped into the cell.

'I'll be back in ten minutes,' Haddad said and left.

Haddad paced in front of the closed cell door. To make any deal with a man like Sorokin was certainly a last resort. This situation demanded desperate measures, Haddad told himself. He glanced at his watch, took a deep breath and pushed open the door. 'Well? What's your answer?'

'We need access to our mobile phones ...' explained Sorokin calmly.

'I'll arrange it,' said Haddad.

Horst and Sorokin spent hours on the phone tracking down their Ethiopian contacts. Haddad was still sceptical, but he had little choice. 'Here's my deal,' he said, unlocking Horst's handcuffs. 'If your associates are as reliable as you claim and they can deliver ... well, you and the Colonel will be allowed to stay in Ethiopia when we're finished. Clear so far?'

'Absolutely,' said Horst, winking at Sorokin standing next to him.

'If we come under attack, you are under attack. If we fail, well ... In short, your lives depend on the success of this mission, understood?'

'Perfectly,' said Sorokin. This was the kind of talk he liked; no room for misunderstandings. In Haddad's place, he would have done exactly the same. His own contacts in Ethiopia were Russian military 'advisers'. Sorokin had dealt with them before; their cooperation was for sale. Self-interest and greed were always reliable.

Horst was in a similar position: he had to promise the rebels another arms deal in return for safe passage across Ethiopian airspace and entry into Axum.

'Now, put these on.' Haddad pointed to the black battle fatigues on the table in front of him. 'We're leaving in two hours.'

106

The brooding, rock-fortress-like hill – pink during the day, now silver in the ghostly light of the full moon – reminded Carrington of Karnak. A thunderstorm was approaching from the south, sending dark clouds racing across the night sky. Thunder rumbled some distance away.

'We have to walk from here,' Habakkuk said, handing out lanterns with large candles. 'You'll need these; there's no light in the churches, or along the way.'

'Is that the entry to the site?' Jack asked, pointing to a narrow breach in the rock wall towering above them.

'It is. The Keeper will meet us at Beite Medhane Alem. We saw it from the plane, remember? The big, free-standing rock church. It's just through here.' Habakkuk led the way; Krakowski fell in beside him.

'I first came across the Grail legend in your father's papers as a young priest in Rome just after the War,' Habakkuk said. 'His ideas were the inspiration for my own work later on.'

'In what way?' asked Krakowski, surprised.

'Your father made an important connection: he pointed out that the Holy Grail made its first appearance in France in 1182 in a poem by Chretien de Troyes. Three years later, in 1185, Prince Lalibela left Jerusalem and returned to Ethiopia to regain his crown – your father believed he had help from the Templars. A few years after that, around 1195 or so, Wolfram von Eschenbach wrote his epic dealing with the same subject.'

'Parzival,' interrupted Krakowski, 'and he took so much from de Troyes' unfinished work.'

'Exactly. But ...' Habakkuk continued, 'Wolfram put in specific references not only to the Templars, but to Ethiopia, and made other important changes.'

'The Holy Grail – no longer a cup – became a stone,' Krakowski said, remembering his father's notes.

'Quite. And your father was convinced that the stone was the tablets. The tablets and the stone were one, you see.'

'Are you suggesting the Templars knew this?'

'Yes, I do.'

'Astonishing,' mumbled Krakowski to himself, 'it all fits!'

'You said earlier that Lalibela was once called Roha ...' said Carrington.

'Quite. And what is particularly interesting is the fact that one short passage in Wolfram's poem specifically refers to Roha ...'

'What? Wolfram knew about Roha?' asked Jack.

'Yes. Many scholars still think it's a reference to the Rohischer Berg – a mountain in Austria – but I think that's nonsense. And so did Maestro Krakowski's father, by the way. I have no doubt he was right. He came to the view that Parzival was a carefully crafted literary map showing the way ... for the initiated ...'

'The way to what?' Jana asked.

Habakkuk stopped and turned around. 'The Grail Stone, the Tablets of the Law, resting inside the Ark of the Covenant,' he replied, 'and the Rohischer Berg is not in Austria, but right here in front of you. This is Roha.'

107

Haddad knew he was taking a huge risk. Flying low and without lights the two unmarked helicopters crossed the border into Ethiopian airspace. The official cover story was that Haddad was following a lead on the recent terrorist attack at Sharm el-Sheikh. As officer in charge of the investigation he had the authority to do that. However, crossing the Ethiopian border was always tricky, especially at night, and could easily trigger an embarrassing incident, or worse. Everything depended on speed and timing, but having to rely on only four handpicked commandos, Haddad had to admit, was almost reckless.

Horst sat behind Haddad – wedged between two burly soldiers. He looked subdued; trying to make contact with his former business associates had almost ended in disaster. At first, no one wanted to help. If it hadn't been for Zelelew, the mission wouldn't have gone ahead. Zelelew, the son of a rebel leader Horst had befriended during an arms deal, would be meeting them at Axum; he would provide access and be interpreter and go-between with the monks.

Sorokin, unlike Horst, appeared calm and in control. Everything was going to plan. His plan. He was out of jail and out of Egypt. In return for clearing the way for the sortie with both the military and the rebels, he would be allowed to go free.

Suddenly, Haddad's helicopter veered sharply to the left and dropped altitude. A blinding light raced past outside.

'What was that?' Haddad shouted into his microphone.

'Rocket attack, from down there, eleven o'clock,' replied the pilot calmly, taking evasive action. Haddad turned around and looked angrily at Horst sitting behind him. Horst shrugged. They were under missile attack – most likely by the very ones Sorokin had sold to the rebels the year before. Then another blinding light exploded out of the darkness, this time from a different direction. At first the light raced towards them just like before. The pilot nosedived, confusing the rocket's heat sensor. The rocket changed direction. The second helicopter with Sorokin on board was directly behind, but flying a little higher. The rocket slammed into its fuselage from below and exploded, ripping the helicopter apart. Spiralling to the ground like a giant catherine wheel, the burning wreckage sent showers of sparks into the night as a fiery farewell to the four souls on board.

Axum was calm and in darkness. The pilot put the helicopter down at the end of the airstrip. Expecting an ambush, the two commandos jumped out and looked around. All appeared calm.

Haddad evaluated his position. With Sorokin, the pilot and two commandos dead, the mission was now severely compromised. However, turning back was out of the question.

'Well?' barked Haddad. 'Where are they?'

'There,' replied Horst, pointing to a flashing light at the other end of the runway. 'It's a signal. I need a torch.' Within minutes of Horst's reply to the signal, a jeep materialised and stopped in front of the helicopter. Horst walked across to the vehicle and spoke to the driver.

'Chief Inspector, please, over here,' Horst called out, waving at Haddad. 'There's someone who wants to speak to you.'

As he approached the jeep, Haddad smelled the familiar notes of frankincense. He switched on his torch to see an old man wearing a pillbox-shaped hat sitting in the passenger seat.

The Guardian, his prayer stick held with both hands, looked calmly at Haddad and smiled.

'We've missed them,' Haddad announced, hurrying back to the chopper. 'We must leave at once.'

'Where to?' asked Horst, looking worried.

'Lalibela.' Haddad pointed to the Guardian and Horst's contact, Zelelew, who'd translated for him. 'These two are coming with us. Let's go!'

On the flight to Lalibela, the Guardian listened patiently to Haddad's account of Habakkuk's betrayal. Suddenly, everything that had troubled him about his brother's death appeared to fall into place. However, more troubling still, he thought, was the fact that Habakkuk appeared to have accomplices among the monks. Seeking guidance, the Guardian closed his eyes and began to pray. After a while, he opened them again, looked at Haddad and spoke in his tell-tale high-pitched voice.

'The Ark is waiting, we must hurry,' Zelelew translated.

108

The Protector of Secrets greeted them in front of the church. Behind him, holding lanterns just like their own stood a small group of monks, chanting.

'These will keep you warm,' said Habakkuk, pointing to a bundle of neatly folded woollen cloaks on the stone steps. 'Please, put them on.' Dr Rosen draped one of the cloaks – the same as those worn by the monks – over her shoulders. She instantly resembled a giant bat.

'Ready for Gotham City?' joked Krakowski, struggling with his own cloak.

Gebra Christos, the Protector of Secrets, said something in Tigrigna.

'The Keeper is expecting you; he's waiting inside, by the Amd,' Habakkuk translated.

'What's the Amd?' Jack asked.

'A pillar in the middle of the church,' replied Habakkuk. 'It's a symbol of the unity of faith. There's a legend that in one of his visions King Lalibela saw Christ touch the pillar. The past and the future of the entire world is written on it. But, since man is too weak to face the truth, the pillar has to be covered to protect the faithful.'

The monks formed two long rows and, led by the Protector of Secrets, entered the church.

'Time travel is possible after all,' Jana whispered, reaching for

Carrington's hand. 'Look, we've just stepped into the Middle Ages.' The church – hollowed out of solid rock with mallet and chisel – was illuminated by dozens of lanterns. Long shadows – crazy demons trapped above the altar – danced along the arches and the barrel vault. Jack looked across and noticed Jana and Carrington's linked hands. *It's my own fault, she's moved on*, he thought, unable to stop a large twinge of regret.

In the middle of the nave stood a pillar covered with cloth. Leaning against it, and holding on to the cloth with one hand, was an old monk with his eyes closed. His long hair – white as the first winter snow – was tied together at the back of his head. This was the Keeper of the Ark.

Slowly, the circle of monks surrounding the pillar opened. The Protector of Secrets walked up to the old man and kissed the large crucifix hanging from his neck. When the old man raised his hand, the chanting stopped. For a while, the voices continued to echo along the soaring walls of the nave before giving way to silence so complete that Jana thought she could hear her heart beating under the coarse woollen cloak.

The Protector of Secrets waved them closer.

As she walked towards the Keeper, Professor Khalil noticed a large slab of stone had been lifted out of the floor, exposing a narrow shaft. The slab was propped against the pillar, like a massive lid removed.

Eventually the Keeper spoke, but his voice sounded strangely distant; as if it came straight out of the Amd behind him.

'The day of great joy has arrived,' Habakkuk translated. 'After much suffering and deprivation the faithful can rejoice at last – the tablets have returned. It is written,' the old man paused, pointing to the Amd behind him, 'right here.' Smiling calmly, he added: 'I have been expecting you.'

Holding his prayer stick firmly in his right hand, the Protector of Secrets stepped forward and began.

'You have been found ... worthy. You are about to be granted a great honour, a rare privilege bestowed through the ages on but a chosen few ...' Habakkuk looked momentarily confused. He was struggling with the translation. Gesturing for permission to go further, the Protector of Secrets paused and looked at the Keeper. Habakkuk watched intently. The Keeper nodded and pointed to the shaft. 'The Keeper will now take you to the Ark of the Covenant,' continued the Protector of Secrets. 'Do not be afraid of what you may find along the way ... God will give you courage. Follow me.'

'Sounds ominous,' whispered Jana.

'Too late,' Carrington replied, squeezing her hand.

The chanting resumed and the Keeper walked slowly over to the edge of the shaft. Two monks – one on each side – helped him take the first step into the darkness below.

This is surreal, thought Jack, lining up with the others to follow the Keeper. *Even if I could write about it, no one would believe me.* Already, excitement was beginning to replace the ache of regret.

109

The pilot turned on the spotlights, aimed them at the rock-hewn churches below and set the helicopter down next to the old bus. Brandishing sticks, a group of monks came running towards the chopper. Haddad helped the Guardian get out of his seat and opened the door.

'What's going on?' asked Horst, watching the angry mob surround the helicopter.

'Just leave it to him,' said Zelelew, pointing to the Guardian. 'Watch.'

Leaning on his prayer stick, the old man addressed the crowd. The monks recognised the Guardian and fell silent.

'The Guardian said we must hurry,' Zelelew translated, turning to Haddad, 'the others have already gone down into the catacombs ...'

'Catacombs? Great!'

Haddad left the pilot and a commando to guard the helicopter. This left him only one soldier to take into the unknown. He had to take Horst as well, and Zelelew would have to do the translating.

Horst recognised Haddad's dilemma. 'You're short of men,' he said calmly. 'You can't do this on your own.' Haddad looked at him but didn't reply. 'We should join forces ... we both want this to succeed, right?'

'I'm listening.'

'I'm on your side, Chief Inspector. Self-preservation ...' he added, a crooked smile creasing his face. 'Surely you must see that. And then there's my sister ...'

Haddad checked his gun. 'What's on your mind?'

'I could watch your back; it's your weakest point.' Haddad looked at Horst. He was right. *Allies of necessity?* he thought.

'All right, but no weapons.'

'No weapons are needed,' replied Horst, 'only courage and resolve.'

I hope you have plenty of both, Haddad thought and hurried after the Guardian.

110

'Did you hear that?' Jana asked, following Carrington down the slippery stairs. A dull thud echoed along the narrow passage from above.

'I think the tomb's just been sealed,' Jack observed from the back. 'I hope it isn't ours.'

'We better pray there's another way out of here,' said Krakowski, looking anxiously over his shoulder. 'You saw the size of that slab; we'll never shift it from below.'

'Thanks, Ben, that's most reassuring,' said Dr Rosen, holding on to Krakowski's belt from behind to steady him. With barely enough room to walk upright, they had to bend low to avoid hitting their heads against the roof of the tunnel. Krakowski found it difficult to negotiate the narrow passage let alone keep hold of the leather portmanteau slung over his shoulder.

The Keeper was waiting for them in a small chapel at the bottom of the stairs. Several passages fanned out from the chapel, reaching deep into the mountain like the abandoned shafts of an ancient mine. Sparkling droplets of water ran slowly down the walls making the floor treacherous.

Next to the Keeper stood a young monk, his face ghostly from the pungent cloud of frankincense rising from the silver burner in his hands.

'This is the burial chapel,' Habakkuk explained. 'All the Keepers and Guardians of the Ark are laid to rest in these catacombs. You will pass some along the way ... they're in niches cut into the walls.'

'See, I told you; it's a tomb,' Jack whispered.

'Great,' Jana said, bracing herself. She glanced at the Keeper kneeling in front of the altar, eyes closed, lips moving in silent prayer. At last he looked up and pointed to one of the passages. Habakkuk held up his lantern and smiled. Carrington adjusted his backpack with the wooden box inside. *I don't like this*, he thought, watching Habakkuk walk into the passage. *If anything happens to us in here, no one will ever know ...*

'What is he doing?' asked Haddad, following the Guardian twice around the Amd.

Zelelew shrugged. 'A ritual ...'

Something cold touched Haddad's neck and tingled down his back. He recognised the feeling – danger – and checked his gun.

The Guardian stopped and pointed with his prayer stick to the large flagstone marking the entry into the catacombs. Using crowbars, the monks went to work. Slowly, the stone was lifted out of the floor. The Guardian, holding the lantern high to spread the circle of light, began to descend.

'He obviously can't walk any faster,' said Haddad, pointing to the Guardian shuffling along in front of him, 'but he seems to be the only one who knows the way. I'll stay with him in the front with Zelelew; you watch the monks ...'

'Okay,' replied Horst.

The Guardian stopped at a small chapel at the bottom of the stairs and looked anxiously around. He closed his eyes and began to chant.

'What on earth is he doing?' asked Haddad, turning to Zelelew standing behind him.

'Praying. I don't think he knows which way to go ...'

'Great!'

The monks formed a tight circle around the Guardian and

began to chant as well. Suddenly, the candles in the lanterns started to flicker. A draught of cool air, like the breath of a hidden giant, was blowing into the chamber through one tunnel. Smiling, the Guardian opened his eyes and pointed with his prayer stick to the passage on his right.

Dr Rosen bent down low to avoid an overhanging rock, lost her footing and almost fell. Trying to regain her balance, she found herself face to face with the broken skull of a past Keeper reposing on a rock ledge. She dropped her lantern.

'He won't harm you,' said Carrington, picking up the lantern. 'It's the live ones we have to watch.'

'Can you hear that noise?' asked Professor Khalil. 'What do you think it is?' A distant rumble rolled through the passage from deep within the mountain.

'Water,' replied Jack. 'Lots of it.' Turning a tight corner, they reached a steep, narrow set of steps chiselled out of the virgin rock. The steps were wet, slippery and it was difficult to climb down without any hand support. The distant rumble turned into pounding thunder.

'Up there – look!' shouted Krakowski, pointing to the soaring ceiling with his lantern. The tunnel opened into a large cave.

'What a place,' said Dr Rosen, holding on to Carrington's arm. Water gushed out of a crack in the rock high above them and cascaded down into a deep pool below. The chamber was filled with spray rising from the boiling torrent and the water disappeared in a whirlpool at the bottom. Carrington thought it looked like the gaping mouth of a hungry basilisk waiting to devour the damned. The noise was deafening.

The foaming water, racing along the polished sides of the cave, would have washed away anyone foolish enough to venture too close. They had suddenly entered an underground cathedral, thought Carrington, built by giants.

'You must be joking!' shouted Jana, pointing to a narrow suspension bridge strung across the steep chasm. Wooden slats, some broken, served as the walkway, and two thick, plaited ropes – one on each side of the bridge – provided the only hand support. The main load-bearing ropes holding the slats together were tied to iron rings set into the rock on either side. At its lowest point in the middle, the sagging bridge cleared the deadly water by only a whisker.

'We must cross,' shouted Habakkuk, pointing to the opposite side, 'there's no other way.'

One of the first monks to cross the bridge almost lost his balance, but then managed to pull himself onto a narrow rock ledge.

'I can't do this,' complained Dr Rosen, swallowing hard and biting the sides of her cheeks. Neither did much to control her rising panic.

'It's not too bad. He made it – see?' Krakowski said, 'I'll come with you.'

'Let the others go first,' suggested Habakkuk, 'I'll help you with your bag ...'

Krakowski caught Carrington's eye. Carrington shook his head. 'It's all right, he can come with me,' he said.

The Keeper and the Protector of Secrets crossed next.

'I can take Bettany,' Jack offered, reaching for Dr Rosen's hand. 'Come, just hold on.' Jack guided Dr Rosen safely across; Professor Khalil and Jana followed.

Habakkuk watched Krakowski adjust Carrington's backpack and smiled: the opportunity he had been waiting for had arrived all by itself. He could hear the Cardinal's instructions: 'Destroy the tablets. You must not fail.' He would not fail!

'You two, next,' Habakkuk snapped. 'We'll steady the bridge for you from here and then bring the lanterns. Go. Quickly!'

'Come on, Ben, here. Let's sling the bag over your shoulder,' said Carrington, helping Krakowski with the portmanteau. 'That's it. Let's go.'

Krakowski stepped onto the slippery slats, tightly gripping the hand ropes on either side. The handles of the leather portmanteau cut deep into his neck but left his hands free. 'Don't look down,' Carrington shouted from behind. When they reached the middle, the bridge suddenly lost tension and began to sag. The slats hit the water.

'Look!' shouted Jana, pointing to the collapsing bridge.

The two monks on the other side had dropped the ropes and were attacking them with knives. One of the ropes snapped, hurling Carrington and Krakowski into the foaming torrent. Carrington's treasured hat flew off and disappeared.

Krakowski managed to keep hold of the severed rope with both hands as he was sucked under. Struggling under the water, Carrington held on to him from behind. He too had kept his grip on the rope, with one hand. They were being swept along towards the whirlpool at the far end of the cave but surfaced just a few feet from the gaping hole. The icy water sent a bolt of searing pain racing through Carrington's neck and shoulders to his brain, like tentacles trying to extinguish the struggling spark of life. Numbed, he almost let go of the rope.

'There they are,' Jana shouted, pointing down. Dr Rosen lent forward to look and almost fell over the edge.

'No!' bellowed Jack, grabbing her from behind. 'Jesus, keep back!'

'Hold on, Ben!' Carrington yelled, gasping for air. The rushing water was dragging them relentlessly towards the abyss. Their knuckles turned white and, slowly, their hands began to slip, losing their grip in the icy water.

'I can't,' shouted Krakowski, closing his eyes. For an instant, the pain disappeared and he felt calm and serene. *I'm about to die*, he thought, his mind racing. Then he heard his father reprimanding him: 'You're not dying, Ben, you're losing. Fight!' Krakowski opened his eyes. The pain returned, and so did the fear, giving him strength to hold on a little bit longer.

Carrington felt it first – the rope pulling him slowly, ever-so-slowly upwards, against the current and away from the dark hole snapping at his feet. Krakowski felt it too, and began to pray.

Jack, helped by Jana, was pulling the rope like a tug of war – man against current – steadily upwards. Terrified, the Protector of Secrets and the Keeper fell to their knees and began to pray.

'He's got a gun!' shouted Professor Khalil. 'Look out!'

At the edge on the opposite side of the chasm, stood Habakkuk aiming at the struggling pair in the water below.

'Did you hear that?' shouted Haddad, looking over his shoulder.

'A gunshot?' said Horst from behind. Pushing the surprised Guardian aside, Haddad pulled his gun from its holster and ran. 'Come, quickly!'

Habakkuk's first shot missed. As he took aim again, Haddad burst into the cave.

'Drop it! Now.'

Habakkuk spun around and stared at Haddad in disbelief, but didn't let go of the gun.

Looking over the edge, Haddad spotted Carrington and Krakowski hanging on to the end of a rope, their heads barely above water. As he took a step forward he was struck with an incense burner from behind and dropped his gun. When it hit the floor, the gun went off and then bounced over the edge. Before the monk could strike again, the commando following Haddad wrestled him to the ground.

Habakkuk lifted his hand, took aim and began to fire into the water below.

'My God, it's Haddad!' shouted Jack, tightening his grip on the wet rope. When Jana looked across, she saw Haddad lunge at Habakkuk and tackle him from behind. The gun went off again, and Habakkuk and Haddad plunged into the dark water – intertwined like a pair of puppets in a deadly embrace –

and disappeared.

'No, God, no,' cried Dr Rosen, pointing down into the boiling cauldron. For an instant, the water turned crimson where the torrent had swallowed the struggling pair.

Haddad surfaced first, trying in vain to kick Habakkuk off his ankle and keep his head above water. He was bleeding, but managed to grab hold of Carrington's backpack. Haddad's strong kick brought him face to face with Habakkuk – teeth bared, eyes bulging with hatred and fear.

Carrington, unable to support the extra weight, lost his grip on the rope. As he was sucked under by the current, his woollen cloak got snagged on a piece of wood wedged between two rocks. Exhausted, Haddad bent his knee and then kicked back as hard as he could, digging his heel deep into the side of Habakkuk's face. Stunned by the blow, Habakkuk let go of the ankle. As he was sucked into the gaping swirl and inevitable oblivion, the Cardinal's words rang in his ear: 'You failed; damn you!'

Still clinging to Carrington's backpack, Haddad could see Carrington's cloak beginning to rip apart under the strain. 'See you in paradise, my friend,' he whispered. 'Inshallah,' and let go.

111

Krakowski marshalled all his remaining strength and managed to pull himself out of the water. Slowly, he crawled onto a narrow rock ledge – the portmanteau still wrapped tightly around his neck – and sat, mouth open, drinking in large gulps of air.

'What are you doing?' Dr Rosen shouted, as Jack climbed over the edge.

'Marcus is drowning – can't you see? I'm going down!' Jack snapped back. Carrington's body had gone limp and only his shoulders and backpack were being kept above water by the entangled cloak.

'Don't be crazy!' Jana shouted, grabbing Jack's arm. 'I know how, you don't. Give it to me!' she said, trying to wrench the rope out of Jack's hands. She threw off her cloak and pulled up her trouser legs. 'You steady the rope from up here, I'm going down. Now!'

She's right, Jack thought, and threw her the rope, which she wound expertly around herself and began to abseil. 'And throw down the other rope when I get to him. Quickly!'

Horst rubbed his aching shoulder and watched Jana from the opposite side. The two monks – Habakkuk's accomplices – were kneeling on the wet stone floor in front of the commando. The Guardian and the Keeper were pointing to Carrington in the water below, and talking excitedly to the other monks lined up along the edge. To get to Carrington, Jana had to move backwards, jump-by-jump down a slippery, almost vertical rock face until she reached the water's edge and steadied herself, the burning rope cutting into the palm of her hand.

Taking a deep breath, she arched her back like a cat, reached down and pulled Carrington's head out of the water by his hair. His eyes were closed, his mouth open; she wasn't sure if he was still alive.

Jack threw down the other rope with one end still attached to the iron ring in the wall behind him. A piece of wood wedged between the rocks provided a narrow foothold just above Carrington's shoulders. Jana crouched down low – her own rope wound tightly around her left leg and waist – and tried to slip the other rope under the shoulder straps of Carrington's backpack. Jack held his breath as Jana, nimble as a trapeze artist, tried again. On the fourth go, she managed to secure the rope. 'Now; pull!' she called out to Jack. The body wouldn't budge.

'His cloak is stuck on the other side,' Jack shouted back.

'I can't reach it!'

'Try again.'

Ignoring the cramp in her shoulder, Jana extended herself as far as she could, but still couldn't reach across. The pain grew unbearable.

'It's no use! I can't hold on much longer.'

'I'm going down,' shouted Horst, turning to Zelelew. 'Get me that rope over there, quickly!' The severed rope from the bridge – also still attached to the iron ring in the wall – was too short. 'We need something else.'

'There's nothing else.'

'Use their cloaks.' Horst pointed to the monks. 'Tie them together; that should do it!'

Dr Rosen stood near the edge, and kept staring across to the other side. *What is he doing?* she thought, watching the man kneeling on the ground in front of the monks. Something about the man looked familiar. The way he ran his fingers through his hair reminded her of someone ... The man turned his head towards her; their eyes locked.

'Horst?' muttered Dr Rosen, surprise and disbelief clouding her face. 'No ...'

Mouthing something, the man stood up, pointed down to Jana struggling at the water's edge and held up a long piece of cloth.

'Horst?' shouted Dr Rosen.

Nodding his head, the man lowered the cloth into the water.

Jana had lost all feeling in her hand and her strength had ebbed away. *This is what defeat feels like*, she thought as large tears rolled down her cheeks. Carrington was slipping away from her.

Then, out of the corner of her eye, she caught a glimpse of something hitting the water with a splash – a piece of dark cloth. Looking up, she saw someone holding on to what looked like a flag or a long curtain, being lowered down on the opposite side.

'Hang on, I'm almost there,' shouted Horst from above. Using the large knots as support, he slid down the improvised cloak ladder until he reached the water's edge. There was nowhere to stand; the vertical rock was as smooth as glass. Horst had to lower himself up to his waist into the icy water before he could reach Carrington's twisted cloak, entangled in a crack in the rock.

'There,' he shouted, 'done. Pull him up.'

'Hurry,' shouted Jana. Slowly, Carrington's heavy, waterlogged body began to rise out of the water. Jana let go of Carrington's hair and looked across to Horst clinging to the cloak ladder on the other side. When Horst turned his head towards her, she almost lost her grip on the rope.

'It can't be,' she whispered, certain she was hallucinating. Ignoring the pain and the little white stars dancing in front of her eyes, she began to climb back up.

Dr Rosen attempted mouth-to-mouth. Jana, kneeling on the ground beside her, began to cry. Jack draped his cloak around her shivering body and held her close. 'He's dead, isn't he?' she sobbed. Dr Rosen didn't reply. Instead, she looked down at the body again and repeated the procedure.

'Ssh,' said Jack, trying in vain to comfort Jana.

Krakowski had made it to the top with the help of the monks. Coughing furiously, he was trying to get the water out of his lungs.

Dr Rosen put her ear against Carrington's chest. Looking pale and defeated, she shook her head and stood up. Jana closed her eyes and began to stroke Carrington's wet hair.

The Keeper pointed to Carrington lying motionless in a puddle of water. The monks walked over to him and began to lift him up.

'What are they doing?' Jana cried, holding on to Carrington's hand. One of the monks pushed her gently aside.

Jack pulled her away. 'Let them.'

The monks lifted Carrington onto their shoulders and carried him slowly into a dark passage. Leading Jana by the hand, Jack picked up one of the lanterns and followed them into the darkness. Krakowski limped after the others.

'They've taken the tablets,' Jana whispered, 'did you see?'

'I did,' Jack replied calmly.

'Can we trust them?'

'Do we have a choice?'

'Jack, tell me this is just a bad dream and it will all go away when I wake up.'

'I wish I could.'

112

The passage narrowed and the ceiling was so low the four monks had to kneel down, their arms scraping against the wet rock. Without lifting Carrington off their shoulders, they moved slowly forward on their knees like repenting pilgrims hoping for salvation. Suddenly, the tunnel turned sharply to the right and they found themselves on a ledge overlooking a small, rectangular chamber. The monks staggered to their feet and followed the Keeper down six wide steps.

'What's that?' asked Jack, pointing to the middle of the chamber.

'A sarcophagus, I'd say,' replied Professor Khalil, 'chiselled out of solid bedrock.'

'The legendary tomb of King Lalibela, you think?' said Krakowski, his voice sounding weak.

'Could be.'

The Keeper stood in front of the sarcophagus, praying. Holding an incense burner, he faced an alcove cut deep into the rock wall. Small, wispy clouds of frankincense drifted into the opening.

'Look, over there,' Jana said, pointing to the sarcophagus, 'the tablets ...'

Lying side by side on top of the massive stone lid, the tablets glowed like two beacons showing the way into the netherworld. The monks lifted Carrington off their shoulders and placed him carefully beside the tablets. Bowing their heads, they stepped away. The Protector of Secrets walked across to the sarcophagus, picked up the undamaged tablet and handed it to the Keeper.

Krakowski reached for Dr Rosen's hand, Jack put his arm around Jana's shoulder and Professor Khalil leant forward to see what was inside the cavity behind the Keeper. Holding the tablet in front of him, the Keeper walked towards the alcove. Hands folded in prayer, the Protector of Secrets remained next to the sarcophagus. Two of the monks stepped forward, lifted up their lanterns and began to chant. The Keeper walked slowly past them, bowed his head and stepped inside.

Professor Khalil gasped and Krakowski squeezed Dr Rosen's hand so hard she almost cried out. Jack stared in wonder; Jana held her breath.

On top of a polished stone plinth shrouded in frankincense stood a large object crafted out of solid gold.

'The Ark,' whispered Krakowski, tears streaming down his ashen face. The scent of frankincense became so overpowering that it made them all feel light-headed and dizzy.

Rubbing her eyes, Professor Khalil moved a step closer. 'But this is an Egyptian shrine!' she exclaimed, 'just like the ones in my museum. Well, not quite ... There, look, can you see it?'

'What?' asked Krakowski.

'The relief on the front; it's a sun disk, that's the symbol of Aten ... This is extraordinary!'

When the Keeper approached the golden chest, Krakowski saw a small door set into the side of the shrine. It was open, and the inside was empty. The Keeper lifted up the tablet and placed it carefully inside. Without turning his back to the chest, he stepped away, bowed his head and stood quite still.

'Do you see what I see?' said Krakowski, turning to Professor Khalil. 'After seven hundred years the Tablets of the Law are returning home.'

'To an Egyptian shrine?' Professor Khalil asked, shaking her head.

'Does that really make a difference?'

'Perhaps not.'

The Protector of Secrets put the broken fragments of the second tablet back into the wooden box Carrington had carried in his backpack. Holding the box in front of him, he walked slowly into the alcove and approached the Ark just as the Keeper had done. After placing the box inside the chest, he closed the little door, stepped back and knelt down. The Keeper and the two monks holding the lanterns did the same. As the clouds of incense became denser, and the chanting louder, the sun disk began to glow.

'Look, there,' Krakowski cried out, pointing into the gloom. 'Can you see it?' A strange light had appeared on top of the golden chest.

'What?' Dr Rosen asked, barely able to speak.

'The light ...'

'What is it?'

'A reflection?' suggested Professor Khalil, holding up her lantern.

'I wonder,' said Krakowski.

'What's happening here, Jack?' Jana asked, unable to stop shaking. 'I feel ... as if ...' She was interrupted by a faint moan coming from the sarcophagus below. Jana looked down. Carrington's chest began to move; a very gentle but visible rising and falling. 'Look!' she cried. 'He's breathing!'

'I think you're right!' Jack replied.

Jana flew down the steps and reached for Carrington's limp hand. She closed her eyes and began to pray in Polish. It was a simple prayer her adopted mother had taught her a long time ago:

Love is always patient and kind.
It is never jealous.
Love is never boastful or conceited.
It is never rude or selfish.
It does not take offence and is not resentful ...

When Jana opened her eyes again, she looked straight into Carrington's smiling face.

'Marcus,' she whispered, bringing her lips close to his, 'can you hear me?'

'Yes,' he sighed. 'Am I dreaming?'

'Oh no; I am.'

'I'm sure he wasn't breathing,' muttered Dr Rosen, looking confused. 'It can happen you know. There was this strange case ...'

'It's all right,' Krakowski interrupted her, stroking her hand. 'You must stop thinking like a surgeon, Bettany. If we don't believe in something greater than ourselves, we are destined to remain forever small. Remember?'

Two months later

Carrington pointed towards the entry to the Vatican Museum. 'Hurry,' he said, looking at his watch. 'They're already lining up and the doors aren't even open yet.'

'What's the big rush?' asked Jana, trailing along behind.

'I want to get there before all the tourists.'

'You want to surprise me in private, is that it?'

'That's part of it.'

'Let me get this straight. What you're about to show me has only been on display for a short time, but we've both seen it before?'

'That's right. Look, they're opening up.'

'I'm intrigued. Any more clues?'

'Definitely not. Come.'

Carrington pushed past the tourists milling around in the foyer and rushed to the stairs. 'You must promise me to close your eyes when I tell you,' he said, taking Jana by the hand.

Carrington's excitement was rubbing off. 'This isn't like you, Marcus; you're acting like a child,' Jana said, laughing. 'I really don't know what's got into you.'

'Patience, we're almost there. Now, close your eyes and follow me.' With Jana's hand firmly in his, Carrington entered a small annex at the back of the Egyptian section.

'Oh ... this is unbelievable,' Carrington whispered, squeezing

551

Jana's hand.

'Can I open my eyes now?'

'Not yet. Come, stand over here.' Carrington guided Jana across the room. 'Now.'

Jana opened her eyes and gasped. On a pedestal in front of her – illuminated by a shaft of sunlight from above – stood a black statue. The head was strangely elongated, the long face serene, the lips full. 'Akhenaten,' she whispered, moving closer. 'There, look.' Jana pointed to a hairline crack running along the bottom of the false beard. It was barely noticeable; the restorer had done a great job. 'It's him! Here? How?'

'Well, it's quite a story. A crafty Sir Eric was behind all this. He negotiated the release of his son; it's all tied up with that.'

'How do you know?'

'Haddad told me. Just before we left Luxor ...'

'Why didn't you say anything?'

'So much was going on ...'

'How did Newman pull this off?'

'Politics and money.'

'In what way?'

'After Omar died, the Egyptians didn't want a high profile trial dragging everything through the courts again. Imagine what it would have done to tourism, for a start.'

'What about the statue? What about London and the auction?'

'That's all part of it, you see. The theft of the statue and Horst's involvement with the terrorists ... they're all related.'

'How did he end up here, then?' Jana asked, pointing to the statue.

'Enter, Sir Eric.'

'I don't understand.'

'It's very clever, listen. Newman offered the Egyptians a solution to a thorny problem. First, there was the pending court case in London about the auction debacle, with Horst in the middle of it all. Then we have his arrest in Egypt along with allegations of terrorist activities involving Omar. Now Omar's dead; more complications ...'

'How does Newman fit into all this?'

'In return for his son's release – all charges dropped in Egypt and in London – he offered to pay the Egyptian government ten million pounds for the statue.'

'Is that it?'

'Well, think about it. The auctioneers are happy; no embarrassing court case dragging their reputation through the mud and a fat commission to boot. The Egyptians are happy. No court case in London and no sensational trial of a westerner accused of terrorist activities in Egypt. And besides, their own hands weren't quite clean either. The money from the sale went straight to the Egyptian Museum in Cairo; much needed funds for overdue renovations, I believe. Professor Khalil will be happy too.'

'Incredible.'

'However, there was one nasty little fly in the ointment.'

'What?'

'The Egyptians didn't want the statue to fall into private hands and then just disappear. Once again, Newman offered them a solution.'

'He did? How?'

'He agreed to bequeath the statue to the Vatican Museum, effective immediately.'

'To the Vatican? And the Vatican was acceptable to the Egyptians?'

Smiling, Carrington pointed to Akhenaten. 'Life's full of compromises. Here he is. It's all rather brilliant, you must admit.'

Jana walked slowly around the statue. 'Do you think the idea of one all-powerful God was the inspired idea of this man?' She stopped and pointed to Akhenaten. 'This king, so far ahead of his time ... 3500 years ago?'

'The only thing set in stone is his smile,' replied Carrington.

'As for the rest, who knows?'

'Ah, yes. Keep an open mind; I do remember ...'

'Good. Now, are you ready for more?'

'There's more?'

'Follow me.' Carrington took Jana by the hand and guided her back to the exit. 'All we need now is a taxi.'

'You're a dark horse, Marcus Carrington ... Where are we going?'

'Piazza Navona.'

'Too many tourists,' explained the taxi driver, shrugging apologetically as they sat in gridlocked traffic. Carrington asked him to stop and paid the fare. 'We can walk from here,' he said, 'it'll be faster.'

The narrow, cobblestoned alley was packed. Almost everyone appeared to be heading in the same direction – towards Piazza Navona.

'How much further?' asked Jana.

'We're almost there. Can you hear it?'

'Water? A fountain?'

'Yes; three actually – Bernini masterpieces.' They turned a corner and found themselves in a large, sun-drenched square thronging with tourists.

'Well, what's the surprise?' asked Jana, laughing. 'Fountains?'

'No. Your surprise is waiting over there.' Carrington pointed to an open air restaurant facing the square. Jana looked across and saw someone waving in their direction. Carrington waved back.

'It can't be!' said Jana, pulling Carrington towards the restaurant. 'Benjamin? Bettany?'

'Who else?'

'Marcus was behind all this,' explained Dr Rosen, kissing Jana on the cheek. 'He arranged it all.'

Jana looked at Carrington. Shrugging his shoulders, he smiled back.

'It's a great idea, Marcus,' said Krakowski, patting Carrington on the arm. 'What about Jack?'

'I spoke to him in New York a couple of days ago; he said he'd come.'

'We heard about your father,' said Jana, turning to Dr Rosen. 'I'm so sorry.'

'Thank you ... yes, quite sudden, but not unexpected. The funeral was last week,' replied Dr Rosen. 'There's something about it you should know ...'

'Not now, Bettany, please,' said Krakowski.

'It's all right, Ben, I want to tell them.'

'What is it?' asked Carrington, reaching for Dr Rosen's hand.

'There was a codicil in his will; a recent one. He asked to be buried wearing the Ritterkreuz and the Totenkopf ring ...' Dr Rosen was interrupted by loud shouting and a policeman's whistle, coming from somewhere in the crowd in front of them.

A Vespa pushed slowly through the parting throng and stopped in front of the restaurant. Jack jumped off the pillion seat, kissed the girl on the motor scooter on the cheek, and began to look around. The girl took off before the angry policeman could reach her.

'Jack, over here,' shouted Jana, waving. Jack hurried towards her.

'I made it,' said Jack, looking rather pleased with himself. 'But only just; what a ride.'

'New girlfriend?' asked Jana.

'Not quite. There were no taxis at my hotel and I got talking to this girl in the lobby; she'd just delivered some flowers. I told her I had to get to Piazza Navona in a hurry ... and, well, she was going the same way; the florist is somewhere over here ...'

'You lead a charmed life, Jack,' said Dr Rosen, laughing.

'What were you doing in New York?' asked Jana.

'Just signed a book deal; Nazi gold and hidden Swiss bank

accounts are quite the rage at the moment ...'

'The big story, at last, eh? Well done, Jack! You'll definitely need a new wardrobe now, surely,' said Jana, lowering her voice. 'Outback Armani in New York? It won't work; trust me!'

'That's what my publisher said.'

'Well?'

'Well what?'

'What are you going to do about it?'

Jack shrugged. 'What do you think?' he replied, running his hands over the smooth lapels of his beloved bomber jacket. 'There's nothing wrong with this – see?'

Jana rolled her eyes. 'Just don't tell me later I didn't try, okay?'

'It's really good to see you all,' said Jack, changing the subject. 'I need a drink.'

Krakowski ordered champagne.

'Tell them about the Foundation, Ben,' prompted Dr Rosen.

'Lord Ashburton made me a co-trustee ...'

'That's great; congratulations,' interrupted Carrington. 'We should drink to that.'

'I would like to propose a toast,' said Krakowski, his eyes misty. 'To my dear father's violin.' Krakowski reached for his glass and stood up. 'He was right; the Empress held the key. To the Empress. May she continue to enchant forever.' The others stood up as well. 'To the Empress,' they chorused, and touched glasses.

Touring the concert halls of the world, the Empress had become famous. But by giving up her secrets, she had become a legend.

***

Coming soon

THE DISAPPEARANCE OF ANNA POPOV

by Gabriel Farago

Author's note

I first came across the story of Jandamarra and the Bunuba Resistance in the remote Kimberley in Western Australia. Leaning against a seven hundred year old boab tree with my Aboriginal guide – a Bunuba elder – I was looking up at the tall cliffs guarding the entrance to Windjana Gorge; his country. We had just visited some stunning Aboriginal rock art – haunting paintings thought to be more than twenty thousand years old. Rising like a fortress out of the glare, the tall cliffs – remnants of an ancient Devonian reef – formed a forbidding barrier between his world and mine.

'This is where it all happened,' the old man said, pointing into the deep gorge cut through the rock by the Lennard River. 'And it wasn't that long ago. Jandamarra's cave is just up there.'

Jandamarra was an Aboriginal freedom fighter in the 1890s who refused to surrender his country and his freedom to the white settlers pushing relentlessly north.

As the shadows lengthened, I listened to the remarkable story of first contact between the Bunuba and the early Australian pastoralists. It was a stirring tale of heroism and despair, unspeakable brutality and acts of great courage. It was the final chapter in the long history of a proud people. With the story ending in tragedy, the painful words turned into a whisper of defeat, falling from the lips of one of its last true elders. Caught between two worlds, Jandamarra had tried to find a way of embracing the new, but the old was in his blood and could not be denied.

This conflict is by no means over. It exists today. Colliding cultures send ripples of discord far into the future and affect generations. It is as relevant today as it was in Jandamarra's time. The stage is the same, so is the plot. Only the actors are different.

As the embers of our camp fire turned slowly to ash, I began to wonder ... What if Jandamarra had lived today? What if ...

Gabriel Farago
Leura, Blue Mountains, Australia

Prologue

Alice Springs, January 2005

Anna was dancing in The Shed the night she disappeared. The Shed was a notorious watering hole frequented mainly by thirsty truckies. It called itself a bush pub, but that was an exaggeration. It was more like a long wooden bar with a corrugated iron roof held up by gnarled fence posts and barbed wire. There were no walls. The floor, hard as rock, was red desert earth compacted by thousands of feet shuffling to the bar for a drink. Because the beer was always cold and the steaks huge and cheap, the place was always packed. More recently, however, there was one more added attraction: backpackers, mainly girls, touring the Outback. Looking for cheap grog and adventure, the young nomads had made The Shed their own. Located three kilometres out of Alice, it was within easy walking distance of the youth hostels and budget motels popular with tourists.

A local bush band was playing country and western music and the mouth-watering aroma of frying onions and sizzling sausages drifted across from the BBQ. It was very hot and very late.

'Beer, mate?' asked the barmaid, sizing up the tall dark stranger. The handsome Aboriginal took off his broad-brimmed drover's hat, wiped his forehead with a red handkerchief and nodded. 'One for your friend as well?' she

561

asked, pointing to the huge snake wound around his neck and shoulders.

'No thanks, she's driving,' he said, affectionately stroking the exquisite python.

Standing at the other end of the bar, a group of truckies were eyeing off the girls on the improvised dance floor. 'Look, the sheilas have to dance with each other 'cause there're no blokes here having a go,' said one, downing another beer.

'I bet you can't get them to dance with you, mate; not even one,' said another, patting his friend on the hairy beer gut bulging over his shorts. 'Just look at you, you slob.'

'Sure can.'

'Oh yeah? You're all talk. What's it worth?'

'Ten rounds.' The others laughed.

'You're on.'

The man slammed down his glass, wiped his mouth with the back of his hand and belched loudly. Pulling down his singlet to cover part of his protruding gut, he slipped his thongs back on and shuffled unsteadily towards the dance floor.

Barefoot and wearing the briefest of shorts and a tight-fitting pink t-shirt accentuating her firm breasts, Anna, silky blonde hair swishing against the tips of her tanned shoulder blades, was dancing with her friend Julia. Anna was looking for freedom, Julia for the adventure and novelty that travel to remote places invariably offered. The Shed had it all: excitement, danger, and the lure of the unknown, far away from the watchful eyes of fretting parents and curious friends. Enjoying her favourite Dixie Chicks song, Anna swayed from side to side with her eyes closed, letting the familiar beat of the music carry her away. When it stopped and she opened her eyes, she almost bumped into the grotesque fat man towering over her.

'How about a dance, luv?' said the fat man, his bald head glistening with sweat.

'No thanks,' she snapped, turning away. 'He's gross,' she whispered to Julia. 'Let's take a break.'

As his mates at the bar roared laughing, a flash of anger raced across the face of the fat truckie.

'Come on, sweetie, just one. Be a good sport,' he persisted, putting a heavy, sweaty hand on Anna's shoulder.

'Get off me!' shouted Anna, pushing the fleshy hand away in disgust.

His mates at the bar began to whistle and hoot. Instead of walking away, the fat man grabbed Anna from behind, spun her around and lifted her up like a rag doll. Pressing her against his huge chest, he lumbered awkwardly around the dance floor like a dancing bear, performing his tricks at the fair. Anna, the man's hot beer breath in her face, began to retch.

The man with the snake sipped his beer and watched the odd couple stagger across the dance floor. Slowly, he unwound the python, lifted it over his head and gently put it down on the bar.

'Look after her for me, luv,' he said to the barmaid. 'She's harmless. I'll be right back.'

He walked slowly over to the dance floor. 'That's enough, mate. Put her down,' he said, patting the fat man on the back.

The truckie turned his head and glared, his bloodshot eyes slightly unfocused.

'Fuck off, darkie, this is none of your business,' he hissed angrily.

The snake man's right hand shot up in silent reply and grabbed the fat man's ear like a vice.

'I don't think you heard me,' he said, twisting the ear. 'Let her go.'

The fat man let go of Anna, clenched his fists and spun around.

The tall man let go of the ear and stepped back.

The fat man charged like a crazed bull – 120 kilos of rage.

Like most professional fighters, the tall man had the waist of a ballerina and the shoulders of a weightlifter. Rocking back and forth on the balls of his feet, he stood poised like a cat watching its prey. He sidestepped the charge easily, letting the fat man crash into the bar.

'Fight, you fucking coward!' bellowed the fat man, picking himself up.

'Okay.'

The tall man moved like lightning. The first punch, delivered by his left fist, landed on his opponent's beer gut and went deep. The second, delivered by his right, caught the fat man on the left cheek and broke a bone. The fight was over in an instant. Two more massive blows, one to the chin and one to the nose, finished the truckie off.

'Anyone else?' the tall man asked, squaring his shoulders. No one stepped forward. 'He had it coming. It's over. Get back to your beers.'

The tall man walked to the far end of the bar, uncoiled the snake which had wound itself around a post, and slung it over his shoulders.

'Thanks for looking after her, luv,' he said to the barmaid. 'One more for the road, please.' Gulping down his beer, he reached for his hat, threw a few coins on the bar and walked out into the darkness.

Julia put her arm around her friend. 'Are you alright?' she asked, a worried look on her face. Anna nodded. 'Come on, let's get out of here before they all have a go at each other and we're caught in the middle.' The two girls left the dance floor and hurried outside.

'Shouldn't we wait for the others?' asked Anna. 'One of the guys from the hostel had a car.'

'No. They're out the back, eating. We can walk. It isn't far.'

The road leading into Alice was deserted. The girls took off their shoes and walked along the warm asphalt.

'Did you see that guy with the snake? What a hunk! And I couldn't even thank him. Pity.'

The powerful V8 of the ute purred into life after the girls had walked past. Inching slowly forward without lights, it left the car park behind The Shed and headed slowly for town. Startled by the engine noise coming towards them out of the dark, the girls turned around. The headlights came on suddenly, momentarily blinding them.

'Get off the road!' shouted Anna, pushing her friend into the bushes. The ute accelerated and screeched to a halt next to them.

'Walking along the road after midnight isn't such a great idea. Especially round here,' said a voice through the open driver's window.

'Look who it is,' whispered Julia excitedly.

'Hop in. I'll give youse a lift back to town.'

'Come on,' said Julia, pulling Anna out of the bushes.

'Julia, don't!' cried Anna. 'No hitchhiking, remember?'

'It's all right ... he's your hero.' Julia walked over to the car and opened the passenger door. 'You scared us,' she said, climbing in.

The snake man smiled at her, revving the engine. Reluctantly, Anna climbed in after her friend and closed the door.

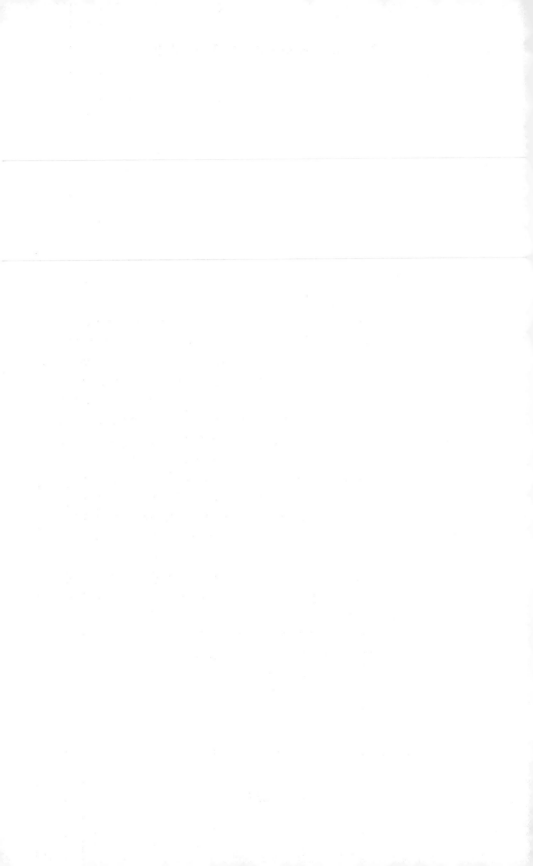

1

Sydney Harbour, New Year's Eve 2009

The old year was dying. 'Five, four, three, two, one ...' counted the cheering crowd as the final seconds of 2009 tumbled through the hourglass. Suddenly, the massive steel arch of the Sydney Harbour Bridge erupted, forming a dazzling tiara of sparks. As it raced along the girders from both sides towards the centre like fire-breathing dragons, the fireworks spectacular lit up the night sky. Meeting in the middle between the main deck and the top of the arch, light and colour engaged in a breathtaking duel, heralding a turbulent year to come.

'Happy New Year, Jack!' shouted the stunning young woman standing next to Jack Rogan on the crowded yacht. Rebecca Armstrong reached up, threw her slender arms around his neck and kissed him passionately on the mouth. It was the first time she had kissed her famous client.

'Wow! I thought a kiss like this was strictly the province of the writer's imagination,' said Jack, coming up for air. 'Happy New Year, Becky!'

Rebecca flicked her glossy dark hair from her flushed face – as women who know they have beautiful hair often do – and took him by the hand. 'Don't get used to it. Tonight's an exception. Come on. I have a surprise for you,' she said.

'I like surprises.'

Heads turned as Rebecca pushed through the crowd with Jack by her side. Radiating sophistication and style in her New

GABRIEL FARAGO

York designer clothes, she made straight for the stern of the yacht.

As the captain navigated the pitching vessel through the tightly packed spectator fleet under the Harbour Bridge, the yacht almost collided with an ostentatious motor cruiser. Sounding like a warning, the deep, throaty foghorn of a large ocean liner tied up at Circular Quay added to the crazy cacophony welcoming the New Year. An acrid, phosphorous, eye-watering gunpowder smell of spent fireworks cartridges filled the balmy air as a smoke haze drifted past the Opera House.

'Who are all these people?' asked Jack, waving a hand at the crowd on the deck.

'The Sydney literary set. Don't you recognise anyone?' asked Rebecca, frowning.

'I'm new to all this, remember?'

'They all seem to know you ... '

'Am I paying for it?' Jack asked anxiously.

'No, Jack. Your publisher is. Relax. Look who's over there.' She pointed to a tall, sandy-haired man in a crumpled checked shirt leaning casually against the mast with a bottle of beer in his hand.

'China!' yelled Jack, walking over to his friend. 'What are you doing here?'

'Spinner! Your girlfriend invited me. Cheers!' They touched glasses. 'And a few of your other neglected mates as well.' The sandy-haired man pointed to the bow of the crowded vessel.

'She isn't my ...' said Jack, lowering his voice.

'China?' asked Rebecca. 'He told me his name was Will.'

'It is,' replied Jack, laughing. 'China's his nickname.'

'China? How come?'

'My little mate, rhymes with china plate; china. Simple – see?'

'You Aussies are something else,' said Rebecca, shaking her head. 'I can see I've a lot to learn.'

'Thanks Becky,' said Jack, giving her a hug, 'very thoughtful of you.' Her firm, toned body sent a ripple of excitement racing up his spine.

During his whirlwind book-signing tour across the US, Jack had repeatedly complained that he missed Sydney and his Aussie friends. The surprise New Year's Eve party on Sydney Harbour was his publisher's response.

'You've got to watch Will, he's quite a lad,' warned Jack, a sparkle in his eyes.

'Don't listen to Spinner,' said Will.

'Spinner? Not another nickname!' said Rebecca.

'Sure is,' replied Will. 'He's always spinning yarns –right?

The two men could have been mistaken for brothers, not only because of their rugged good looks, but also because of their good-natured banter suggesting a deep friendship forged by years spent together. Both were clearly outdoor types. Will's tanned face – lined by laughter and a little too much sun – hinted at laid-back good humour, while Jack's piercing green eyes and athletic physique were a magnet for women of all ages.

'You're a lucky bastard, mate,' said Will.

'How come?'

'She's not bad,' said Will pointing with his glass to Rebecca. 'Girlfriend?'

'No, mate.'

'Sure ... Don't tell me you haven't ...?'

'No, seriously. My publishers told me I needed help with PR, book signings, publicity, stuff like that. You know what I'm like. So, they appointed her to look after all that crap for me. You should see her office in New York. She's very good,' said Jack. 'Strictly business.'

Will wasn't convinced. 'I've heard that one before,' he said. 'You and women ... Lucky bastard.'

'Perhaps I am.'

'Perhaps? Jet-setting author with yachts and champagne and classy chicks like this one to look after you? You've come a long way, Spinner.'

'It all happened very fast.'

'I can see that, but you hardly have time for your old drinking buddies anymore,' lamented Will.

'I haven't got time to scratch myself.'

'Just look around, mate. This crowd isn't you.'

As a freelance journalist, Jack Rogan depended on his eclectic network of contacts and friends for leads and inspiration. It was Will who had given Jack the lead to a great story two years before – the trial of a Nazi war criminal that exposed a secret hoard of Nazi gold in the vaults of Swiss banks.

When Jack published *Dental Gold and Other Horrors* it was an international success. The Swiss, embarrassed by the outcries about 'abandoned' bank accounts of thousands of Holocaust victims, finally agreed to open their ledgers. This was seen by many as the first serious step towards compensation. Overnight, Jack had become a celebrated *Time* magazine front page hero, and his book a sensation.

'Come on, Will, it's not that bad,' retorted Jack, handing his friend a glass of champagne. 'Here, drink up!'

The famous Sydney New Year's Eve fireworks were reaching their climax with a multicoloured waterfall of sparks cascading from the deck of the bridge into the ink-blue waters of the harbour below.

'So – what next, mate?' asked Will, draining his glass.

'I'm taking a couple weeks off. First break in two years.'

'Then why don't you come with me?'

'What do you mean?'

'I'm taking some time off too. Going bush, out west ... '

'Fossicking for bric-a-brac and old furniture?'

'Exactly. And I still have the old van.'

'I don't believe it! Just like the good old days, eh?'

'Some things never change, mate. Do you reckon they might have some more beer around here? I'm sick of this foreign crap,' said Will.

Jack pointed an accusing finger at his friend. 'This is Bollinger, you peasant,' he said. 'The best.'

'I don't give a stuff. It's crap.'

'I'll see what I can do. When are you leaving?'

'As soon as I sober up.'

'I tell you what. You clear it with Becky, and I'm in.'

'Well, well! I never thought I'd see the day. Jack Rogan actually in awe of a woman. Asking for permission?' said Will, shaking his head.

'You don't know these Yankee broads, mate. Tough as old boot leather. And besides,' continued Jack lowering his voice, 'they hold the purse strings ... '

'You go and find me a beer, Spinner, and leave her to me.'

'Good luck.' *Poor bastard*, thought Jack, *she'll eat him alive!*

2

Somewhere in the bush near Bathurst, 1 January 2010

The old van lurched alarmingly to one side – tortured gears crunching loudly – and began the steep descent down into the valley. Jack woke with a start. Rubbing his aching shoulder – a constant reminder of the sniper's bullet that ended his stint as a war correspondent in Afghanistan – he turned to Will.

'Where are we?' he asked, reaching for his sunglasses.

'Goldmining country. We just passed Bathurst. Good sleep? A little too much Bollinger, perhaps?' suggested Will good-naturedly. 'You should have stuck to the beer, mate.'

'What did you tell her?' Jack asked. Leaving the party at dawn with Will to go back home and pack was still a blur.

'I suggested she let you go for a month, and after a bit of argy bargy, we settled for a week. Done and dusted. She's taking a few days off as well. Barrier Reef. That helped. But you're right, she's one tough cookie. She even challenged me to a drinking contest – vodka shots – before she agreed. We must have downed a dozen, I reckon.'

'Who won?'

'You're here, aren't you? The things I do for a chum.'

'Where are we staying?'

'Camping, Jack. Just like we used to. I know a good spot up in the hills by the creek. This area used to be Dad's favourite, remember? The gear's in the back,' Will said, 'including the old tent.'

'It leaked like a sieve,' said Jack. He was beginning to have second thoughts. Maybe New Year's Eve nostalgia and a little too much champagne had got the better of him.

As young men, he and Will had been inseparable. Will's family had taken in the fresh-faced Queensland country boy as one of their own. The two lads had accompanied Will's father on many a buying trip, going from farm to farm in remote rural areas and offering to buy old stuff nobody needed. Buy cheaply, take the goods back to Sydney, do them up a bit in the workshop behind the house and then sell them for a handsome profit in the shop at the front.

'Presentation is everything,' Will's dad used to say. 'Remember boys, the wrapping can be more important than the present.' He had made a good living out of this for over fifty years. After he passed away, Will continued the tradition once a year or so, for old times' sake. Jack had many fond memories of those trips: delicious roast dinners with a farmer and his family in the cosy kitchen; sitting on the veranda of a remote homestead with a cold beer at the end of a long hot day; and many a romp in the hay with a farmer's daughter. Even, sometimes, his wife. Or both.

Most of the furniture in Jack's house came from these excursions. It was surprising what curios had found their way to Australia and were waiting in disused sheds or in the back of barns to be discovered by someone with imagination and an eye for value. Jack and Will used to joke about it often. The father's buying trips had turned into a nostalgic treasure hunt for the son and his friend.

After putting up the old tent by the creek, Will made a fire and cooked some sausages.

'What's she really like?' he asked, stoking the fire.

'Becky?'

'Yeah.'

'To tell you the truth, I don't know her that well.'

'How come?'

'We've been flat out these last couple of months travelling together, on and off. All business.'

'She's a good looker, that's for sure. Very sexy; great body. She must be pushing forty; surely.'

'She's a bit of a health buff.'

'What? All carrot juice and push-ups?'

'No. Yoga and karate. She'd deck us both in three seconds flat. I've seen her do it. Very fit.'

'Bodyguard as well. Impressive.'

'She's also very smart, sophisticated and incredibly well connected. She knows all the right people.'

'Single?'

'Yes.'

'Boyfriend?'

'Not as far as I know. Career type; too busy.'

'Well, then?'

'What?'

'Come on, mate, it's me you're talking to. She'd be great in the sack.'

'I don't look at her that way. She's a professional. She takes care of my business interests. The royalties; the financial side of things.'

'Don't give me that crap.'

'No, I'm serious. Never put your dick in the cash register, as my first editor used to say.'

'You must have at least thought about it.'

'Hmm ...There's something about her ... I can't put my finger on it, but ...'

'She sure likes you ...' interrupted Will.

'You can tell, can you?'

'She and I are drinking buddies – remember?'

'Well, that explains it ...'

'We'll see. Here; done.' Will took the pan off the fire and put the sausages on a plate. Accidentally touching the hot pan, he burnt his fingers and almost dropped the pan. 'Shit! Throw us another tinnie, mate, and let's get stuck into it.'

They were both asleep just after sundown.

'There's enough grog in here to get an entire football team pissed several times over, but no food at all,' complained Jack next morning, searching in vain for some eggs and bacon for breakfast.

'I'm the alcohol technician, you're the cook, remember?' replied Will, tinkering with his fishing gear. 'I fixed dinner last night, mate. Breakfast is your job.'

'Sausages. Big deal.'

'If you don't like the tucker, get some fresh stuff. The village is just down the road.'

'Okay.'

The only thing open in the tiny hamlet was the corner store which also served as the post office and petrol station. The man behind the counter turned out to be the local real estate agent minding the store for a mate who'd gone to visit family. Inquisitive by nature, the agent was intrigued by the old van with 'Arthur Hamilton & Son – second-hand furniture bought and sold' prominently painted on its sides. The business logo – a laughing kookaburra perched on the arm of a rocking chair – reminded him of a biscuit tin popular in the 1950s. After half an hour of small talk, Jack had managed to buy some meagre provisions. He had also managed to arrange their first assignment.

By the time he manoeuvred the van back into camp, it was already lunchtime and very hot. Holding a fishing rod with one hand, Will was dozing under a tree by the creek.

'Enjoying your holiday, mate?' asked Jack, unpacking the groceries. 'Here, look at this.' He handed Will a crumpled piece of paper.

'What's that?'

'A map.'

'Oh?'

'Our first assignment. You didn't think I drove this contraption all the way into the village just to buy some eggs?'

'And you didn't think I invited you along just because you're a famous author, eh?' retorted Will. 'Be a good sport and throw us a tinnie.'

They waited until late afternoon had taken the sting out of the sun before setting out to find the farm. Following a rutted track for several kilometres, they turned a sharp corner and stopped in front of a wooden gate which had all but rotted off its hinges.

'What a dump,' said Jack, pushing the gate open with his shoulder. 'The agent did warn me that the place is about to be demolished. No one's lived here in years. A stockbroker from Sydney just bought it and wants to get rid of all the furniture and stuff. The agent said we should grab what we want and meet him in the village tomorrow to make an offer. This could be our lucky day.'

Will looked around the ramshackle yard. 'I doubt it,' he said and shook his head.

The abandoned homestead had definitely seen better days. Part of the wooden structure had been destroyed by fire and was open to the elements. The front door was missing and the corrugated iron roof of the veranda had collapsed. Most of the windows were broken. Coming closer, Jack noticed something shiny and tightly coiled like a sailor's rope on the deck of a yacht, glistening in the sunlight. *Shit! A red bellied black*, thought Jack, watching the deadly snake sunning itself on the warped floorboards of the porch. To Jack it looked like an ominous sentinel, guarding the entrance to a forbidden place. The stone chimney leaning precariously against a rusty water tank looked like it could collapse at any moment.

'You got a bum steer, mate. The place is empty. We're wasting our time,' said Will. He turned around and began to walk back to the van. 'Let's go.'

'The agent said all the stuff's in a barn behind the house – see?' Jack kept an eye on the snake, and picked his way carefully through the tall grass. 'Here, give me a hand.' Together they pushed open the old wooden door and peered inside.

The small barn was filled with all kinds of furniture, kitchen utensils, farming implements and carpentry tools. Broken crockery, pages torn from books and magazines, crumpled old newspapers and an assortment of cutlery and pottery shards littered the floor. Everything was covered in dust.

'Well, well, what have we here then, eh?' asked Jack, squinting into the gloom.

Will picked up a candle from the floor and lit it. 'Look at this,' he said.

'What's that?'

'A harmonium.' Will pulled over a rickety stool, sat down in front of the keyboard and began to operate the bellows with the broken foot pedals. He handed the candle to Jack and started to play. At first, the air in the protesting bellows responded with a tortured, wheezing sound, but it soon turned into a melody, faint and church organ-like. The hymn sounded eerie and out of place in the barn filled with abandoned possessions of generations past.

'I didn't know you could play.'

'Sunday school. You never forget.'

They pushed the harmonium aside and began to explore the barn.

Their curiosity aroused, they opened tea chests, emptied drawers and peered into hatboxes and armoires crammed with vintage clothing. They pored over photo albums filled with sepia portraits of dapper gentlemen wearing their Sunday best and Victorian matrons staring blankly into space. Pulling funny faces, they tried on waistcoats, bonnets and bowler hats and took turns parading in front of the cracked dressing table mirror.

Outside, the afternoon had turned to night, the shrill, monotonous hum of cicadas the only intrusion on the stillness. Exhausted, they lay down on an old double bed next to the window.

'It's a strange feeling, isn't it?' said Will.

'What is?'

'Being surrounded by all this stuff that once belonged to real people. Now long gone.'

'It is a bit,' said Jack.

'It makes you feel ... vulnerable.'

'In what way?'

'Here we are, both in our prime, yet ...'

'What are you getting at?'

'The Ferryman is never that far away ...'

'That's a bit morbid,' said Jack.

'It's true, though. We don't know how much time we've got ...'

'No, we don't. And yes, one day we'll have to pay the Ferryman. But ...'

'What?' asked Will.

'Not yet. Go to sleep.'

Unable to fall asleep, Will looked through the broken window panes at the stars blazing above and listened to the regular breathing of his friend lying fast asleep next to him. Feeling suddenly quite cold, he got up and began to search for something to cover himself with.

This'll do, he thought, reaching for the old moth-eaten Army overcoat he had tried on before. *I wonder what horrors this has seen?*

When Will pulled the coat up to his chin to keep warm, a dank smell assaulted his nose, conjuring up images of trench warfare, whistling shells, mateship and blood. *Smells of death*, he thought, pushing the coat aside. *Would Jack lay down his life to save a mate?* Will asked himself, *like many of the Diggers have done? I think he would.* Will closed his eyes. *Could I do the same? I guess only the real thing can answer that*, he thought and drifted to sleep.

By the time they woke up and began to load up the van, the first rays of morning sun had kissed the tiny beads of dew glistening like tears on the broken window panes.

3

Rose Cottage, Sydney, 9 January 2010

Rebecca Armstrong got out of the taxi and looked at the small sandstone cottage. It wasn't what she had expected. *I should have worn my jeans and a tank top*, she thought, looking at her tight-fitting designer slacks, high heel shoes, and crisp Chanel blouse. She adjusted her hair, and clutching her tiny two-thousand-dollar handbag, walked to the front door and rang the bell.

'So, this is where the world-famous Aussie author lives,' she said, following Jack into the cottage. 'Interesting ... Homes tell us so much, don't you think?'

'They do?'

'About the people inside. Are you ready to give up your secrets?'

'Secrets? What secrets? This is a bachelor pad. A bolthole and sanctuary wrapped in one. It's all I could afford after the divorce. Sorry – I lost track of time.' Jack took off his leather apron and laid it over the back of a chair. 'I was just polishing an old secretaire out in the courtyard.'

'You were doing – what?'

'I'm restoring an antique. My booty from the little buying trip you so kindly allowed me to go on.'

'Your friend was very persuasive.'

'I did warn you about him.'

'I'm a big girl.'

'Here, I'll show you. How did you like the Barrier Reef?'

'It took my breath away.'

The back of the cottage opened into a small courtyard garden with a fountain in the middle. The small ornate desk stood on a drop sheet next to the fountain.

'This is beautiful. What is it?'

'A cedar secretaire, circa 1870, made by one of the early cabinetmakers of Sydney. Here, look at the trade label: "W. Jones & Son of Ross Street, Glebe". Its opening is cantilevered forward and decorated with two blind drawers,' said Jack, folding down the top of the secretaire. 'There are three more drawers under here – see – supported by two turned full columns. There should also be a secret compartment somewhere in there. I was just trying to find it when you arrived.'

Rebecca held up her hand. 'Stop it,' she said, laughing. 'You sound like one of those judges on the Antiques Road Show.'

'Sorry. That's collector's speak, I'm afraid. I don't notice it anymore.'

'You're a dark horse, Jack Rogan ... '

'I like working with my hands. I collect antiques, mainly early Australian colonial furniture. When I can afford it. Ah, here it is,' said Jack, exploring the back of one of the drawers with the tips of his fingers, 'the secret compartment. There must be a brass spring somewhere in here, and a knob. Yes! You pull it out,' he said. 'Who knows what treasures are hidden within?'

'How exciting!' Rebecca reached inside and carefully pulled out the little cedar drawer. 'Empty, I'm afraid,' she said, holding up the exquisite little box.

'Not quite,' Jack said. 'There's something tucked into the corner here. Well, what do you know? Look at this.' He held up a silver bracelet and began to polish it with his handkerchief. 'Here, have a look.' He handed the bracelet to Rebecca.

'How romantic. If only it could talk,' she said, holding it up to the light.

'Perhaps it can. Look over here. There's an inscription on the inside.'

'What does it say?'

'One word – Orokke. How strange. I wonder what it means.'

'Could it be a name, you think?'

'No idea. It really doesn't matter, I suppose,' continued Jack. 'I want you to have it. Here, let me put it on.'

'I couldn't possibly, Jack. It's yours ... '

'Don't be silly.' Jack reached for her wrist. 'I insist. There, it's done. Look. A perfect fit.'

'That's very sweet of you, thank you.' She gave him a peck on the cheek.

'And thanks for the party,' said Jack. 'Come on, let me show you around.'

'You have some exquisite pieces. What's this?' asked Rebecca, running her hand over the gleaming surface of a cedar chest with brass corner plates and brass handles.

'You have a good eye. This is one of my best pieces. A campaign chest.'

'What, for going to war?'

'Not quite. Governor Fitzroy commissioned a Sydney cabinetmaker, Andrew Leneham, in about 1860 – the same year, incidentally, this cottage was built – to make specimen boxes for the presentation of gold samples to Queen Victoria. This is one of them. Gold was discovered in New South Wales in 1851.'

'How fascinating. And this?'

'This is a writing slope. A kind of portable desk, also made of cedar. It's mitre joined at the corners here, with recessed brass carrying handles. It has internal compartments for writing utensils and documents. It also has a secret compartment – here. To hide love letters and gold coins.'

'Drum roll, please. And now comes the surprise; its value? What's it worth?' teased Rebecca.

'You're making fun of me. Am I boring you?'

'Not at all,' said Rebecca, putting her hand reassuringly on Jack's arm. 'You have quite a collection.' Rebecca pointed to the painting above the chest. 'This is fabulous. What is it?'

'Brett Whitely. Do you like it?'

'Fascinating. Antiques and modern paintings. Polished wooden floorboards and sandstone walls. Not at all what I expected.'

'What did you expect?' asked Jack, handing Rebecca a glass of wine. 'Homes tell us so much ... '

'I can't really say. But not this ...' she replied.

'You know this is the first time we've had a conversation like this since you took me under your wing,' said Jack quietly. It had been just over three months since his New York publisher had introduced him to Rebecca Armstrong. It was an unlikely fit. The tall, lanky, suntanned Australian larrikin first-time-author with the funny accent, and the elegant, sophisticated New York PR agent representing several well established writers on the bestseller list. Faded jeans and leather jackets met Hermes and Cartier; the experienced New Yorker taking on the rookie from Down Under. Yet, somehow it worked. It worked, because Jack had written an exceptional book and genuinely needed help in dealing with his success and sudden fame. Rebecca found his inexperience endearing, and his willingness to listen to her advice strangely flattering. And there was one more thing: it was exciting to be around him.

'You know a lot about me. But I know very little about you,' Jack said. 'That's not quite fair, don't you think?'

Rebecca laughed. 'What do you want to know?'

'Surely you didn't just pop up out of nowhere one day as a successful businesswoman in New York? You must have somehow clawed your way through that treacherous jungle first.'

For a while she looked at him pensively.

'Where did you come from, I wonder?' Jack asked, reaching for her hand.

Rebecca wore large glasses, giving her an endearingly studious look which didn't quite go with the designer labels and expensive French accessories. Jack suspected this was deliberate. Somehow, the glasses always stood out. She had several pairs to suit different occasions, just like handbags and shoes. That afternoon, she wore an old-fashioned tortoiseshell pair that kept sliding down her nose. She kept pushing it back up with her index finger while pursing her lips.

'That's quite a question. Have you heard of Lancaster County?' Rebecca asked.

'Pennsylvania. Amish territory ... '

'Well informed, as usual.' She nodded appreciatively. 'My maiden name was Stolzfus. I grew up on a small farm outside Philadelphia with my three brothers. We had no electricity, no television, radio or kitchen appliances. Musical instruments were forbidden and cars not allowed.'

'Buggy?' interrupted Jack.

'Right again. We spoke Pennsylvania Dutch and our only transport was a horse-drawn buggy which took us to the markets in Philly once a week with our produce – eggs and fresh vegetables. I tended a small stall with my mother in my long black dress, apron and starched white bonnet.'

'Very cute. I can just see you ...' Jack teased.

'My brothers were all carpenters making furniture in the barn behind our house when they didn't work in the fields,' Rebecca continued, undeterred. 'Mother and I made quilts in the evenings by candlelight. My father had a long beard but no moustache – that too was forbidden – and always wore a straw hat and baggy black trousers held up by braces.'

'And I'm supposed to be the dark horse here ...' interjected Jack, refilling Rebecca's glass.

'Fun was a barn-raising with lots of laughter, prayer, and games, and enough food to feed the entire county for a year. It was a community event. You know, everyone pulling together to help a neighbour. That's where I met Amos ...' Rebecca paused and turned away, her eyes misting over. It only lasted for an instant, opening a tiny crack in her otherwise carefully controlled demeanour.

'Amos?' asked Jack.

'My first husband. We fell in love and ran away, leaving everything behind ... '

'First husband?'

'I haven't been lucky with men ... '

Jack sensed it was time to change to subject. 'I ran away too,' he said. 'As you know, I left a Queensland cattle station for the big smoke. I started out sweeping floors and running errands for a Brisbane newspaper.'

Appreciating his tact, Rebecca looked at Jack and smiled. *There's a lot more to this guy*, she thought, *than he lets you see*. 'And I started out as a receptionist, working for a fashion magazine in New York ...' she said.

'The Devil Wears Prada stuff?'

Rebecca chuckled. 'A bit like that, but without the free clothes. You saw the movie?'

'Loved it.'

'What was it like? Growing up on a cattle station?'

Jack took his time before replying and looked pensively at Rebecca. 'Lonely and harsh,' he said. 'I learnt to ride before I could walk and helped around the house as soon as I could stand. Our closest neighbour was fifty miles away, and it took three hours on a good day to reach town in the old ute. I used to ride in the back with Bonny and Clyde.'

'I thought you had no siblings,' interrupted Rebecca.

Jack began to chuckle. 'Bonny and Clyde were our cattle dogs. Sharp as a tack,' he said. 'They were my friends. Our enemy was the drought. It was never far away,' said Jack, turning serious, 'and when it came, it lasted for years. That's when the land became a dustbowl, the cattle began to die, and the bank manager came knocking.' Jack looked away. 'Mum hated it with a passion. She was a country girl from Wales. She married my father when she was just eighteen ...'

Realising that she had opened old wounds, Rebecca reached across and put her hand on Jack's. 'What happened to your parents?' she asked.

'Mum left. One day, she couldn't take it anymore and ran off with the publican in town. We never saw her again. And then I ran away too,' Jack said, the sadness in his voice reflecting the heartache of painful memories. 'Dad eked out a living on the cattle station with three Aboriginal stockmen until he got sick ...'

'What happened to him?'

'He lost the farm and died a broken man in a boarding house in Townsville a few years ago.'

'I'm sorry.'

'Such is life,' said Jack, reaching for his wine glass. 'We all have to follow our own path. Often barefoot, and some of it is treacherous and paved with nails.'

Rebecca squeezed Jack's hand. 'Your divorce?' she asked, changing direction.

'Messy, like all of them.'

'Girlfriends?'

Jack shrugged. 'Girlfriends? Are you kidding? With my diabolical schedule? I couldn't keep a canary in a cage ... '

'Interesting comparison ... '

'You know what they say: a rolling stone gathers no moss.'

'Poor boy ... But it wasn't always that way. What about that policewoman in your book?'

'Jana?'

Rebecca nodded, watching Jack carefully.

'She was an old flame. You can't ignite old flames; it doesn't work. The spark isn't there anymore,' Jack said pensively. 'In the end, she fell for the other guy.'

'Marcus Carrington, the lawyer ...'

The look on Jack's face told Rebecca it was time to back off.

'We're still friends,' said Jack. Rebecca wasn't convinced.

'Now, let me show you something interesting.' Jack pointed to a curious piece consisting of three wooden steps leading nowhere.

'What on earth is that?' asked Rebecca.

'Bed steps. That's how you climbed into the feathers in the good old days. The top step here opens up – see – for your jewellery and personal stuff. But the really important part was this.' Jack opened the second step and pulled out a lidded commode seat.

'Is this what I think it is?' asked Rebecca, a sparkle in her eye.

'Sure is! The chamber pot is over there,' said Jack, pointing to the window sill. But enough of the tour. How about some dinner?'

'I was beginning to think you'd never ask.' They linked arms and strolled down the corridor towards the kitchen.

'Unlucky with men, eh?'

Rebecca nodded.

'A woman like you? You're obviously looking in the wrong places,' said Jack.

'Looking under stones would be a wrong place then?' joked Rebecca.

'Definitely.'

'Thanks, Jack. I'll keep that in mind.'

'I promised to cook for you, remember? Well, this is your lucky day.'

'I'm sure it is. You're the first man who ever offered to cook something just for me. I can't wait.'

'You may be sorry.'

'I doubt it.'

'Amish, eh? You'd be used to plain tucker then ...' teased Jack, opening the door to the kitchen.

'We may be known as the Plain People, but the food, I tell you, was never plain.'

'Neither is my cooking; follow me.'

4

At the old farm near Bathurst, 10 January 2010

'Do you know what time it is?' asked Will. He turned to look at the clock on the bedside table and almost dropped the phone.

'It's important, mate! There's something I have to show you!' said Jack urgently.

'Can't it wait till the morning?'

'No, it can't. Please, Will ... '

Will lived in the flat above his antique shop a few hundred metres up the road from Jack's place. It was faster to walk than to try to find a parking spot in the crowded Balmain street. He arrived ten minutes later, wearing a pair of baggy shorts and a crumpled t-shirt he had obviously slept in. Jack was waiting on the front doorstep of his cottage, a glass of wine in his hand.

'I thought you were having dinner with your posh agent last night. What happened? Did you have a blue?' said Will.

'No. She caught the last ferry back to town hours ago. Come in. I've been working on this since she left.' Jack led the way to the courtyard at the back and pointed to the secretaire by the fountain.

'You dragged me out of the sack at two in the morning to show me this? Is that it? You must be blotto.'

'Not quite. Here, have a look.' Jack wiped the desktop with his polishing cloth, switched on his torch and aimed the beam at the top right-hand corner. The desktop was badly marked with deep scratches, indentations, faded inkblots and candle wax stains. All normal wear and tear from more than a century of extensive use. *Colonial patina*, as it was affectionately called in the trade.

'What am I looking for?' asked Will, rubbing his eyes.

'There's something written here – look.' Jack pointed to some letters scratched into the wood.

'What does it say?'

'First, there's a name. Here – "Anna Popov". Can you see it?'

'Sure.'

'And then one more word. A little to the right – "Help".'

'Yes.'

'And then comes the really interesting bit over here in the corner. A date. Well, just the year actually – 07.'

'So? Is this some kind of joke?'

'Far from it. Does the name ring a bell?'

'Should it?'

'Come on, Will. Think back! January 2005. Alice Springs, two girls disappeared ... '

'Popov ... Popov. Oh yeah ... It was in the news for months. They vanished without a trace. Backpackers.'

'That's it. I looked it up on the internet before you came. The police operation was huge at the time with lots of overseas interest and media attention, especially from Britain. Almost as big as Azaria Chamberlain. The police even brought in Aboriginal trackers and a psychic. "Operation Dingo II", it was called. It came to nothing. The case was closed a year later. No leads, no clues. Zilch.'

'What are you getting at, Jack?' asked Will impatiently.

'Aren't you even just a little bit curious? We find this old secretaire here – purely by accident – on an abandoned farm in the middle of nowhere with "Anna Popov – Help" scratched into the desktop. Next to a date – 07. That's two years after she disappeared!' Jack said, jabbing his finger at the numbers.

'You're not seriously suggesting it was this Popov girl who wrote this desktop graffiti two years after she vanished? Are you saying she could be alive, or was at least, in 2007? Come on, mate, I can think of a hundred other explanations. I'm going back to bed.'

'I have a funny feeling about this, Will,' said Jack pensively. 'What if this is for real? What if this is a desperate plea for help and we ignore it?'

'You're a hopeless romantic, Jack, admit it. This is bullshit! Sheer speculation and you know it.'

'The place was spooky, you said so yourself,' argued Jack. 'I think we should at least go back and have another look. Make some enquiries, poke around a little. You know, find out who lived there before, what happened to the place, why it was abandoned, the fire ... The agent acted strange, admit it. He accepted the pittance we offered for the stuff without argument. He was happy – no, relieved – to be rid of it.' Will shook his head. 'Come on, Will, it's only a three-hour drive. We could do the whole thing in a day, easy. There and back.'

'I thought you had to go to London. Pressing author business.'

'I'm leaving on Monday. We could do it today.'

'You're wasting your time.'

'I'll pick you up at six.'

'We're getting too old for this, Jack!'

'Bullshit!'

'Dreamer.'

Scared?'

'Me? What of?'

'I may be on to something ...'

They arrived at the farm just after nine in the morning. It was already very hot and the flies were unbearable. They had to walk the last two hundred metres to the gate because the track was too rutted for Jack's MG. On their first visit, they had completely ignored the house. This time, however, they decided to take a closer look at it.

The fire had obviously started in the kitchen. It was almost completely gutted.

'Here, look at this,' said Jack, picking up an urn with a rubber hose attached to one end. 'And all this junk over here.' He pointed to a rusty stove-like six burner lying on top of a heap of glass tubes, steel clamps and broken bottles.

'Looks more like stuff from a laboratory than a farmhouse kitchen,' commented Will, kicking some metal tubing aside.

The front room was empty. Fingers of sunlight reaching through gaping holes in the roof illuminated intricate cobwebs ready to ensnare the careless and the curious. There were no doors left. All the windows were broken and most of the floorboards had rotted away. Lying on its back, a fly-encrusted rat was decomposing in front of the fireplace.

'Here, have a look at this,' said Jack. He pointed to a timber wall next to the fireplace. The wall was covered in black numbers carved into the wood in neat groups of three: '666' '666' '666'. 'How weird ... Look over there; above the fireplace. What do you reckon it is? A stuffed goat's head?'

The mantelpiece with its forest of black candles reminded Jack of a strange pagan altar waiting for a sacrifice. Pools of hard candle wax coated the floorboards below the mantelpiece.

'This place gives me the creeps,' said Will.

Jack picked up an iron poker and went through the mound of ash in the fireplace. Buried under the ash, charred bones, an iron cross covered in soot and a dagger with a broken blade had escaped destruction by the flames. *Leftovers from a black mass?* thought Jack, glancing at the back of the fireplace. Then something behind the grate caught his eye. It looked like a piece of limp material – burnt around the edges – with some kind of picture in the middle. He lifted it up with the poker and dropped it on the floor in front of him.

'How weird,' he said, examining the strange thing lying on the floorboards. A piece of leather with a picture of a human head cut in half. The left side of the face was a grinning skull, the right, the face of a bearded man. On top of the head sat a conical black hat with strange looking symbols like silver arrows and stars.

'What do you reckon? A magician?' ventured Will, pointing to the head.

'Half dead, half alive?'

'Yea. Something like that.'

'Black magic.'

'Scary place. Let's get out of here.'

'Why don't you track down the agent?' suggested Will on their way back to the village. 'See what you can find out about the farm. I'll try the store and the pub. Let's meet there in an hour.'

Everyone they spoke to had two things in common: suspicion and a reluctance to talk about the farm. The responses varied. Moving from polite evasion via pretended ignorance and obvious lies to rude rebuff, they covered everything but the truth.

'I could do with a cold beer,' said Jack, pulling up a stool next to Will's at the bar. Apart from the publican reading the paper behind the counter, the bar was deserted.

'Any luck?' asked Will.

'Nothing! The bastard didn't want to know me and almost threw me out.'

'Same here,' said Will, lowering his voice, 'except for the vicar. You just missed him. He was having a quiet beer at ten in the morning.'

Jack ordered two beers. 'What did you find out?' he asked.

'About a year ago, there were some rather unusual characters at the farm who caused the village here, and particularly the vicar, a lot of grief. They terrorised the locals for months and only left after the farm burnt down.'

'Not your ideal tenants,' said Jack. He nodded appreciatively and took a sip of his beer. 'Who were they?'

'At first, even the vicar was reluctant to talk. But three scotches later he opened up a little.'

'Well?'

'A bikie gang,' said Will, lowering his voice even further. 'Can you believe it? Here, in this God forsaken place?'

Jack looked up, surprised. 'Yes, I can,' he said, grinning. 'And we have the proof right here.'

'What are you talking about?'

'This.' Jack pulled the piece of leather he'd found in the fireplace out of his pocket and put it on the bar in front of him. 'Do you know what this is?'

'No idea.'

'The penny dropped as soon as you mentioned the bikies. This, my friend, is the colours of an outlaw motorcycle club.'

'You're kidding! Do you know which club?'

'Yes. The Wizards of Oz.'

Will's jaw almost dropped into his glass. 'Let me buy you another beer, mate. You deserve it,' he said.

**

Did you enjoy this sample?
If you'd like to find out what happened in *The Disappearance of Anna Popov*, visit Gabriel's website and sign up to be notified when the book is released.

http://gabrielfarago.com.au/

About the author

As a lawyer with a passion for history and archaeology, Gabriel Farago had to wait for many years before being able to pursue another passion – writing – in earnest. However, his love of books and storytelling started long before that.

'I remember as a young boy reading biographies and history books with a torch under the bed covers,' he recalls, 'and then writing stories about archaeologists and explorers the next day, instead of doing homework. While I regularly got into trouble for this, I believe we can only do well in our endeavours if we are passionate about the things we love; for me, writing has become a passion.'

Born in Budapest, Gabriel grew up in post-War Europe and, after fleeing Hungary with his parents during the Revolution in 1956, went to school in Austria before arriving in Australia as a teenager. This allowed him to become multi-lingual and feel 'at home' in different countries and diverse cultures.

Shaped by a long legal career and experiences spanning several decades and continents, his is a mature voice that speaks in many tongues. Gabriel holds degrees in literature and law, speaks several languages and takes research and authenticity very seriously. Inquisitive by nature, he studied Egyptology and learned to read the hieroglyphs. He travels extensively and visits all of the locations mentioned in his books.

'I try to weave fact and fiction into a seamless storyline,' he explains. 'By blurring the boundaries between the two, the reader is never quite sure where one ends, and the other begins. This is of course quite deliberate as it creates the illusion of authenticity and reality in a work that is pure fiction. A successful work of fiction is a balancing act: reality must rub shoulders with imagination in a way that is both entertaining and plausible.'

Gabriel lives just outside Sydney, Australia, in the Blue Mountains, surrounded by a World Heritage National Park. 'The beauty and solitude of this unique environment,' he points out, 'give me the inspiration and energy to weave my thoughts and ideas into stories which, I sincerely hope, will in turn entertain and inspire my readers.'

Connect with Gabriel

Website: http://gabrielfarago.com.au/

Facebook:
https://www.facebook.com/GabrielFaragoAuthor

Learn more about Gabriel and his writing

If you've enjoyed this book and wanted to know more about how it was written, download a copy of Gabriel's free ebook, *Letters from the Attic*, in mobi or epub, from your favourite ebook store.

Made in the USA
Monee, IL
25 June 2021